My Last Summer with Cass

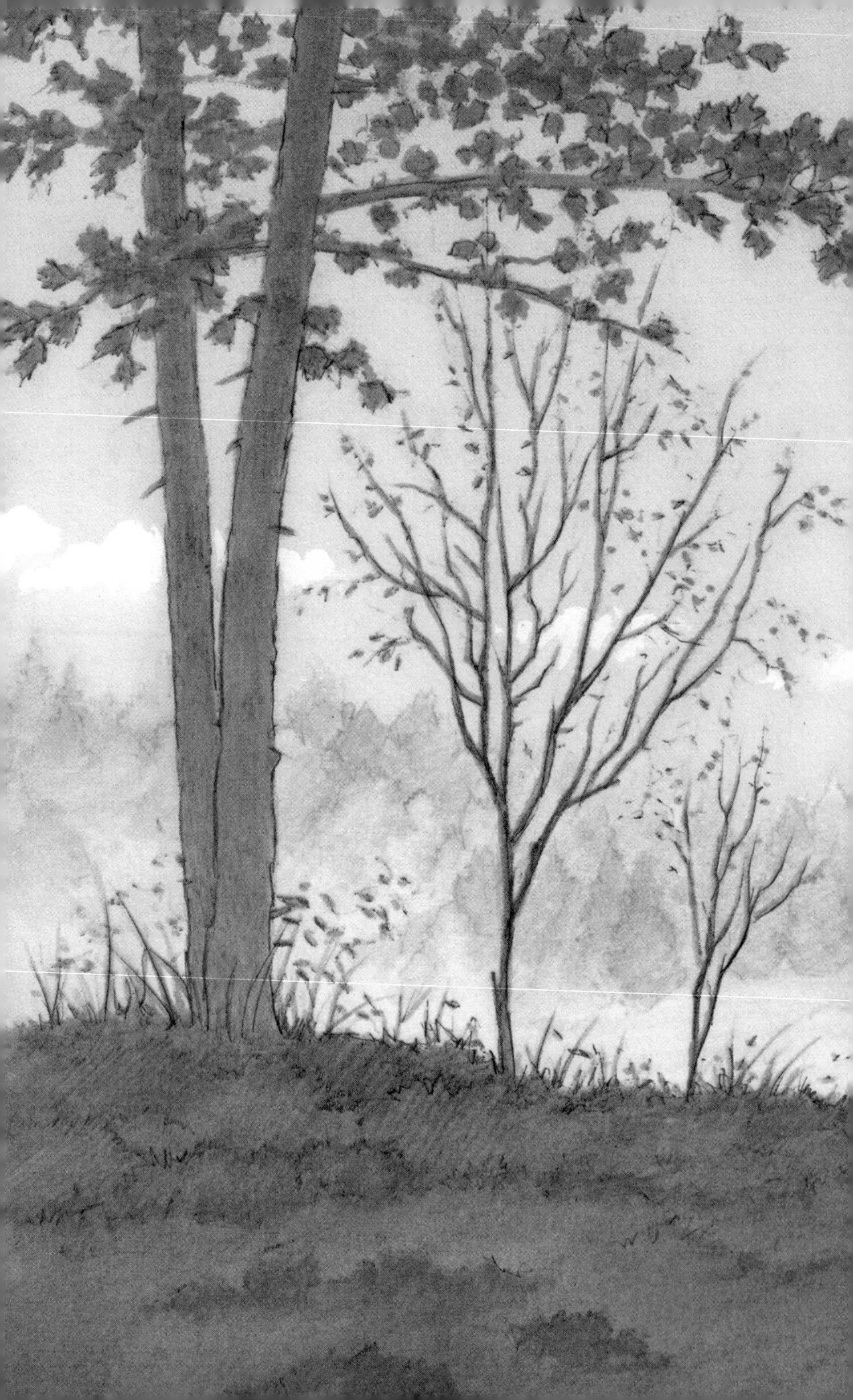

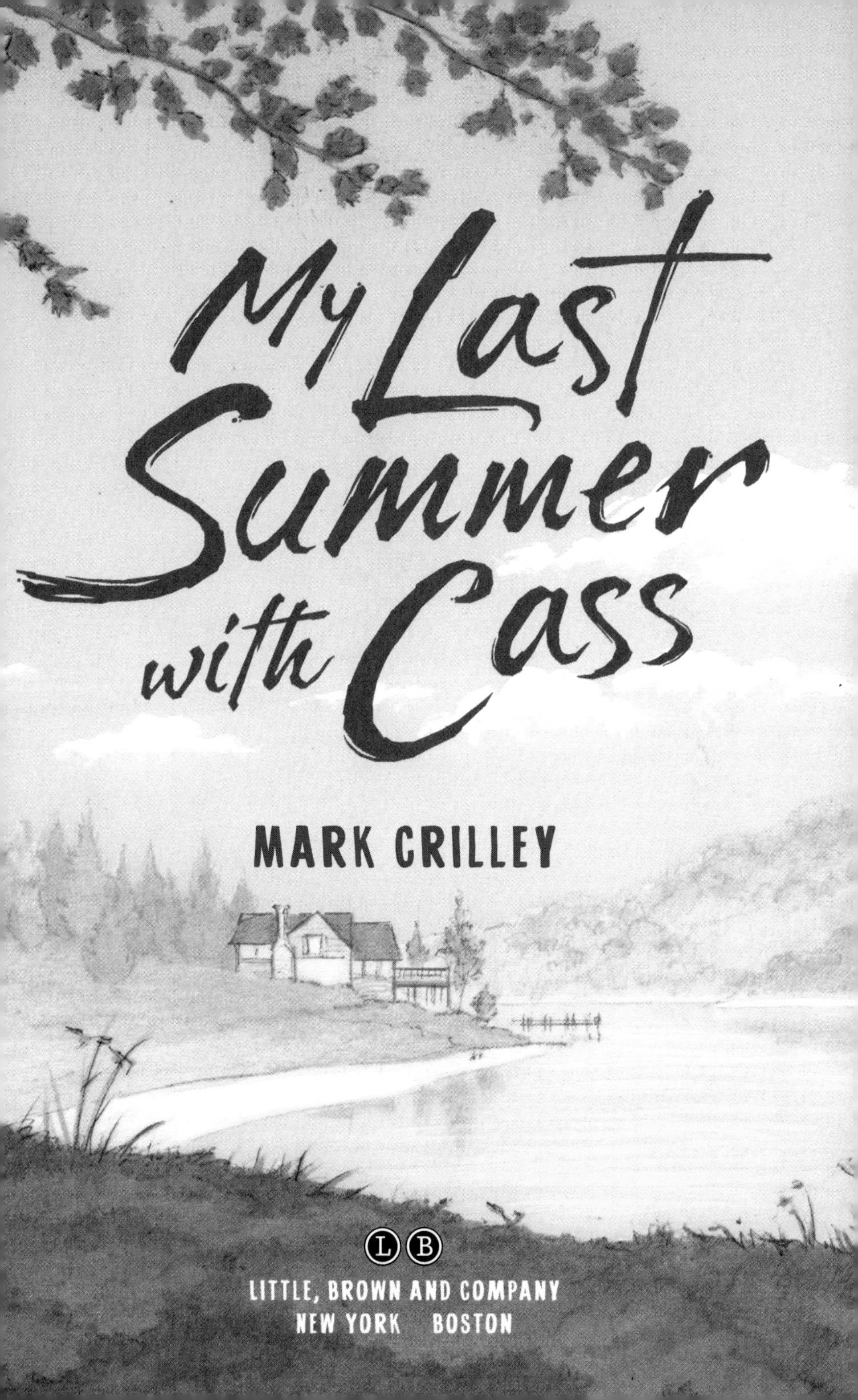

My Last Summer with Cass

MARK CRILLEY

LB
LITTLE, BROWN AND COMPANY
NEW YORK BOSTON

About This Book

This book was edited by Emily Meehan, Hannah Allaman, and Andrea Colvin and designed by Jenny Kimura. The production was supervised by Bernadette Flinn, and the production editor was Lindsay Walter-Greaney. The text was set in CC Wild Words Lower, and the display type is Hillstone Regular.

Little, Brown and Company
Hachette Book Group
1290 Avenue of the Americas, New York, NY 10104
Visit us at LBYR.com

First Edition: March 2021

Little, Brown and Company is a division of Hachette Book Group, Inc. The Little, Brown name and logo are trademarks of Hachette Book Group, Inc.

The publisher is not responsible for websites (or their content) that are not owned by the publisher.

Library of Congress Cataloging-in-Publication Data
Names: Crilley, Mark, writer, illustrator.
Title: My last summer with Cass / Mark Crilley.
Description: First edition. | New York : Little, Brown Books for Young Readers, 2021.
| Summary: "Megan and Cass are at a crossroads in their lives and in their art. Will this summer make or break their friendship?"—Provided by publisher.
Identifiers: LCCN 2020015189 (print) | LCCN 2020015190 (ebook) | ISBN 9780759555464 (hardcover) | ISBN 9780759555457 (paperback) | ISBN 9780316705479 (ebook) | ISBN 9780316705448 (ebook other)
Subjects: LCSH: Graphic novels. | CYAC: Graphic novels. | Friendship—Fiction.
| Summer—Fiction.
Classification: LCC PZ7.7.C75 My 2021 (print) | LCC PZ7.7.C75 (ebook)
| DDC 741.5/973—dc23
LC record available at https://lccn.loc.gov/2020015189
LC ebook record available at https://lccn.loc.gov/2020015190

ISBNs: 978-0-7595-5546-4 (hardcover), 978-0-7595-5545-7 (pbk.),
978-0-316-70547-9 (ebook), 978-0-316-70558-5 (ebook), 978-0-316-70546-2 (ebook)

Printed in the United States of America

LSC-C

Printing 1, 2020

To John Walter,
whose friendship really is a work of art

Part One

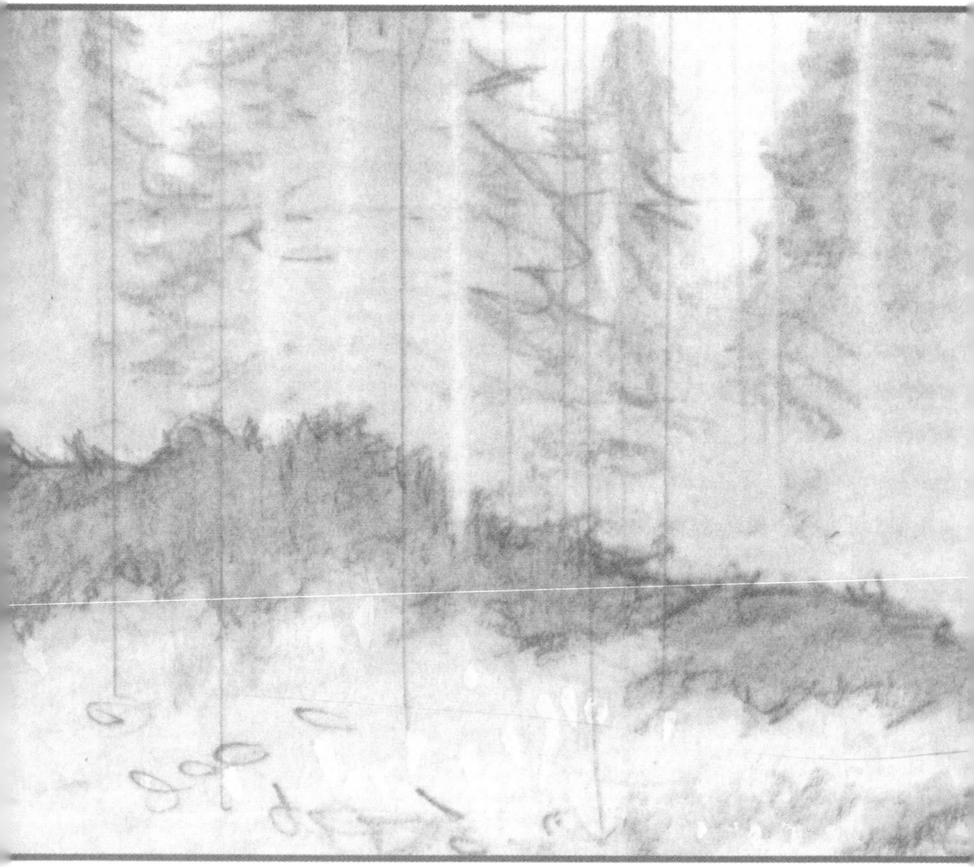

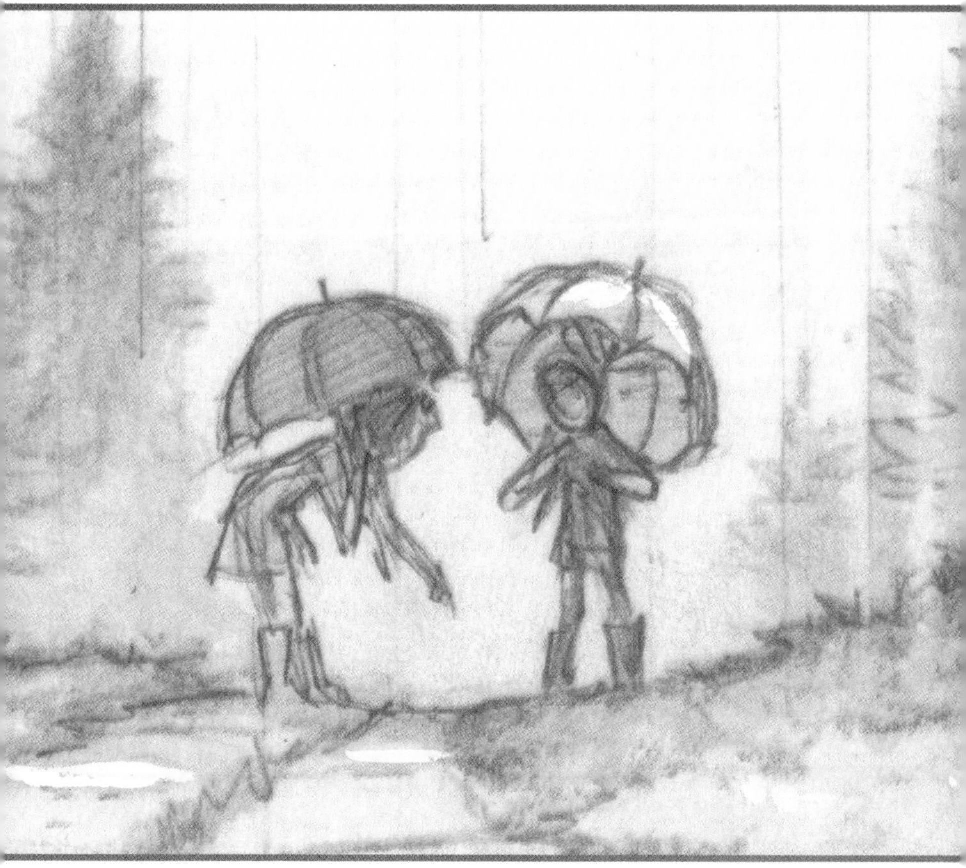

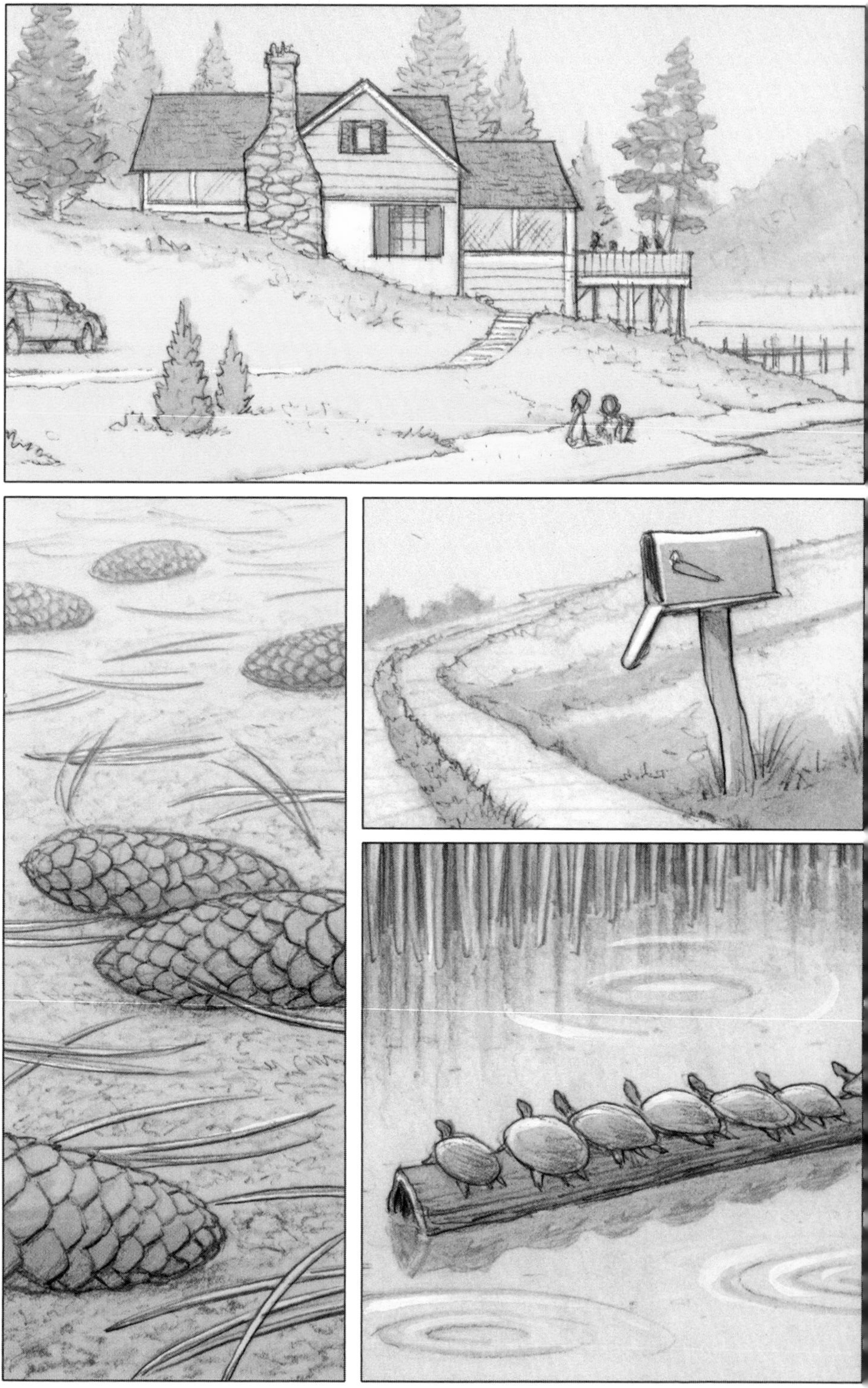

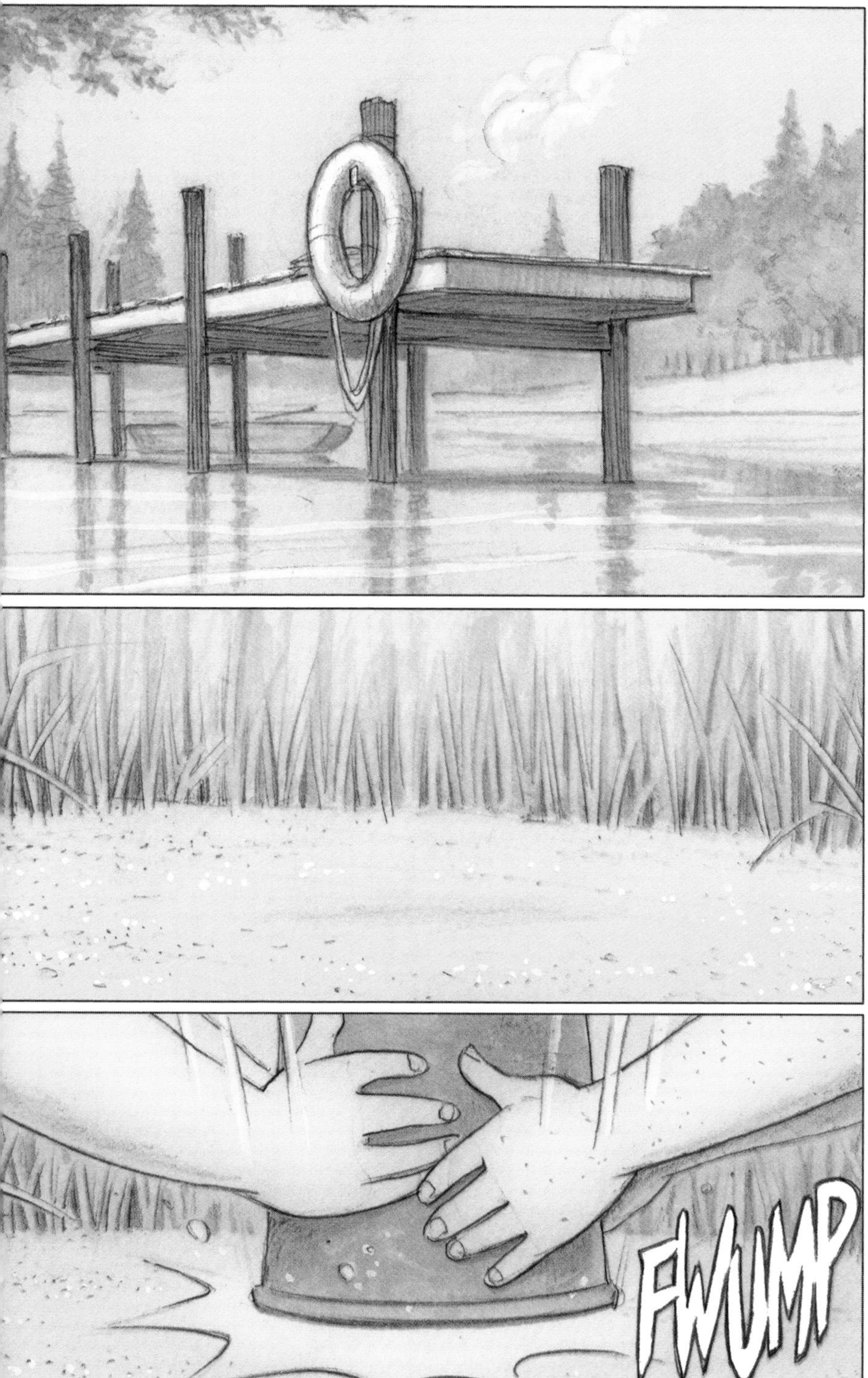
FWUMP

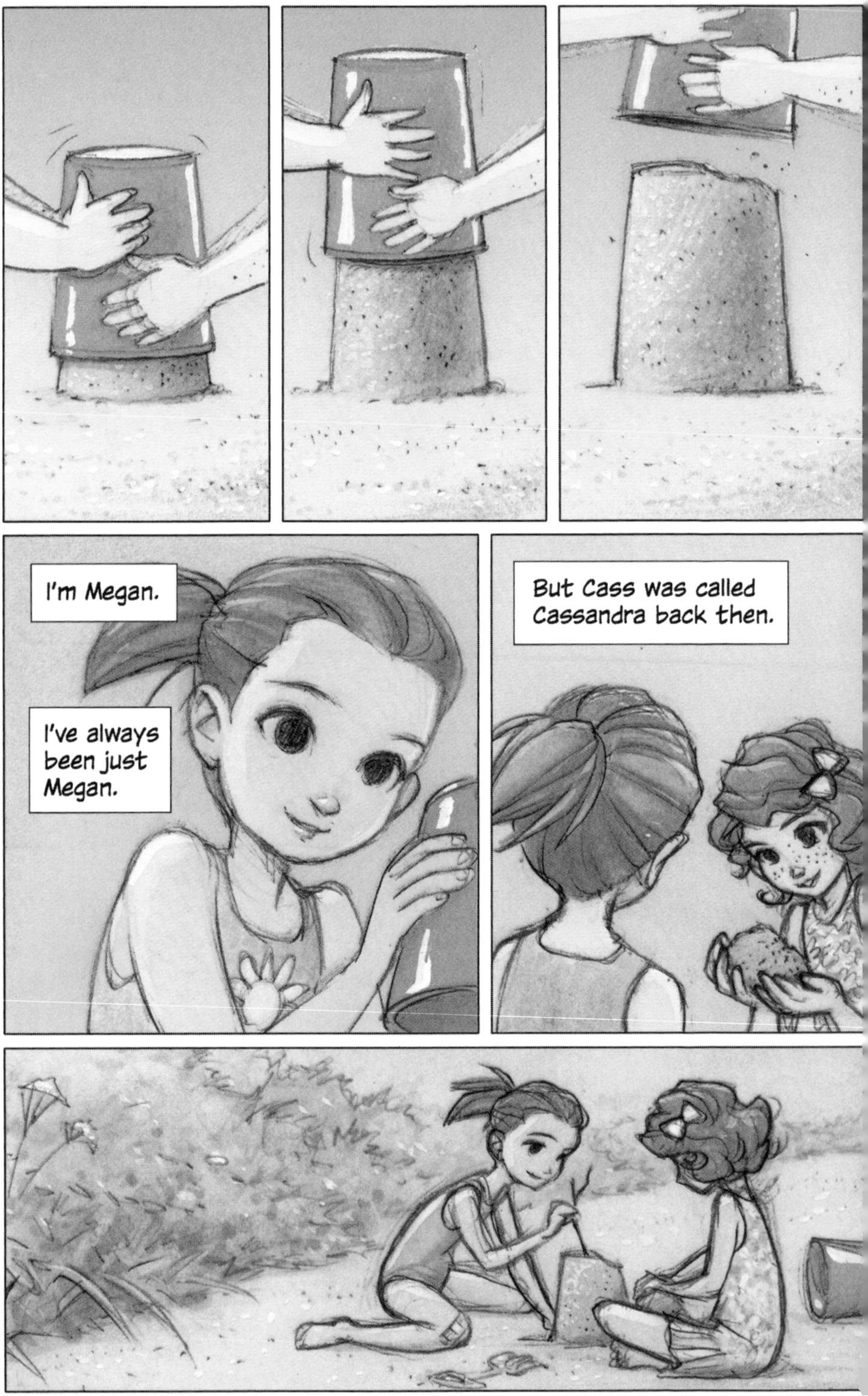
I'm Megan.
I've always been just Megan.
But Cass was called Cassandra back then.

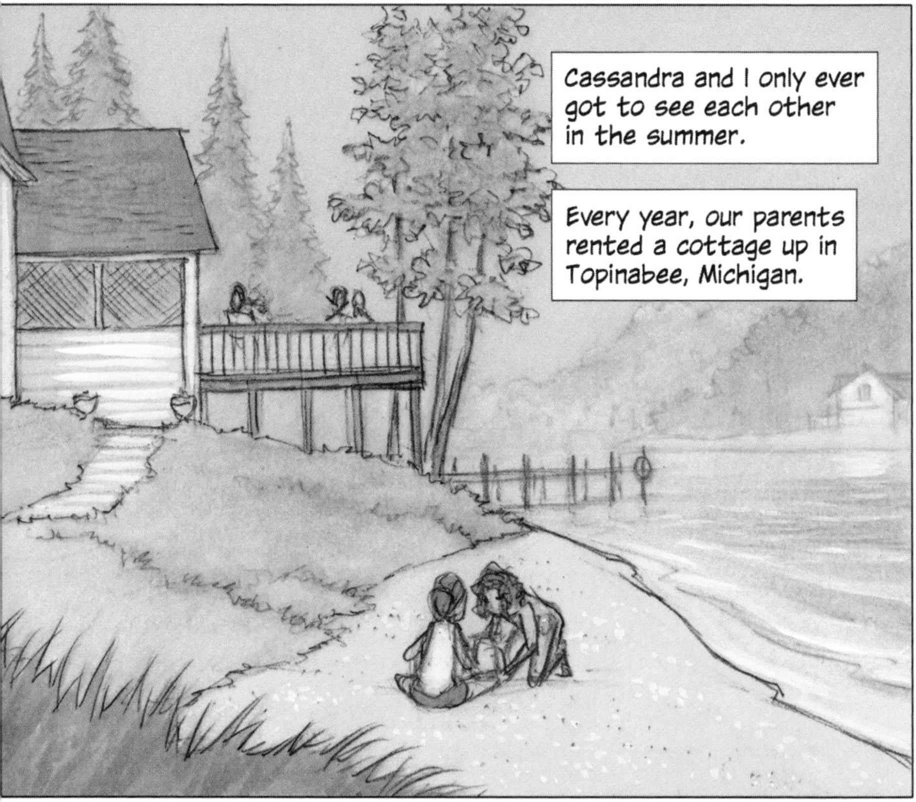
Cassandra and I only ever got to see each other in the summer.
Every year, our parents rented a cottage up in Topinabee, Michigan.

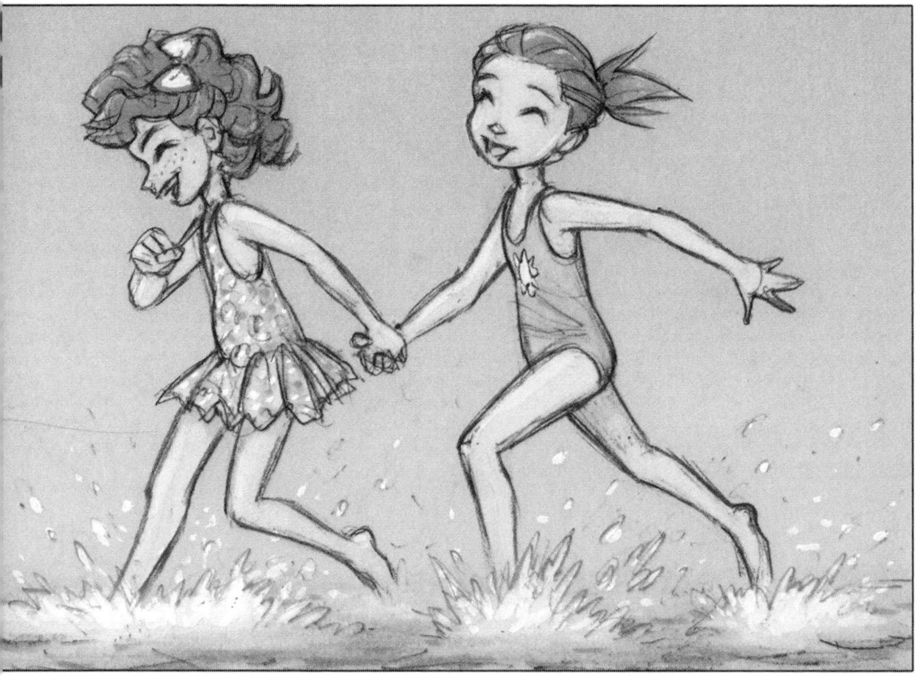

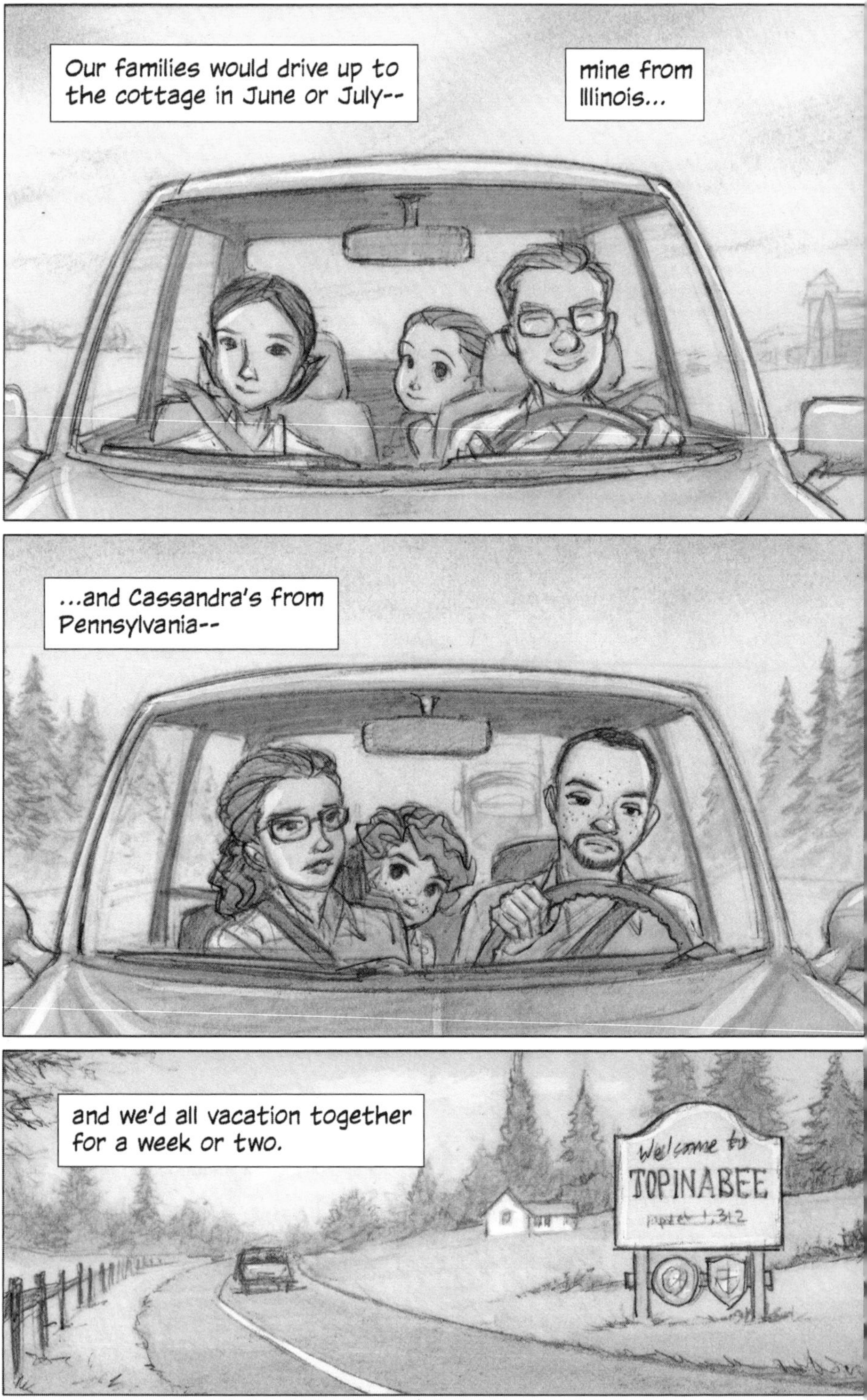
Our families would drive up to the cottage in June or July--
mine from Illinois...
...and Cassandra's from Pennsylvania--
and we'd all vacation together for a week or two.
Welcome to
TOPINABEE

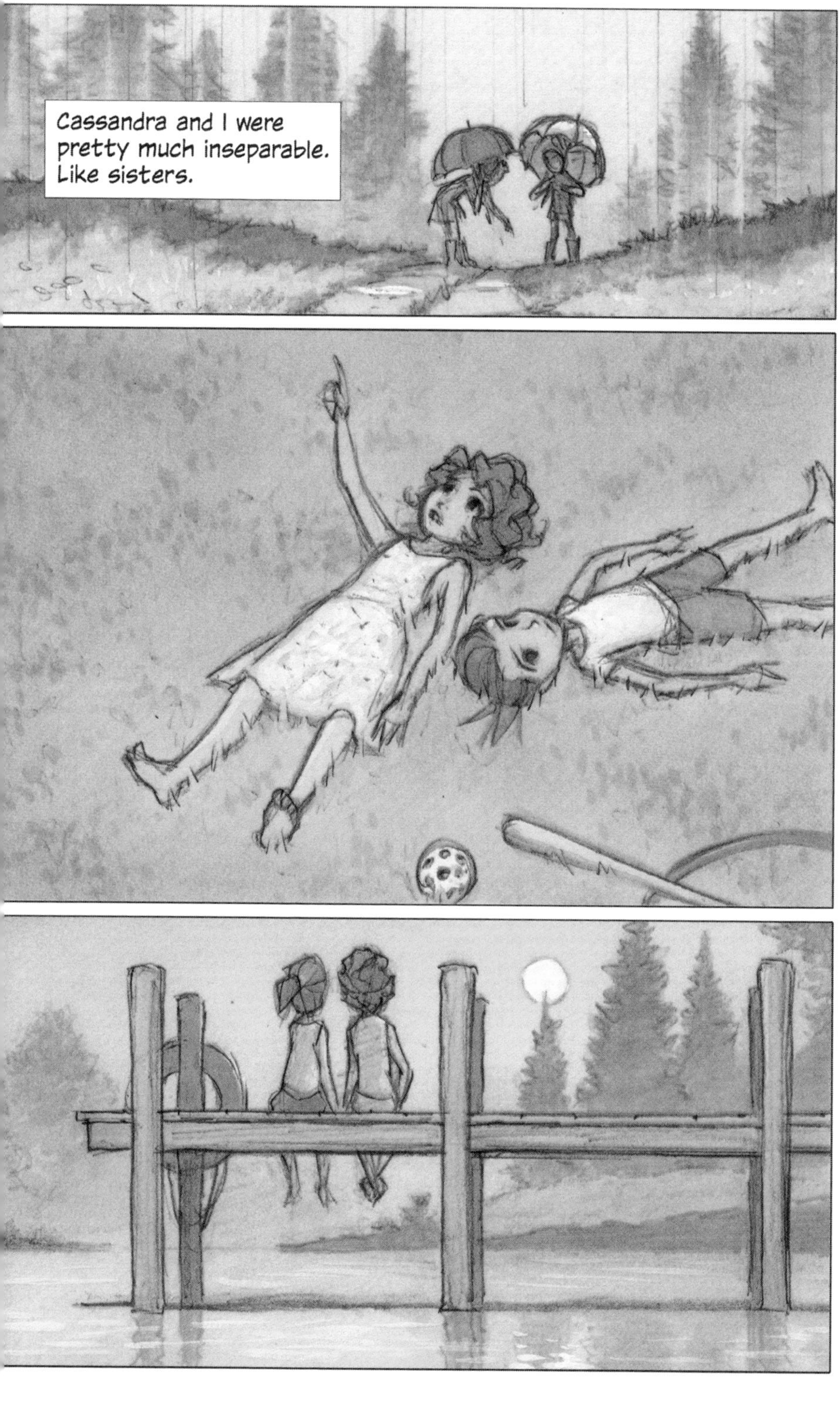
Cassandra and I were pretty much inseparable. Like sisters.

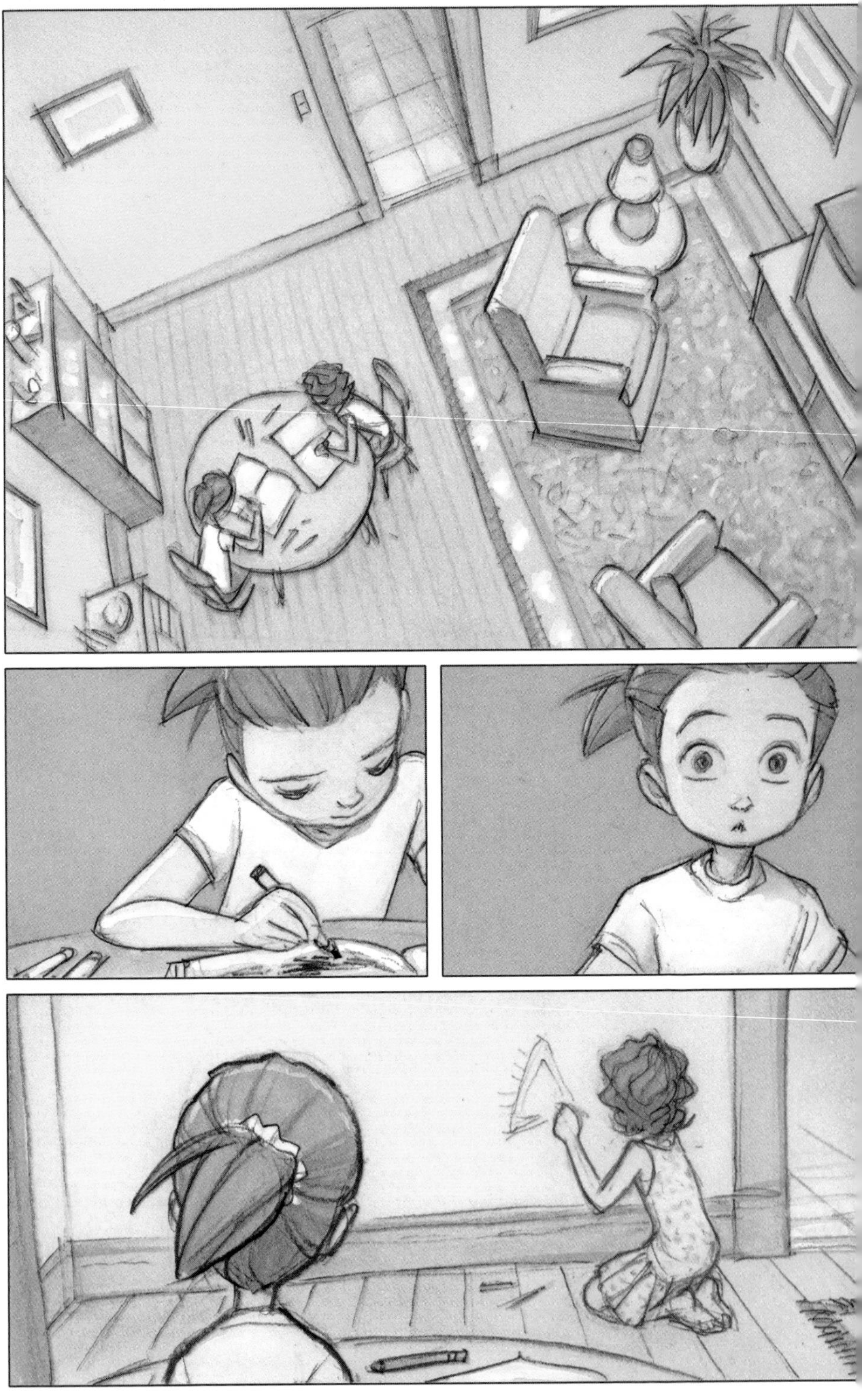

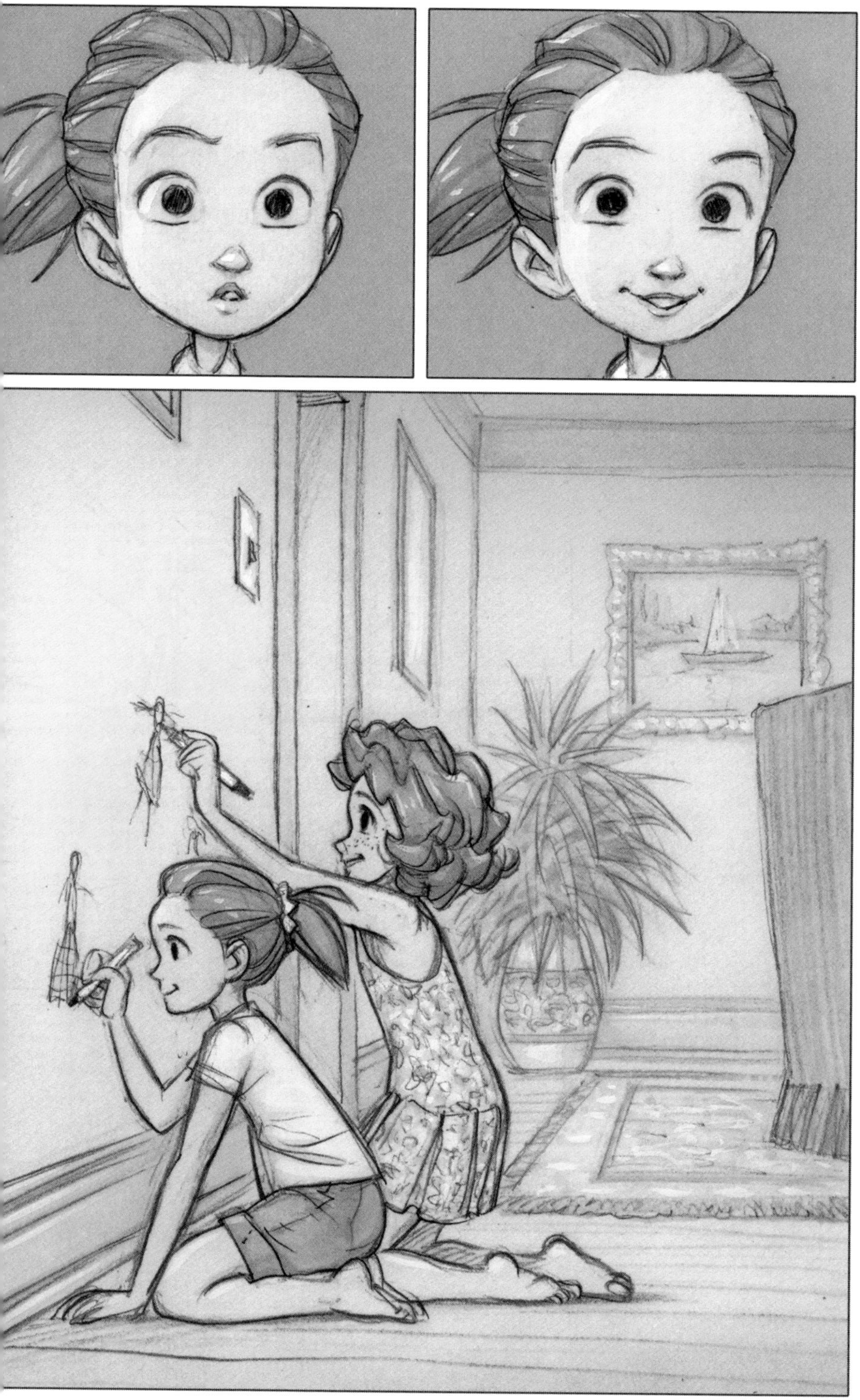

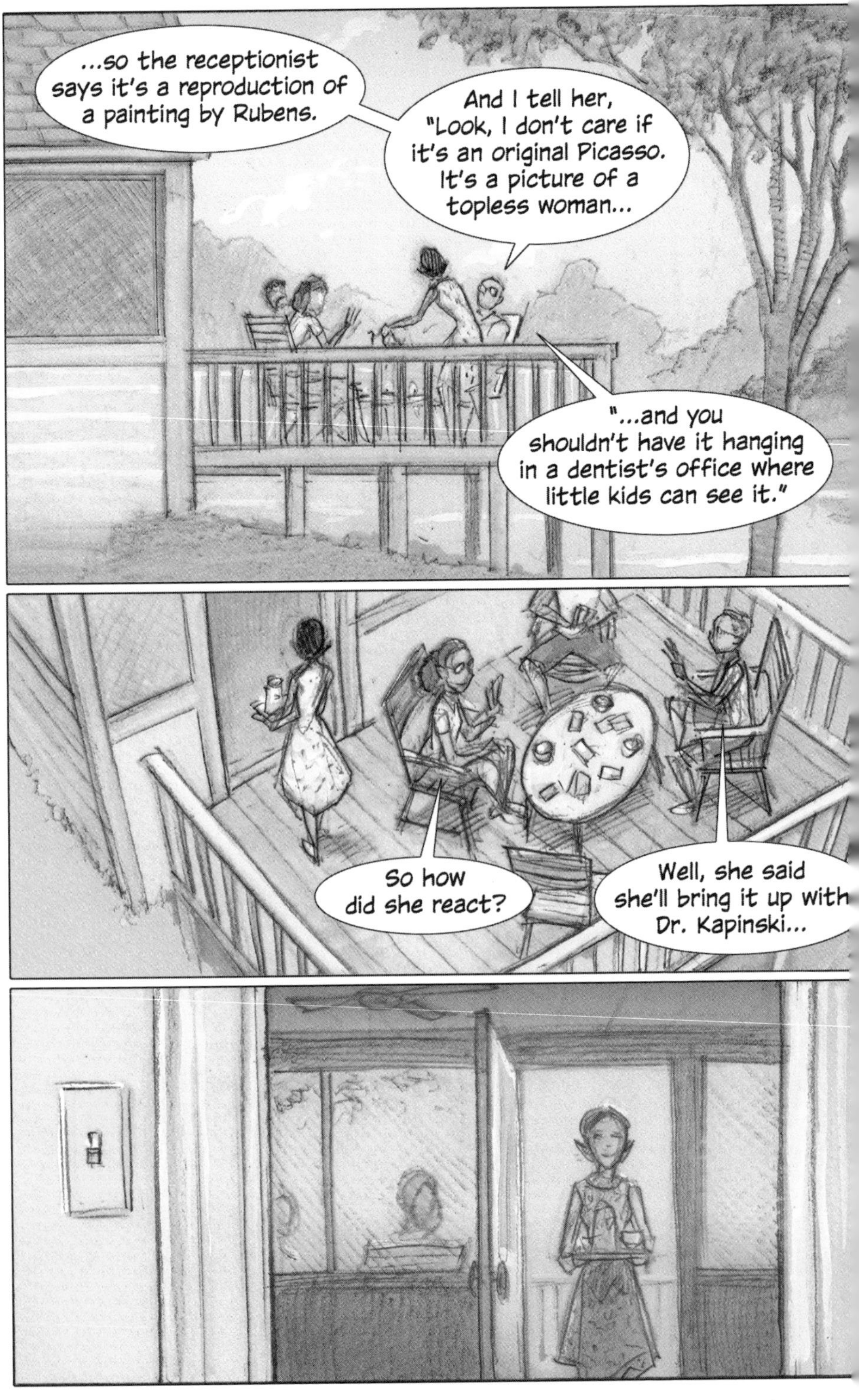
...so the receptionist says it's a reproduction of a painting by Rubens.
And I tell her, "Look, I don't care if it's an original Picasso. It's a picture of a topless woman...
"...and you shouldn't have it hanging in a dentist's office where little kids can see it."
So how did she react?
Well, she said she'll bring it up with Dr. Kapinski...

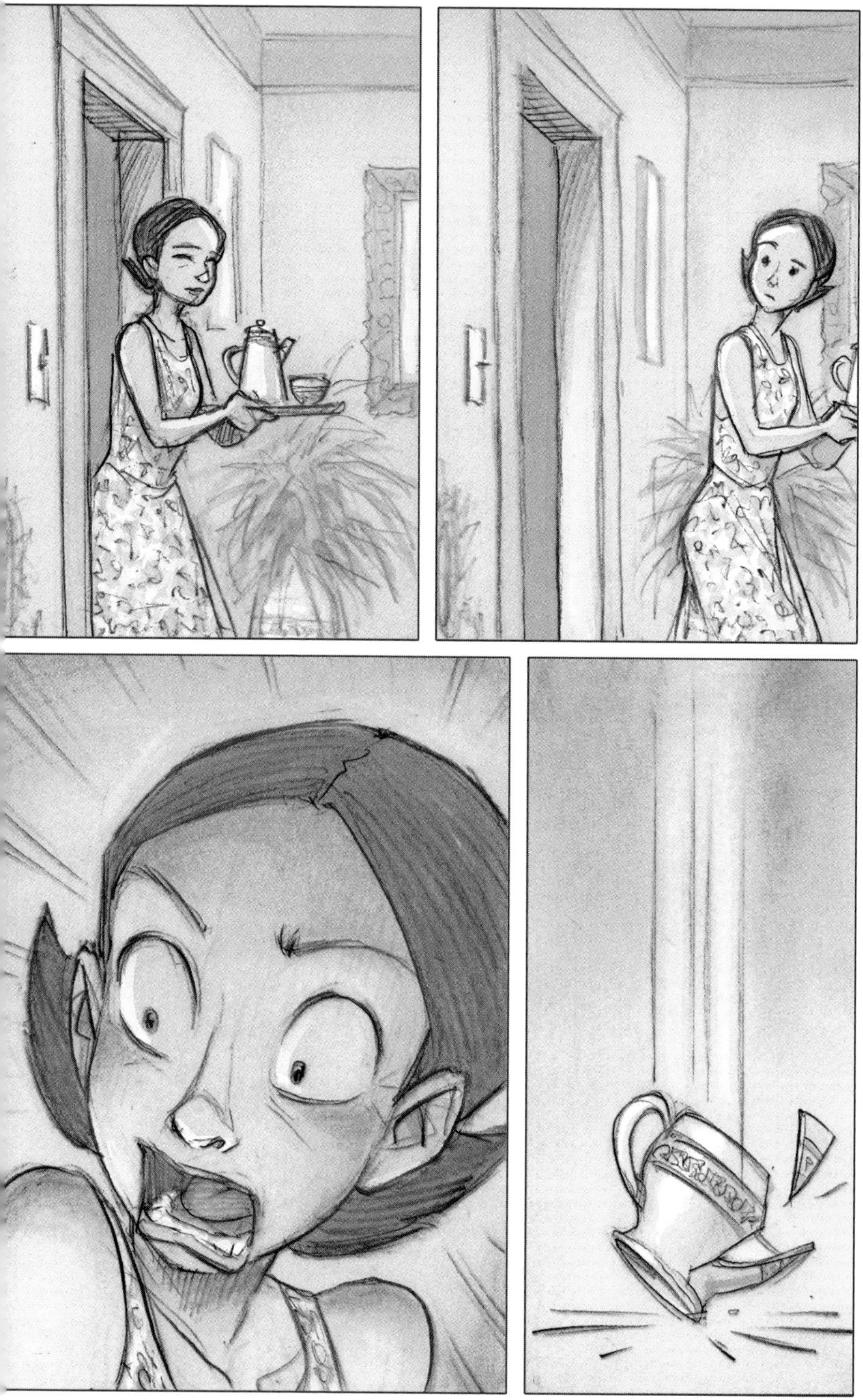

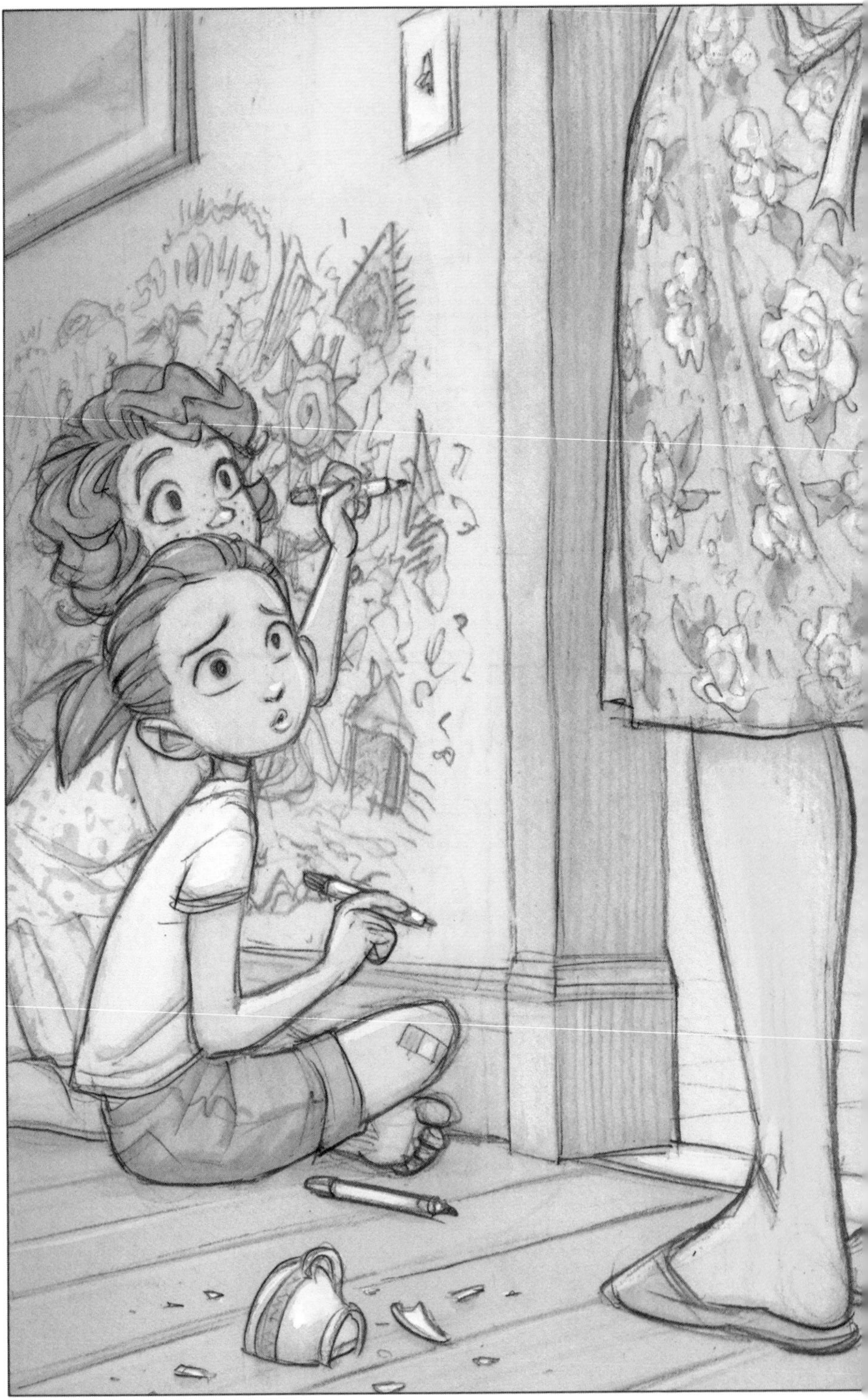

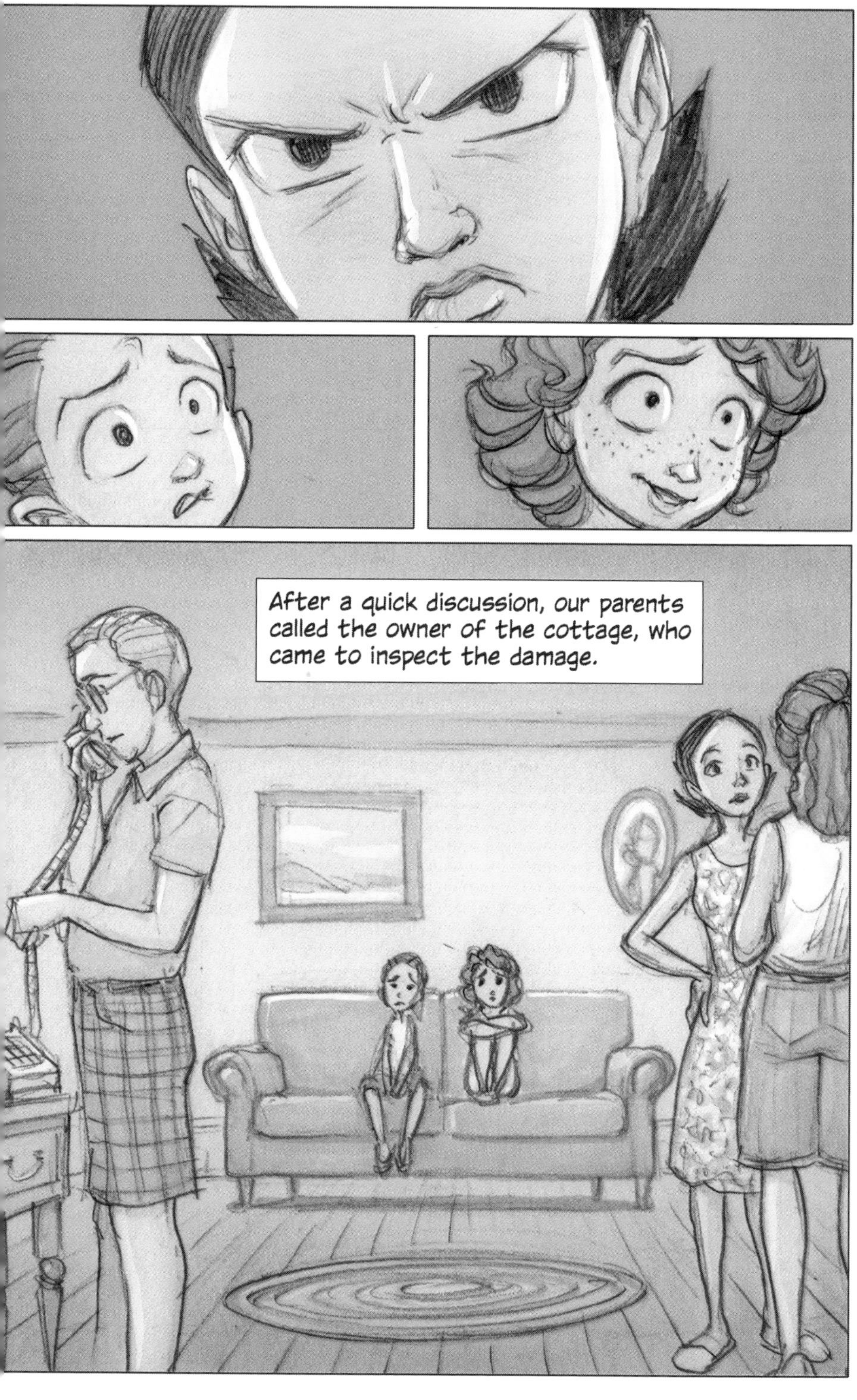
After a quick discussion, our parents called the owner of the cottage, who came to inspect the damage.

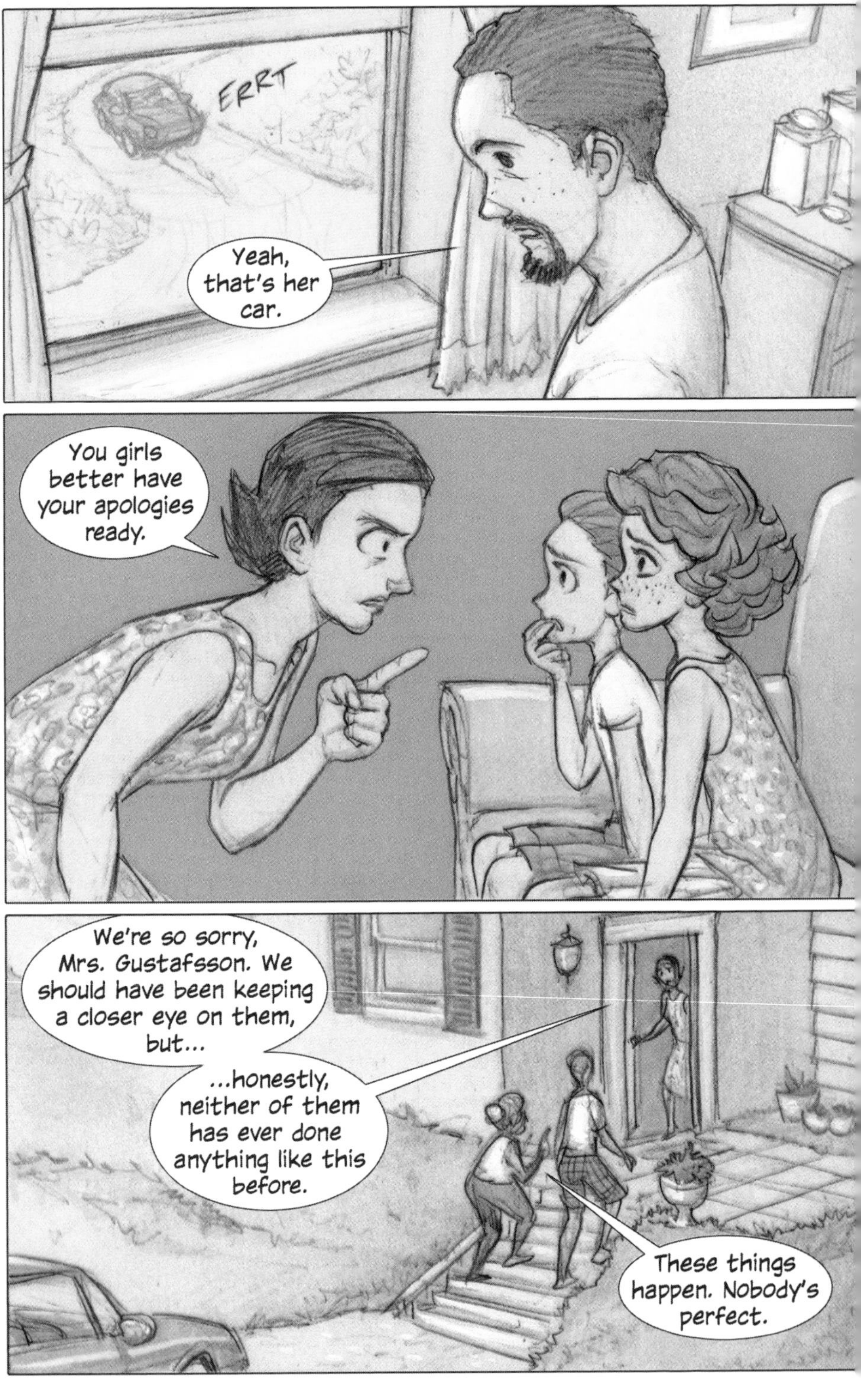
ERRT
Yeah, that's her car.
You girls better have your apologies ready.
We're so sorry, Mrs. Gustafsson. We should have been keeping a closer eye on them, but...
...honestly, neither of them has ever done anything like this before.
These things happen. Nobody's perfect.

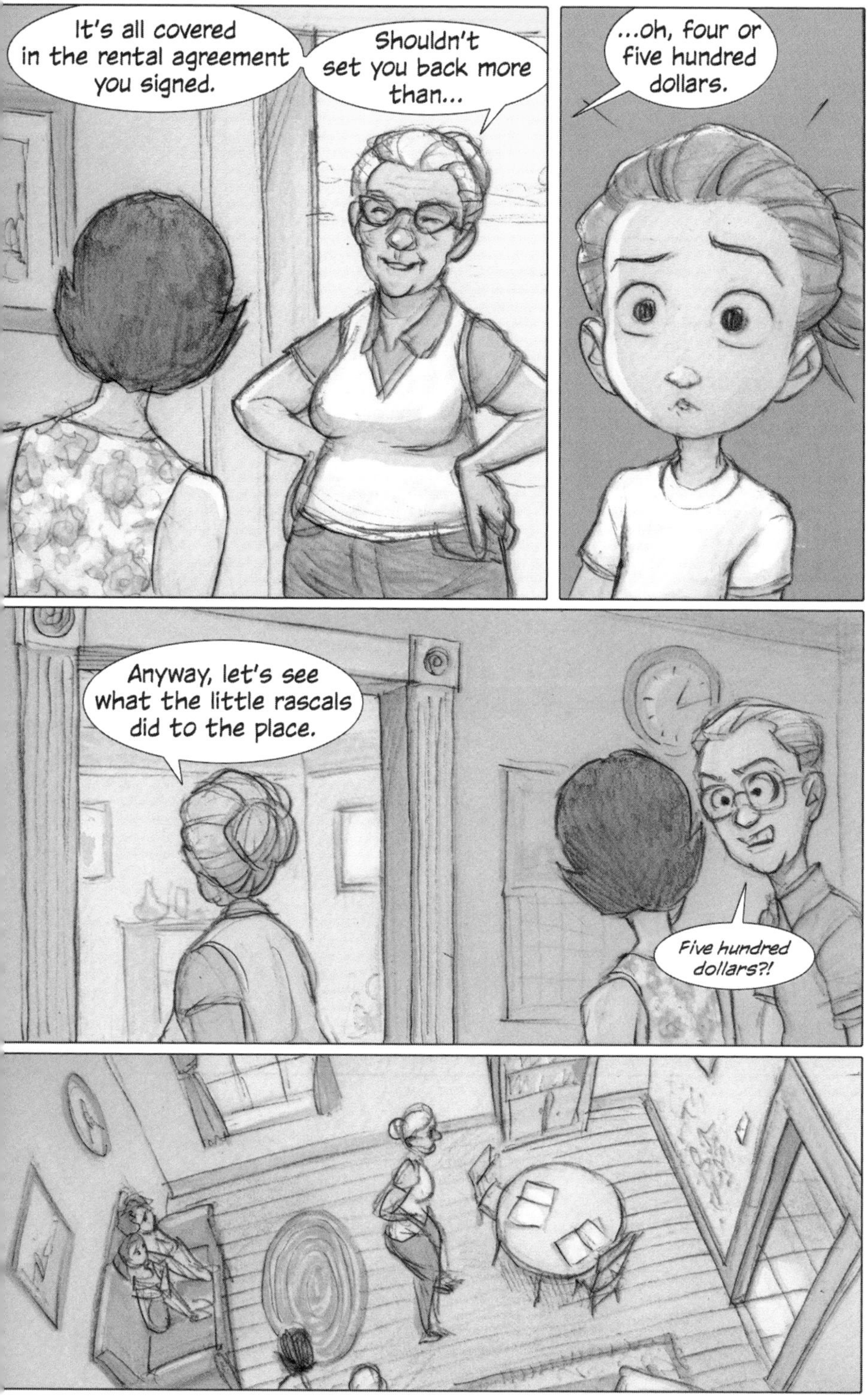
It's all covered in the rental agreement you signed.
Shouldn't set you back more than...
...oh, four or five hundred dollars.
Anyway, let's see what the little rascals did to the place.
Five hundred dollars?!

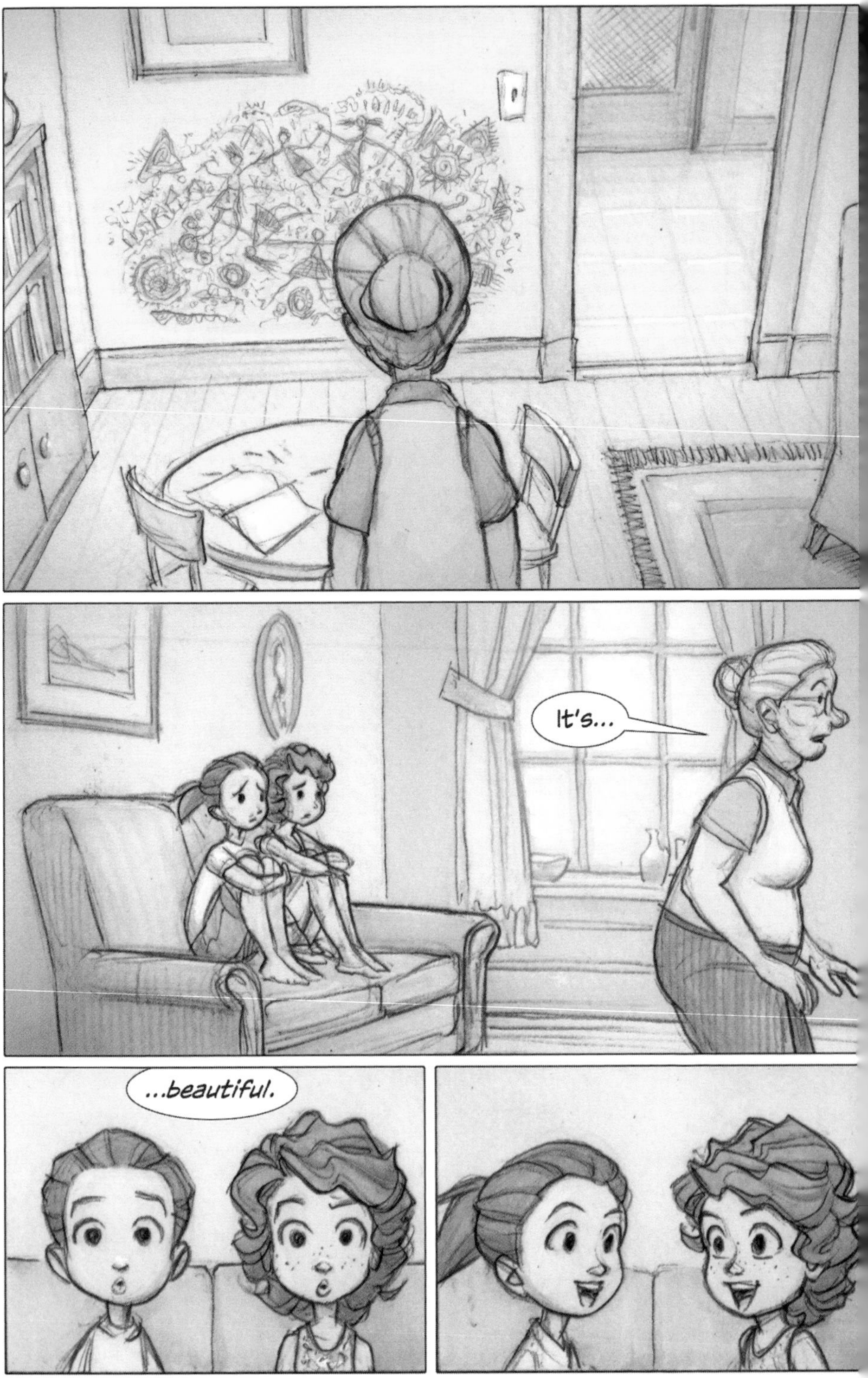
It's...
...beautiful.

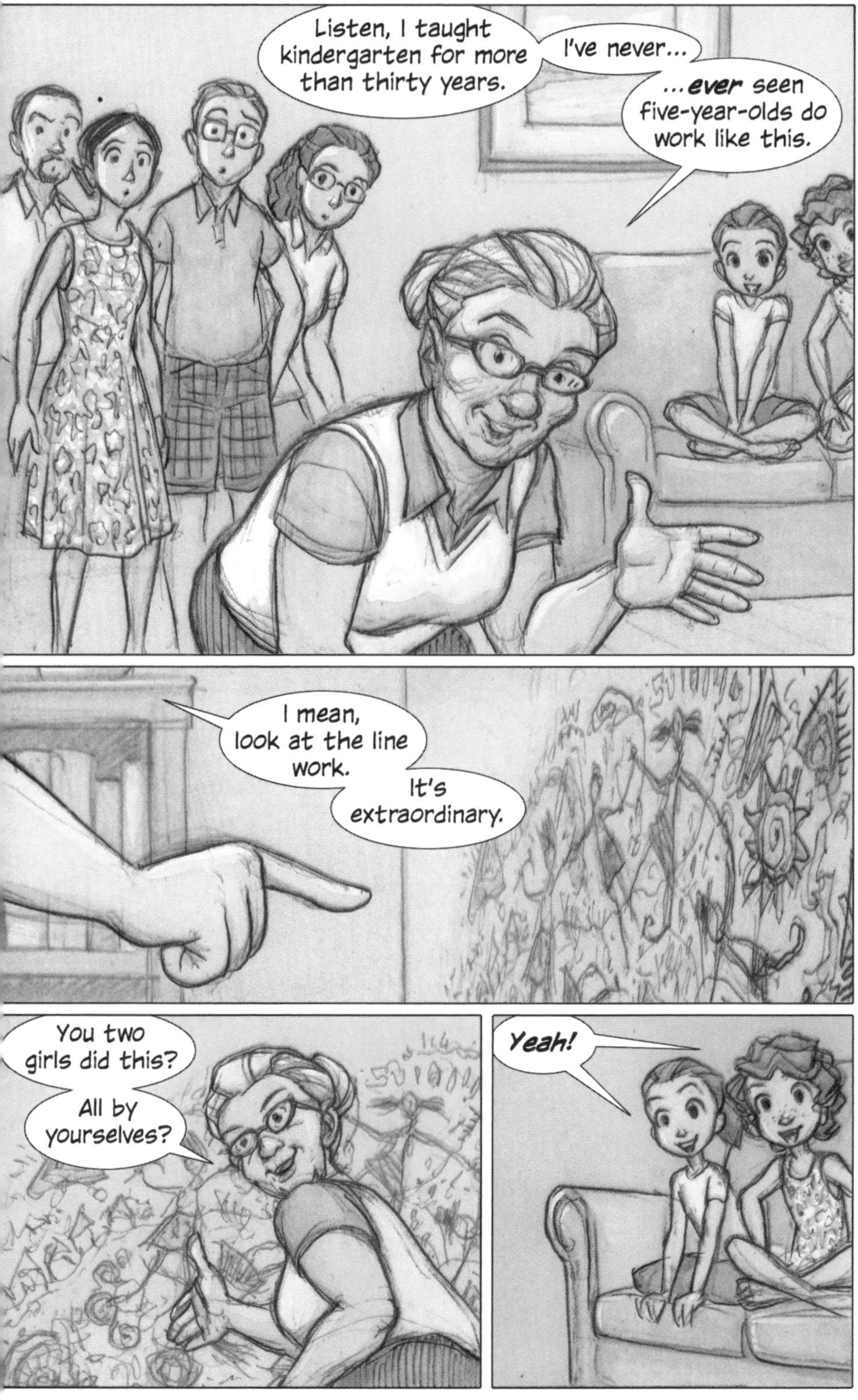
Listen, I taught kindergarten for more than thirty years.
I've never...
...ever seen five-year-olds do work like this.
I mean, look at the line work.
It's extraordinary.
You two girls did this?
All by yourselves?
Yeah!

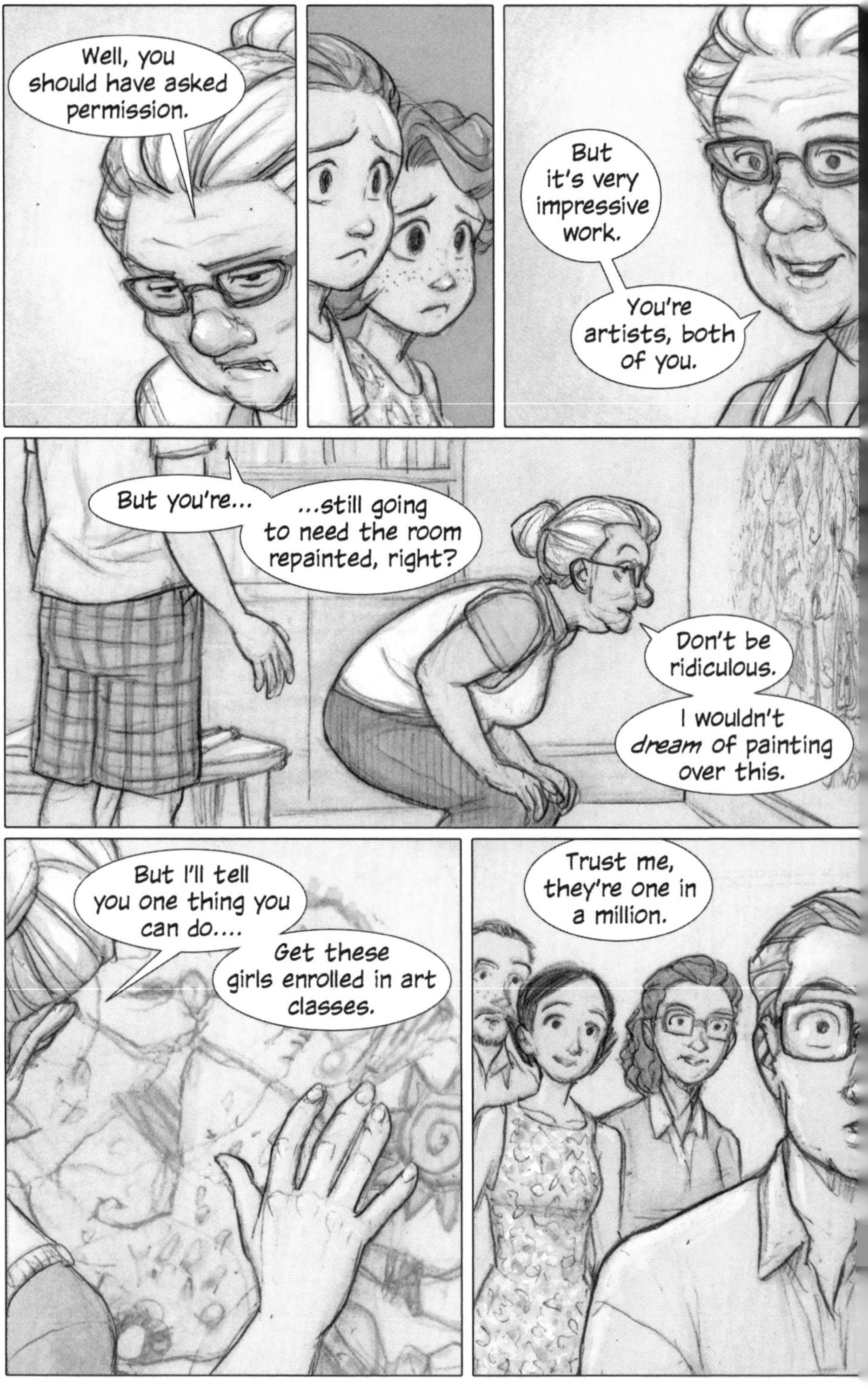
Well, you should have asked permission.
But it's very impressive work.
You're artists, both of you.
But you're...
...still going to need the room repainted, right?
Don't be ridiculous.
I wouldn't *dream* of painting over this.
But I'll tell you one thing you can do....
Get these girls enrolled in art classes.
Trust me, they're one in a million.

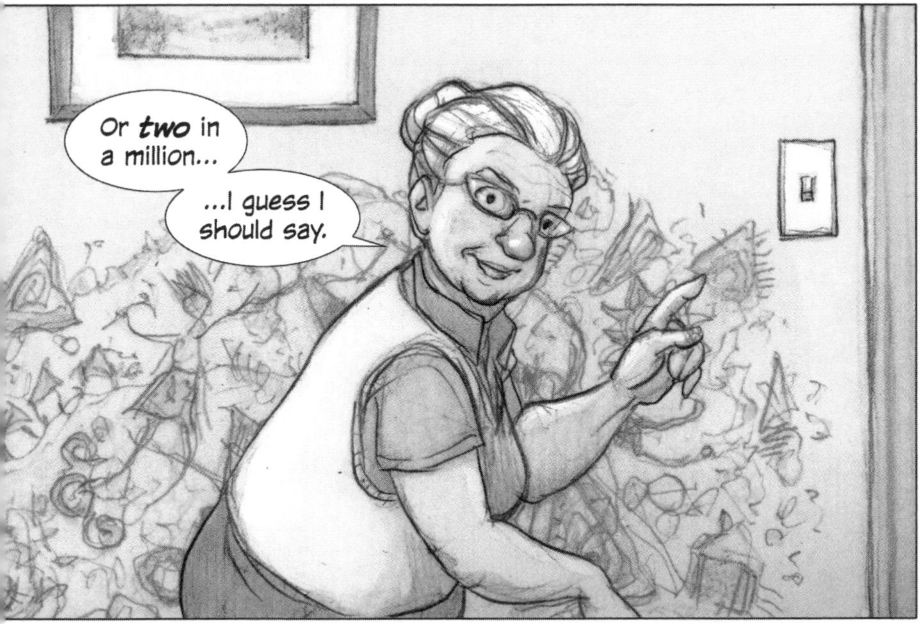
Or *two* in a million...
...I guess I should say.

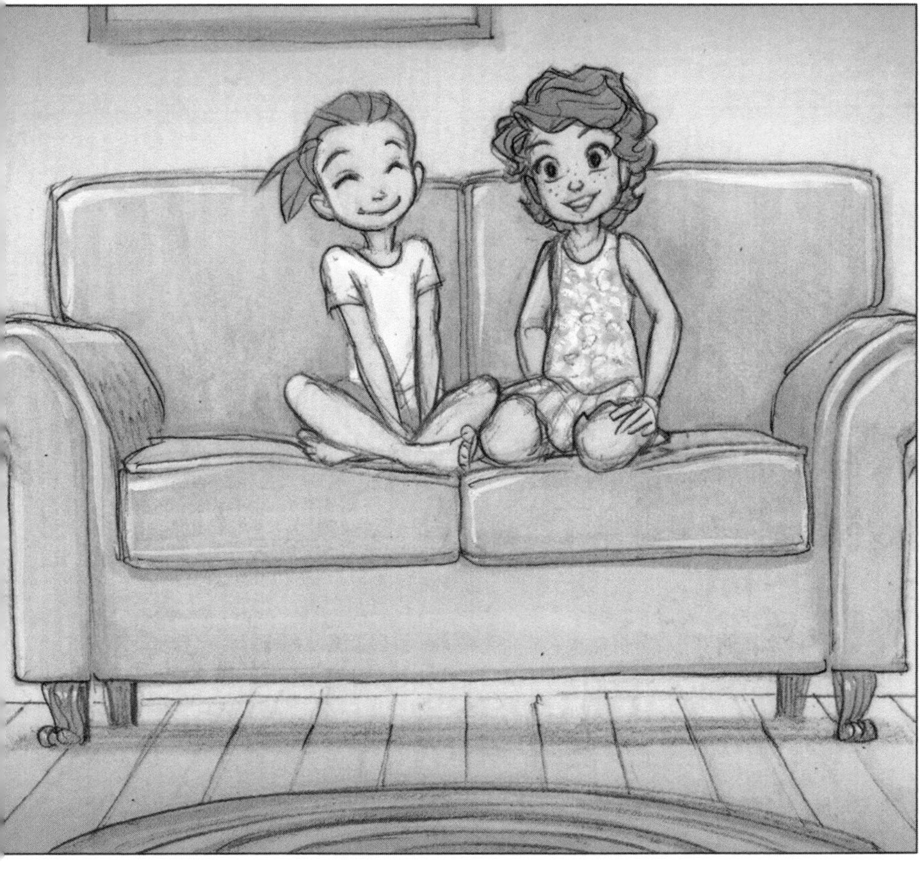

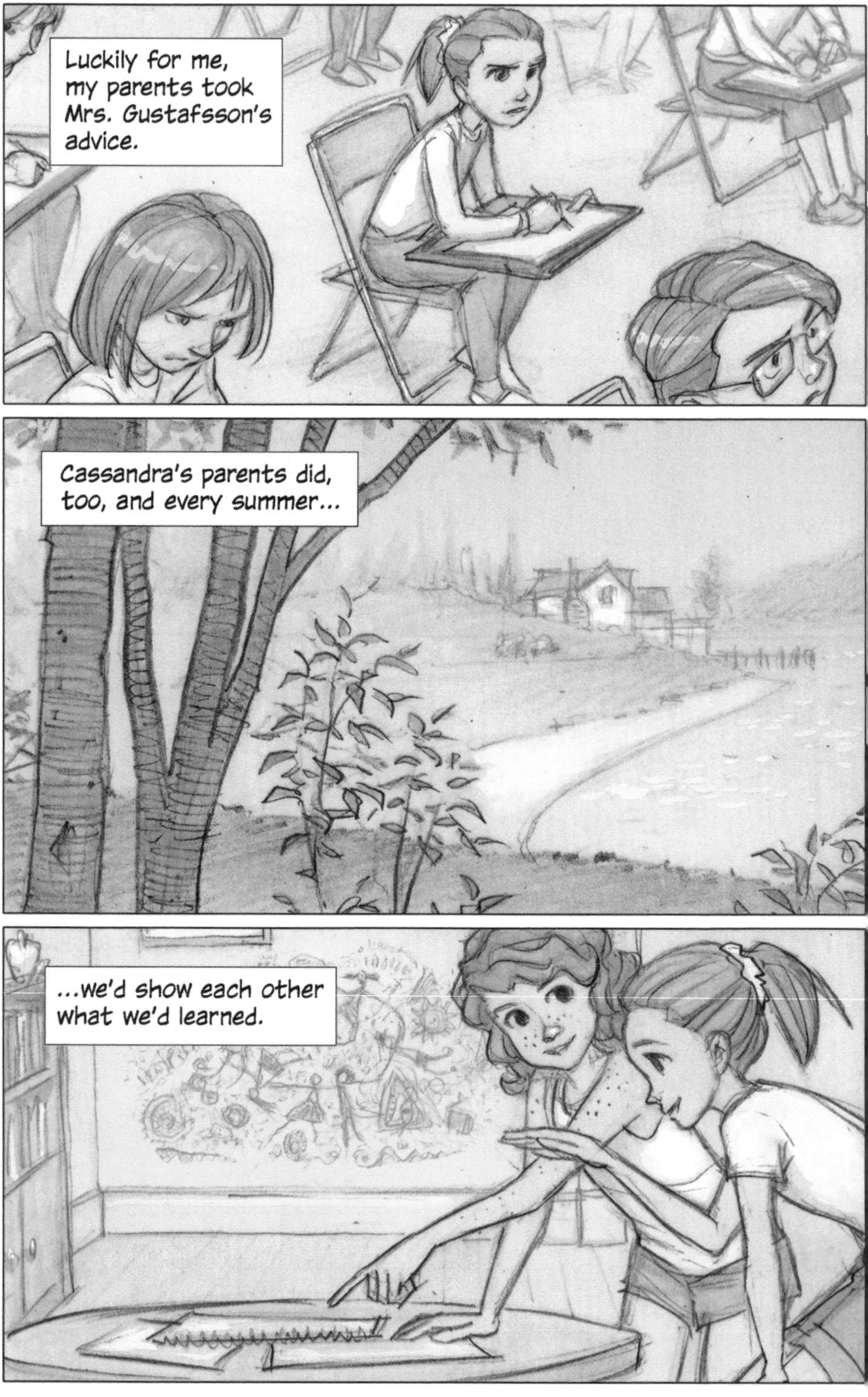
Luckily for me, my parents took Mrs. Gustafsson's advice.
Cassandra's parents did, too, and every summer...
...we'd show each other what we'd learned.

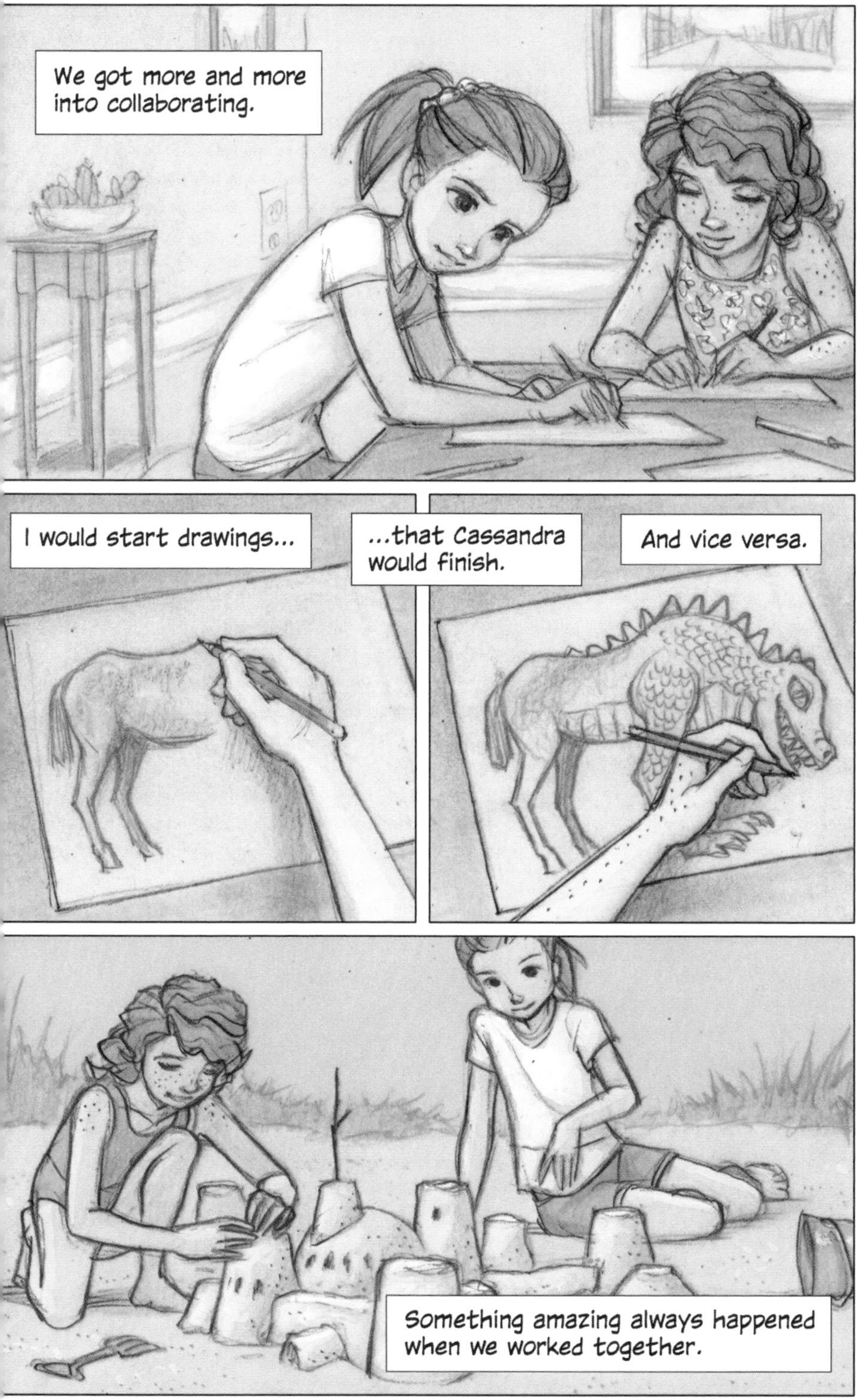
We got more and more into collaborating.
I would start drawings...
...that Cassandra would finish.
And vice versa.
Something amazing always happened when we worked together.

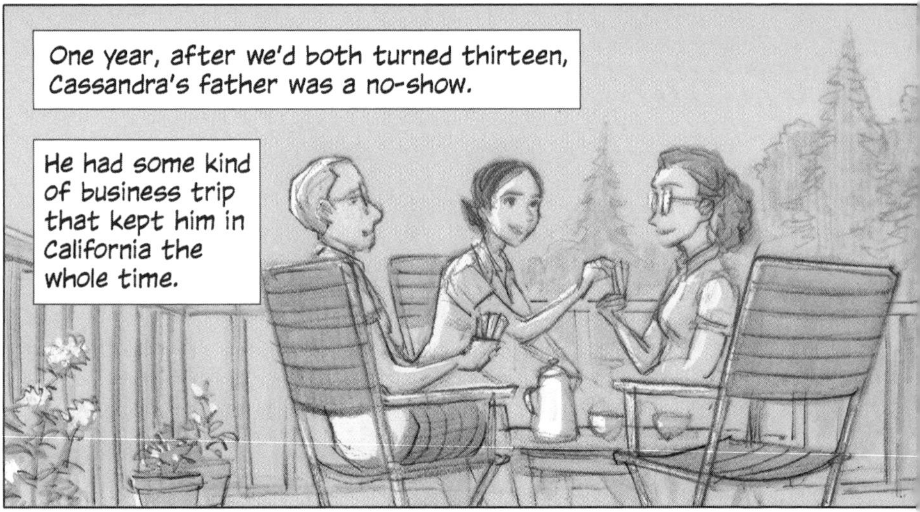
One year, after we'd both turned thirteen, Cassandra's father was a no-show.
He had some kind of business trip that kept him in California the whole time.

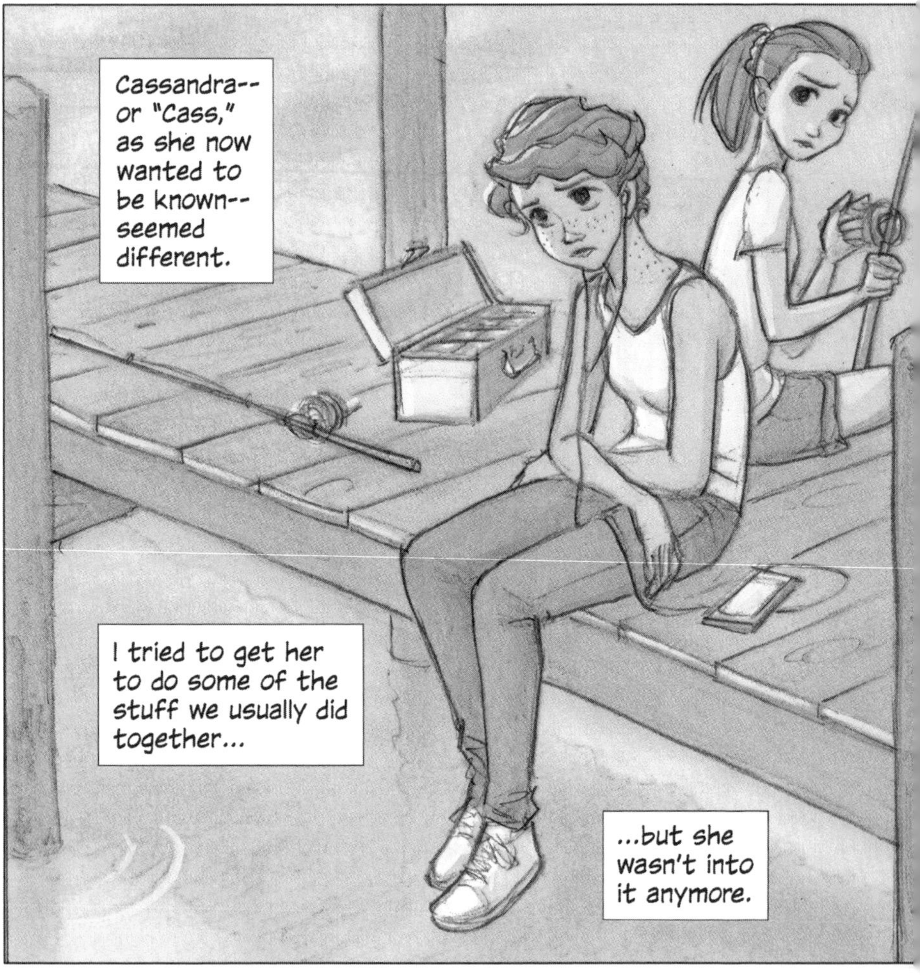
Cassandra--or "Cass," as she now wanted to be known--seemed different.
I tried to get her to do some of the stuff we usually did together...
...but she wasn't into it anymore.

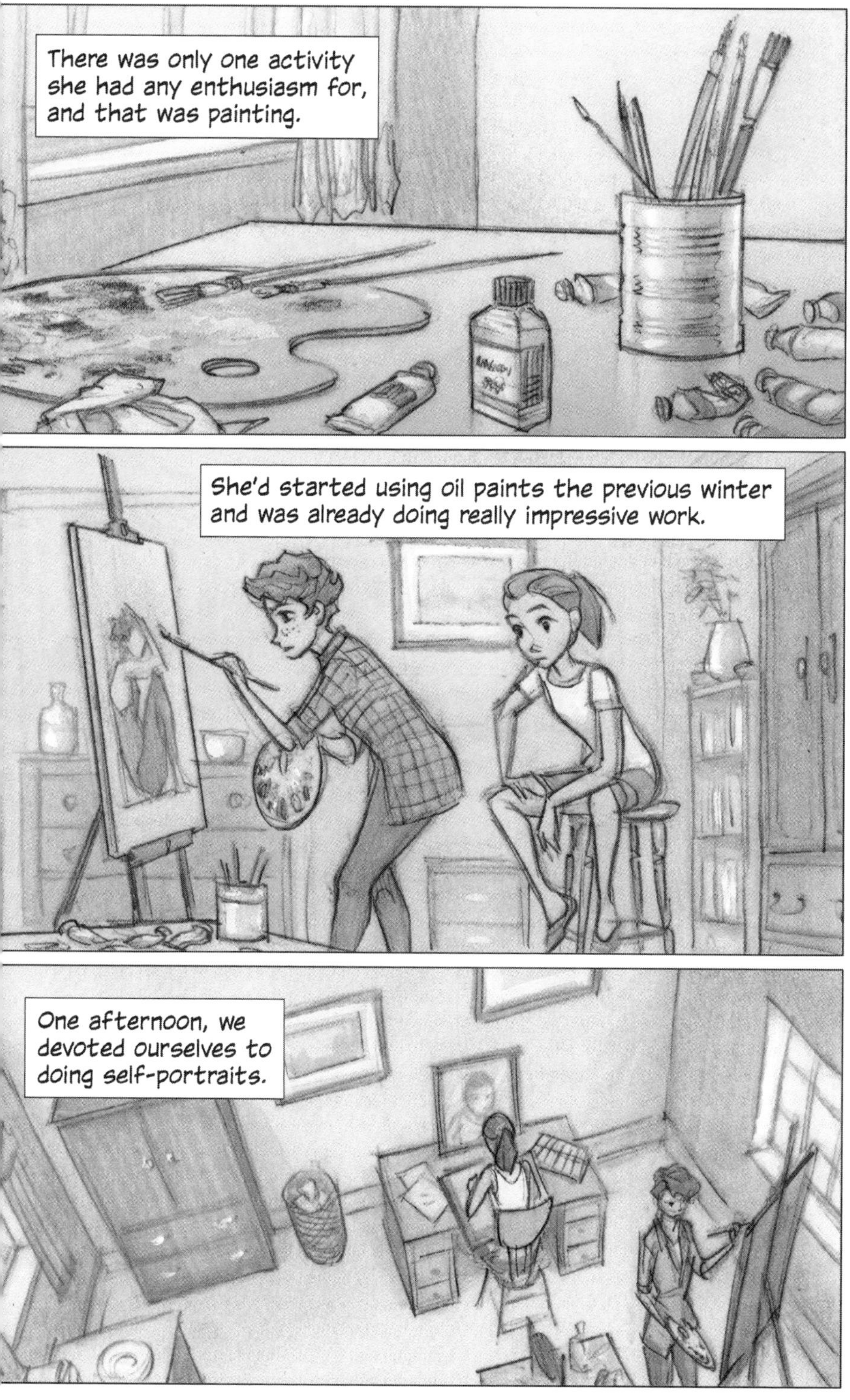
There was only one activity she had any enthusiasm for, and that was painting.
She'd started using oil paints the previous winter and was already doing really impressive work.
One afternoon, we devoted ourselves to doing self-portraits.

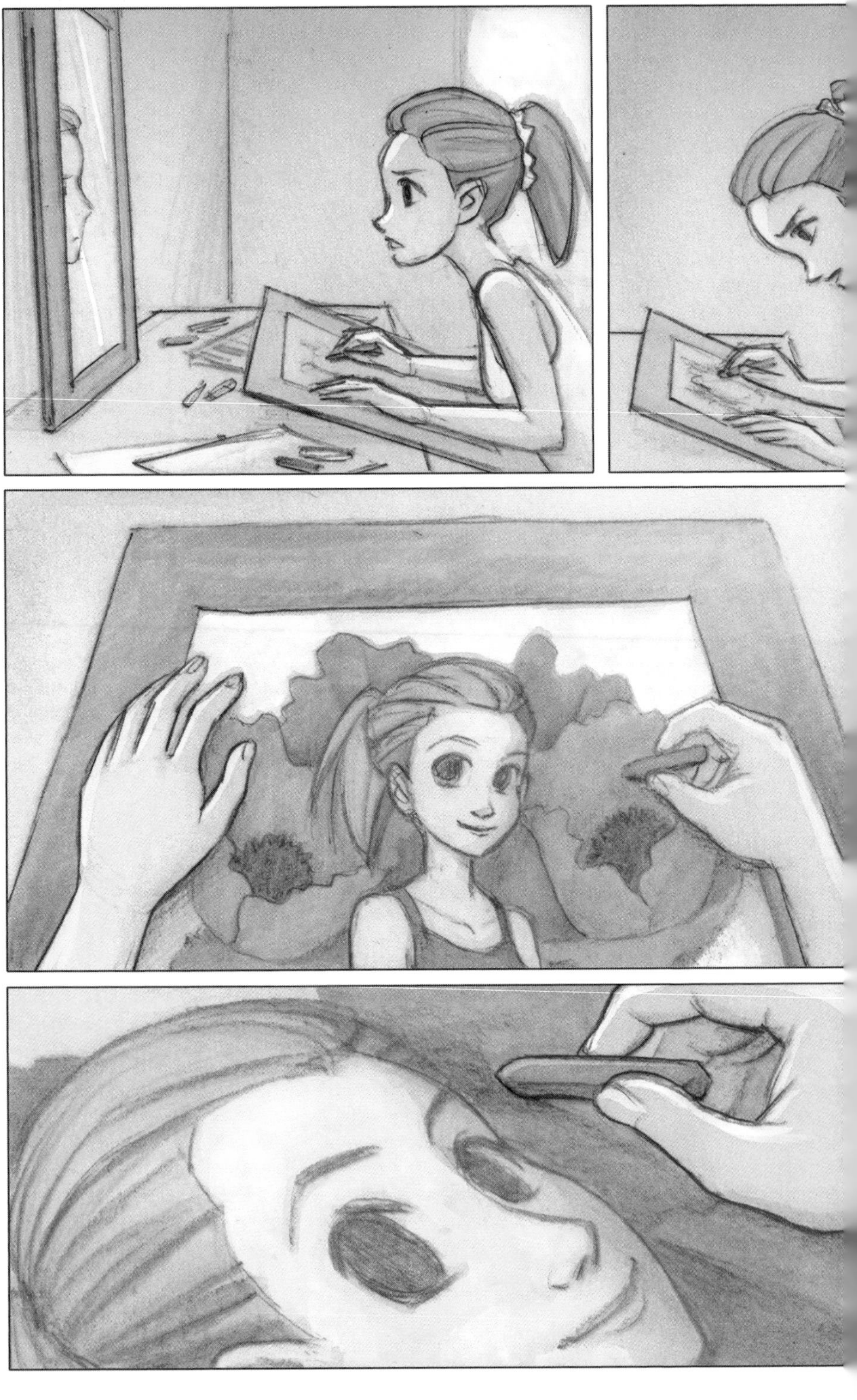

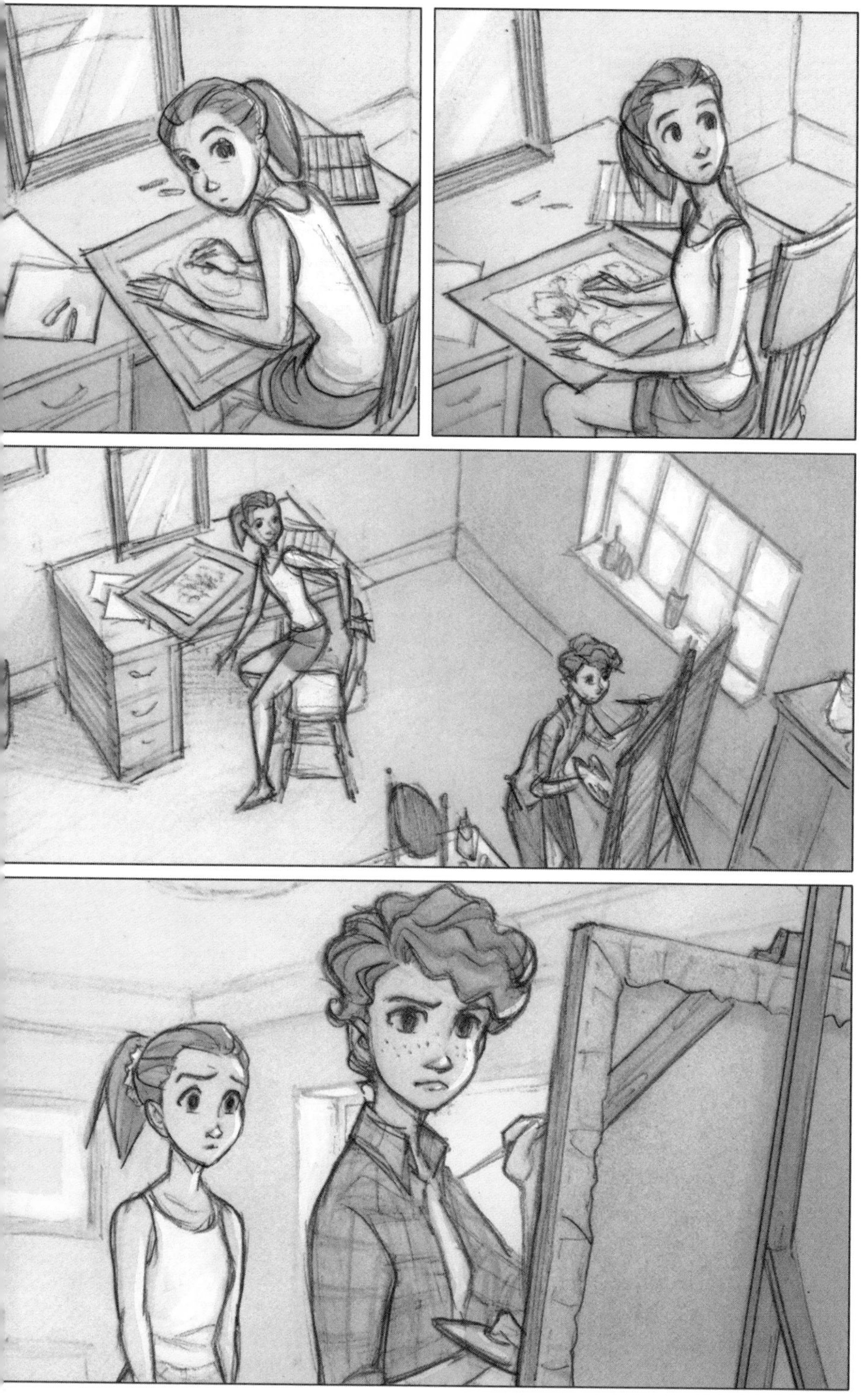

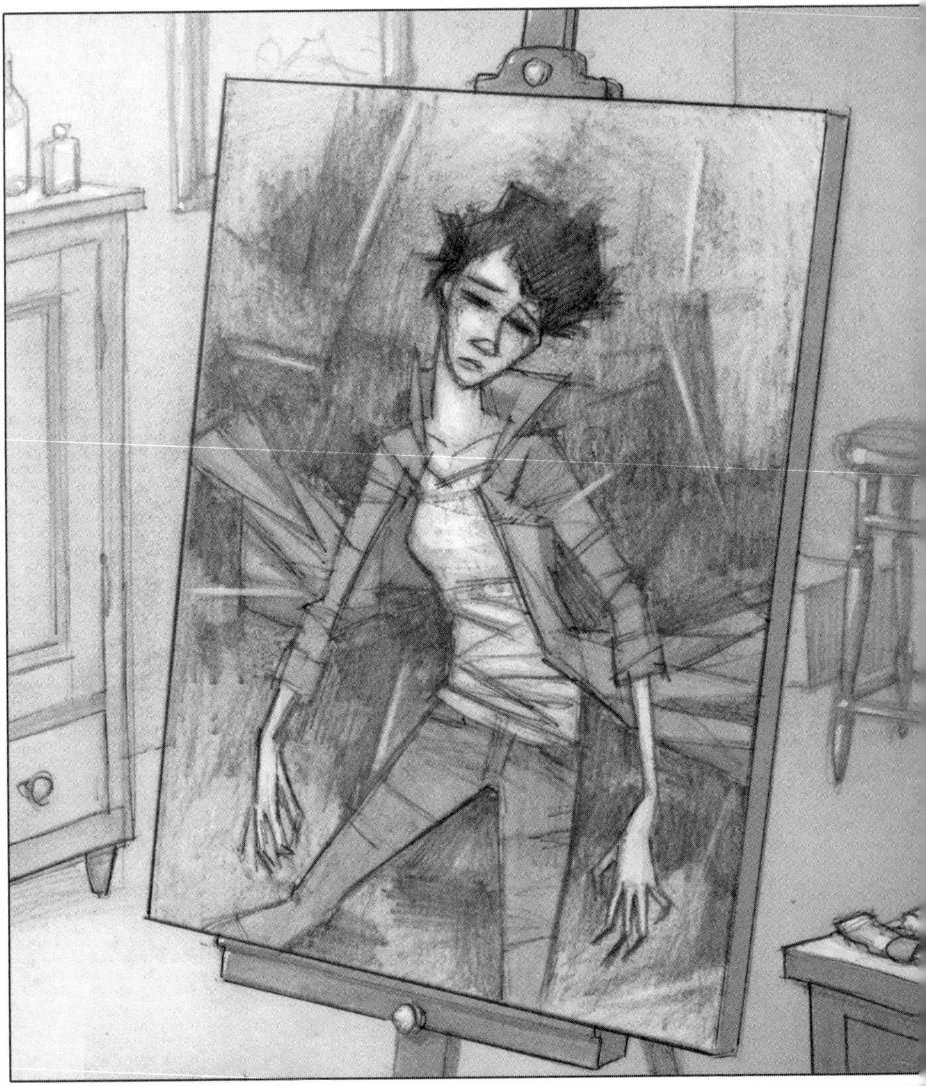

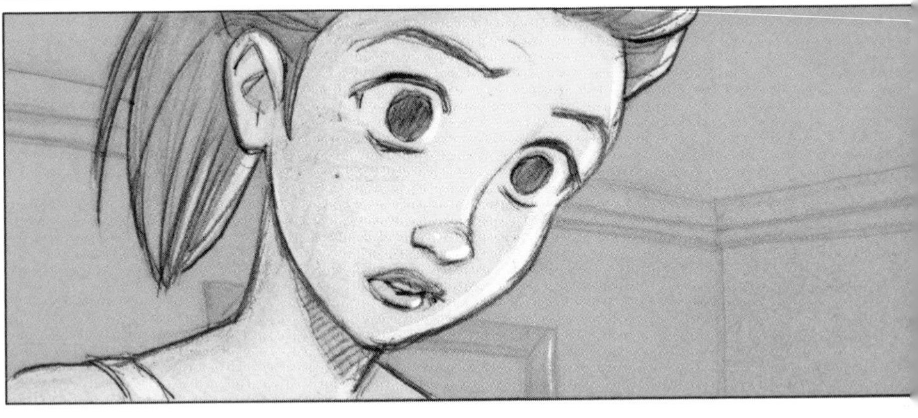

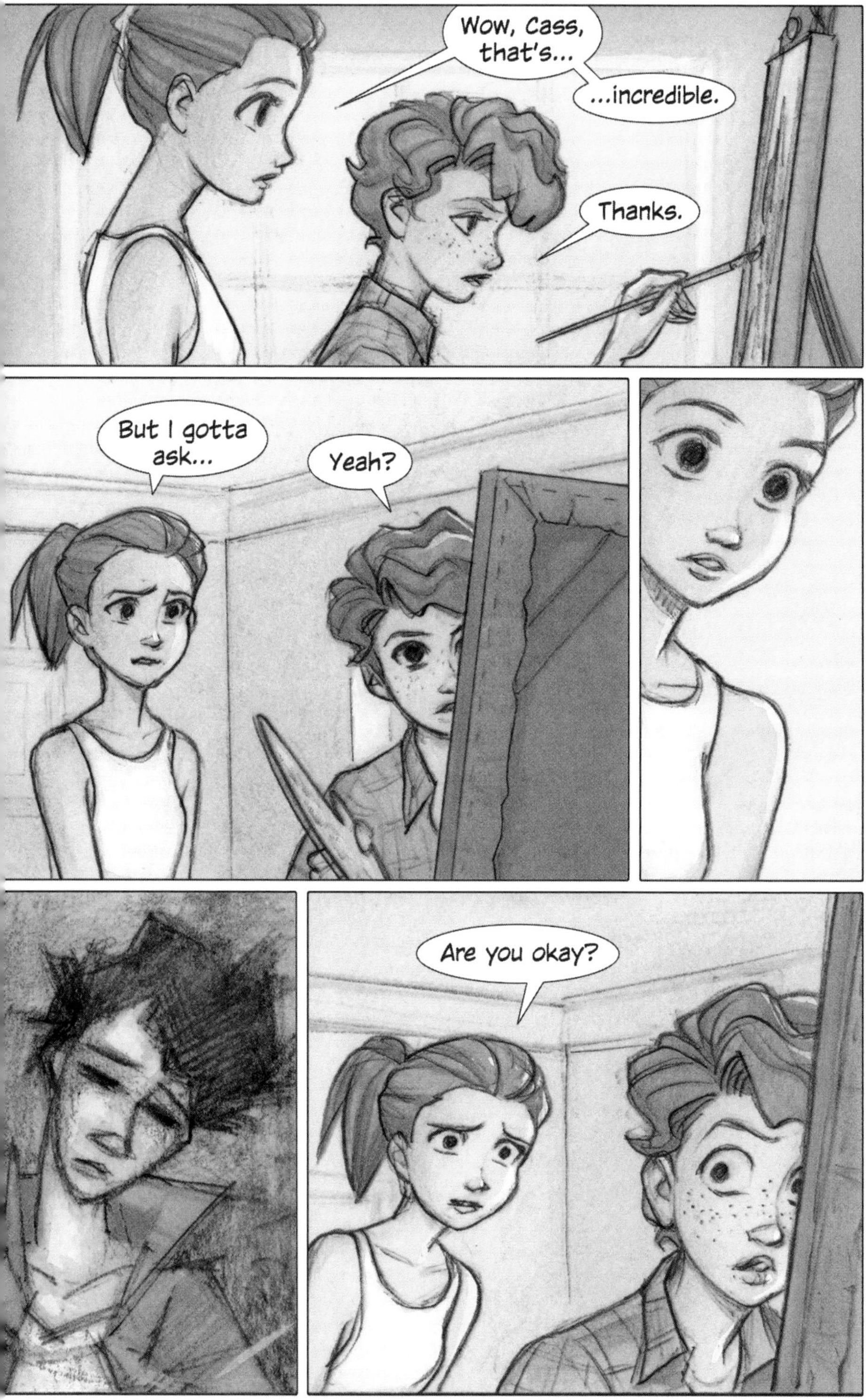
Wow, Cass, that's...
...incredible.
Thanks.
But I gotta ask...
Yeah?
Are you okay?

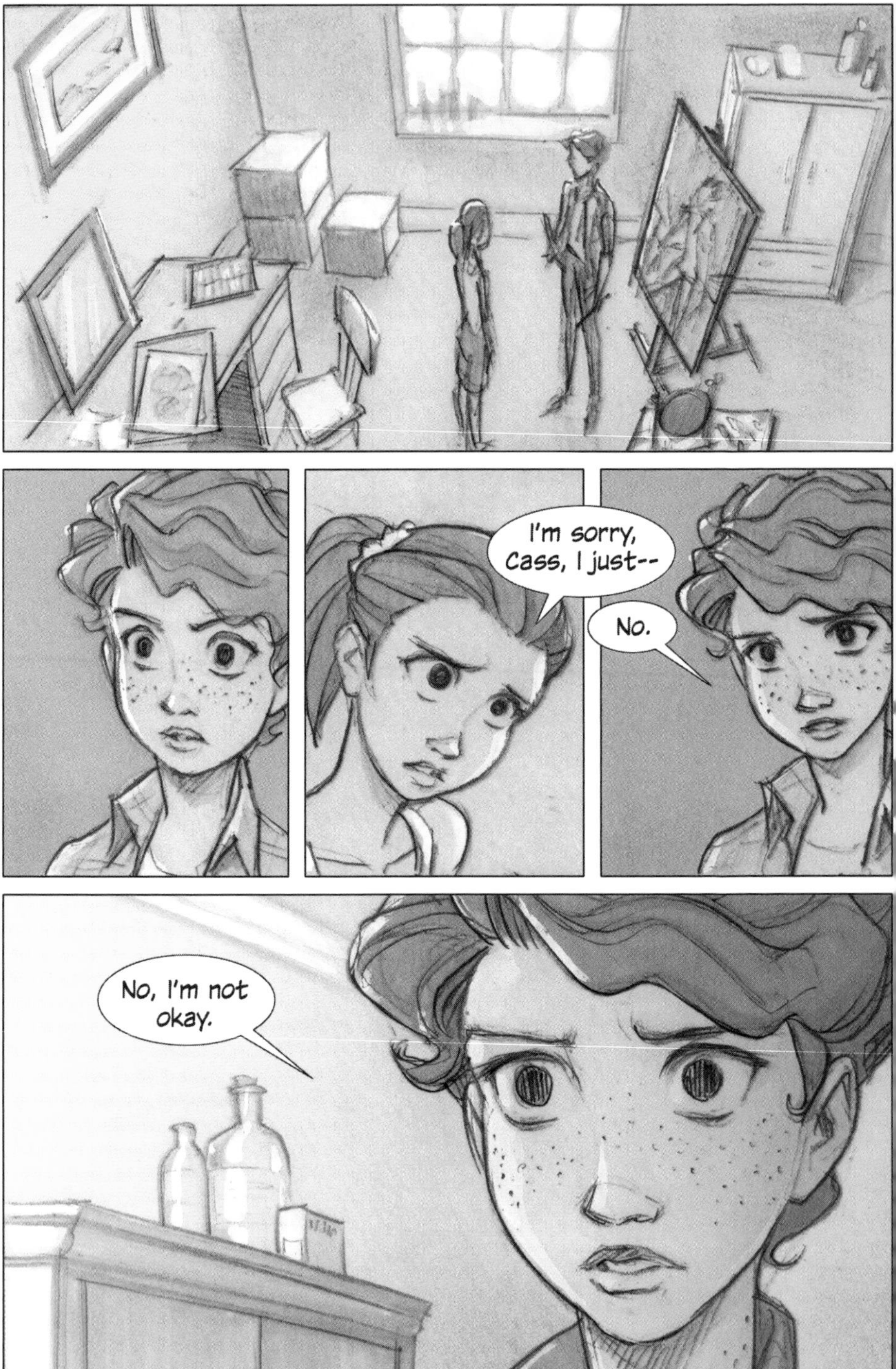
I'm sorry, Cass, I just--
No.
No, I'm not okay.

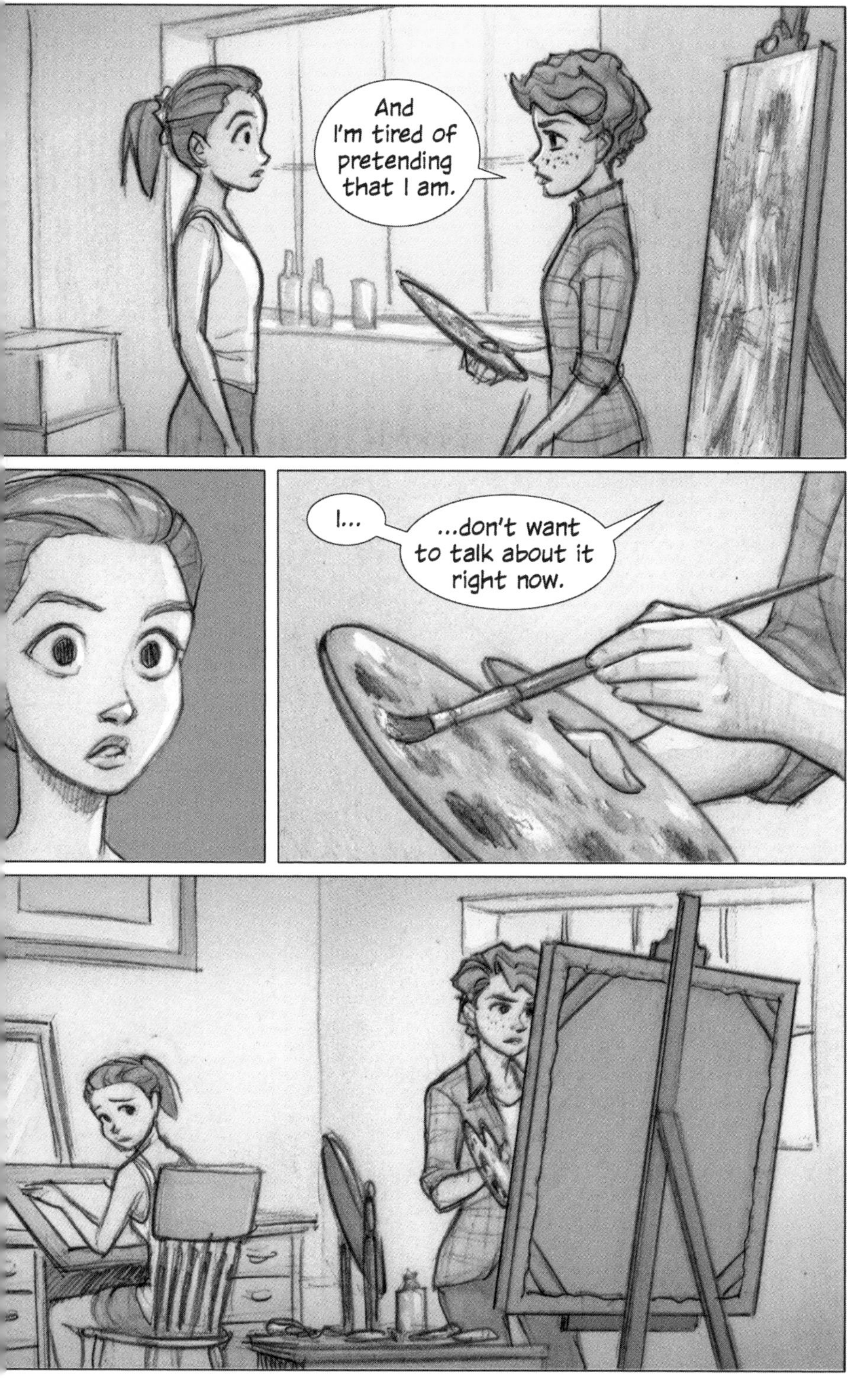
And I'm tired of pretending that I am.
I...
...don't want to talk about it right now.

That night, Cass and I stayed out after sundown, talking about things.
Admittedly, I did most of the talking.
...and he says, "This hardware store has been in the family for three generations."

And I'm like, "Yeah, yeah, yeah. Three generations. I *get* it.
"You've only been drilling that into my head since the day I was *born*.
"Do you have any *idea* how sick to death I am of hearing you say that?"

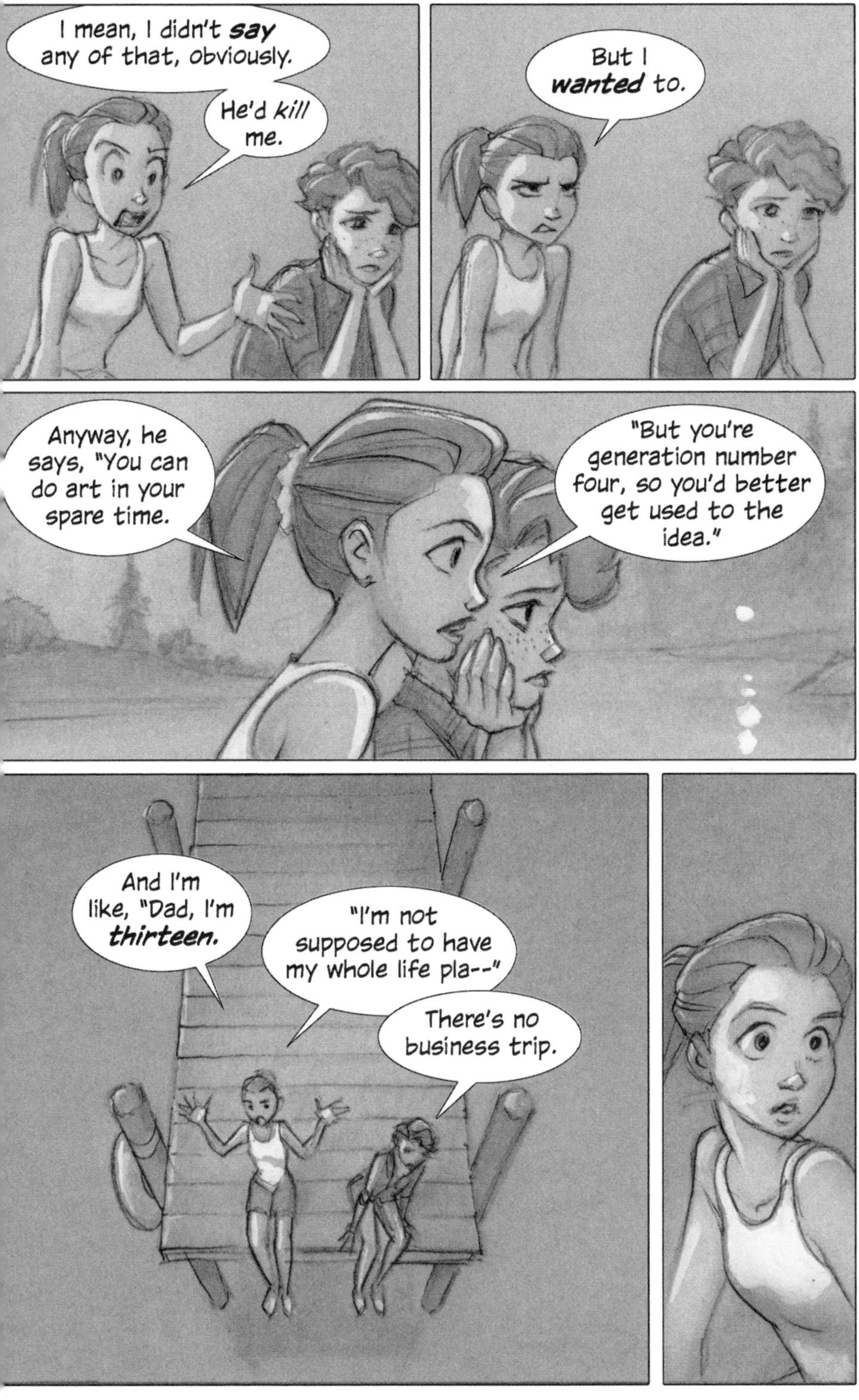
I mean, I didn't **say** any of that, obviously.
He'd *kill* me.
But I **wanted** to.
Anyway, he says, "You can do art in your spare time.
"But you're generation number four, so you'd better get used to the idea."
And I'm like, "Dad, I'm **thirteen.**
"I'm not supposed to have my whole life pla--"
There's no business trip.

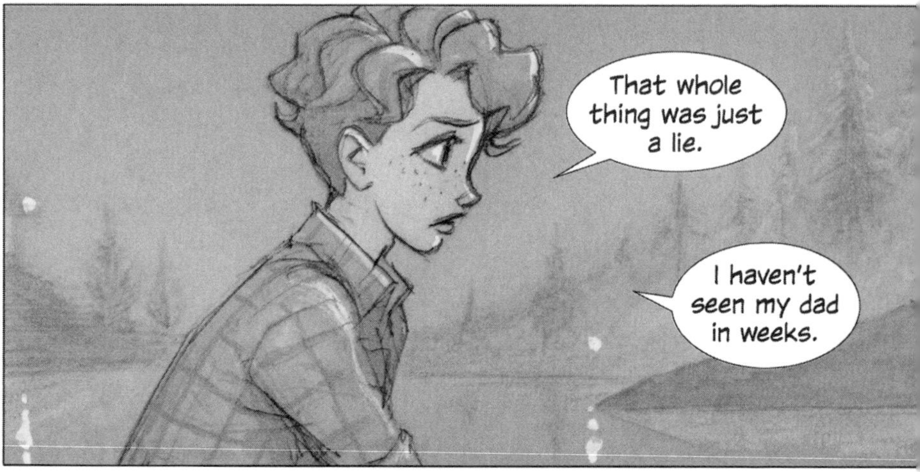
That whole thing was just a lie.
I haven't seen my dad in weeks.

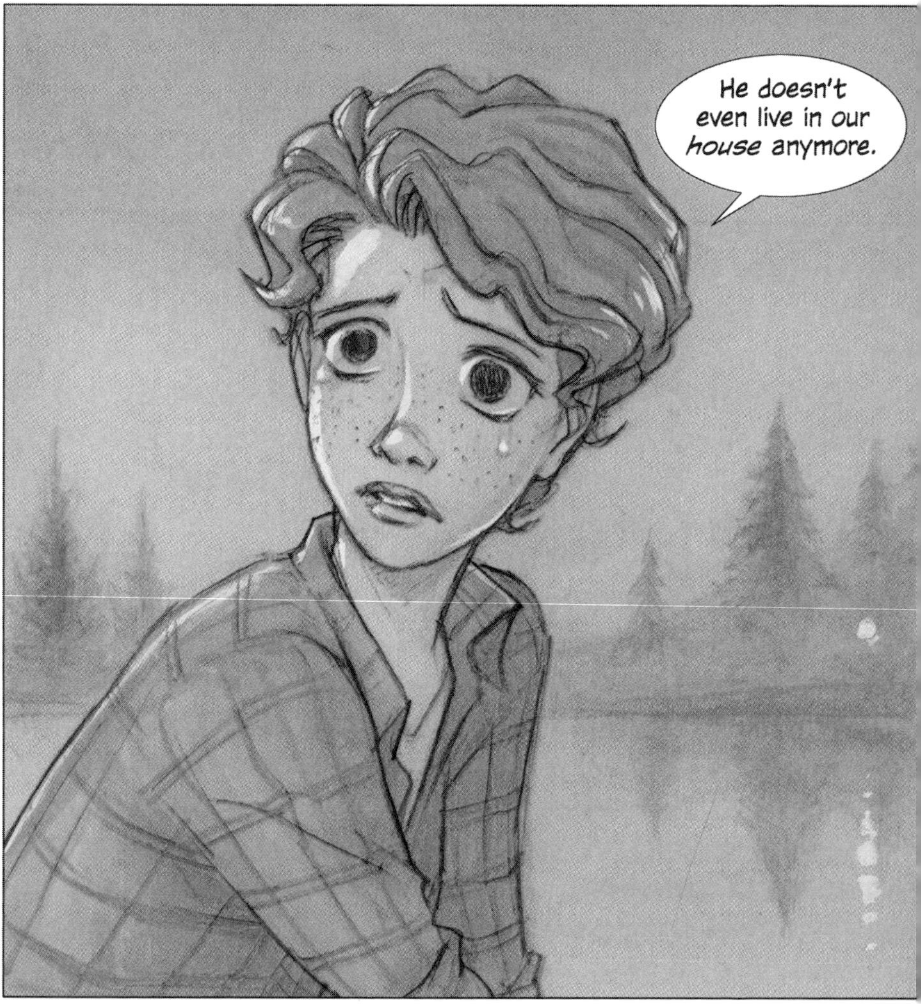
He doesn't even live in our *house* anymore.

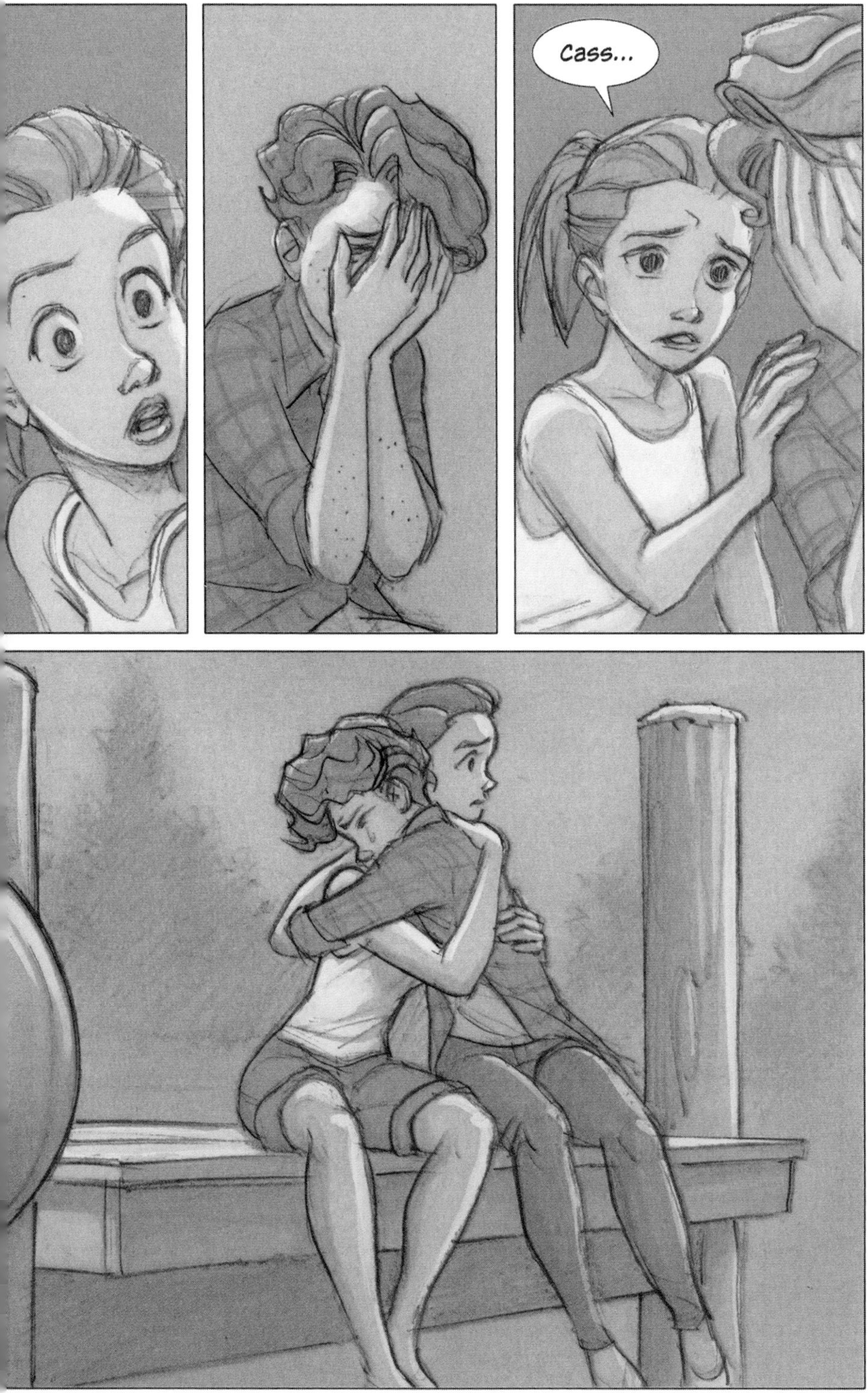
Cass...

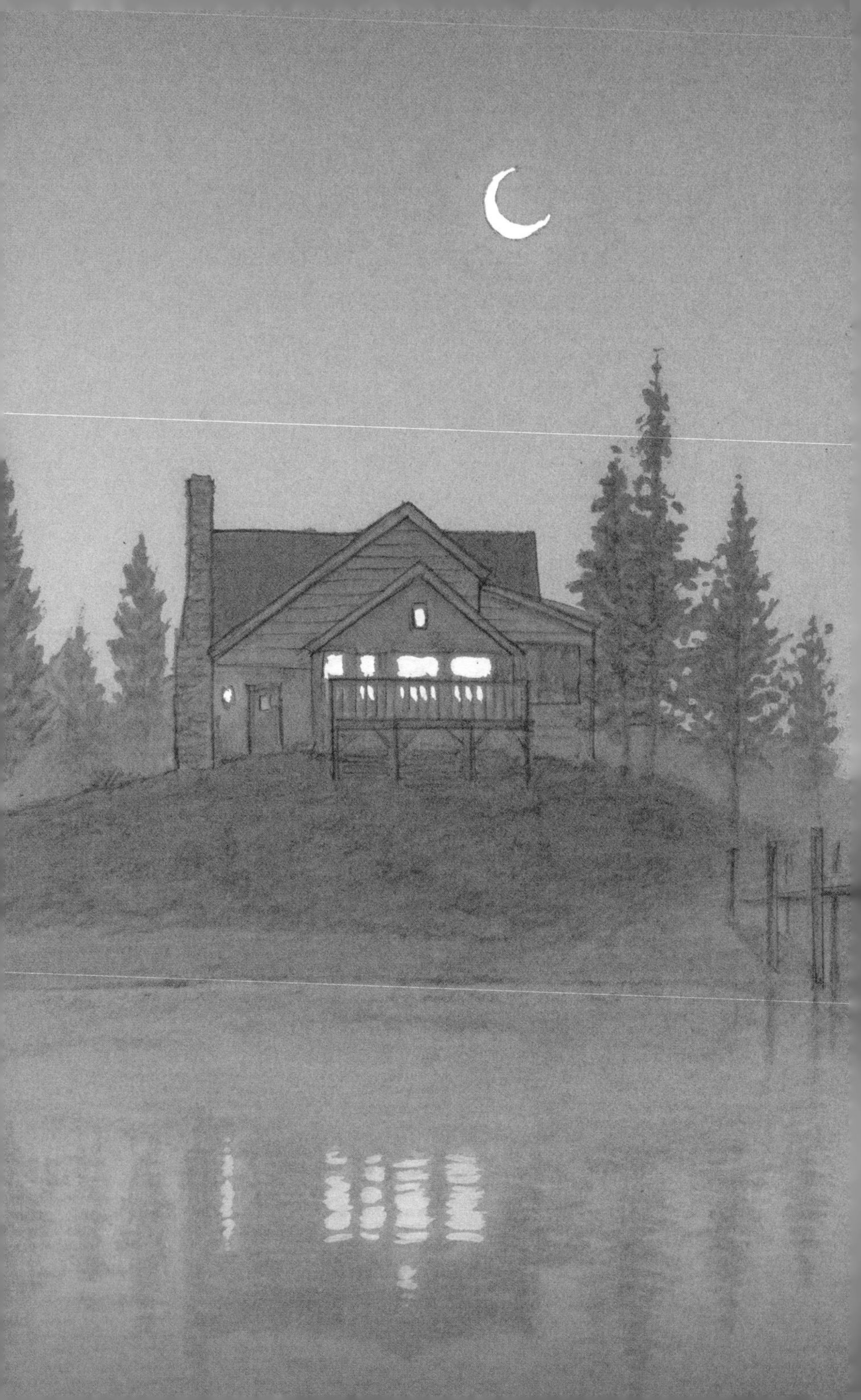

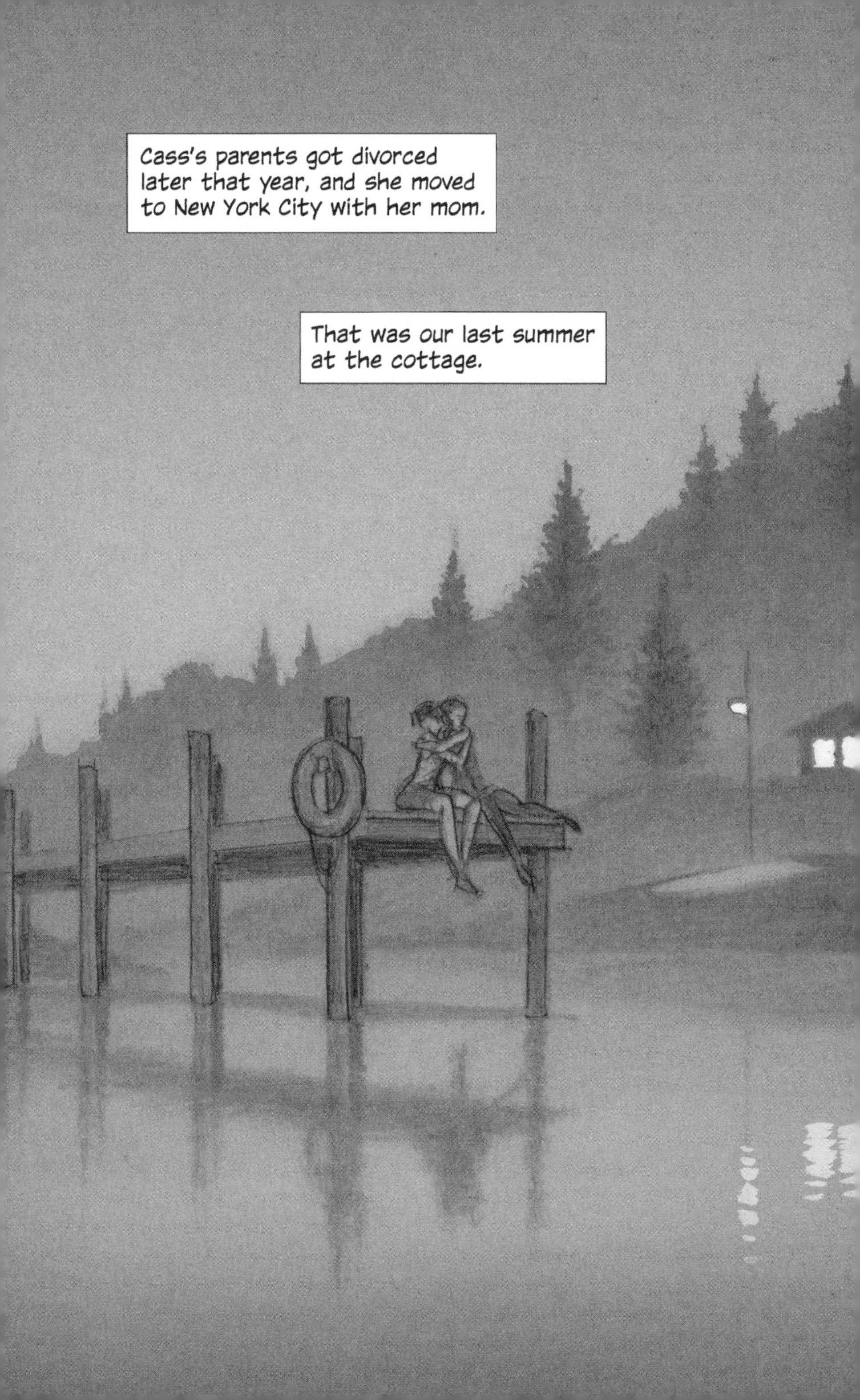
Cass's parents got divorced later that year, and she moved to New York City with her mom.
That was our last summer at the cottage.

Part Two

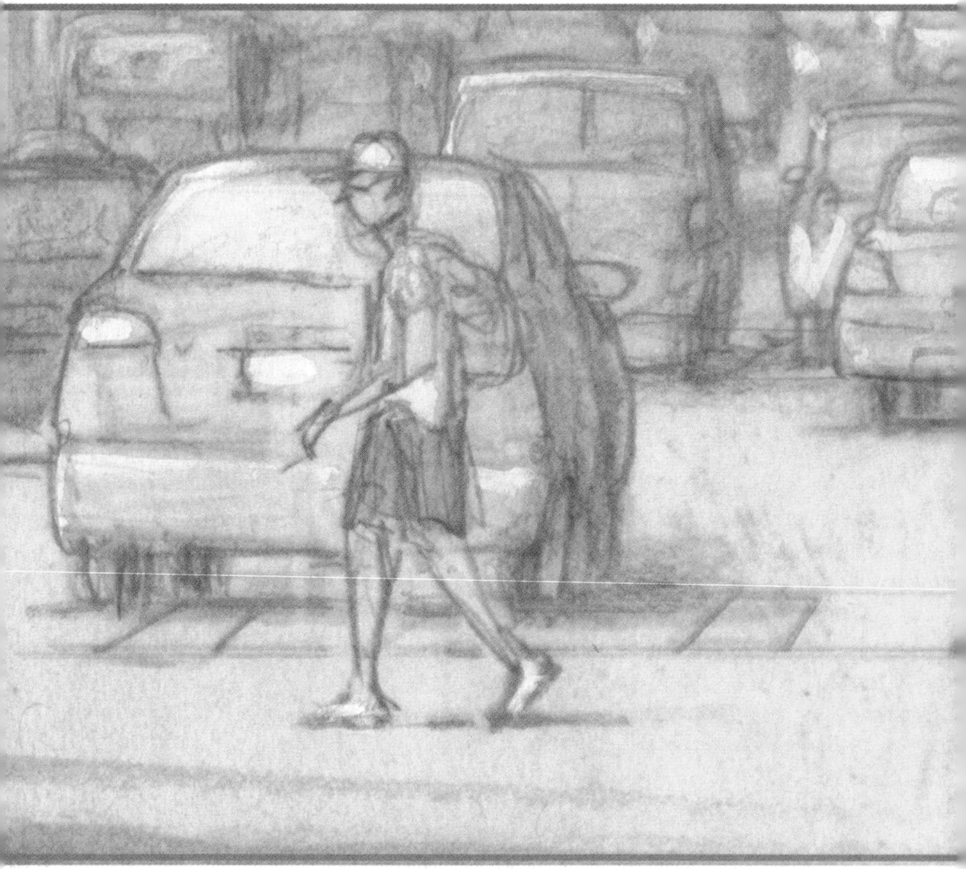

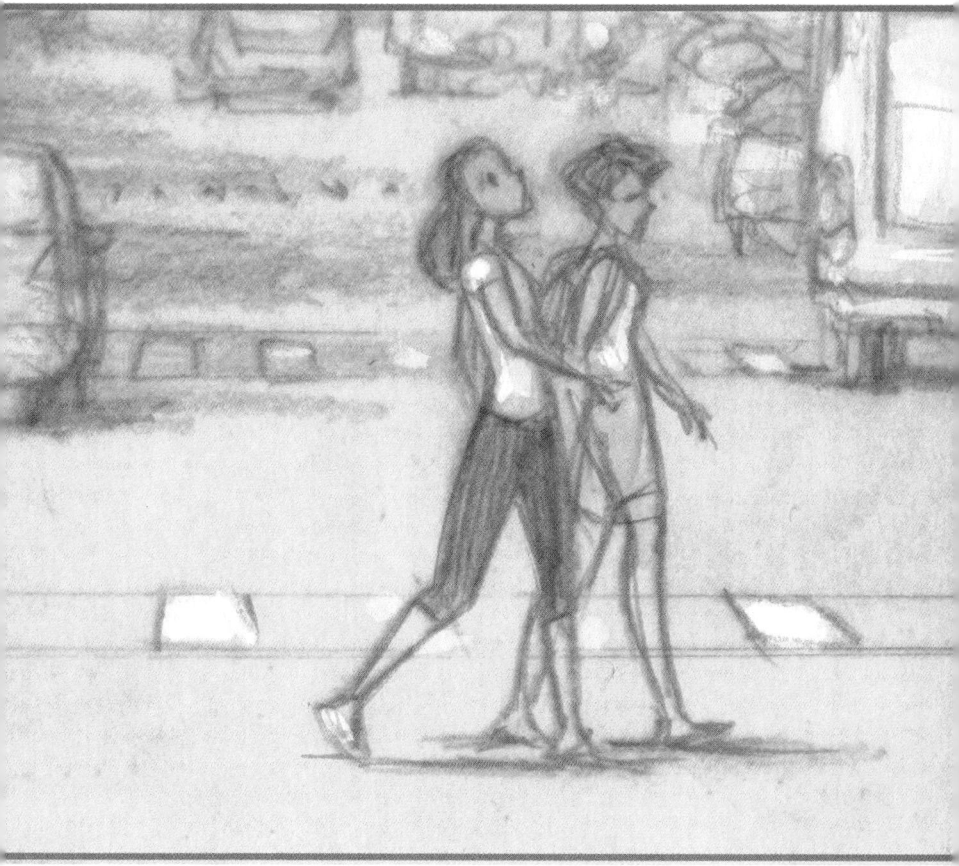

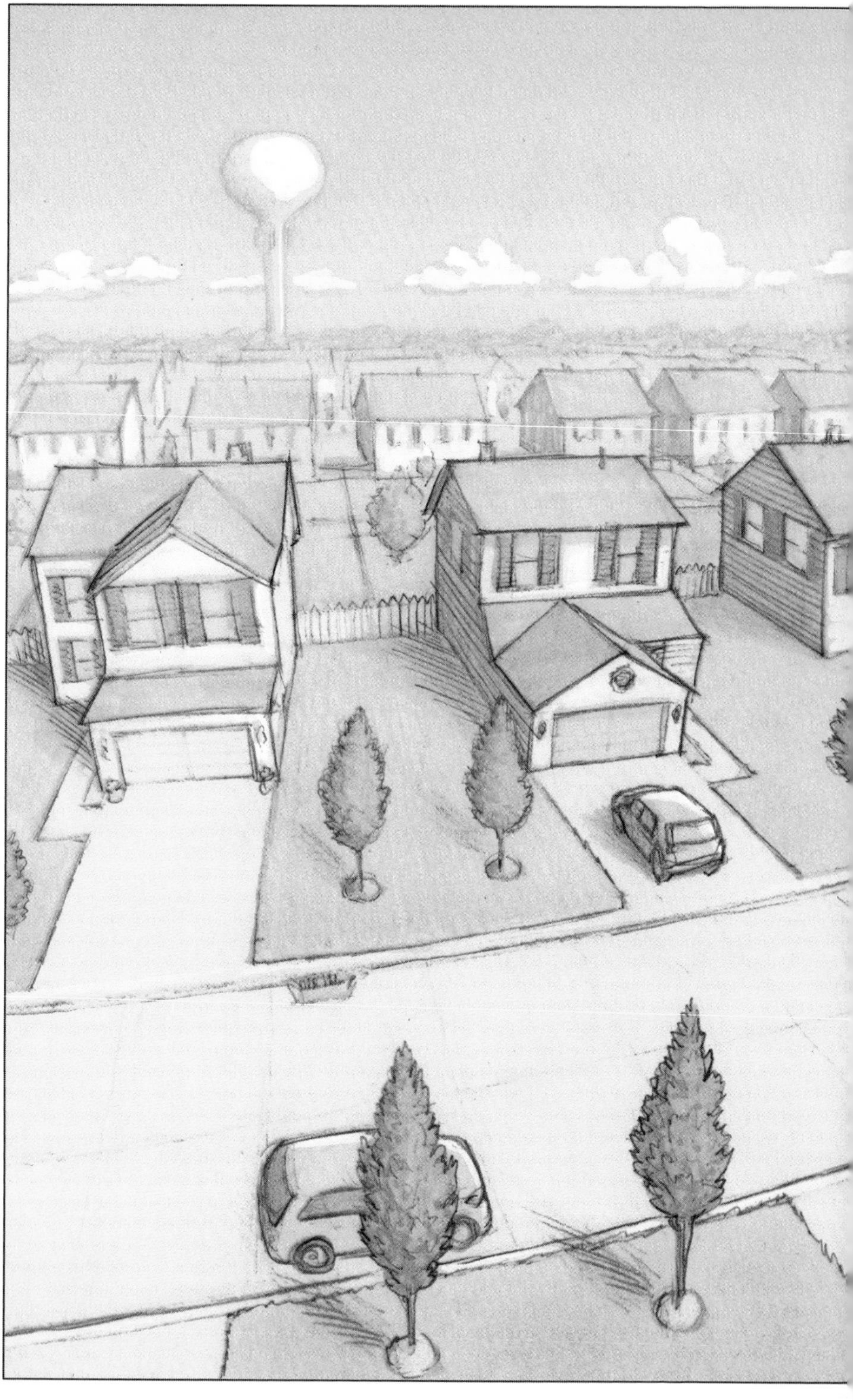

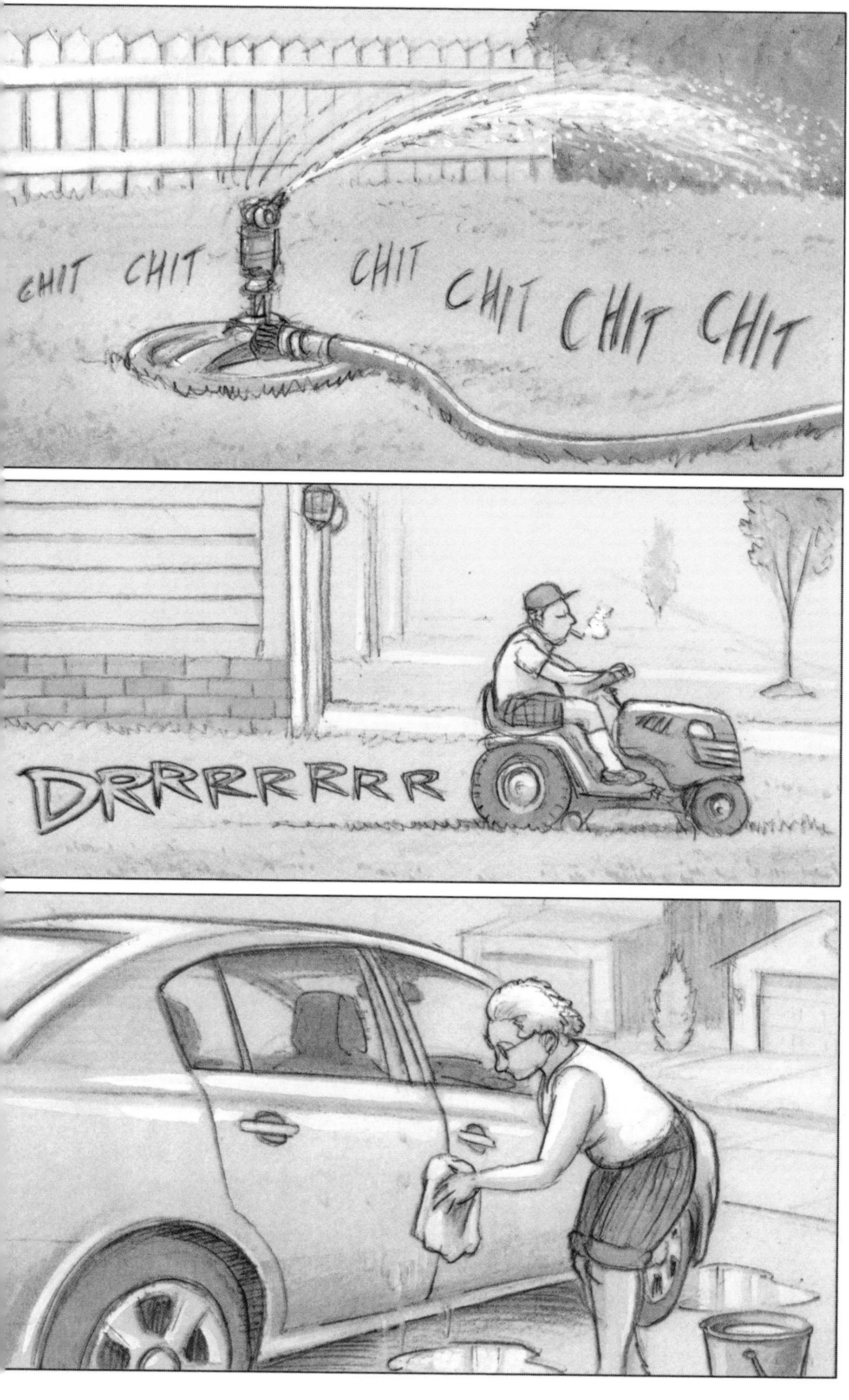
CHIT CHIT CHIT CHIT CHIT CHIT
DRRRRRRR

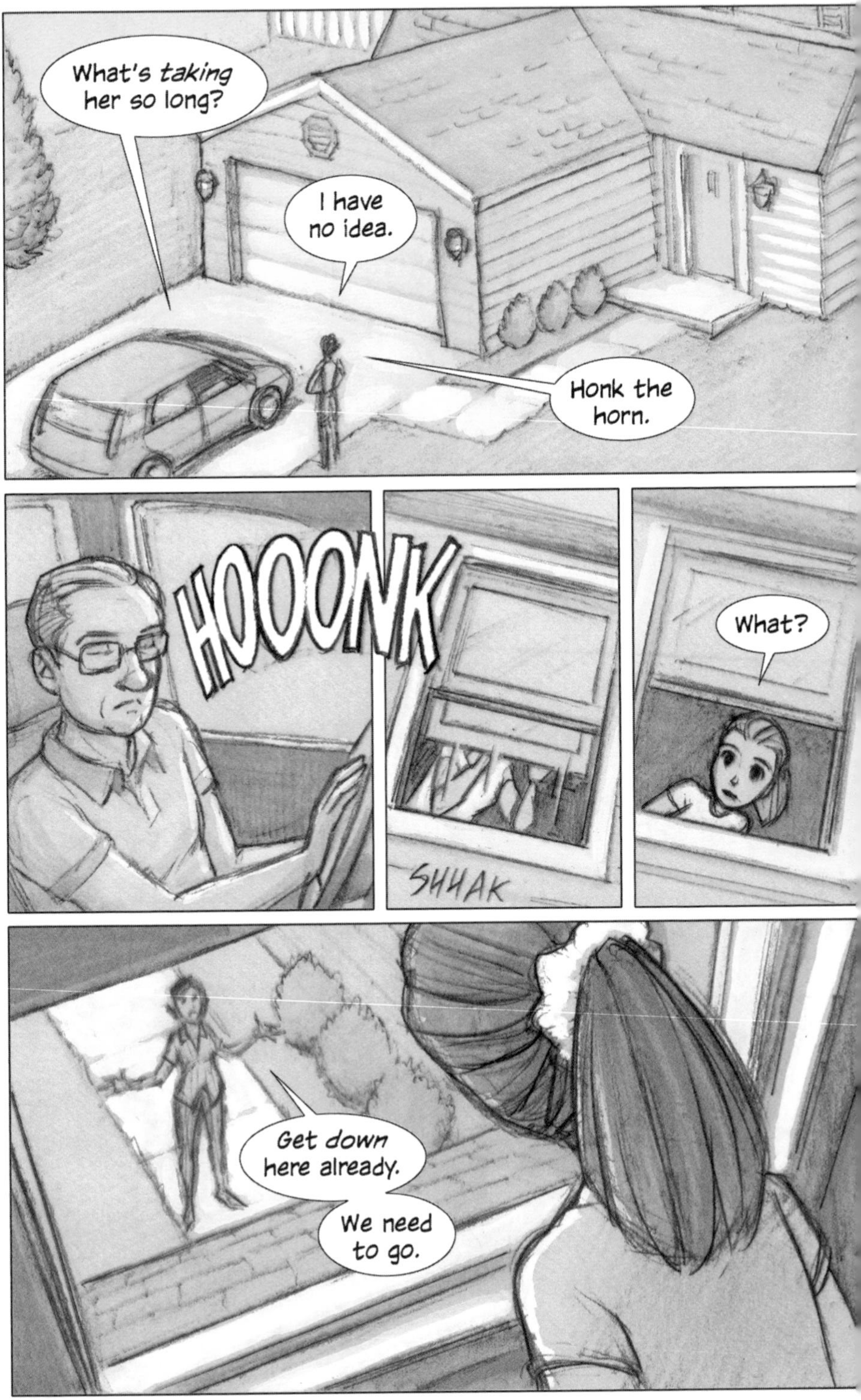
What's *taking* her so long?
I have no idea.
Honk the horn.
HOOONK
SHHAK
What?
Get *down* here already.
We need to go.

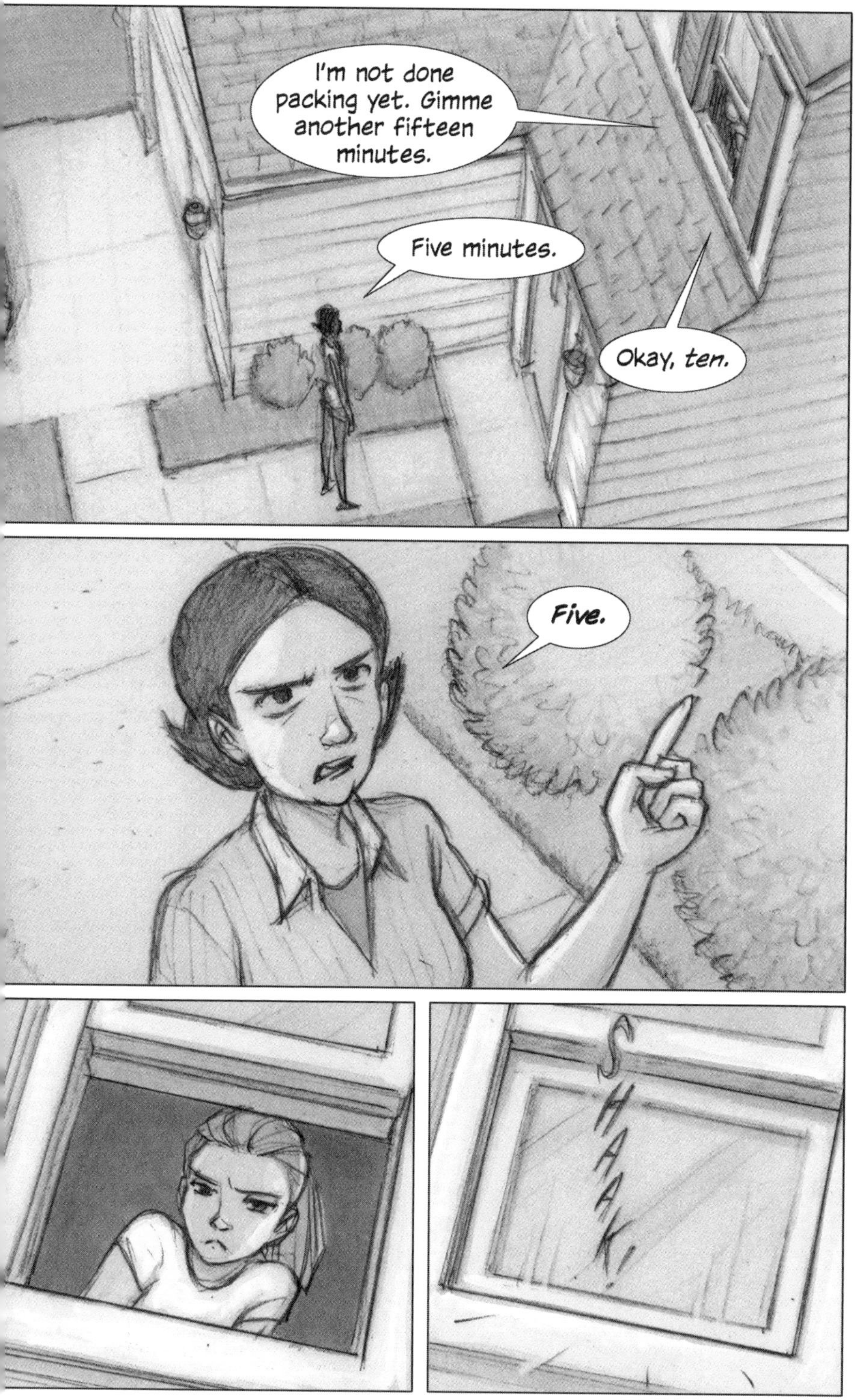
I'm not done packing yet. Gimme another fifteen minutes.
Five minutes.
Okay, ten.
Five.
SHAAK!

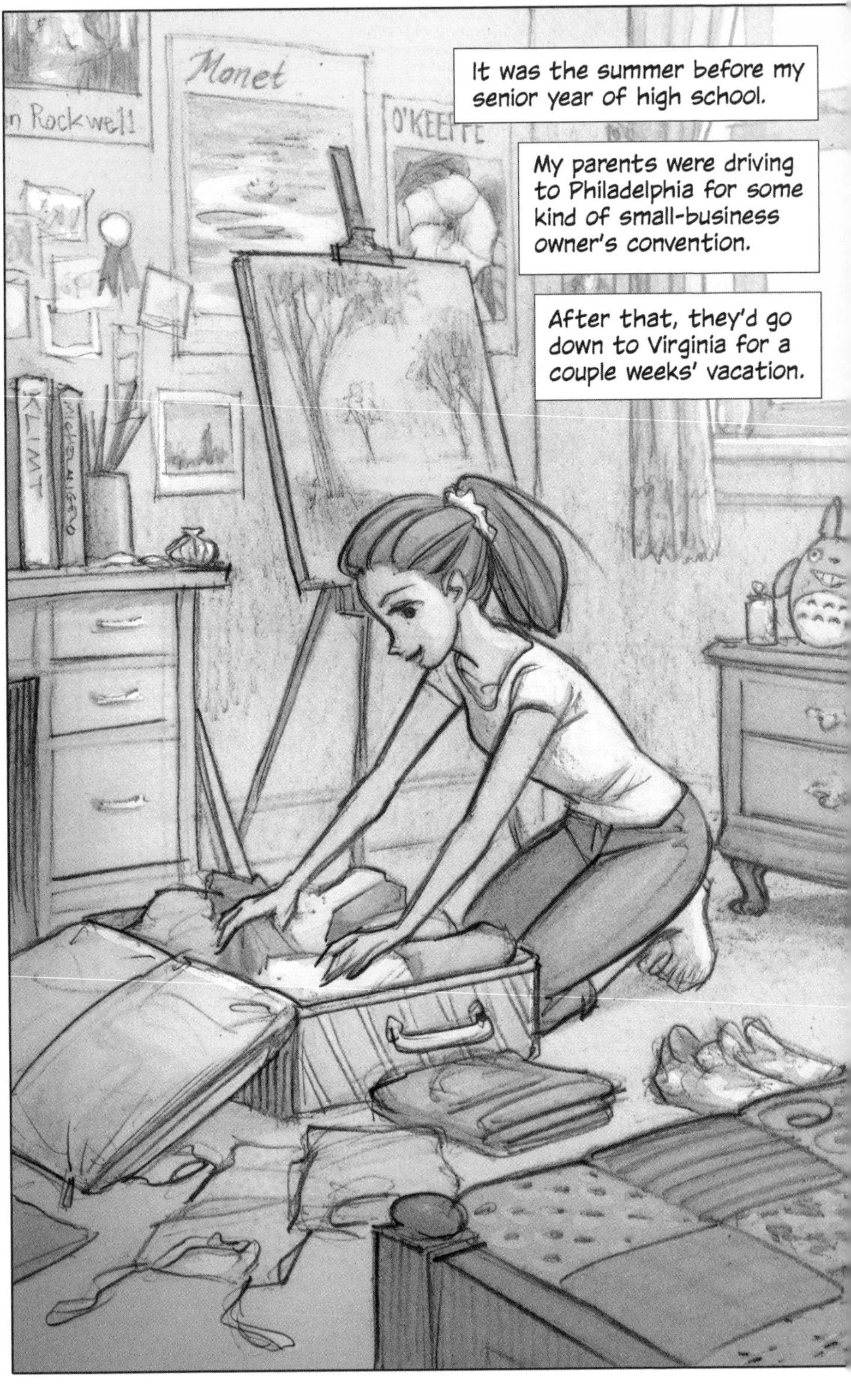
Monet
O'KEEFFE
KLIMT
It was the summer before my senior year of high school.
My parents were driving to Philadelphia for some kind of small-business owner's convention.
After that, they'd go down to Virginia for a couple weeks' vacation.

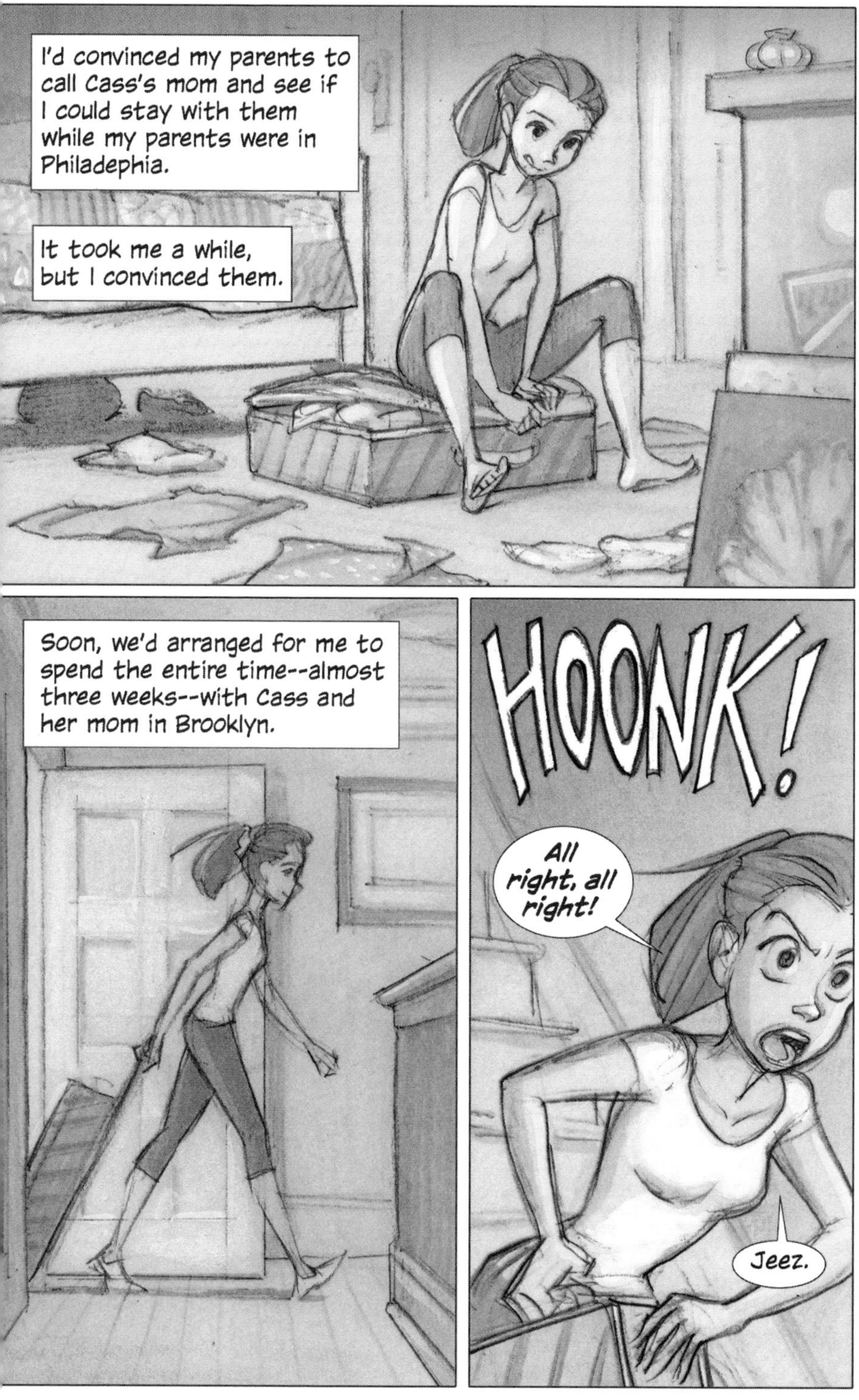

I'd convinced my parents to call Cass's mom and see if I could stay with them while my parents were in Philadephia.
It took me a while, but I convinced them.
Soon, we'd arranged for me to spend the entire time--almost three weeks--with Cass and her mom in Brooklyn.
HOONK!
All right, all right!
Jeez.

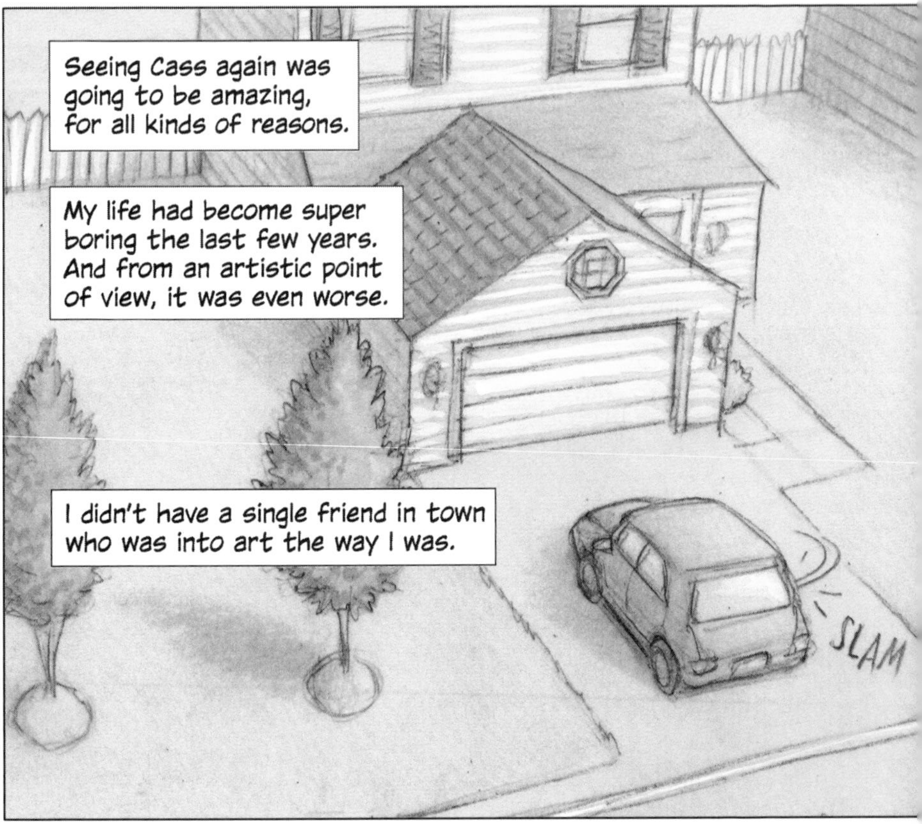
Seeing Cass again was going to be amazing, for all kinds of reasons.
My life had become super boring the last few years. And from an artistic point of view, it was even worse.
I didn't have a single friend in town who was into art the way I was.
SLAM

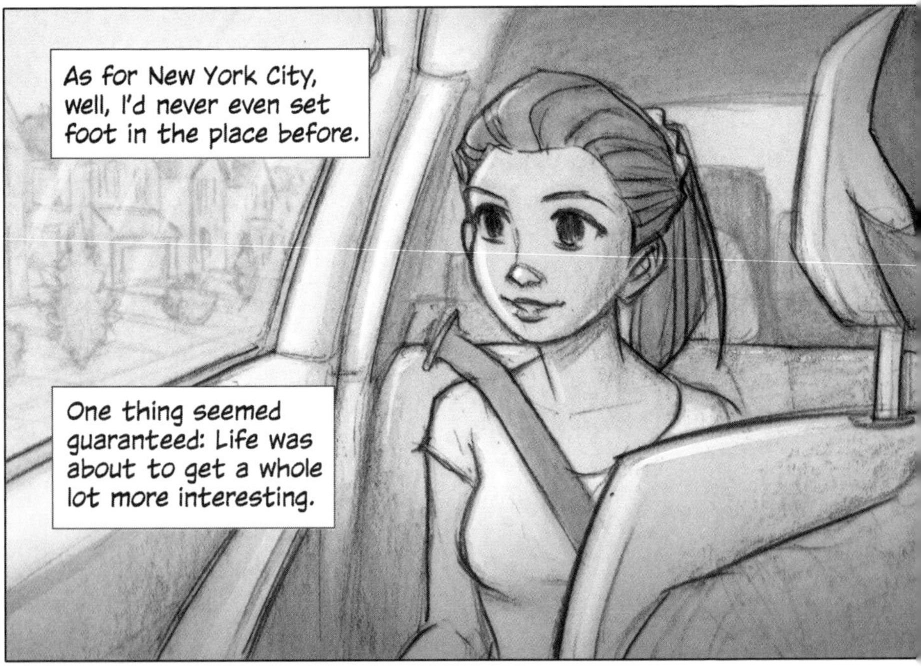
As for New York City, well, I'd never even set foot in the place before.
One thing seemed guaranteed: Life was about to get a whole lot more interesting.

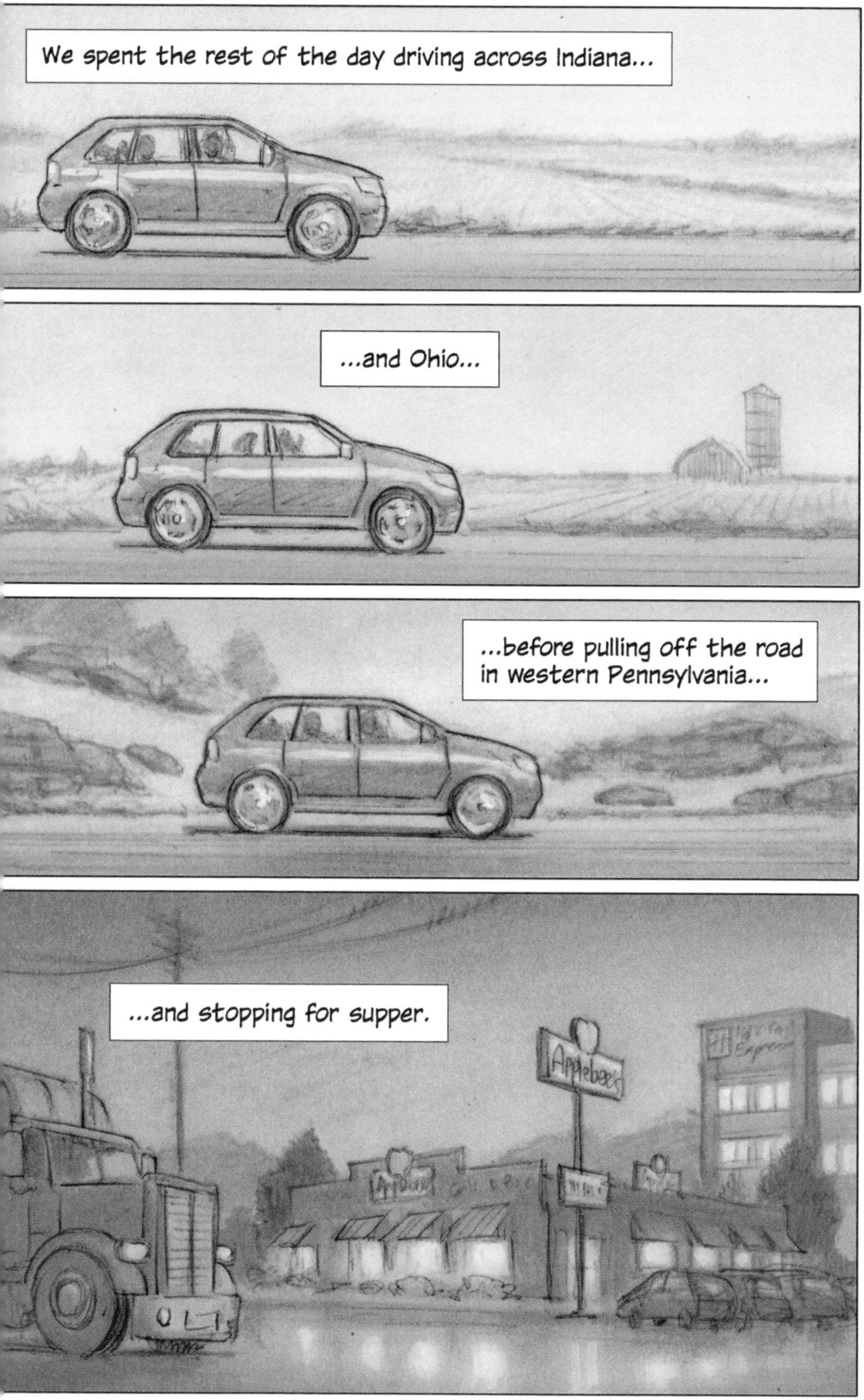
We spent the rest of the day driving across Indiana...
...and Ohio...
...before pulling off the road in western Pennsylvania...
...and stopping for supper.
Applebee's

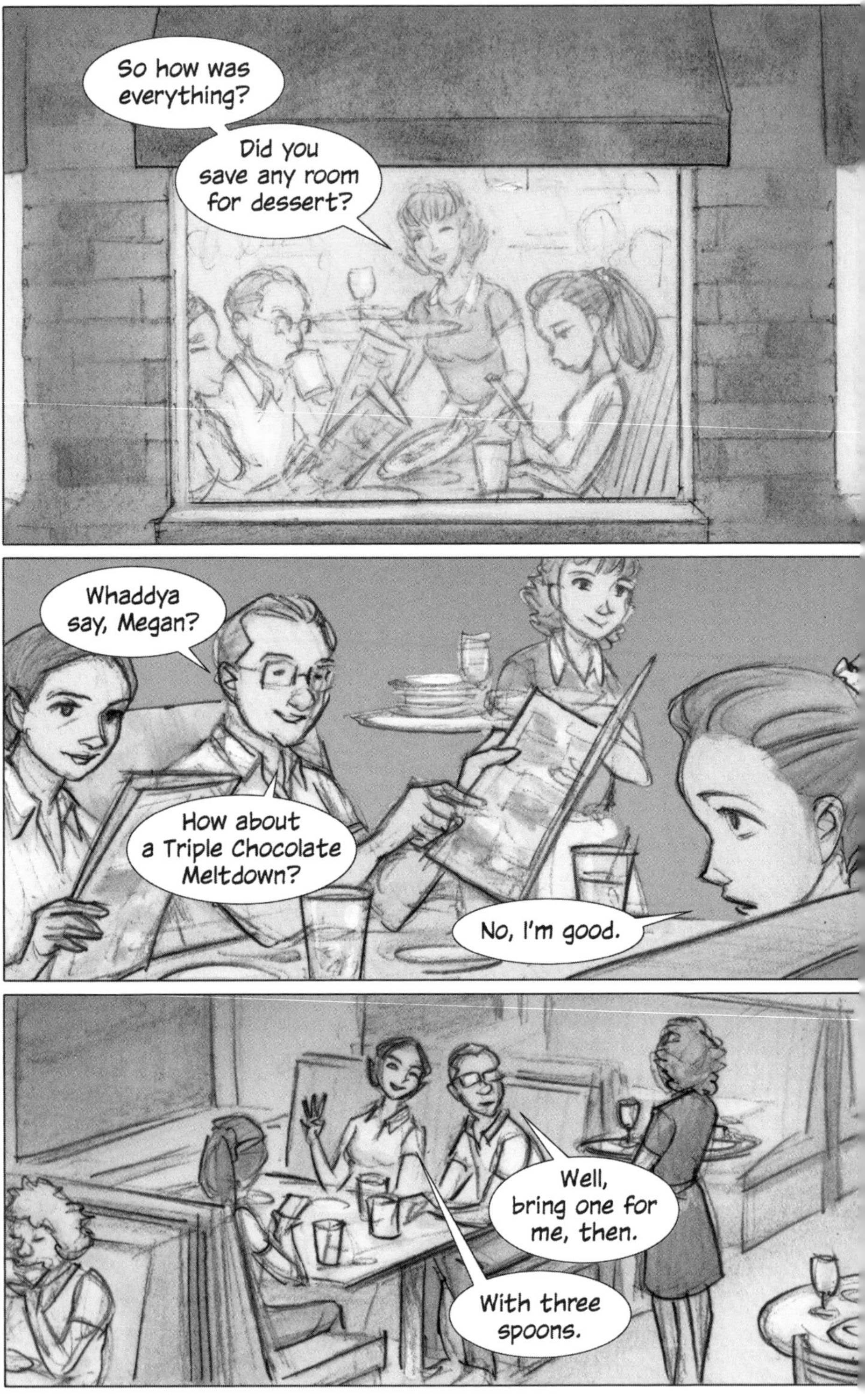
So how was everything?
Did you save any room for dessert?
Whaddya say, Megan?
How about a Triple Chocolate Meltdown?
No, I'm good.
Well, bring one for me, then.
With three spoons.

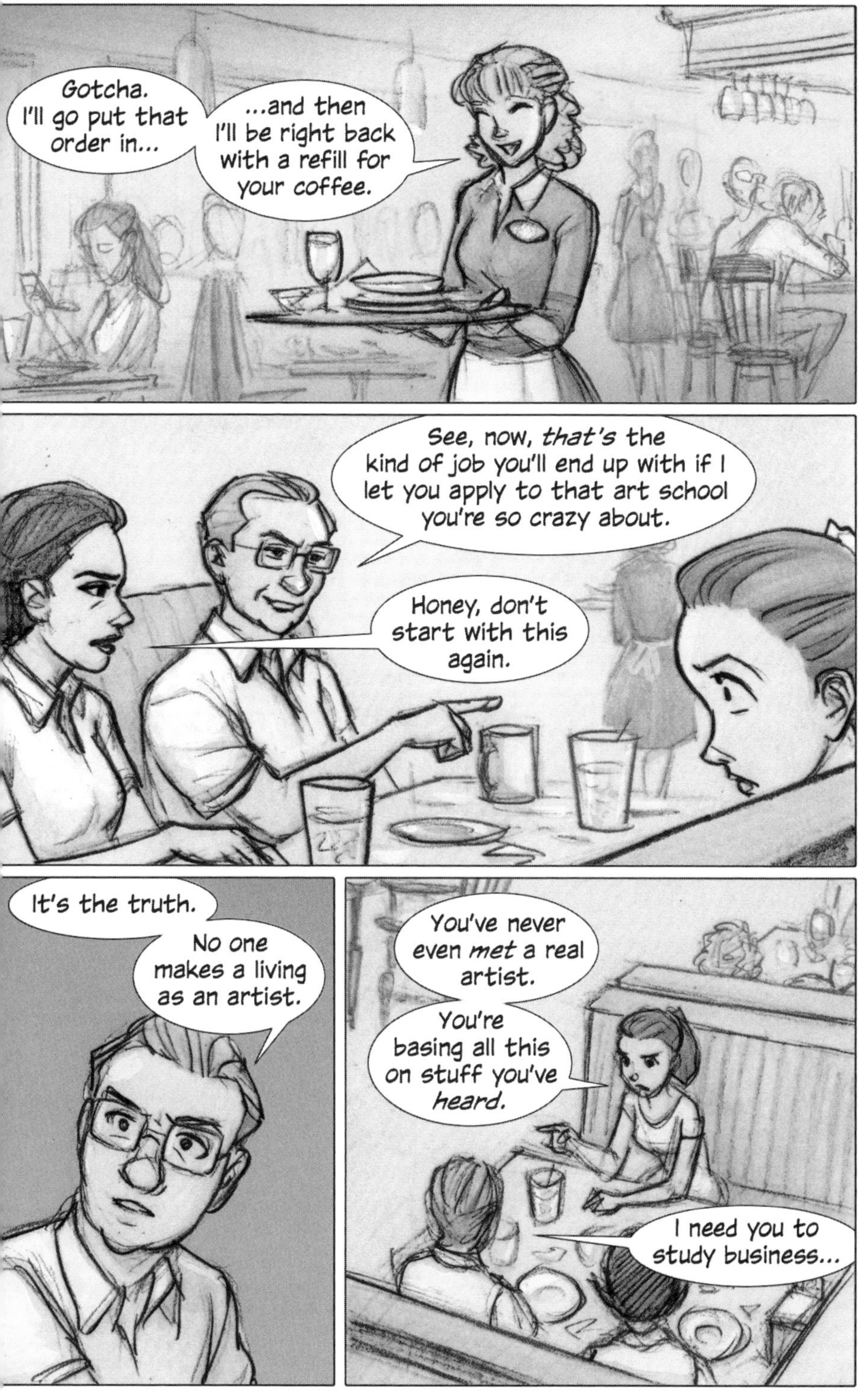
Gotcha. I'll go put that order in...
...and then I'll be right back with a refill for your coffee.
See, now, *that's* the kind of job you'll end up with if I let you apply to that art school you're so crazy about.
Honey, don't start with this again.
It's the truth.
No one makes a living as an artist.
You've never even *met* a real artist.
You're basing all this on stuff you've *heard*.
I need you to study business...

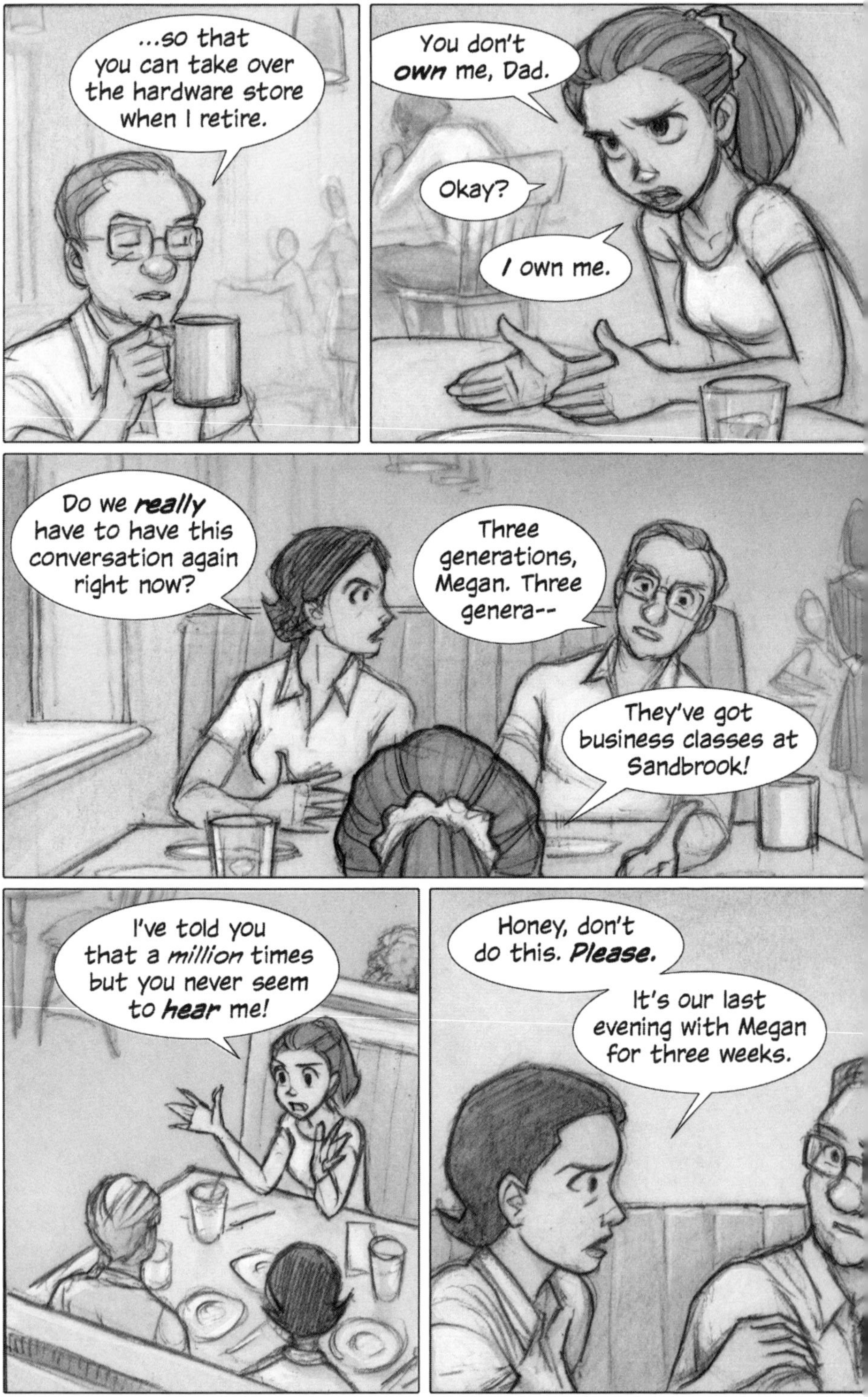
...so that you can take over the hardware store when I retire.
You don't *own* me, Dad.
Okay?
I own me.
Do we *really* have to have this conversation again right now?
Three generations, Megan. Three genera--
They've got business classes at Sandbrook!
I've told you that a *million* times but you never seem to *hear* me!
Honey, don't do this. *Please.*
It's our last evening with Megan for three weeks.

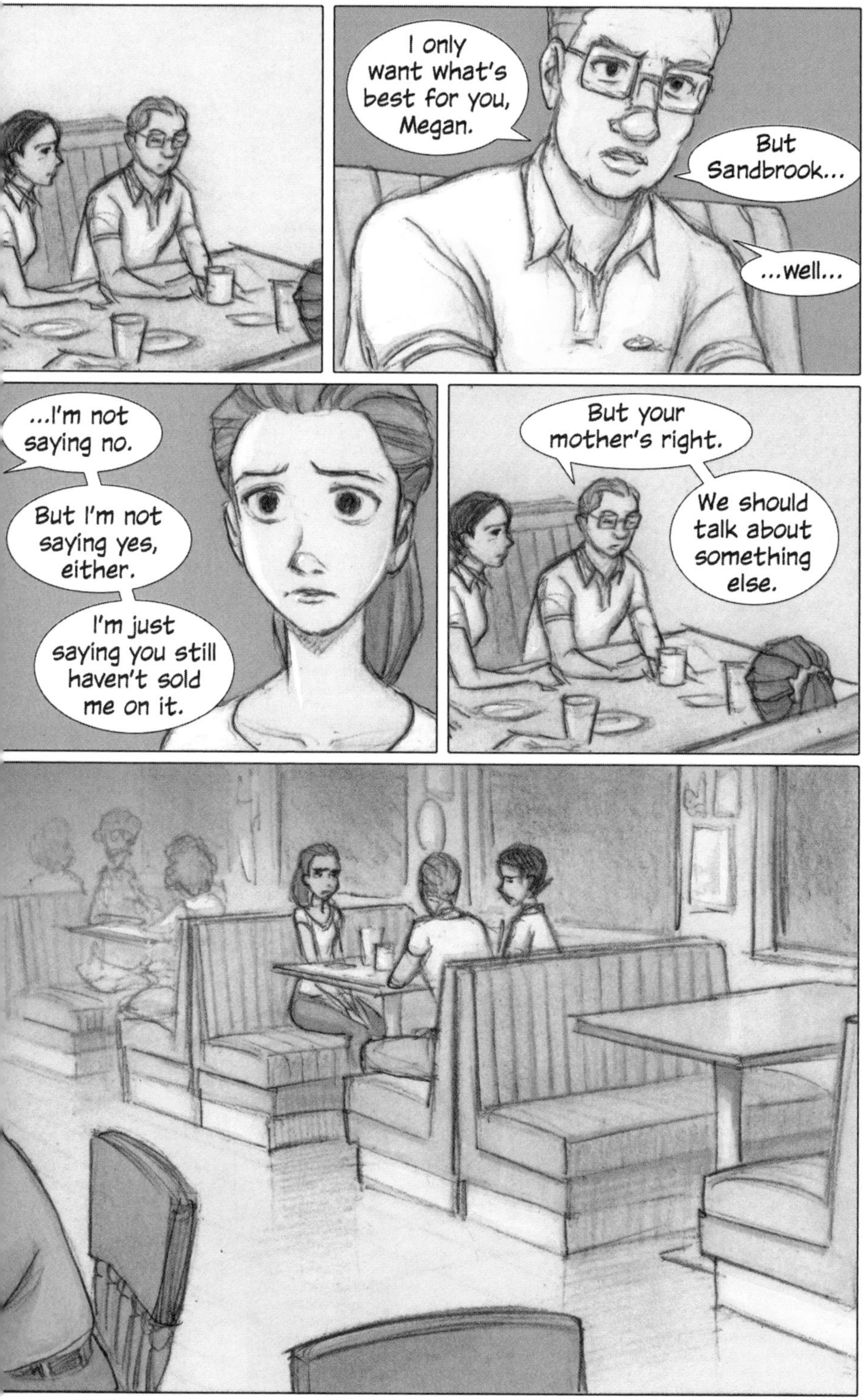
I only want what's best for you, Megan.
But Sandbrook...
...well...
...I'm not saying no.
But I'm not saying yes, either.
I'm just saying you still haven't sold me on it.
But your mother's right.
We should talk about something else.

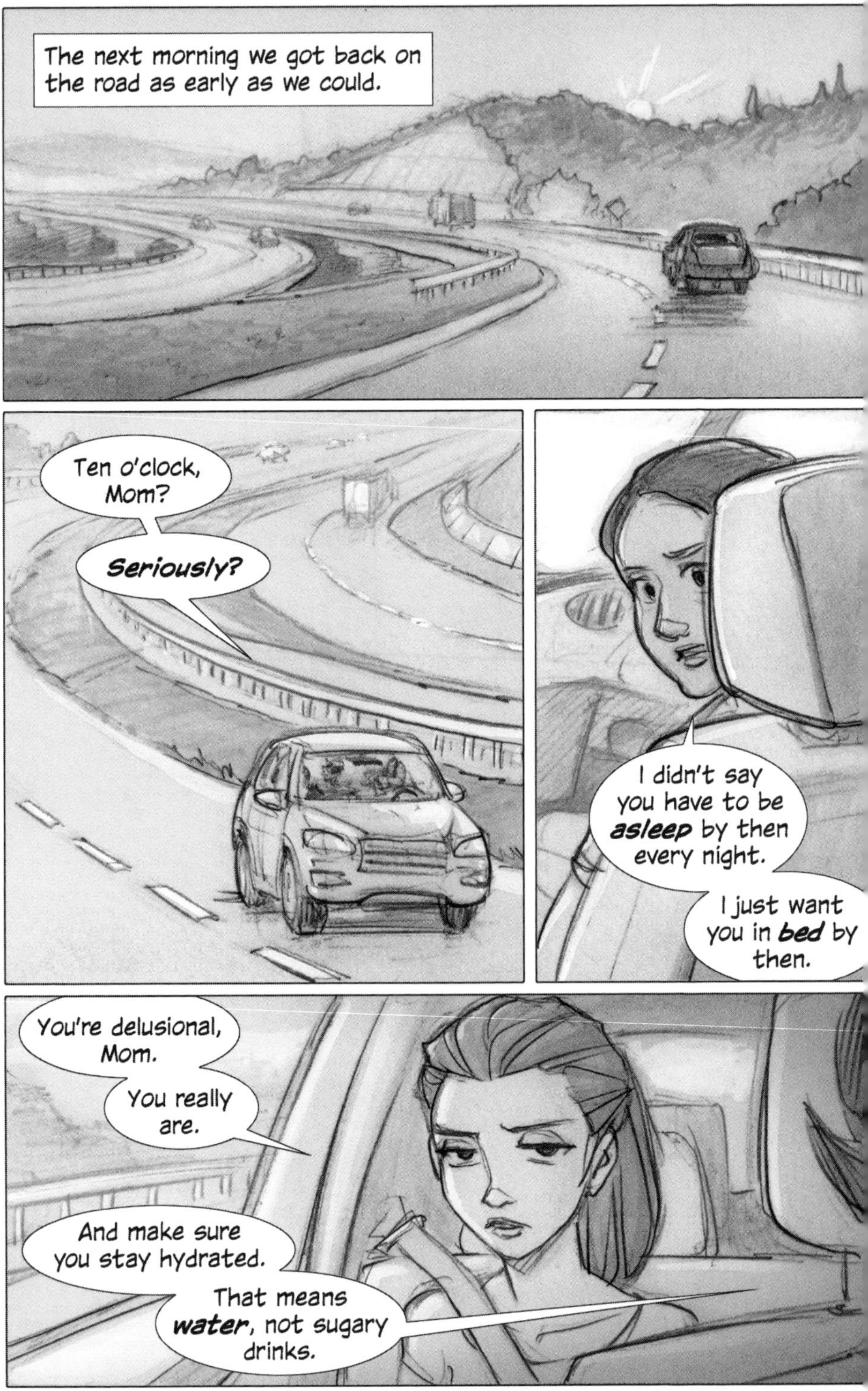
The next morning we got back on the road as early as we could.
Ten o'clock, Mom?
Seriously?
I didn't say you have to be *asleep* by then every night.
I just want you in *bed* by then.
You're delusional, Mom.
You really are.
And make sure you stay hydrated.
That means *water*, not sugary drinks.

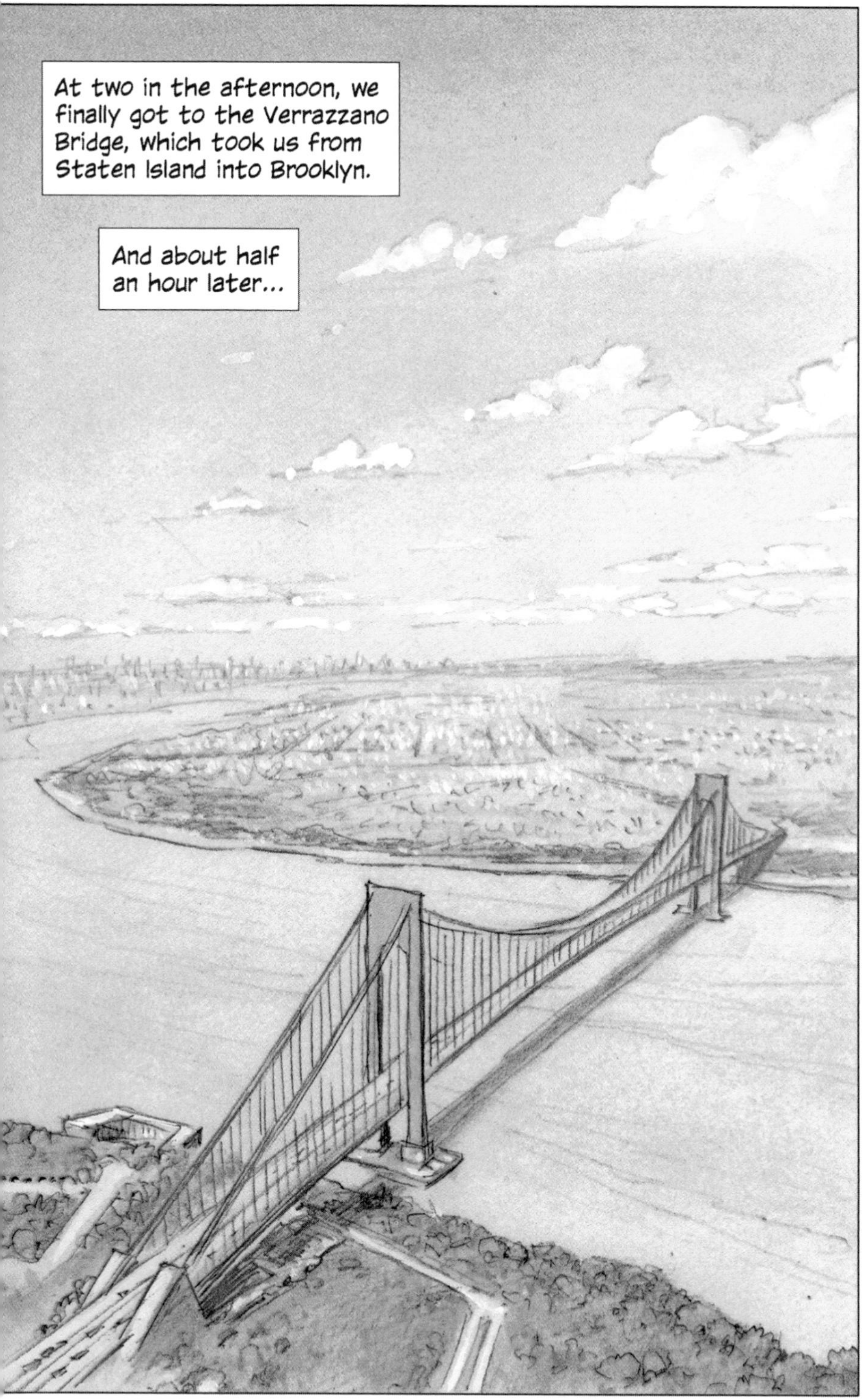
At two in the afternoon, we finally got to the Verrazzano Bridge, which took us from Staten Island into Brooklyn.
And about half an hour later...

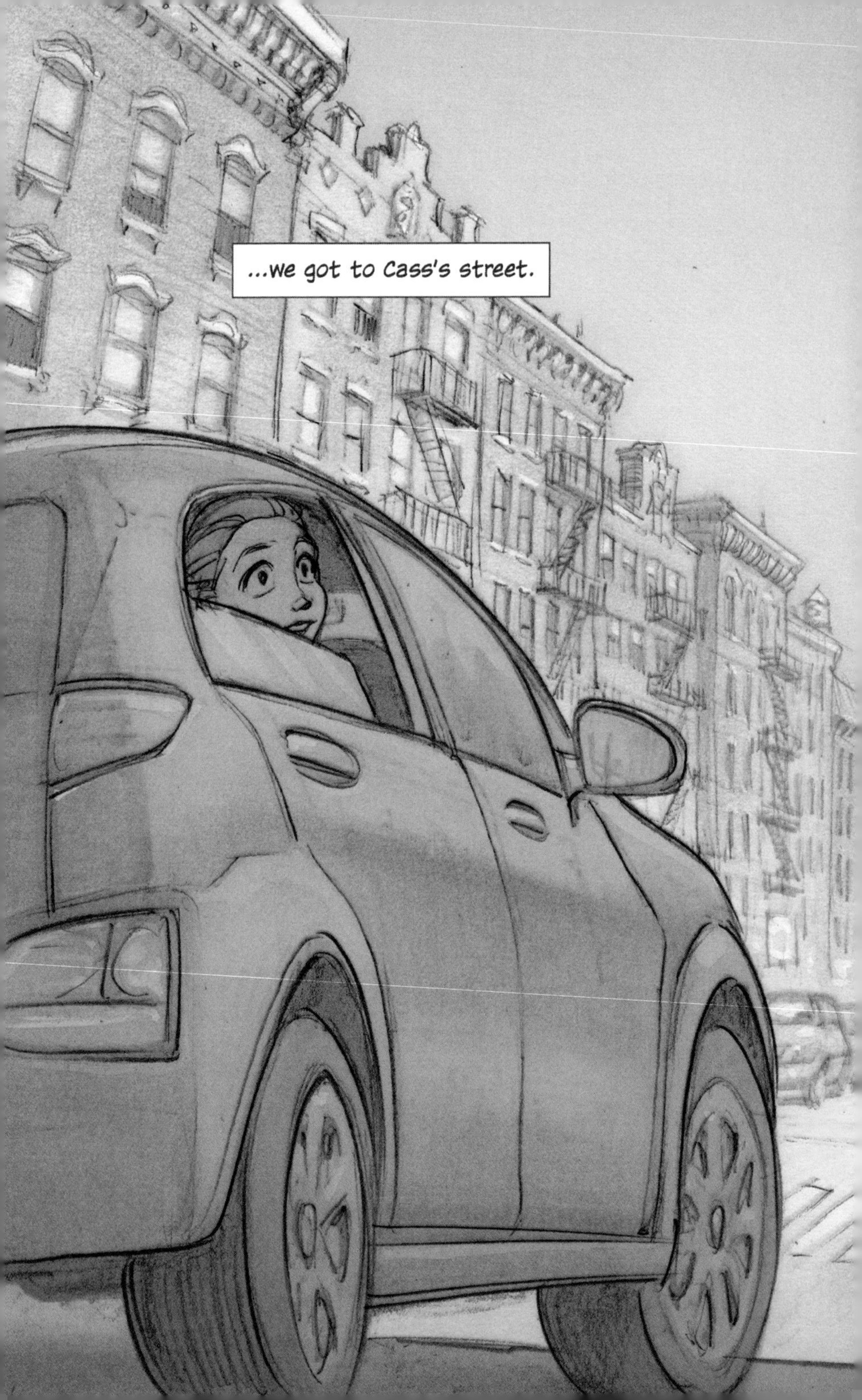
...we got to Cass's street.

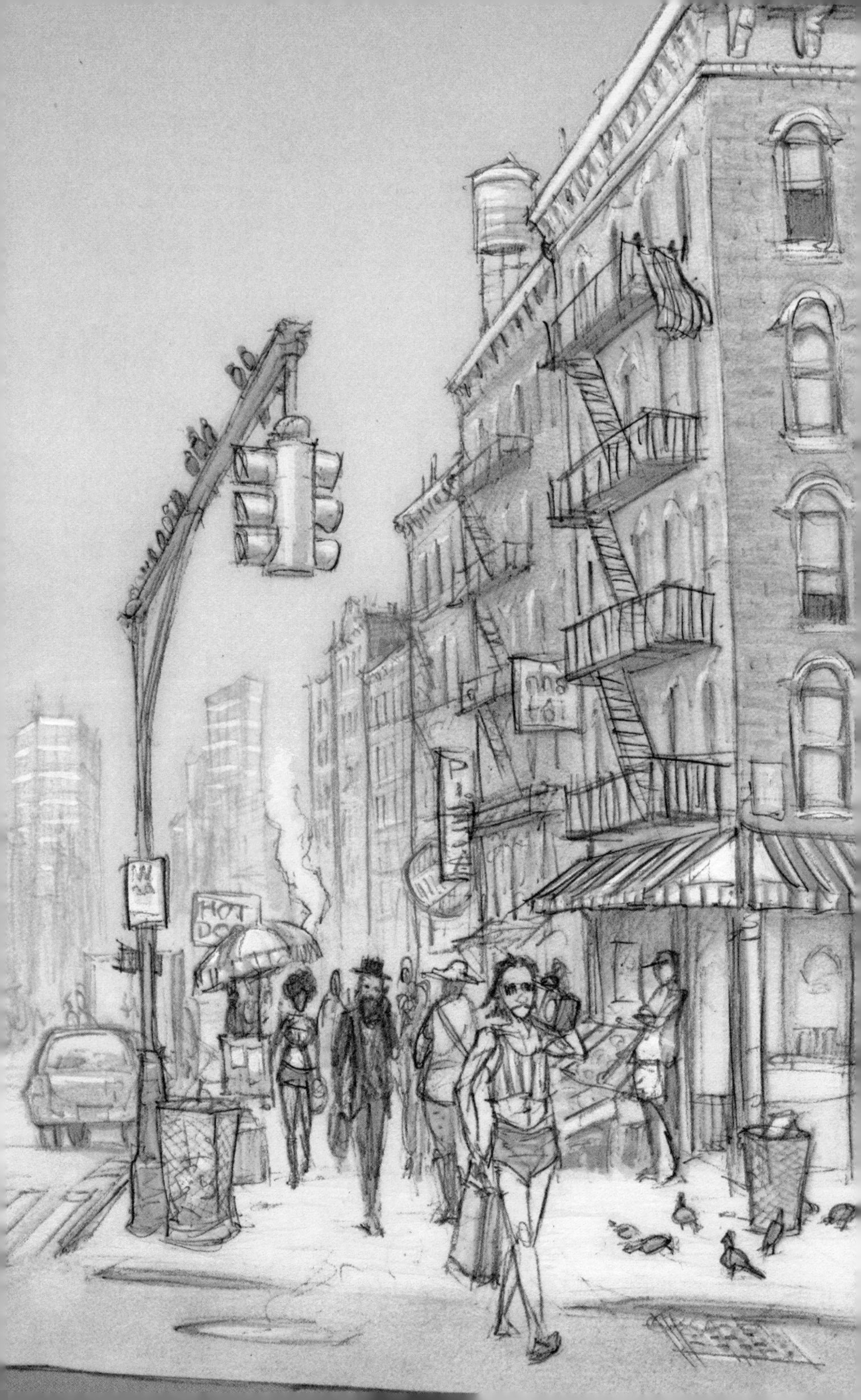
HOT

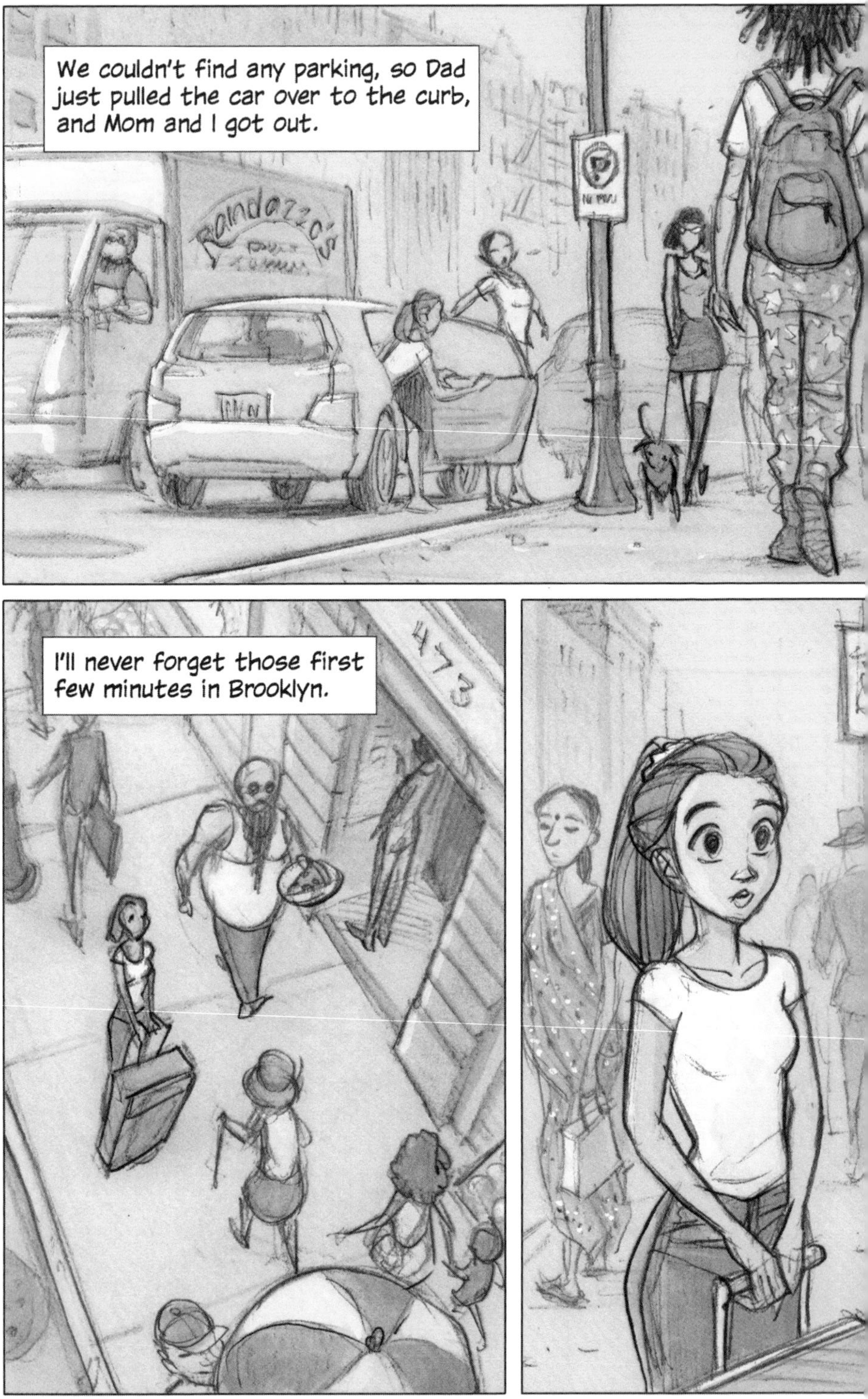
We couldn't find any parking, so Dad just pulled the car over to the curb, and Mom and I got out.
I'll never forget those first few minutes in Brooklyn.

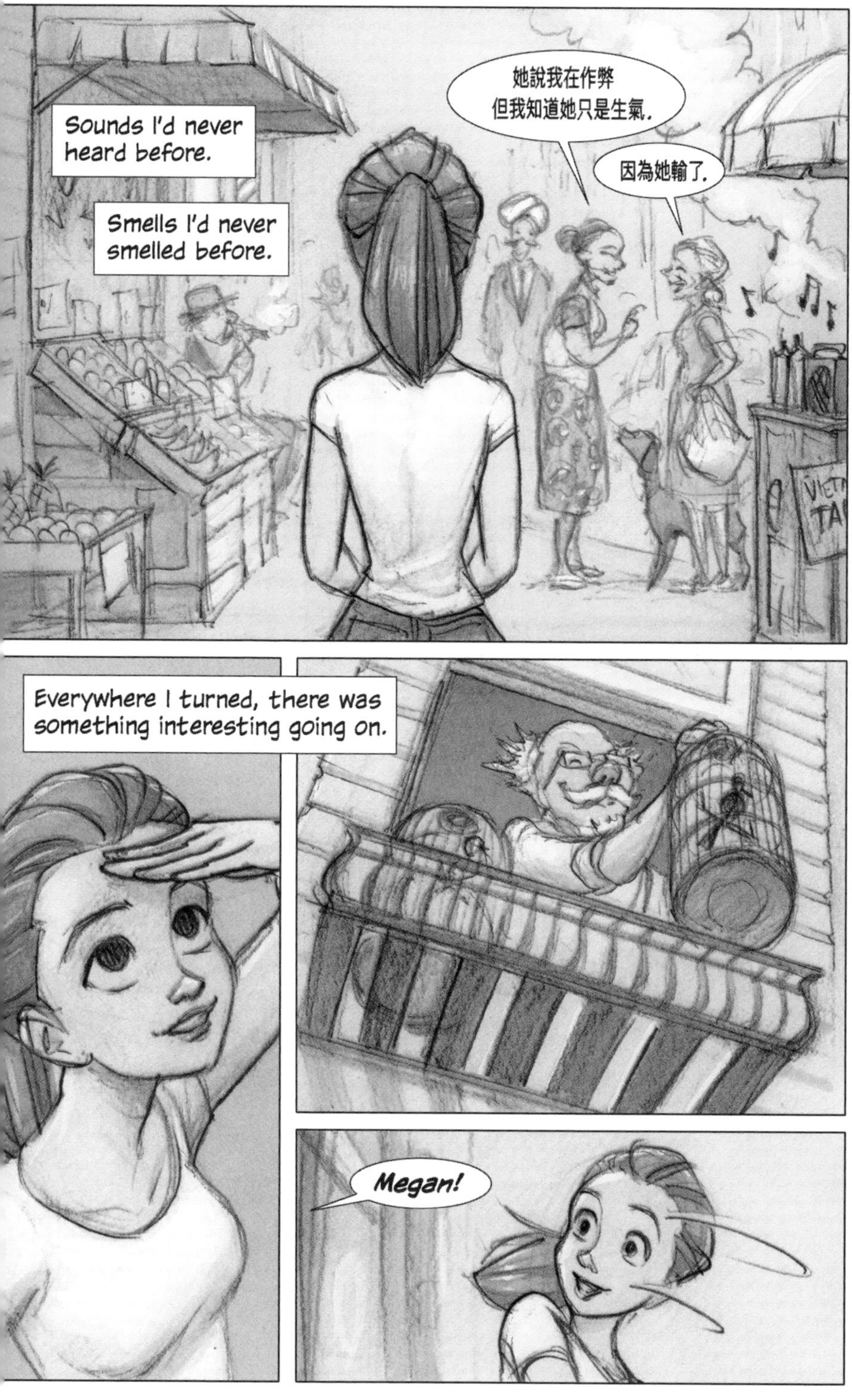
Sounds I'd never heard before.
Smells I'd never smelled before.
她說我在作弊
但我知道她只是生氣.
因為她輸了.
Everywhere I turned, there was something interesting going on.
Megan!

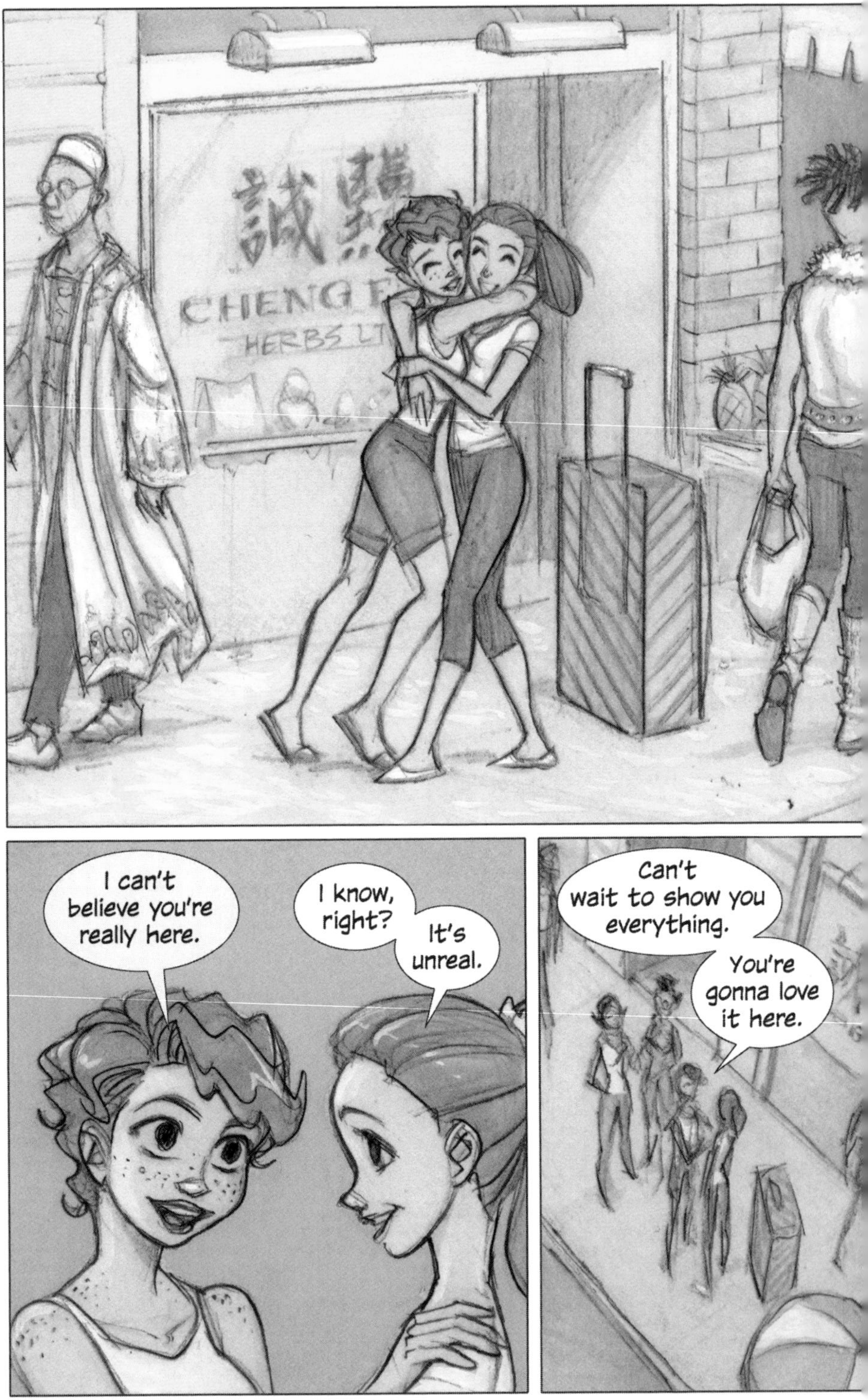
I can't believe you're really here.
I know, right?
It's unreal.
Can't wait to show you everything.
You're gonna love it here.

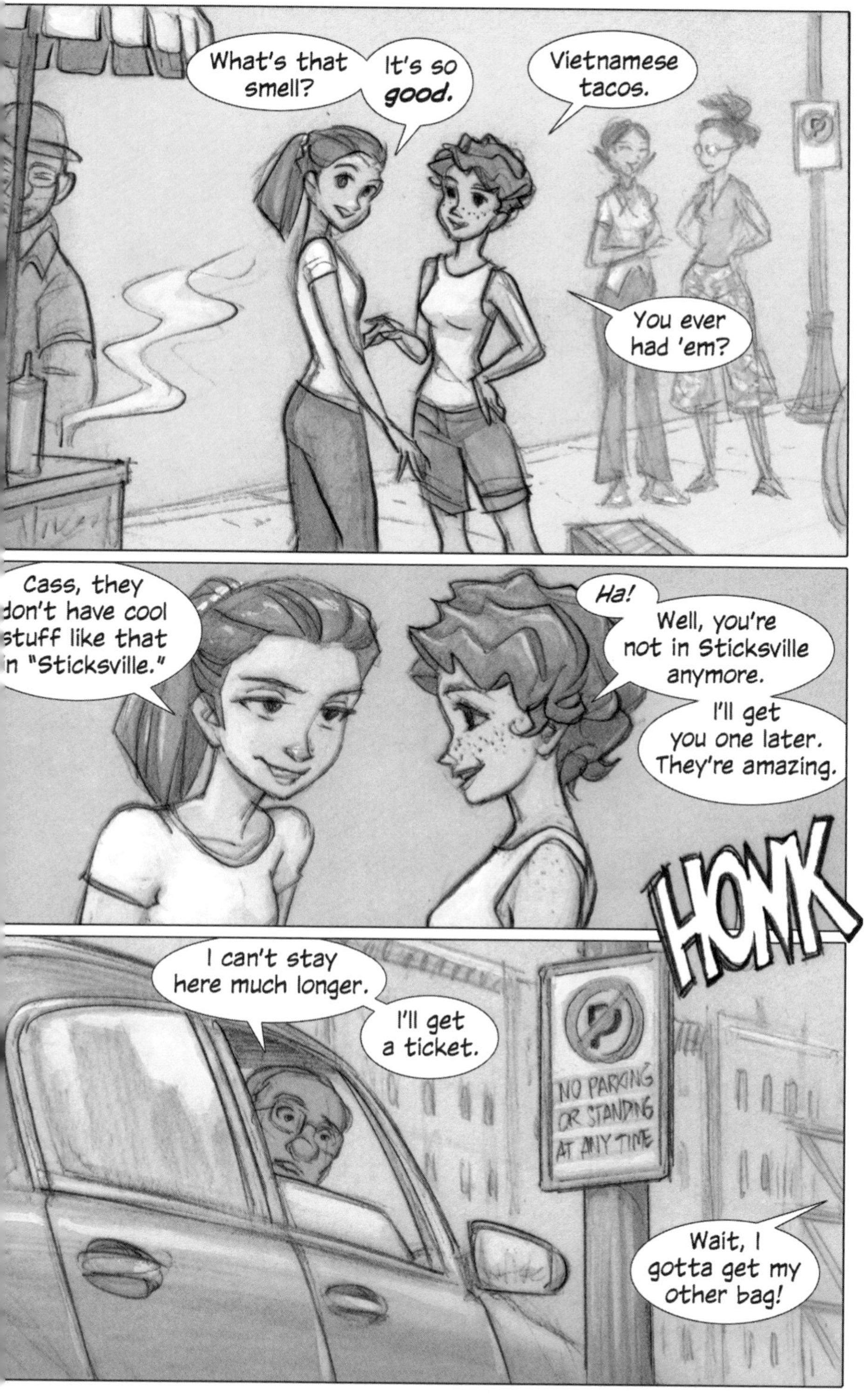
What's that smell?
It's so *good.*
Vietnamese tacos.
You ever had 'em?
Cass, they don't have cool stuff like that in "Sticksville."
Ha!
Well, you're not in Sticksville anymore.
I'll get you one later. They're amazing.
HONK
I can't stay here much longer.
I'll get a ticket.
NO PARKING OR STANDING AT ANY TIME
Wait, I gotta get my other bag!

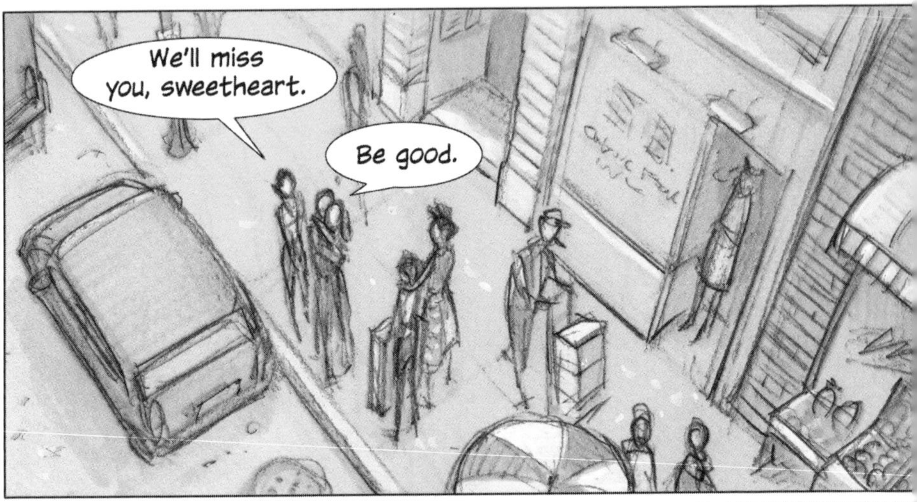
We'll miss you, sweetheart.
Be good.

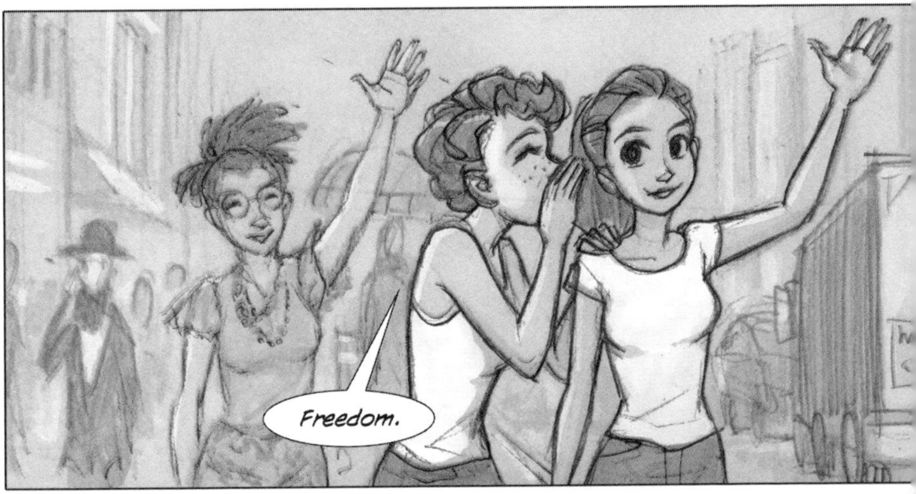
Freedom.

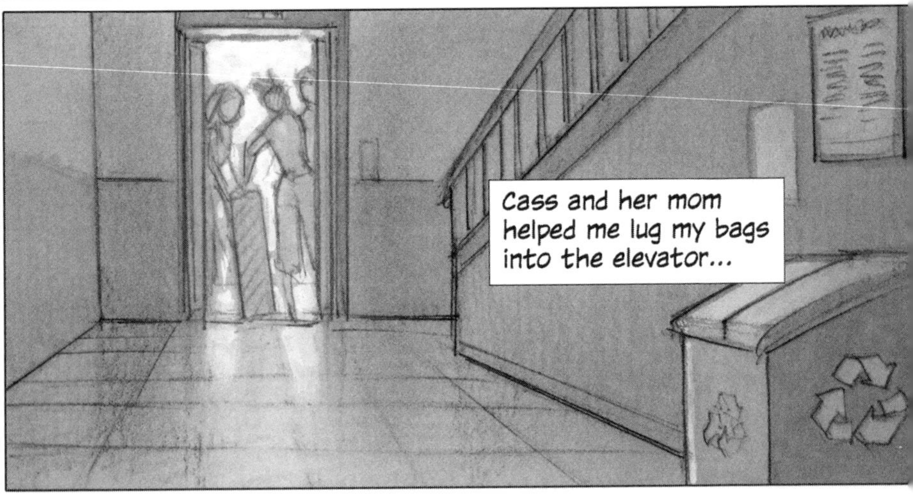
Cass and her mom helped me lug my bags into the elevator...

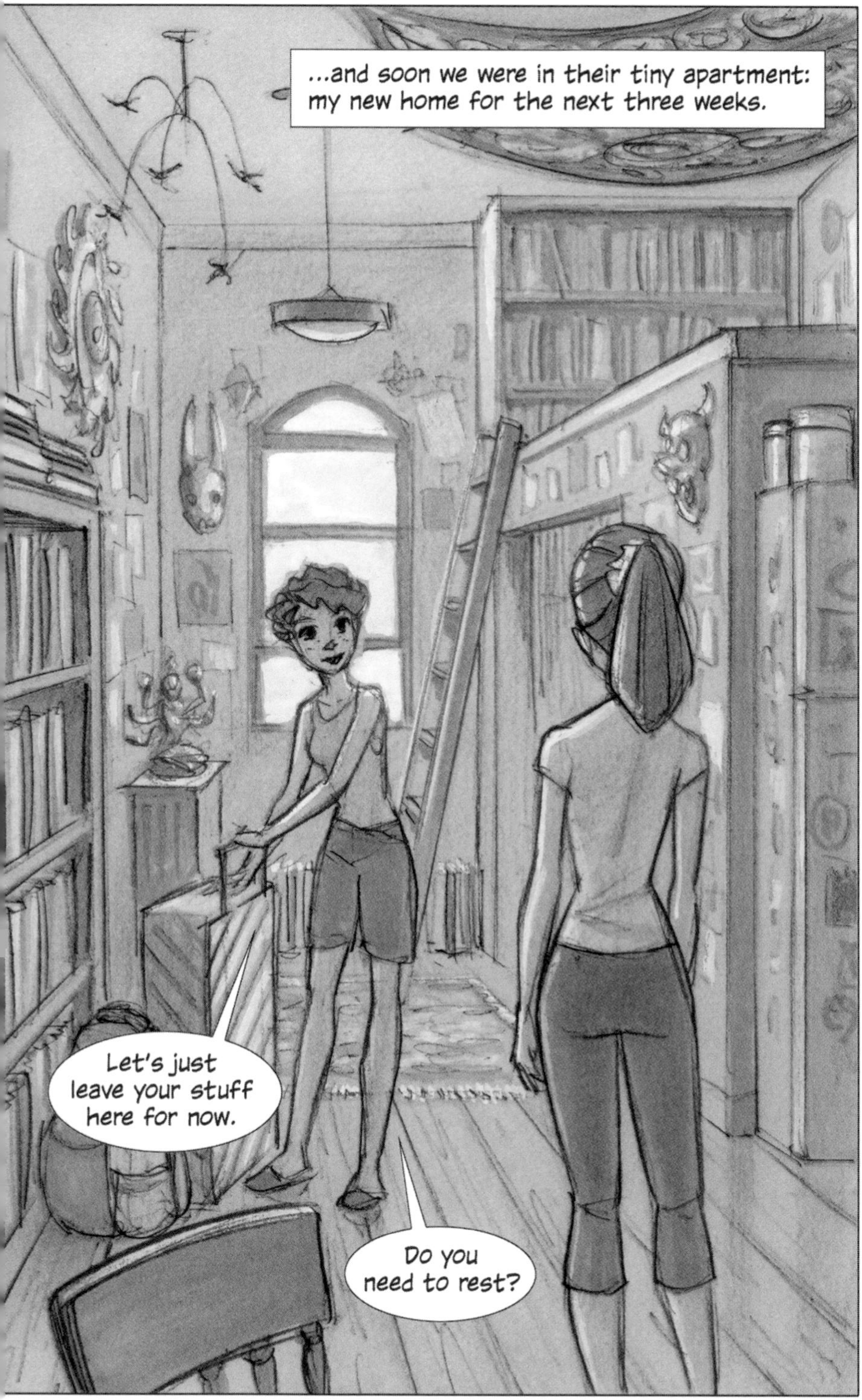
...and soon we were in their tiny apartment: my new home for the next three weeks.
Let's just leave your stuff here for now.
Do you need to rest?

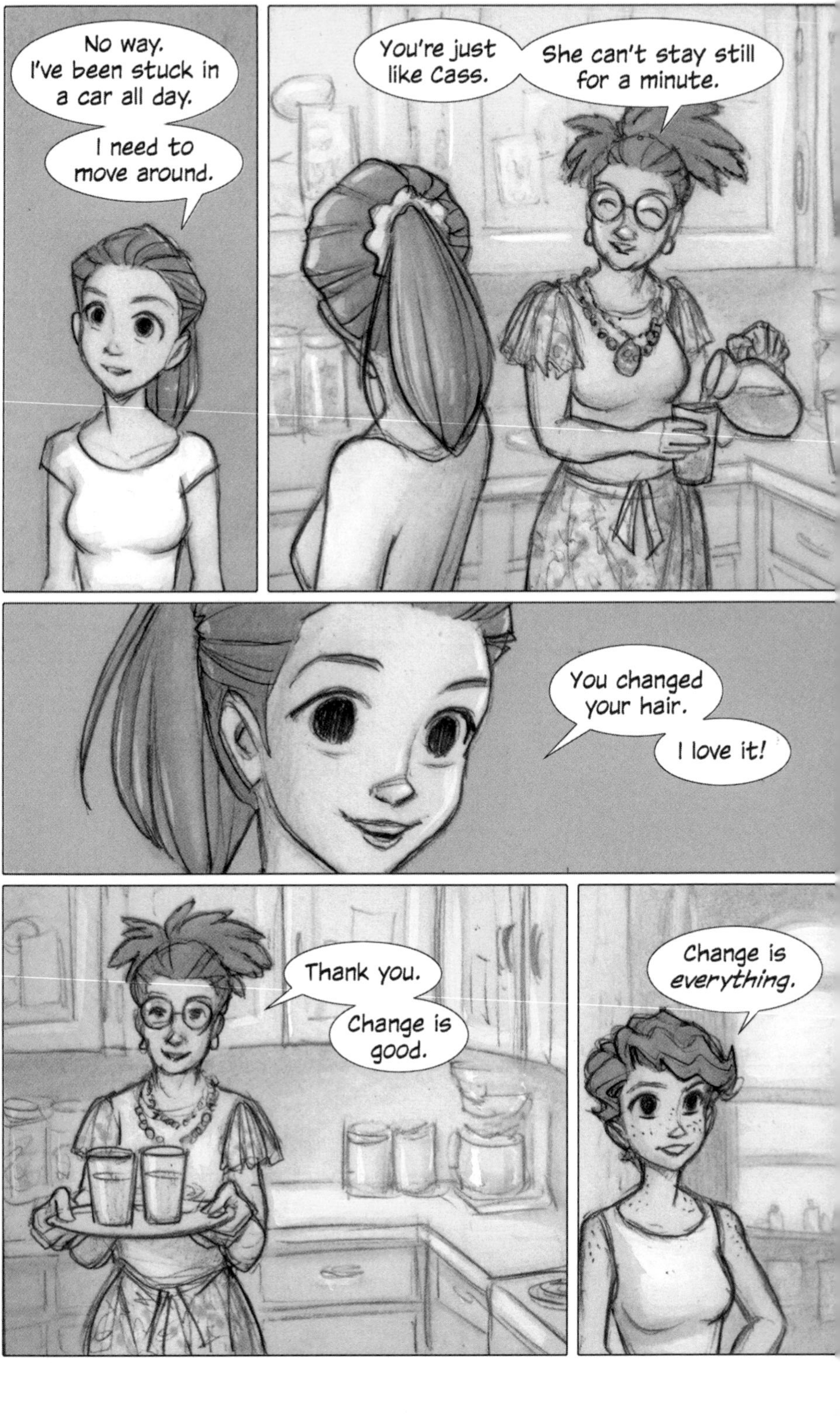
No way. I've been stuck in a car all day.
I need to move around.
You're just like Cass.
She can't stay still for a minute.
You changed your hair.
I love it!
Thank you.
Change is good.
Change is *everything*.

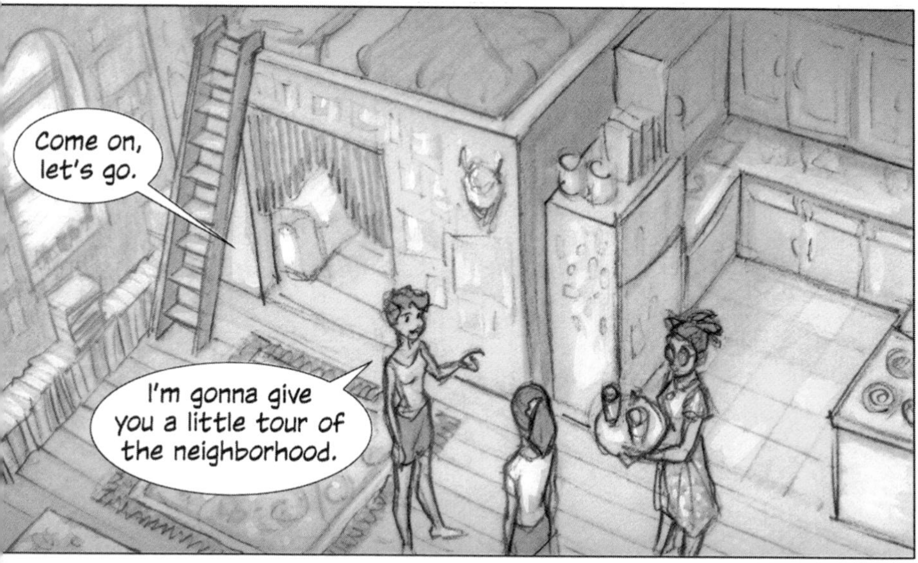
Come on, let's go.
I'm gonna give you a little tour of the neighborhood.

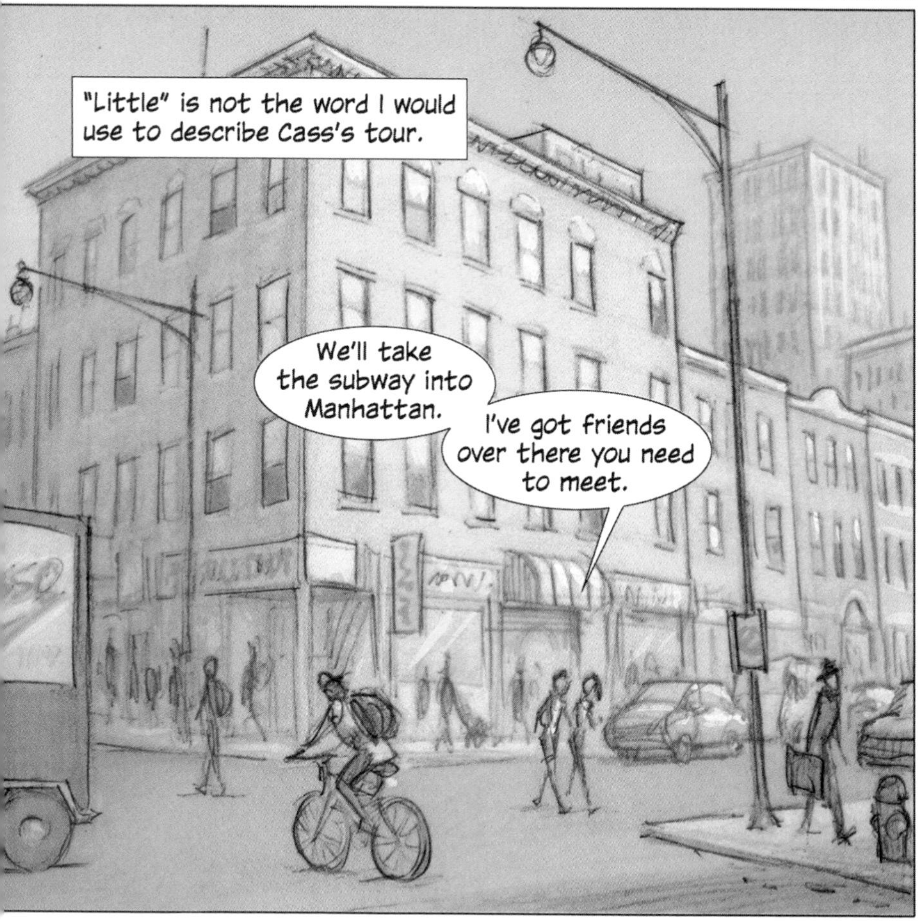
"Little" is not the word I would use to describe Cass's tour.
We'll take the subway into Manhattan.
I've got friends over there you need to meet.

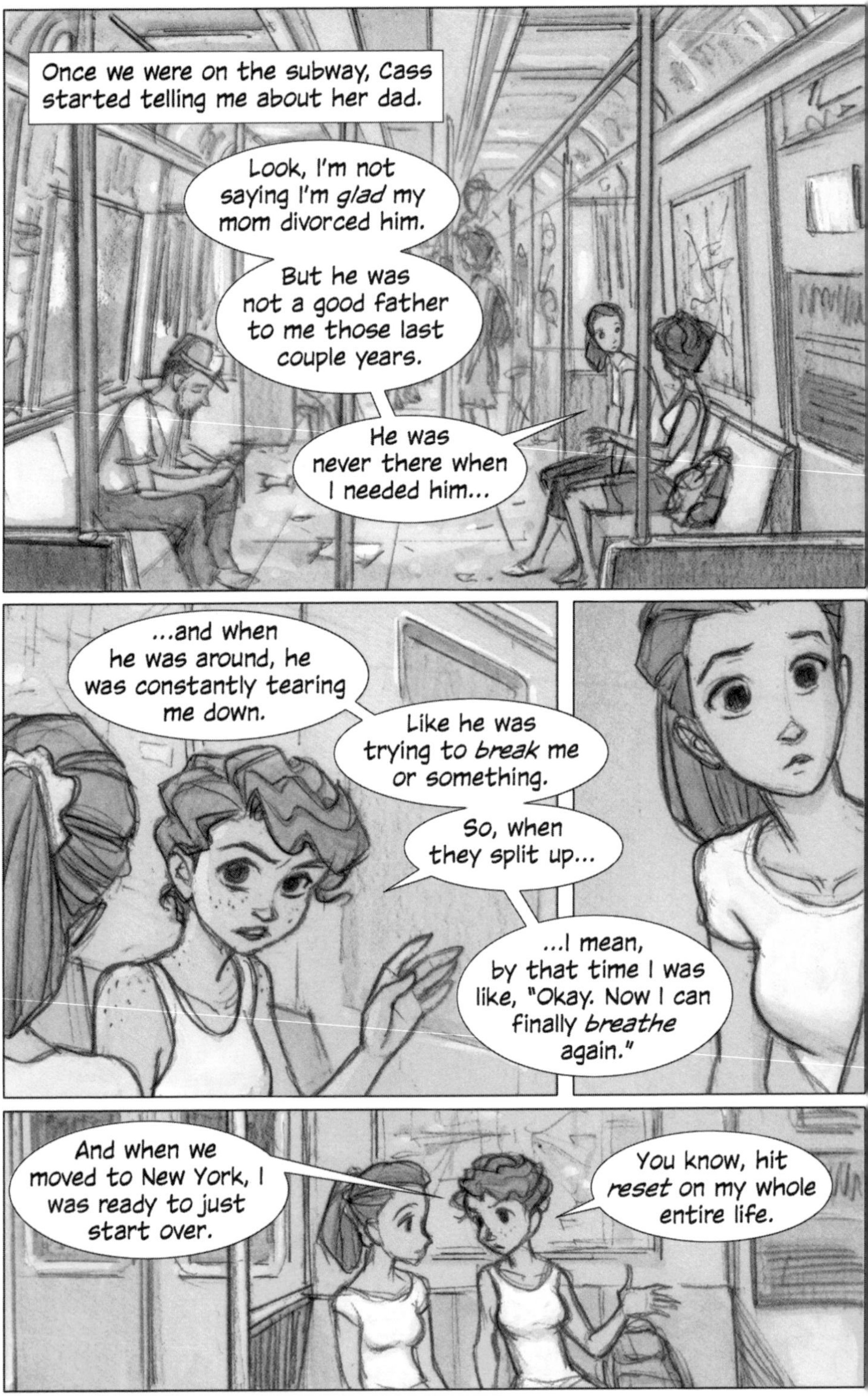
Once we were on the subway, Cass started telling me about her dad.
Look, I'm not saying I'm *glad* my mom divorced him.
But he was not a good father to me those last couple years.
He was never there when I needed him...
...and when he was around, he was constantly tearing me down.
Like he was trying to *break* me or something.
So, when they split up...
...I mean, by that time I was like, "Okay. Now I can finally *breathe* again."
And when we moved to New York, I was ready to just start over.
You know, hit *reset* on my whole entire life.

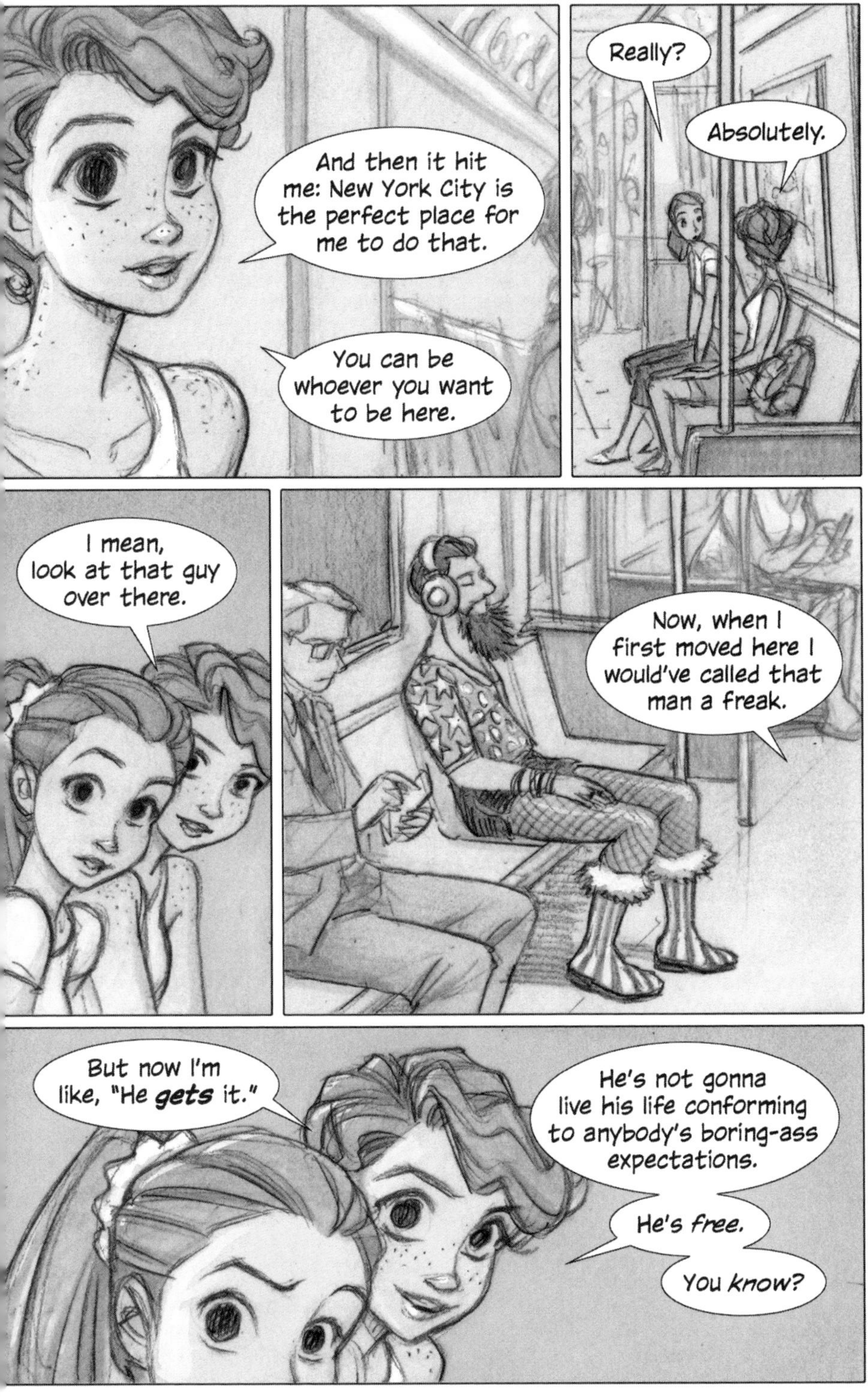
And then it hit me: New York City is the perfect place for me to do that.
You can be whoever you want to be here.
Really?
Absolutely.
I mean, look at that guy over there.
Now, when I first moved here I would've called that man a freak.
But now I'm like, "He *gets* it."
He's not gonna live his life conforming to anybody's boring-ass expectations.
He's *free.*
You *know?*

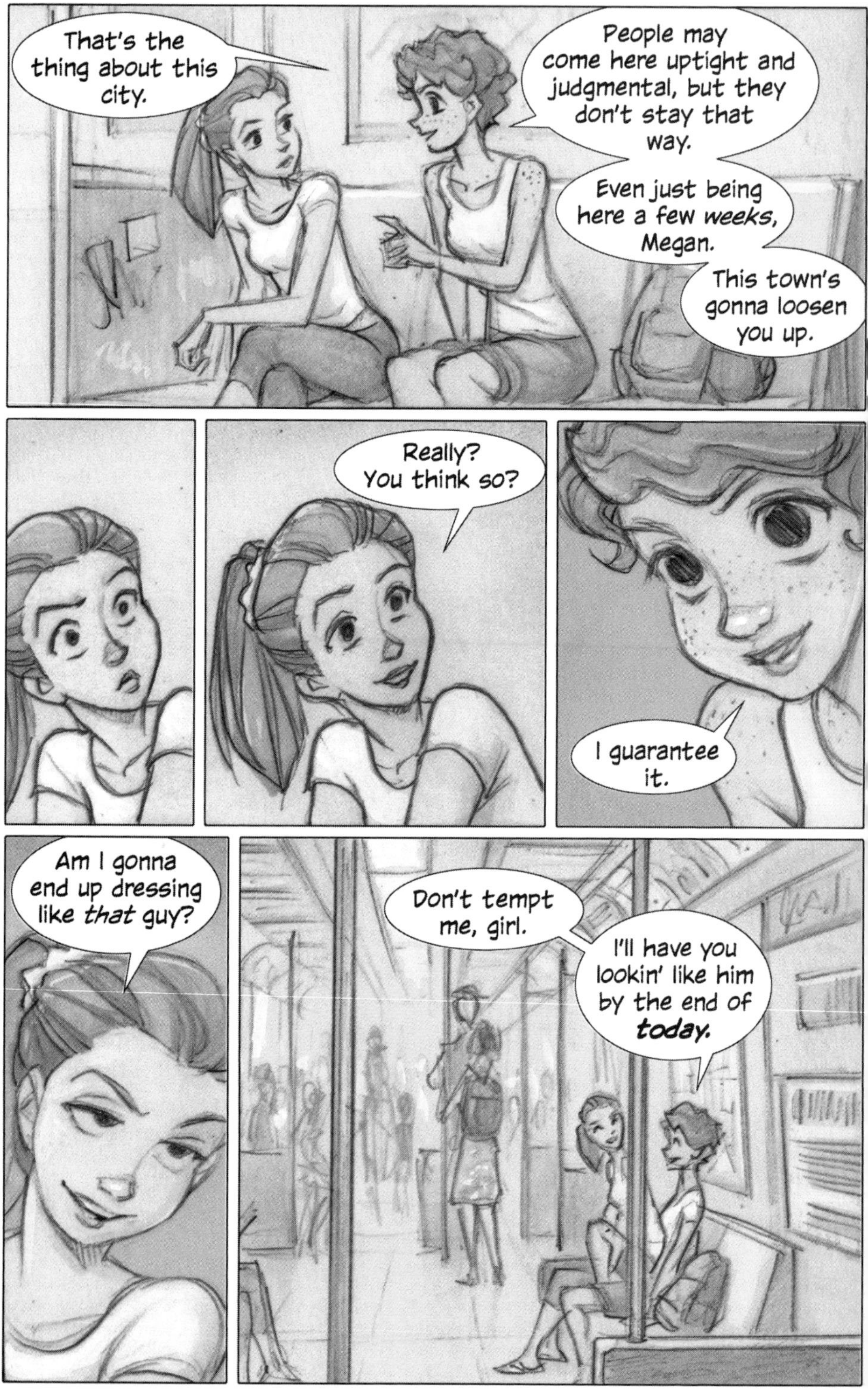
That's the thing about this city.
People may come here uptight and judgmental, but they don't stay that way.
Even just being here a few *weeks*, Megan.
This town's gonna loosen you up.
Really? You think so?
I guarantee it.
Am I gonna end up dressing like *that* guy?
Don't tempt me, girl.
I'll have you lookin' like him by the end of ***today.***

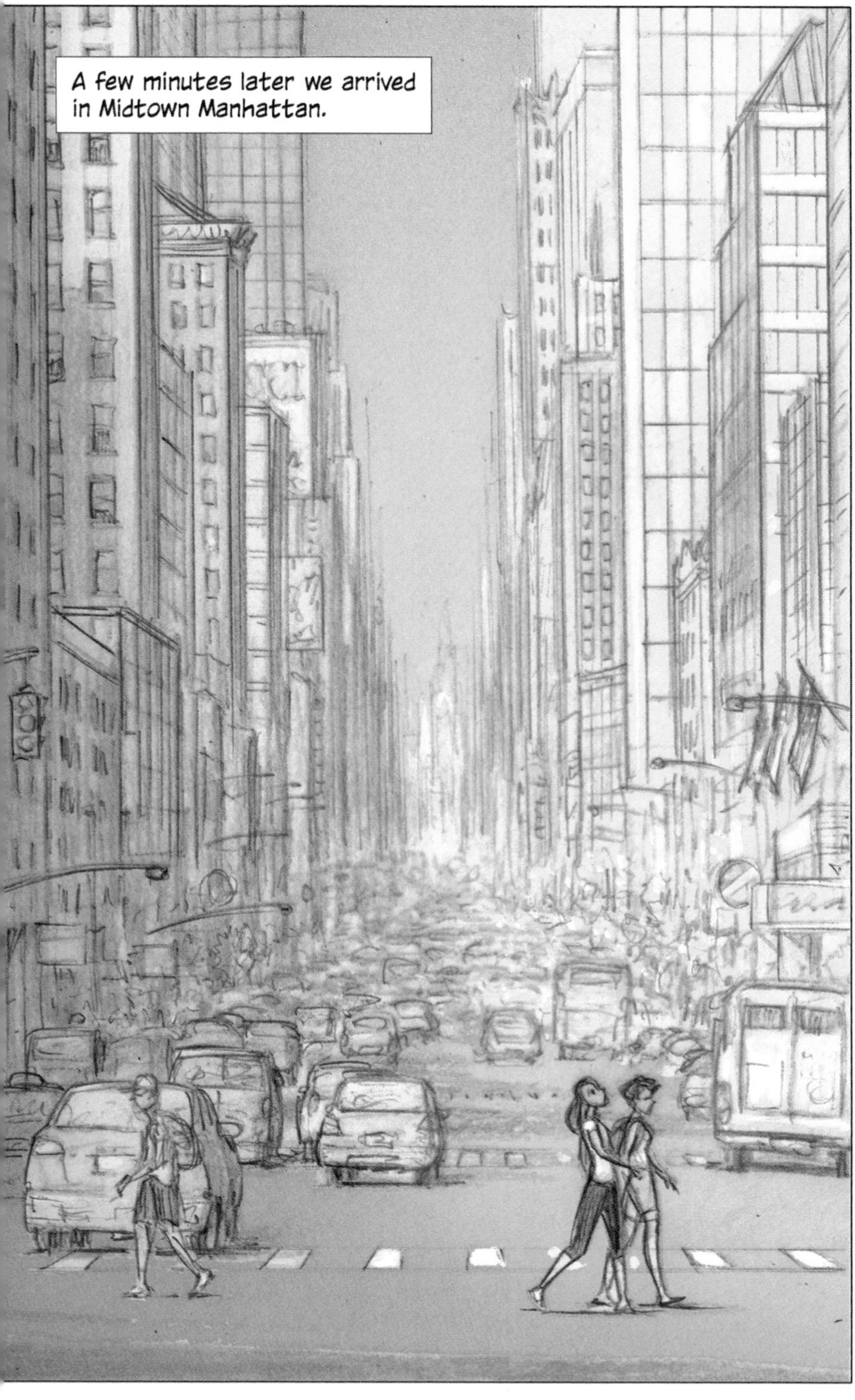
A few minutes later we arrived in Midtown Manhattan.

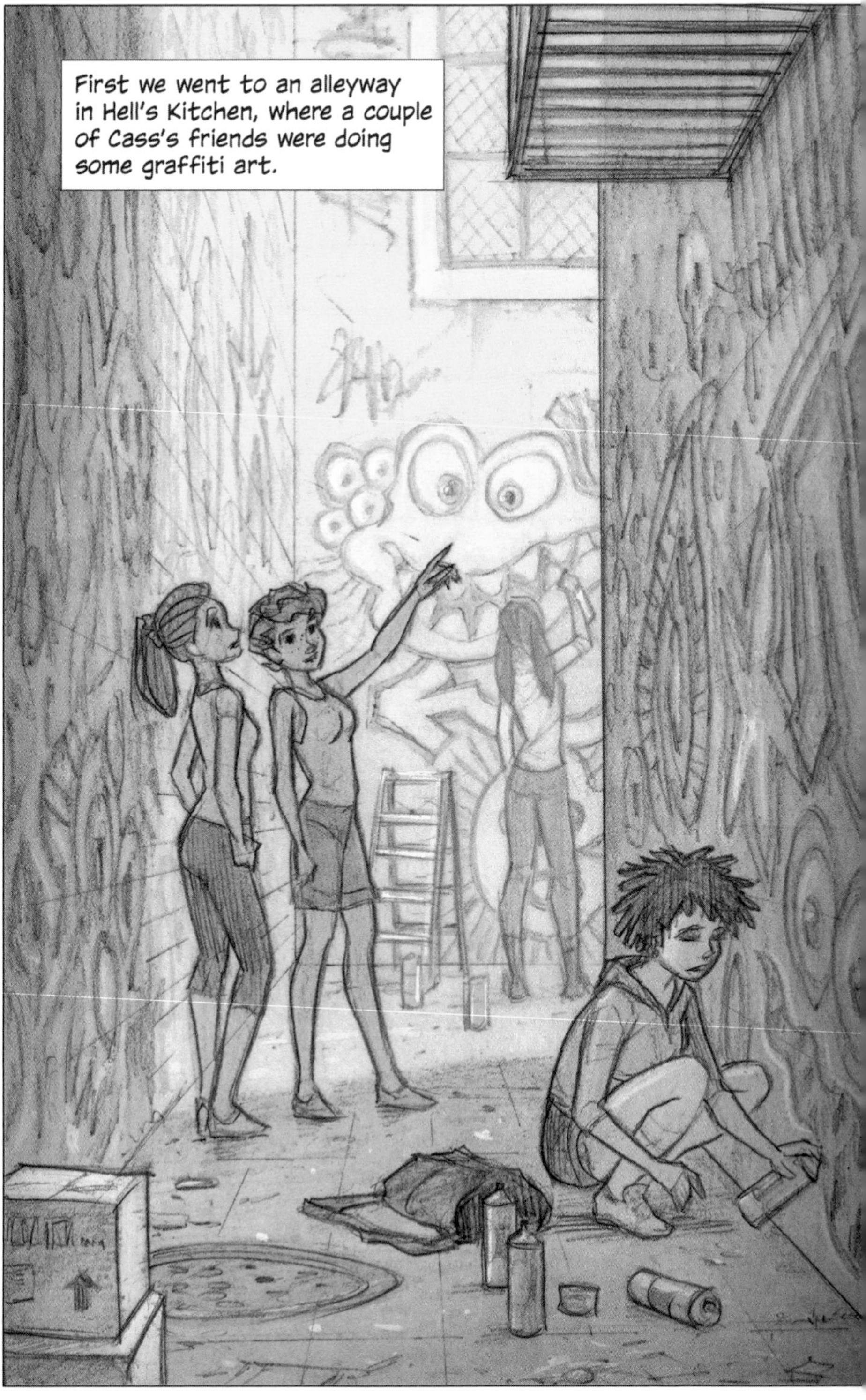
First we went to an alleyway in Hell's Kitchen, where a couple of Cass's friends were doing some graffiti art.

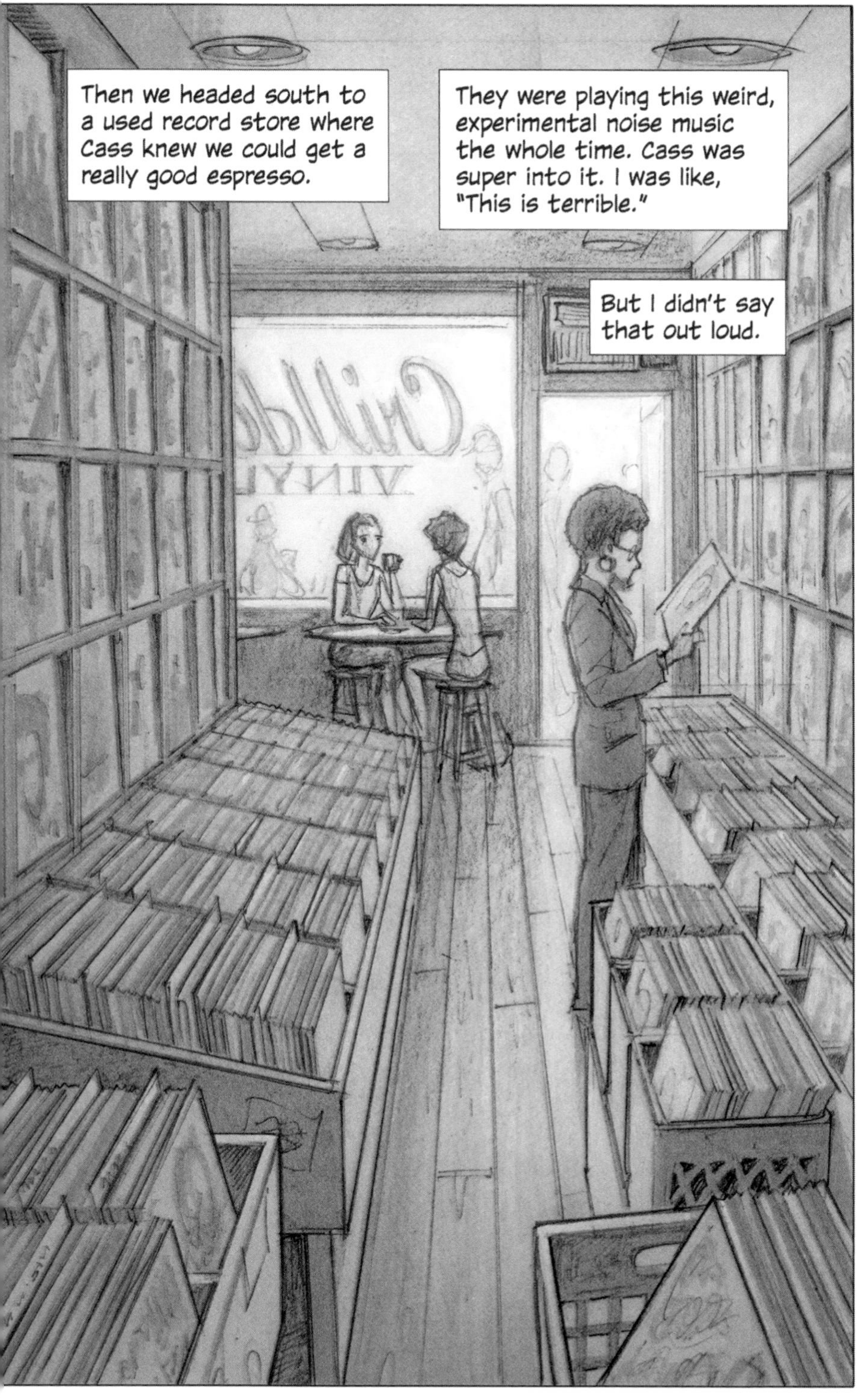
Then we headed south to a used record store where Cass knew we could get a really good espresso.
They were playing this weird, experimental noise music the whole time. Cass was super into it. I was like, "This is terrible."
But I didn't say that out loud.
VINYL

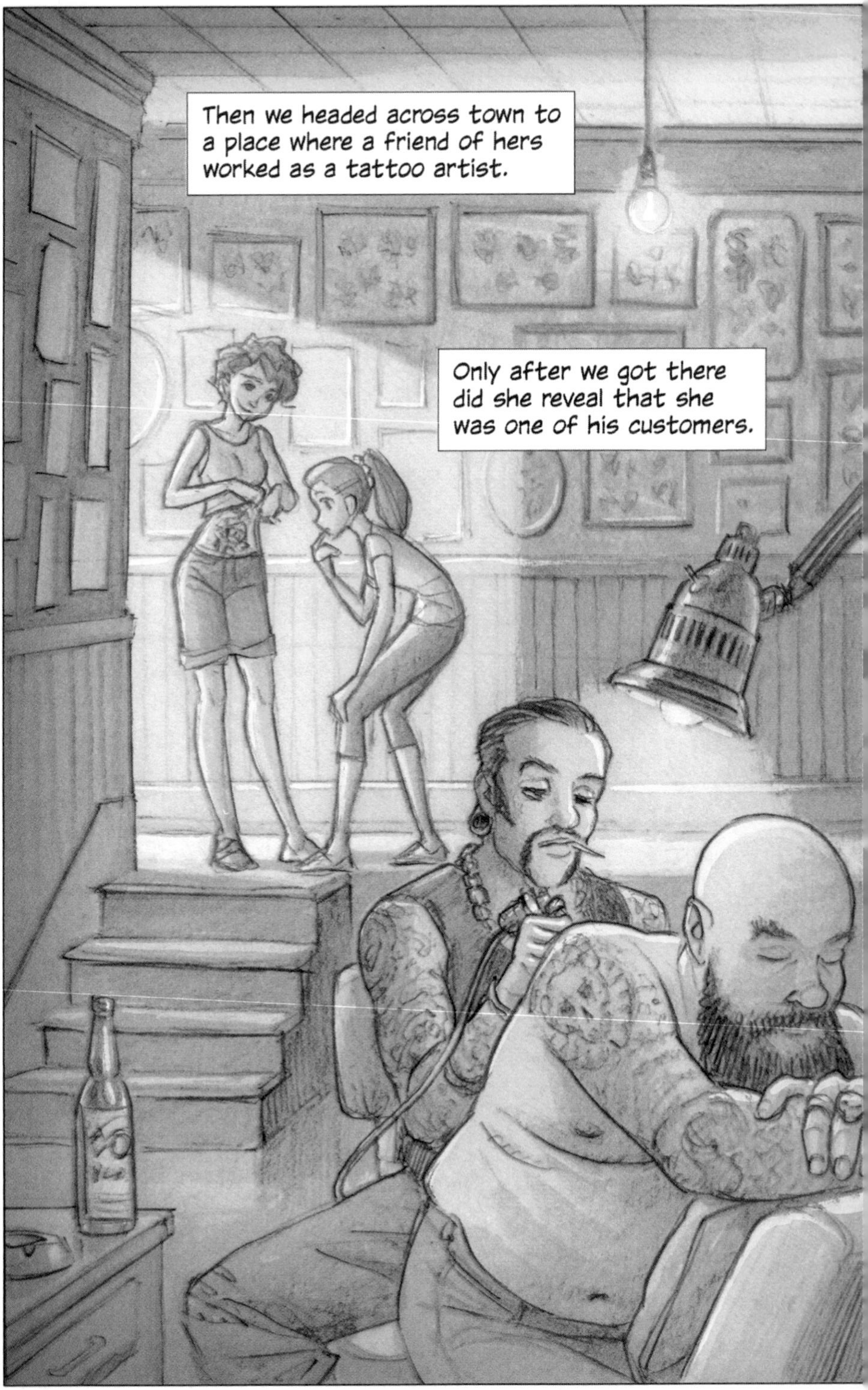
Then we headed across town to a place where a friend of hers worked as a tattoo artist.
Only after we got there did she reveal that she was one of his customers.

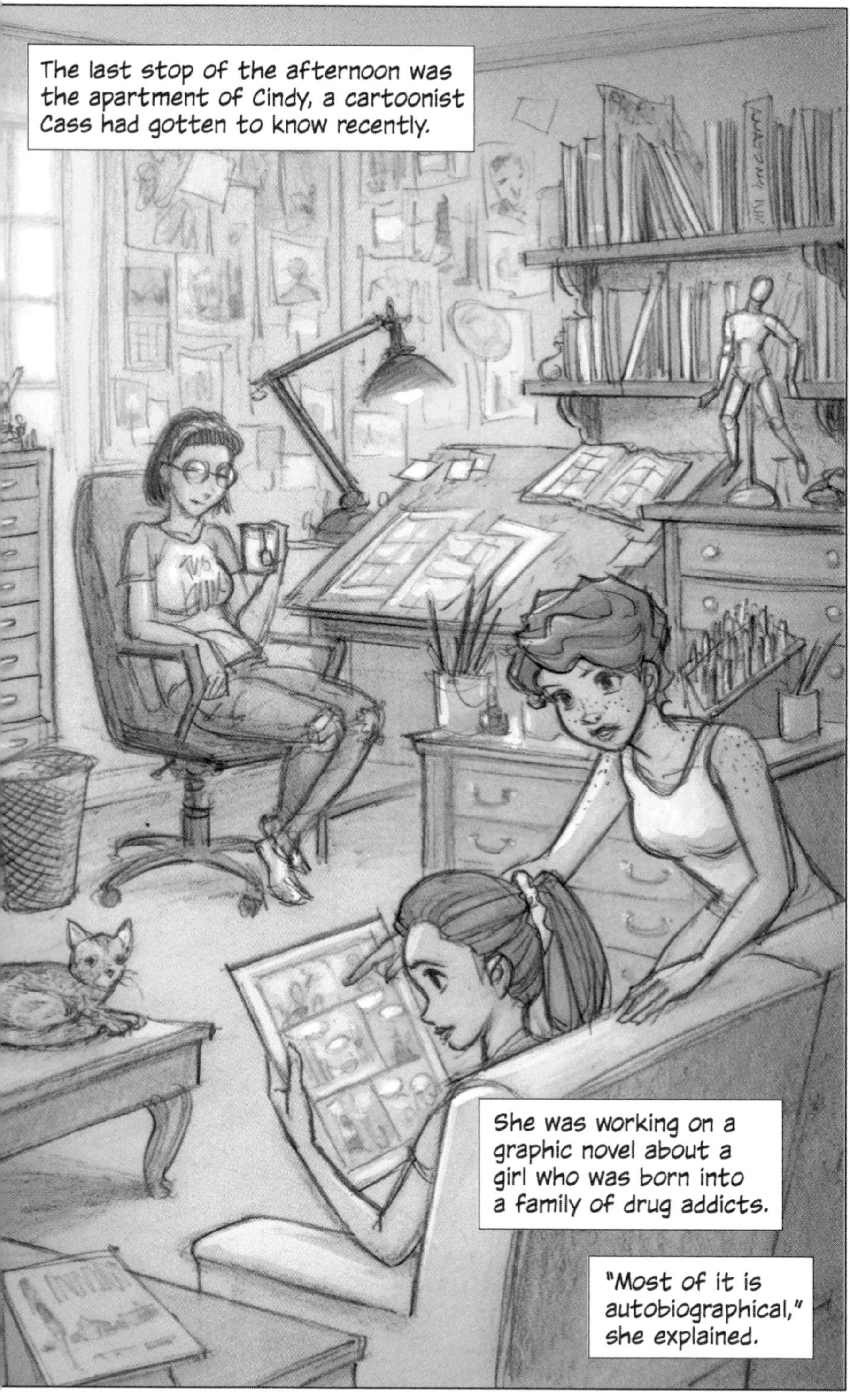
The last stop of the afternoon was the apartment of Cindy, a cartoonist Cass had gotten to know recently.
She was working on a graphic novel about a girl who was born into a family of drug addicts.
"Most of it is autobiographical," she explained.

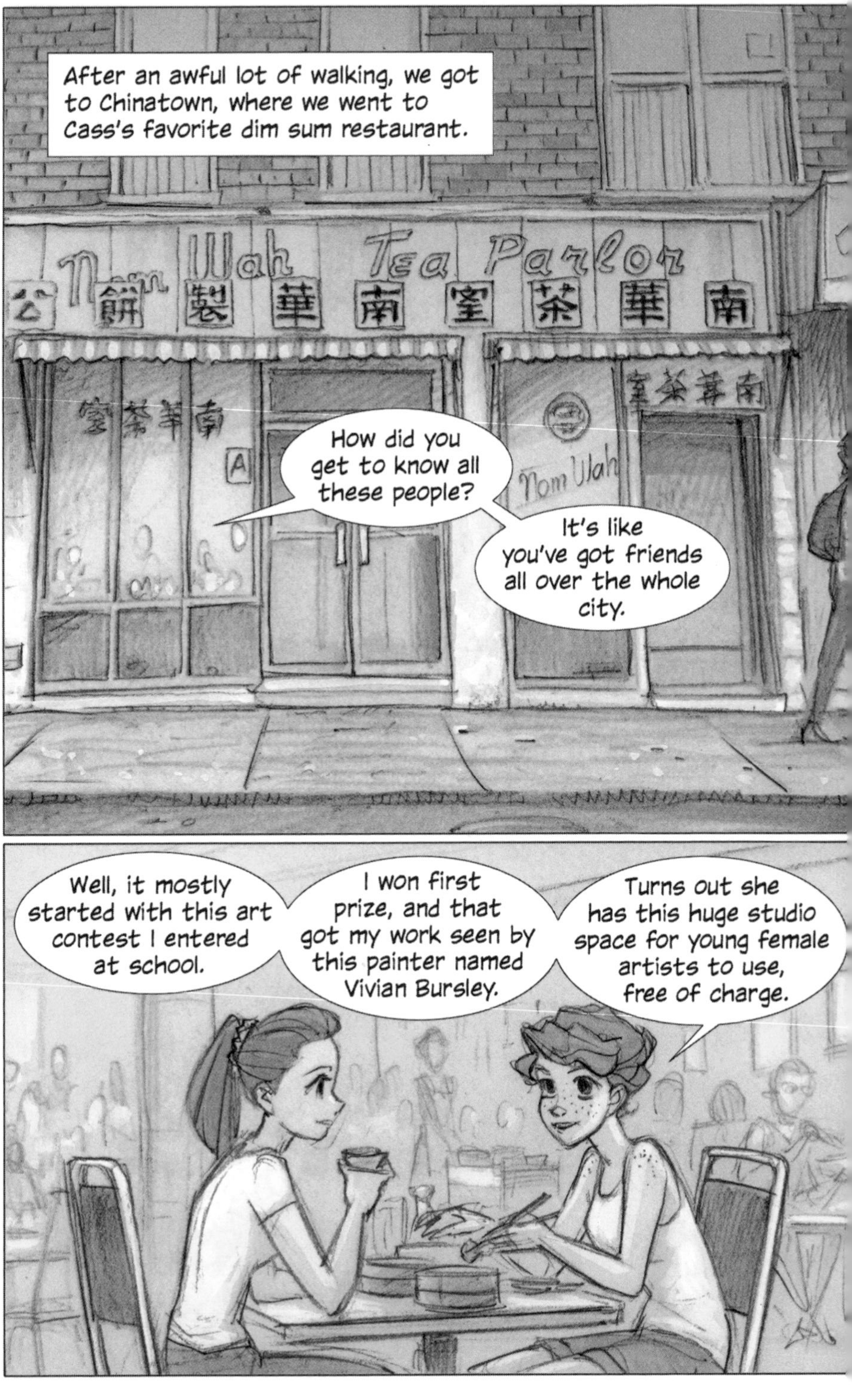
After an awful lot of walking, we got to Chinatown, where we went to Cass's favorite dim sum restaurant.
Nom Wah Tea Parlor
How did you get to know all these people?
Nom Wah
It's like you've got friends all over the whole city.
Well, it mostly started with this art contest I entered at school.
I won first prize, and that got my work seen by this painter named Vivian Bursley.
Turns out she has this huge studio space for young female artists to use, free of charge.

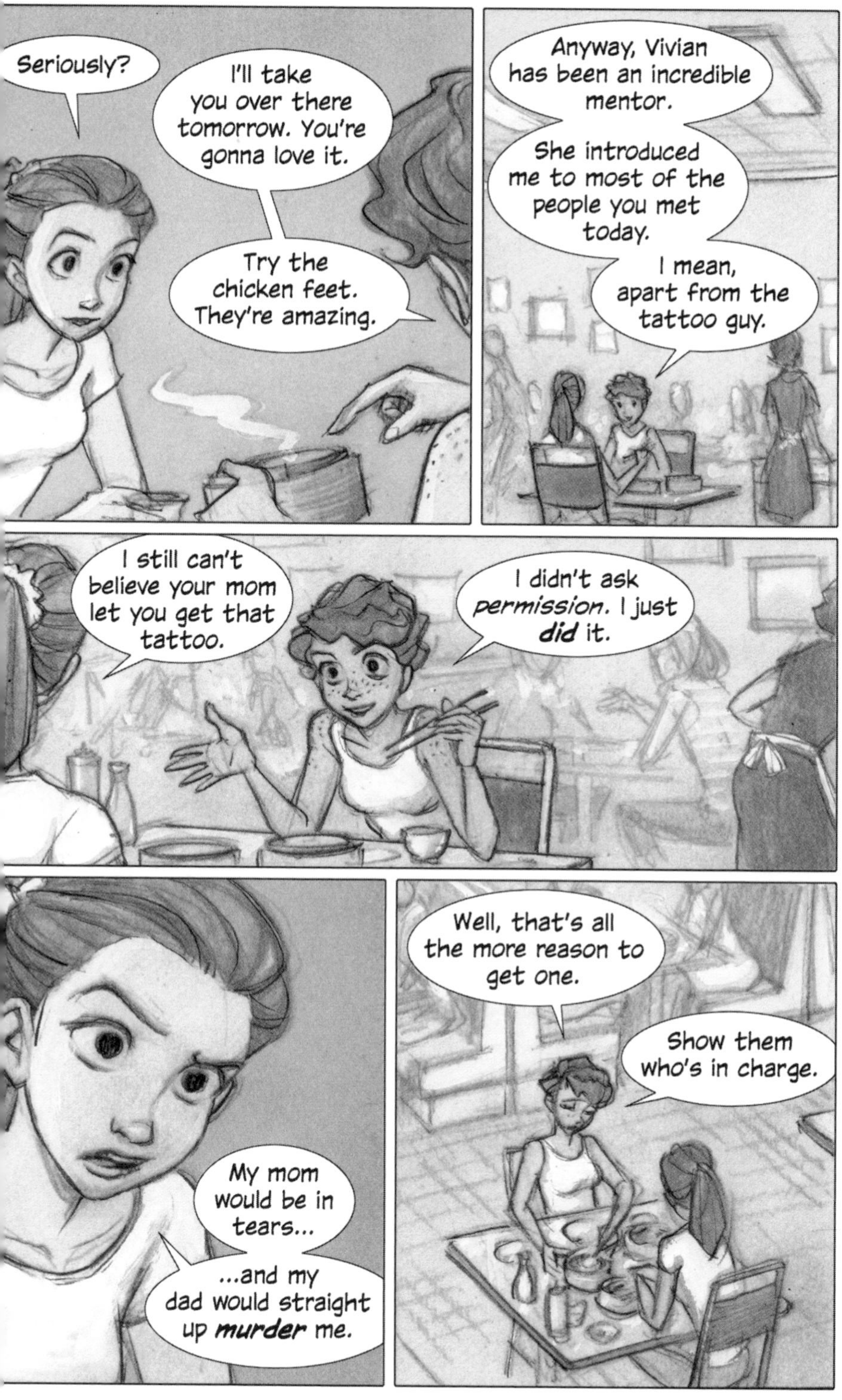

Seriously?
I'll take you over there tomorrow. You're gonna love it.
Try the chicken feet. They're amazing.
Anyway, Vivian has been an incredible mentor.
She introduced me to most of the people you met today.
I mean, apart from the tattoo guy.
I still can't believe your mom let you get that tattoo.
I didn't ask *permission*. I just ***did*** it.
My mom would be in tears...
...and my dad would straight up ***murder*** me.
Well, that's all the more reason to get one.
Show them who's in charge.

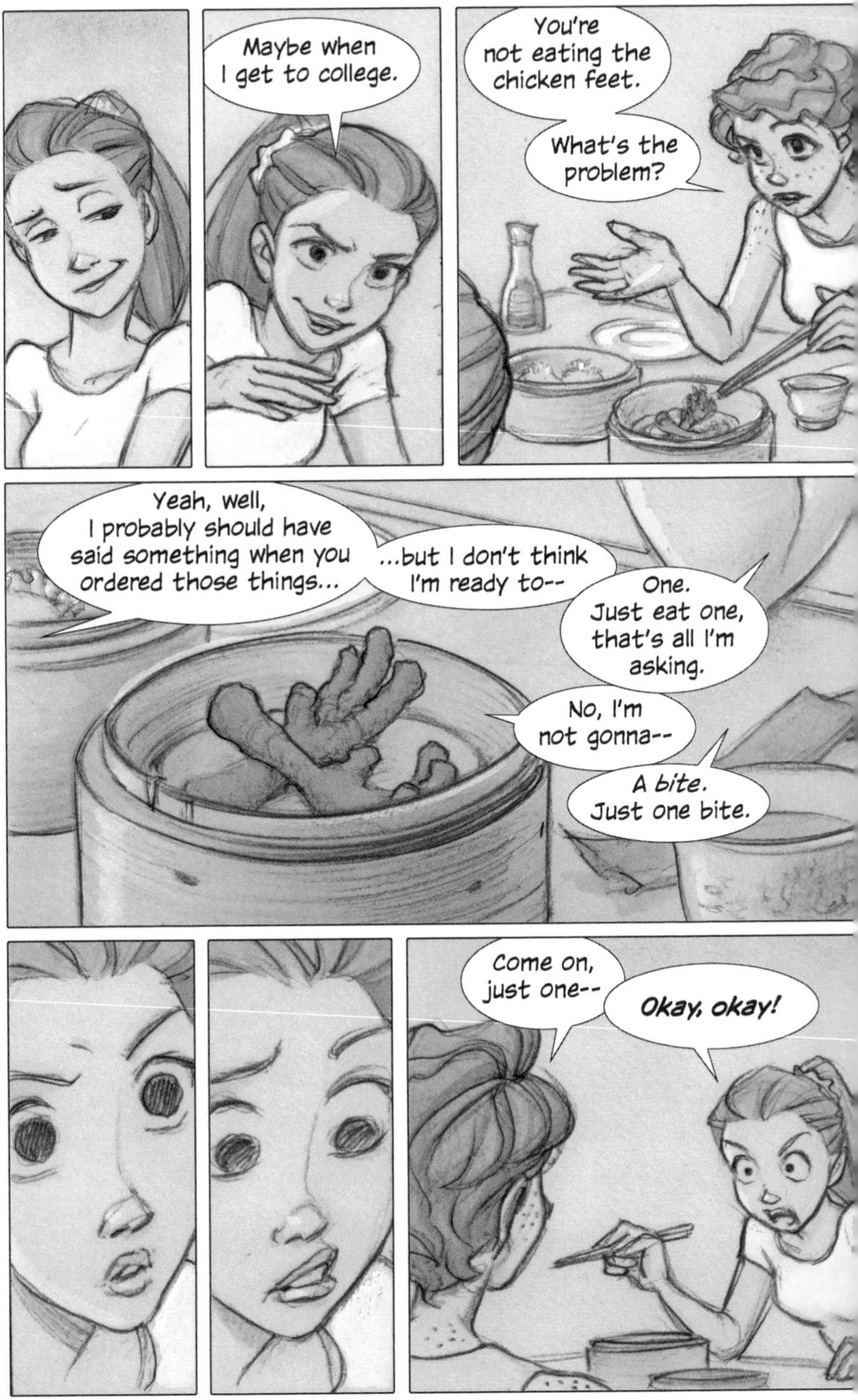
Maybe when I get to college.
You're not eating the chicken feet.
What's the problem?
Yeah, well, I probably should have said something when you ordered those things...
...but I don't think I'm ready to--
One. Just eat one, that's all I'm asking.
No, I'm not gonna--
A *bite*. Just one bite.
Come on, just one--
Okay, okay!

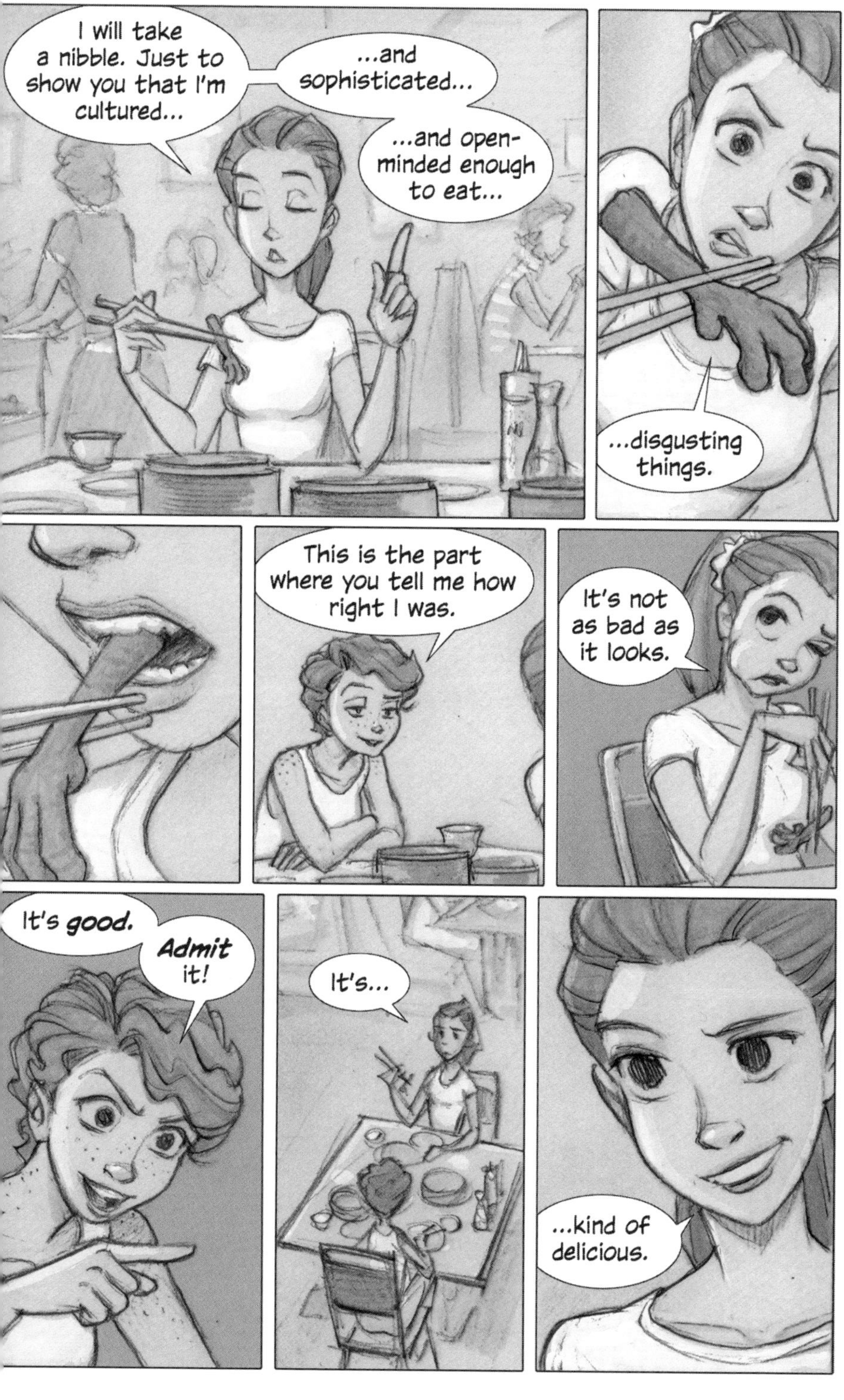
I will take a nibble. Just to show you that I'm cultured...
...and sophisticated...
...and open-minded enough to eat...
...disgusting things.
This is the part where you tell me how right I was.
It's not as bad as it looks.
It's *good.*
Admit it!
It's...
...kind of delicious.

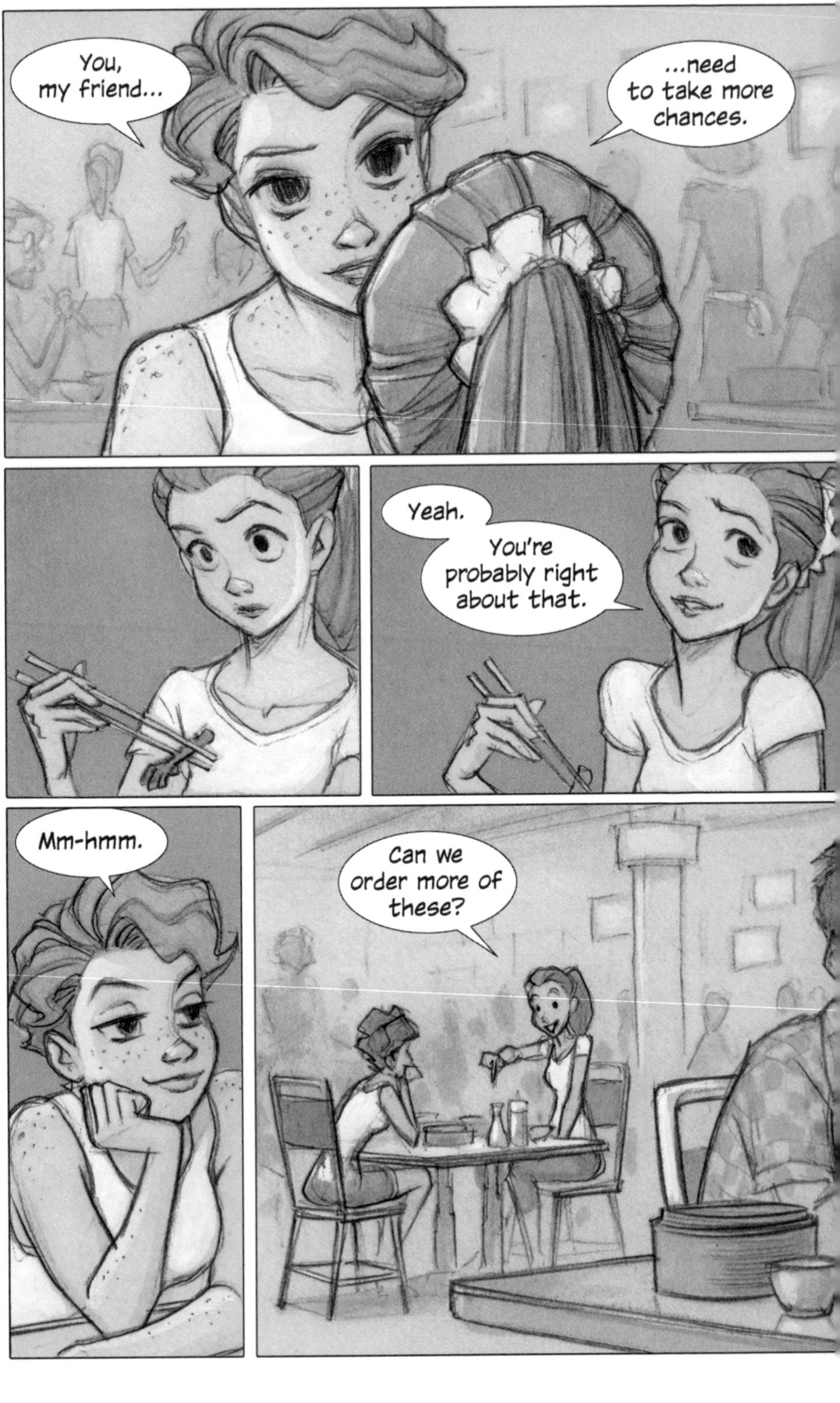
You, my friend...
...need to take more chances.
Yeah.
You're probably right about that.
Mm-hmm.
Can we order more of these?

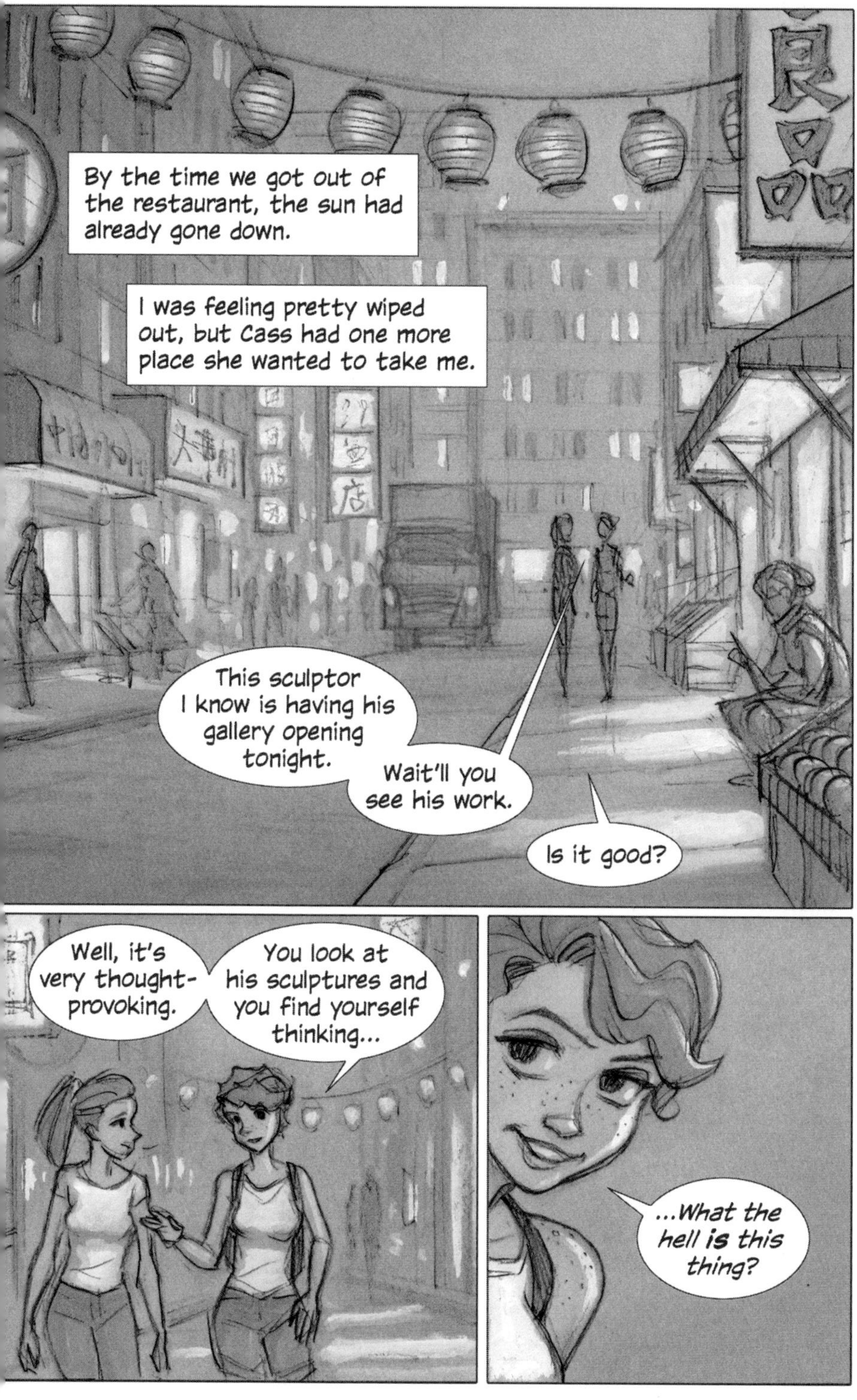
By the time we got out of the restaurant, the sun had already gone down.
I was feeling pretty wiped out, but Cass had one more place she wanted to take me.
This sculptor I know is having his gallery opening tonight.
Wait'll you see his work.
Is it good?
Well, it's very thought-provoking.
You look at his sculptures and you find yourself thinking...
...What the hell *is* this thing?

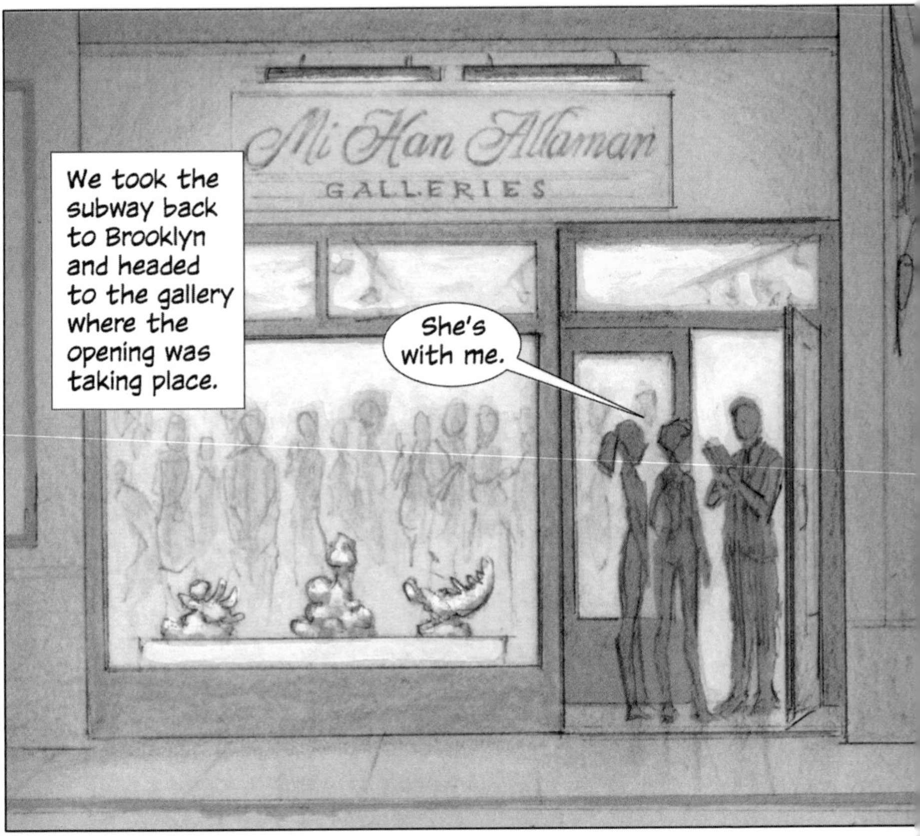
Mi Han Allaman
GALLERIES
We took the subway back to Brooklyn and headed to the gallery where the opening was taking place.
She's with me.

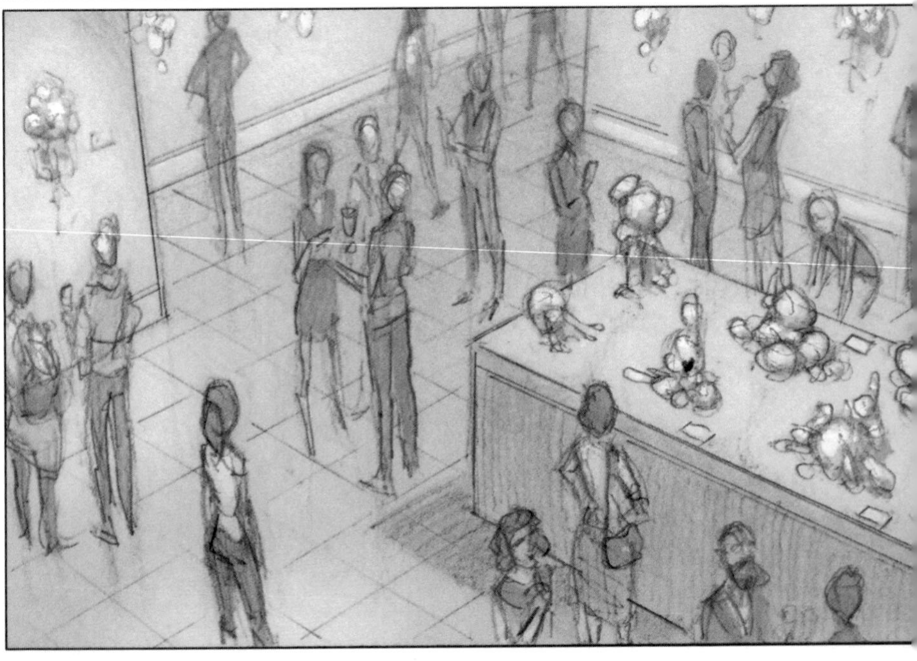

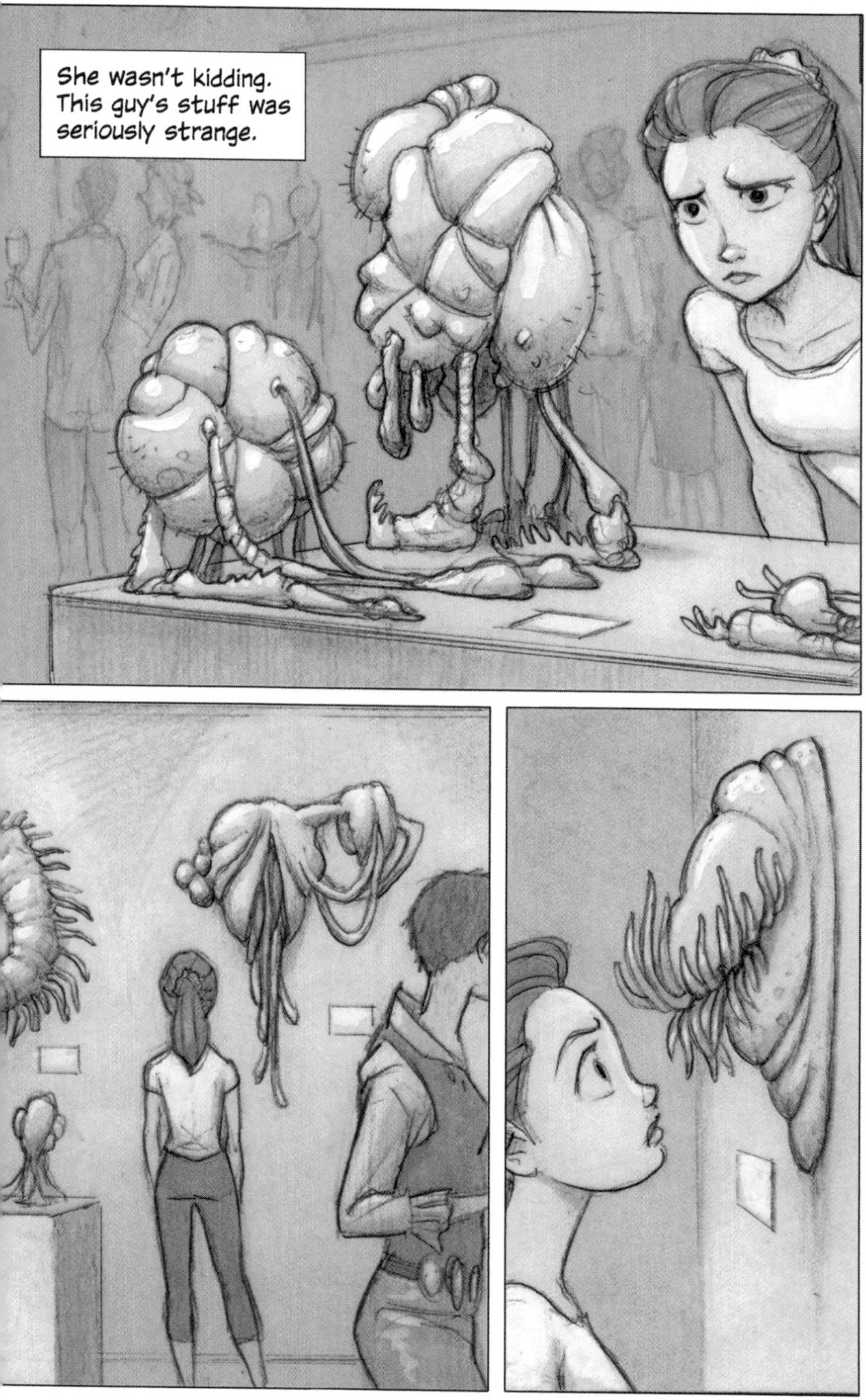
She wasn't kidding. This guy's stuff was seriously strange.

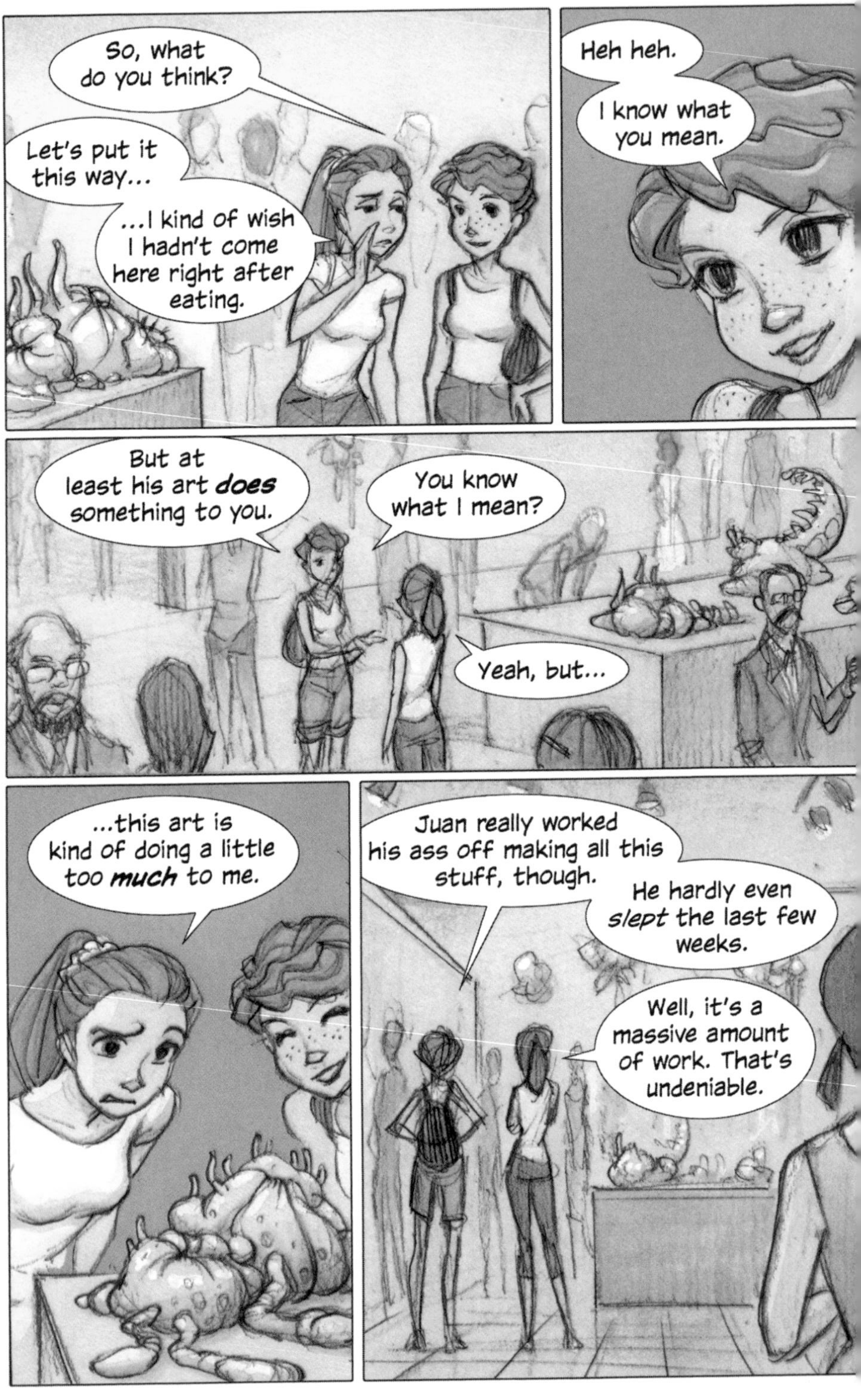
So, what do you think?
Let's put it this way...
...I kind of wish I hadn't come here right after eating.
Heh heh.
I know what you mean.
But at least his art *does* something to you.
You know what I mean?
Yeah, but...
...this art is kind of doing a little too *much* to me.
Juan really worked his ass off making all this stuff, though.
He hardly even *slept* the last few weeks.
Well, it's a massive amount of work. That's undeniable.

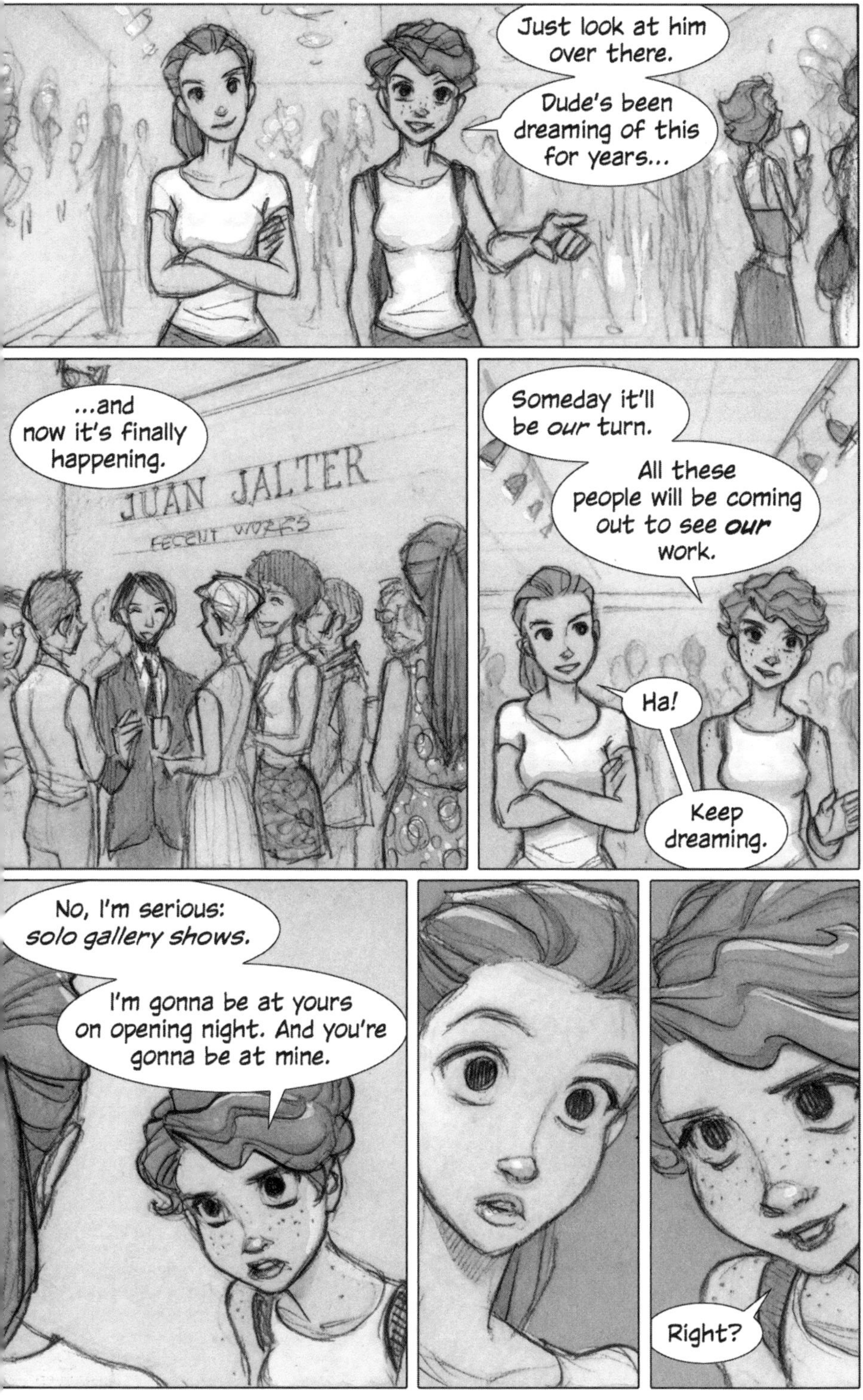

Just look at him over there.
Dude's been dreaming of this for years...
...and now it's finally happening.
JUAN JALTER
Someday it'll be *our* turn.
All these people will be coming out to see ***our*** work.
Ha!
Keep dreaming.
No, I'm serious: *solo gallery shows.*
I'm gonna be at yours on opening night. And you're gonna be at mine.
Right?

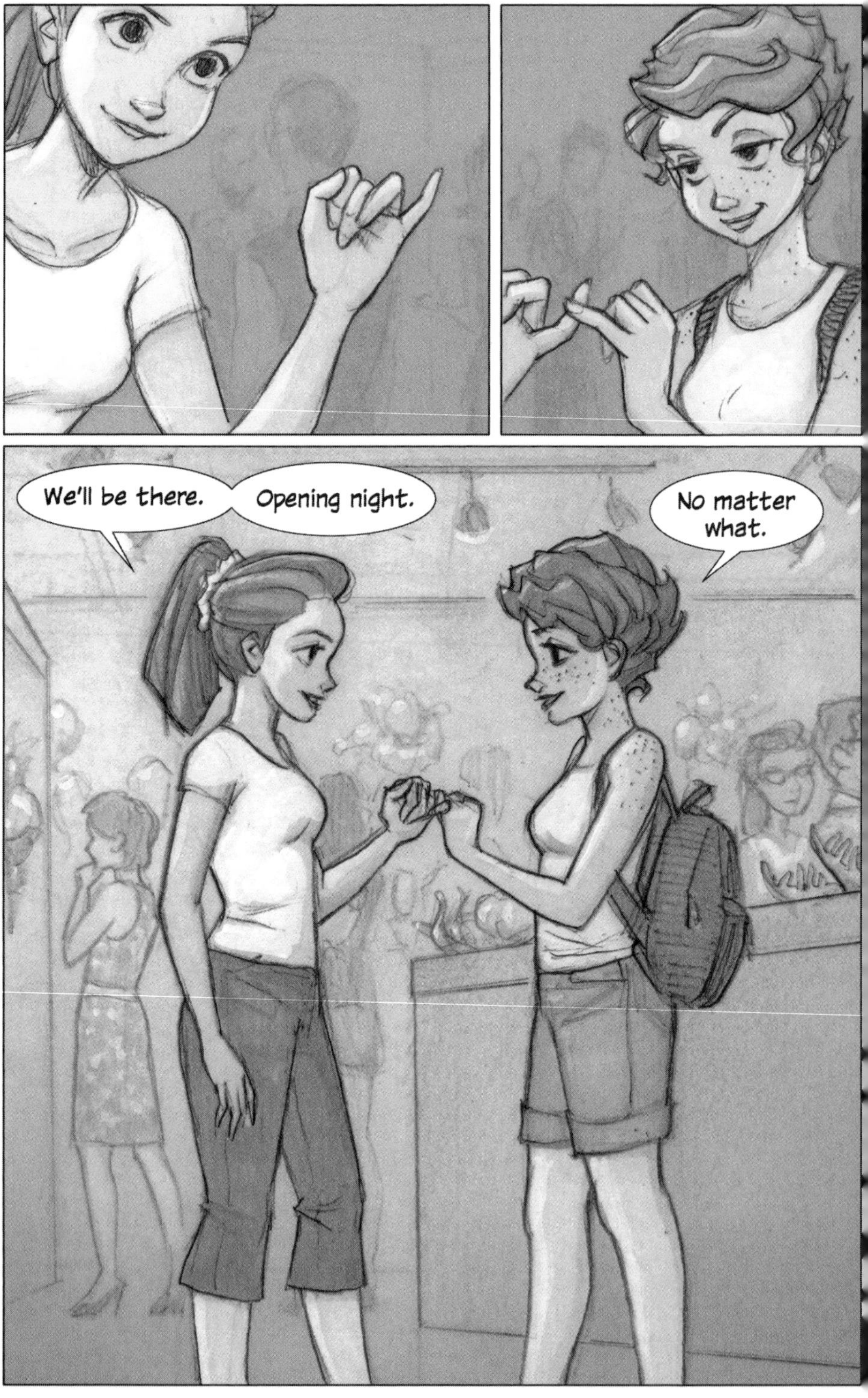
We'll be there.
Opening night.
No matter what.

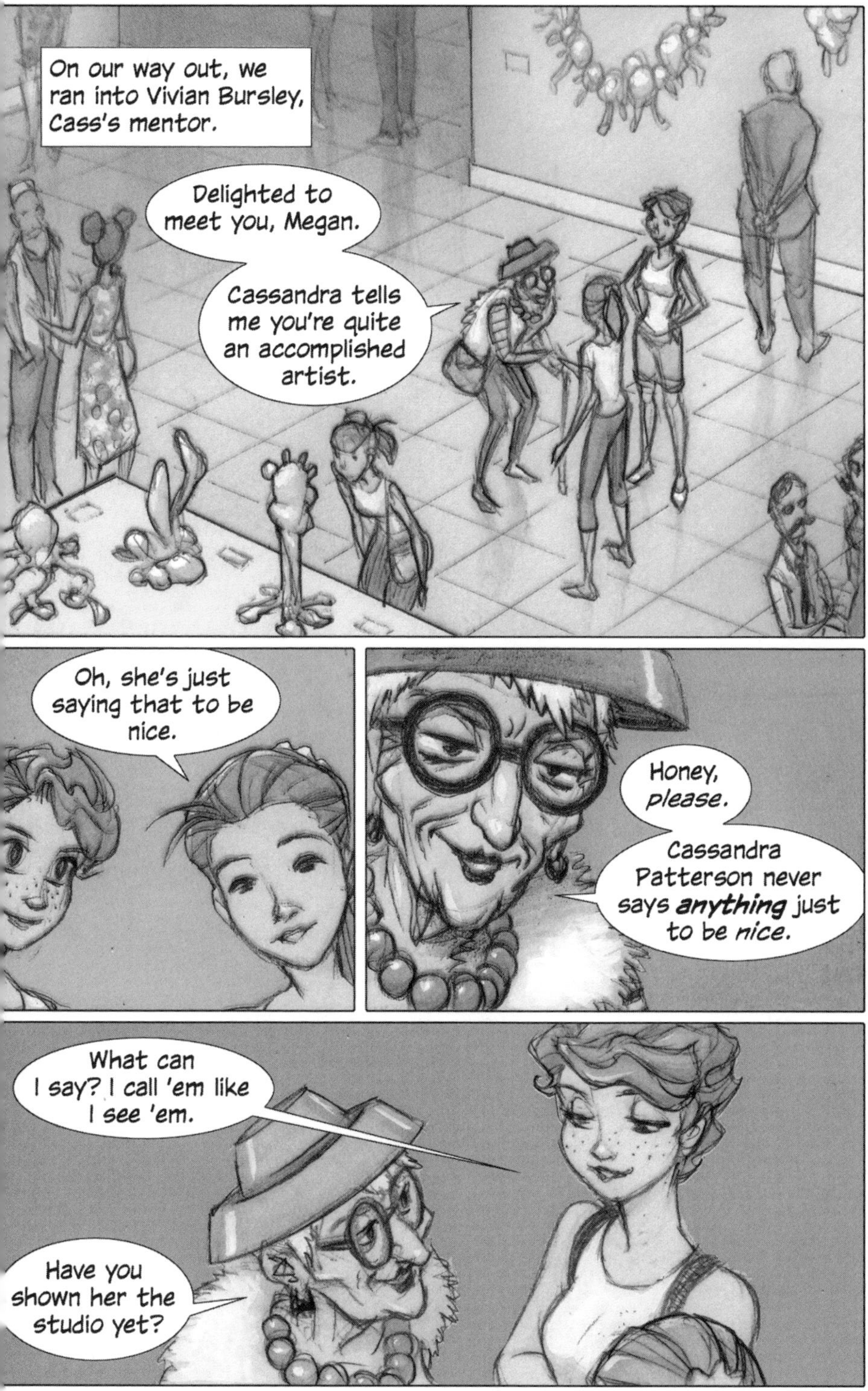
On our way out, we ran into Vivian Bursley, Cass's mentor.
Delighted to meet you, Megan.
Cassandra tells me you're quite an accomplished artist.
Oh, she's just saying that to be nice.
Honey, *please.*
Cassandra Patterson never says ***anything*** just to be *nice.*
What can I say? I call 'em like I see 'em.
Have you shown her the studio yet?

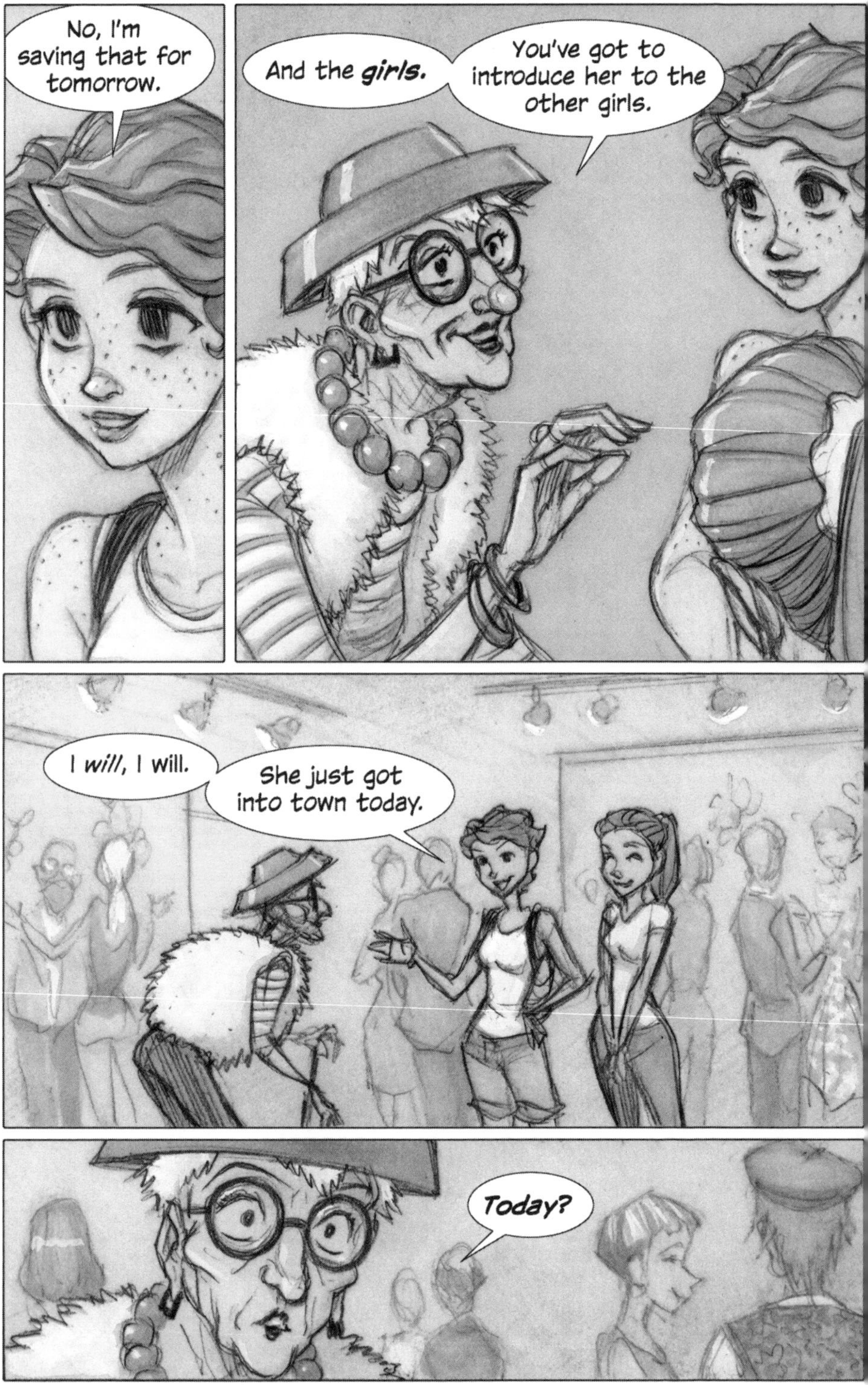
No, I'm saving that for tomorrow.
And the *girls.*
You've got to introduce her to the other girls.
I *will*, I will.
She just got into town today.
Today?

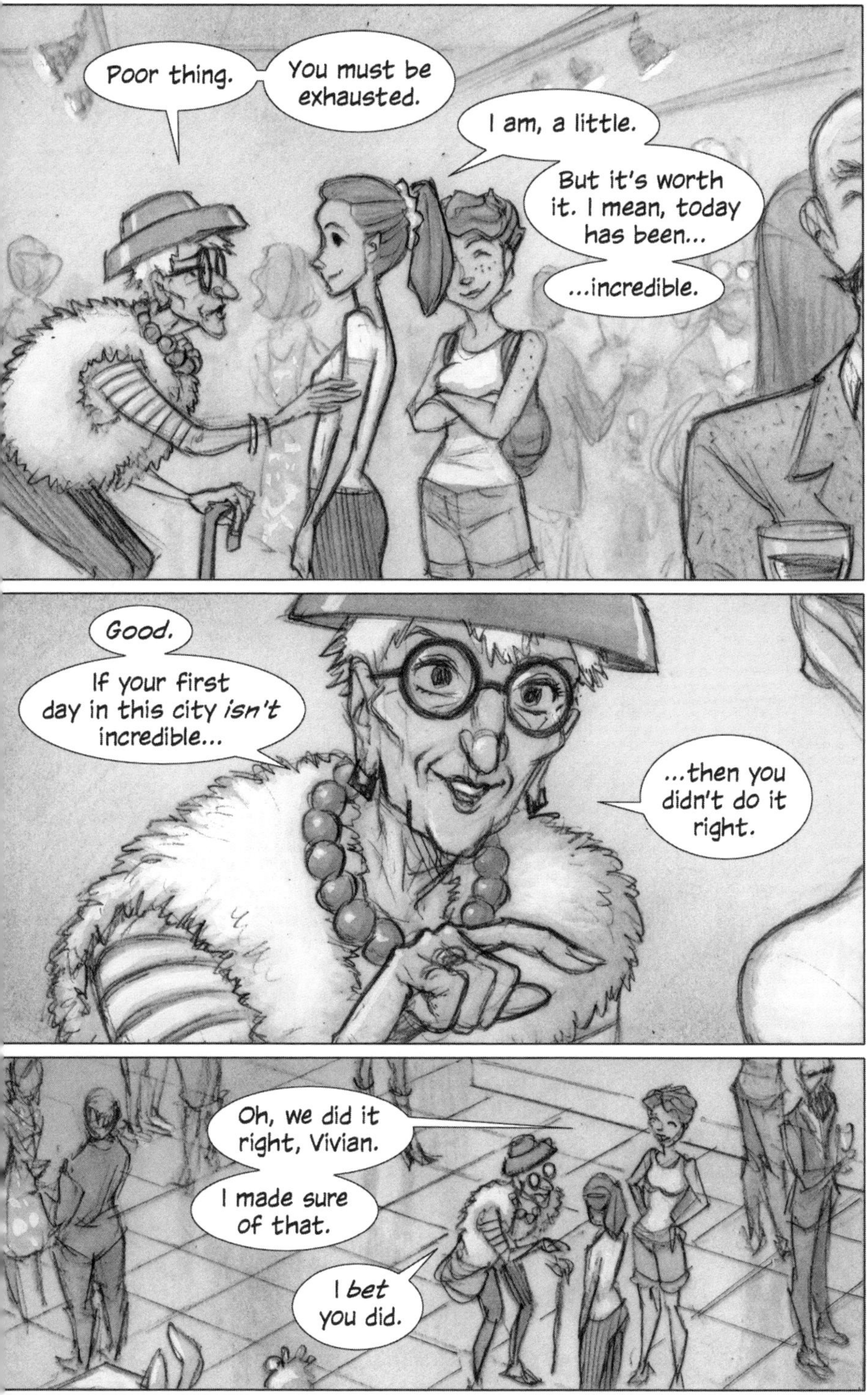

Poor thing.
You must be exhausted.
I am, a little.
But it's worth it. I mean, today has been...
...incredible.
Good.
If your first day in this city *isn't* incredible...
...then you didn't do it right.
Oh, we did it right, Vivian.
I made sure of that.
I *bet* you did.

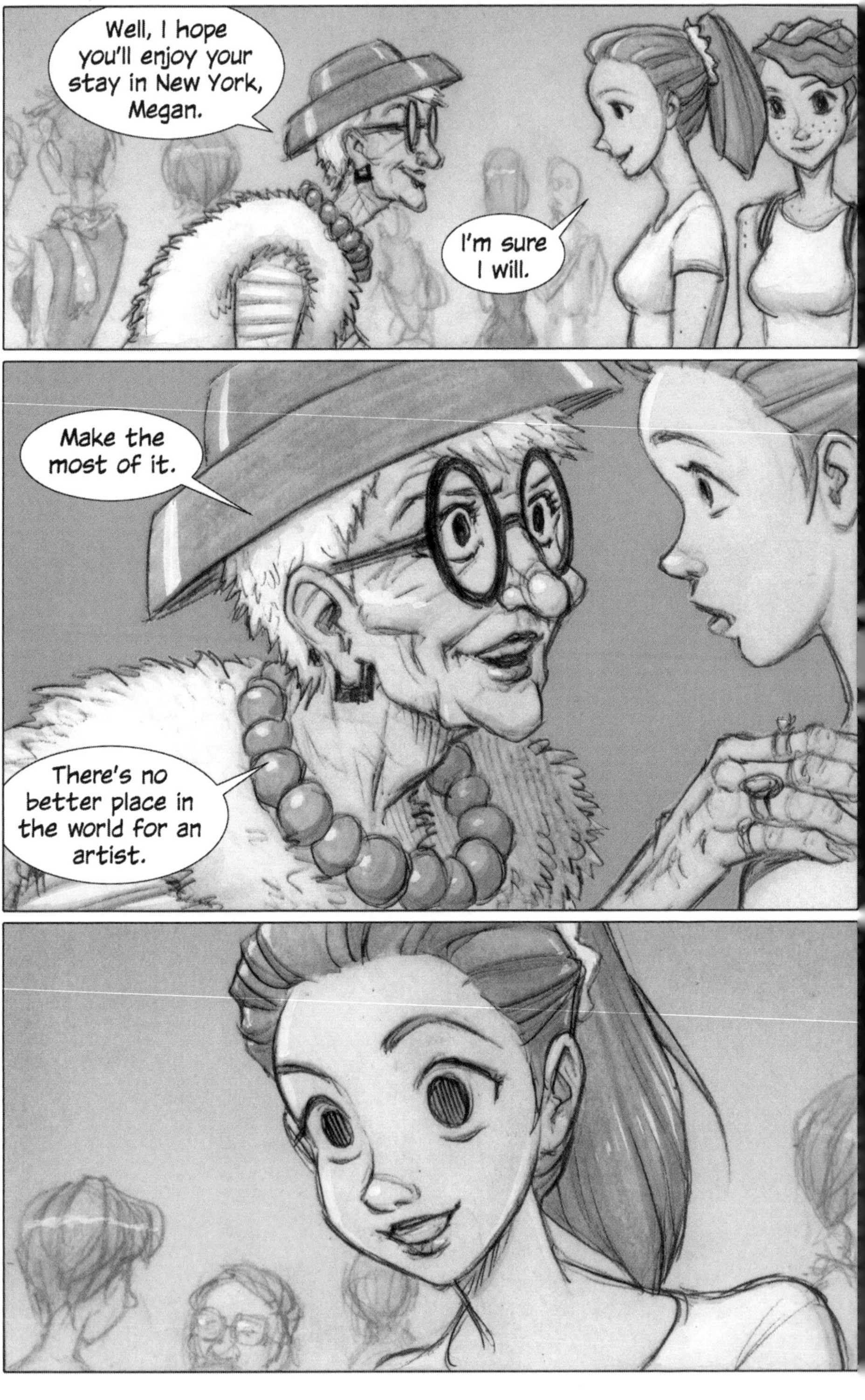
Well, I hope you'll enjoy your stay in New York, Megan.
I'm sure I will.
Make the most of it.
There's no better place in the world for an artist.

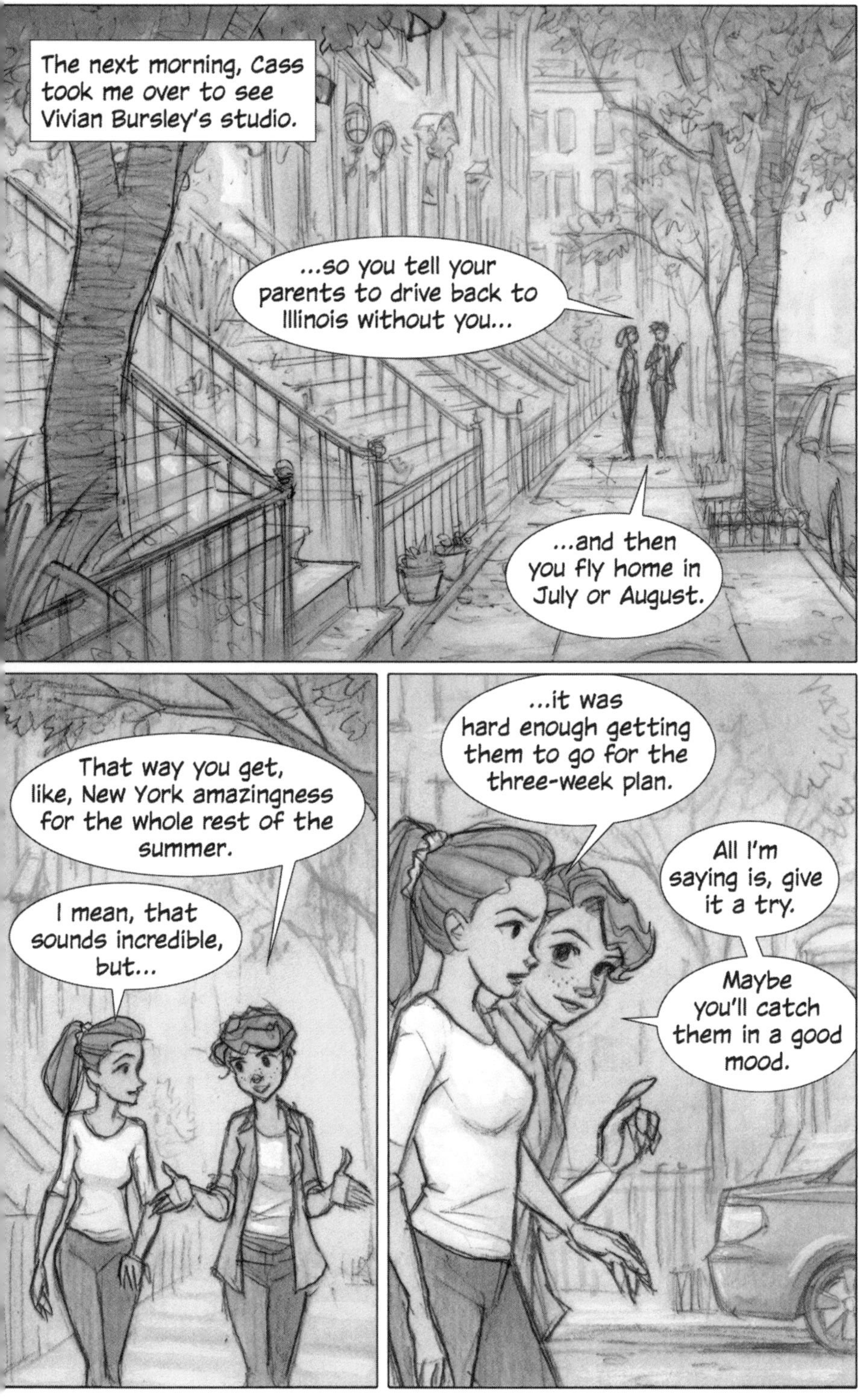
The next morning, Cass took me over to see Vivian Bursley's studio.
...so you tell your parents to drive back to Illinois without you...
...and then you fly home in July or August.
That way you get, like, New York amazingness for the whole rest of the summer.
I mean, that sounds incredible, but...
...it was hard enough getting them to go for the three-week plan.
All I'm saying is, give it a try.
Maybe you'll catch them in a good mood.

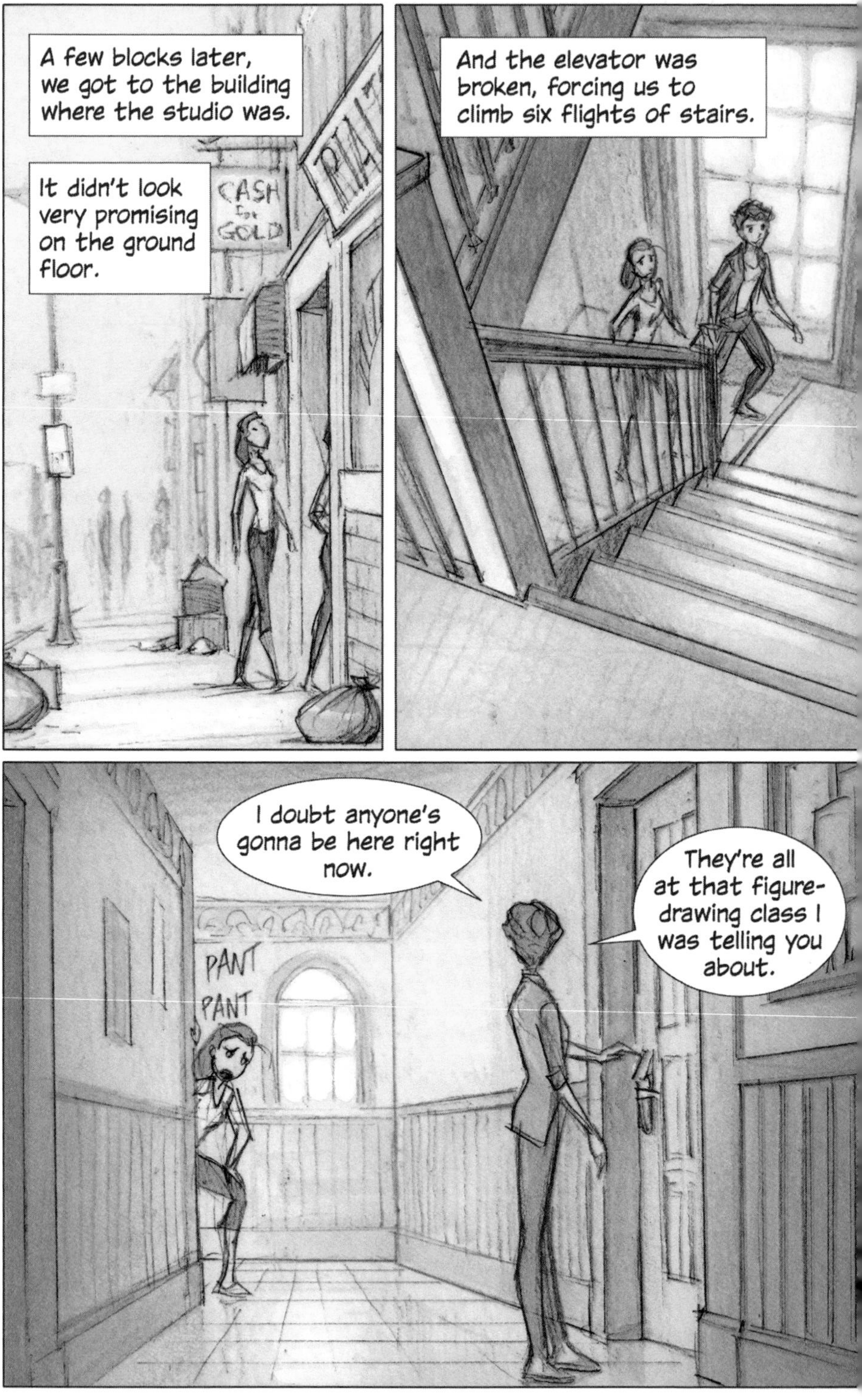
A few blocks later, we got to the building where the studio was.
It didn't look very promising on the ground floor.
And the elevator was broken, forcing us to climb six flights of stairs.
I doubt anyone's gonna be here right now.
They're all at that figure-drawing class I was telling you about.
PANT
PANT

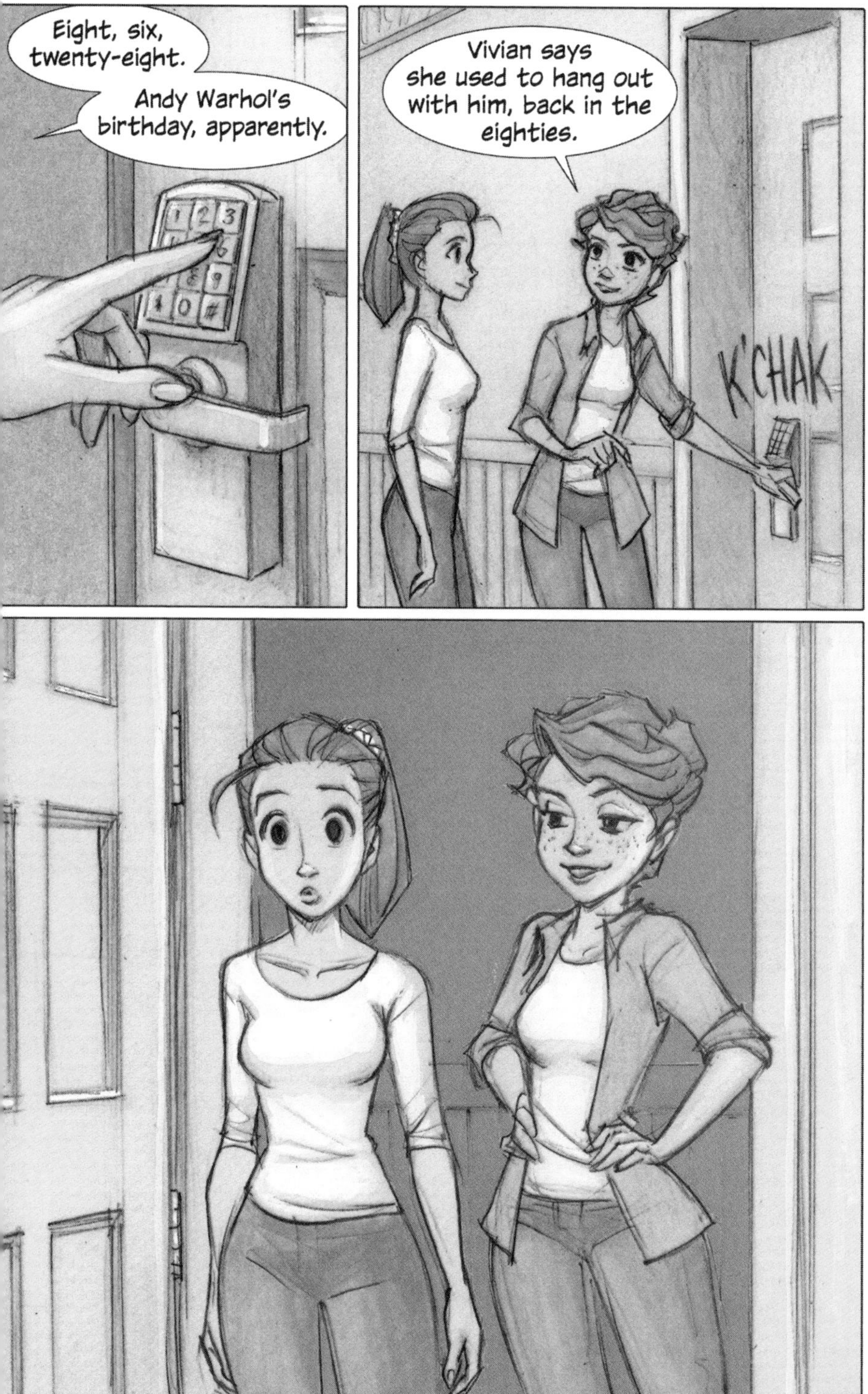
Eight, six, twenty-eight.
Andy Warhol's birthday, apparently.
Vivian says she used to hang out with him, back in the eighties.
K'CHAK

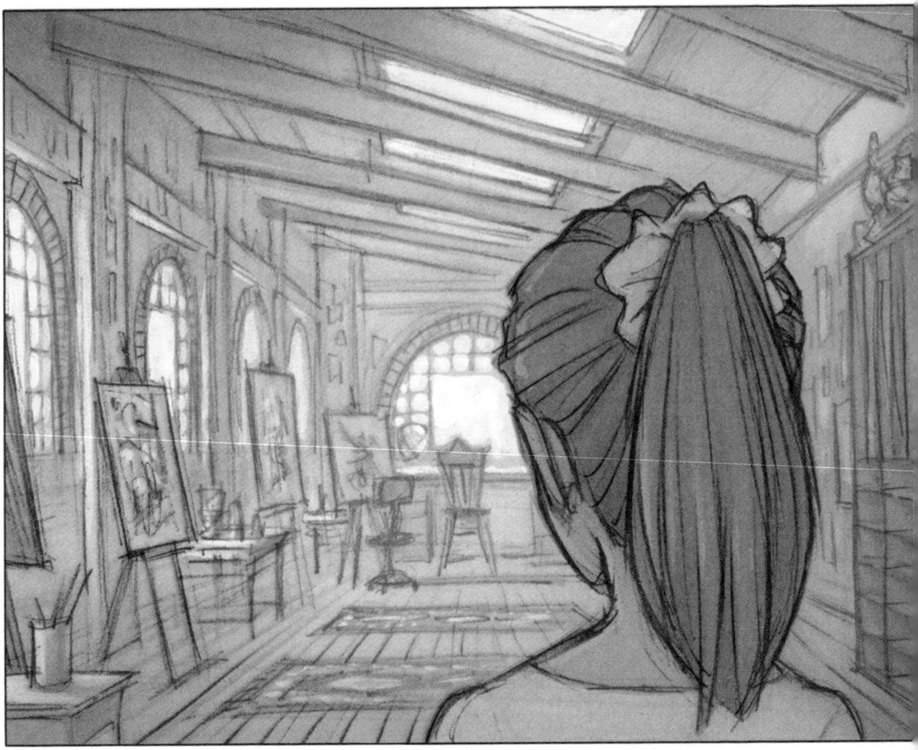

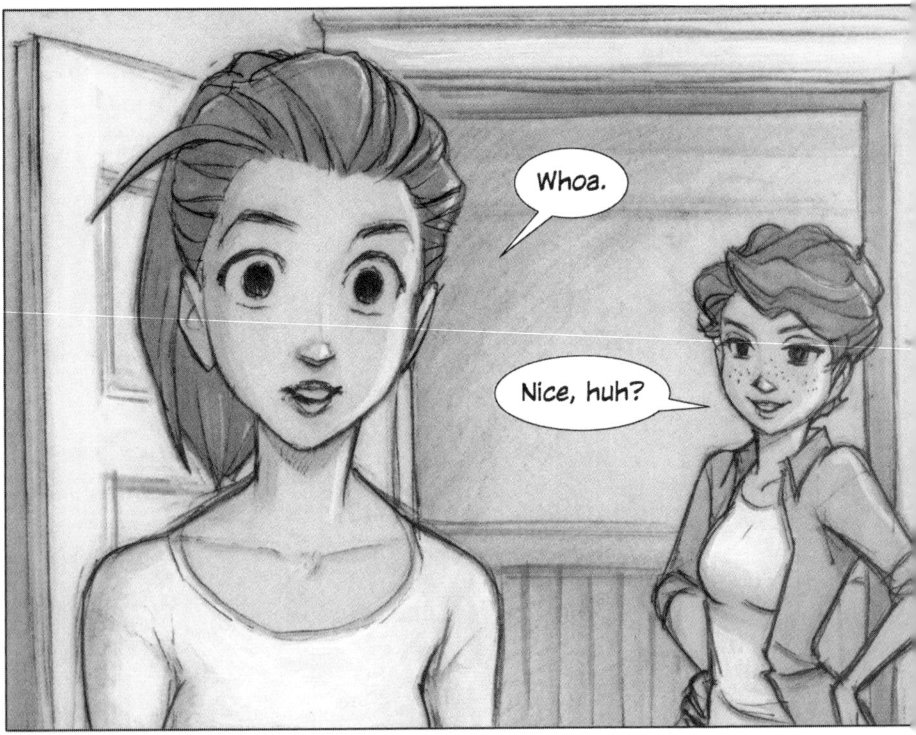
Whoa.
Nice, huh?

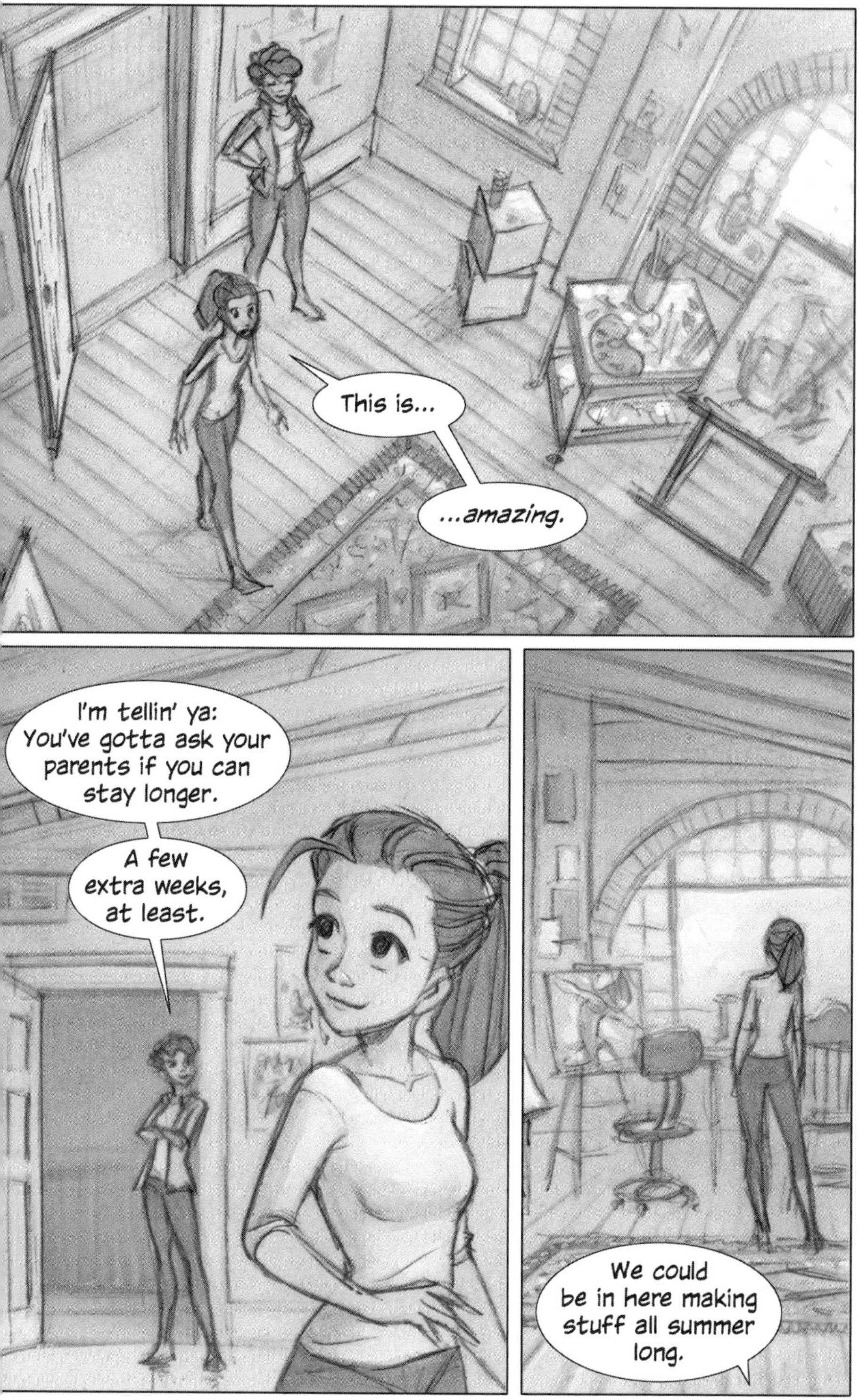
This is...
...amazing.
I'm tellin' ya: You've gotta ask your parents if you can stay longer.
A few extra weeks, at least.
We could be in here making stuff all summer long.

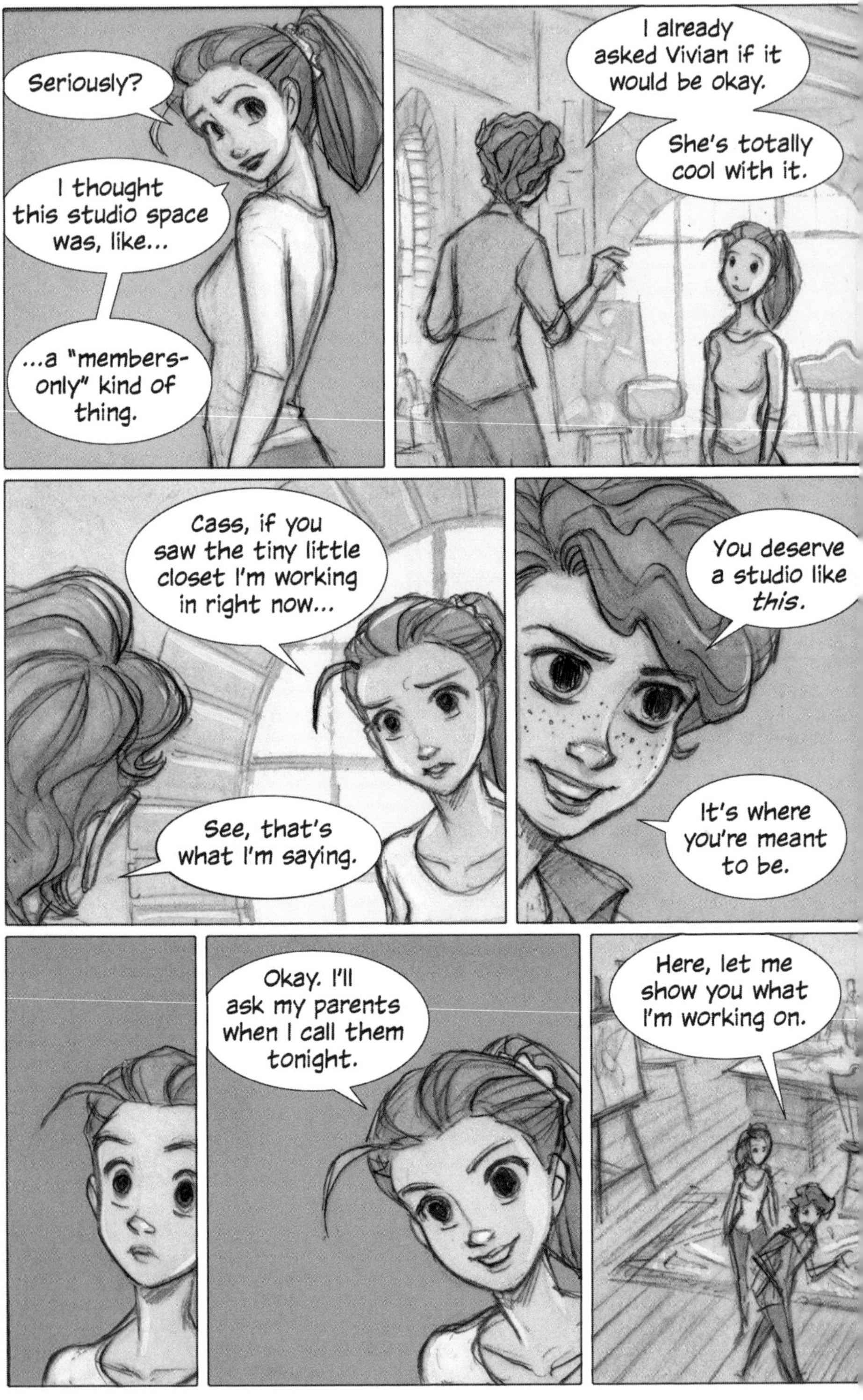
Seriously?
I thought this studio space was, like...
...a "members-only" kind of thing.
I already asked Vivian if it would be okay.
She's totally cool with it.
Cass, if you saw the tiny little closet I'm working in right now...
See, that's what I'm saying.
You deserve a studio like *this*.
It's where you're meant to be.
Okay. I'll ask my parents when I call them tonight.
Here, let me show you what I'm working on.

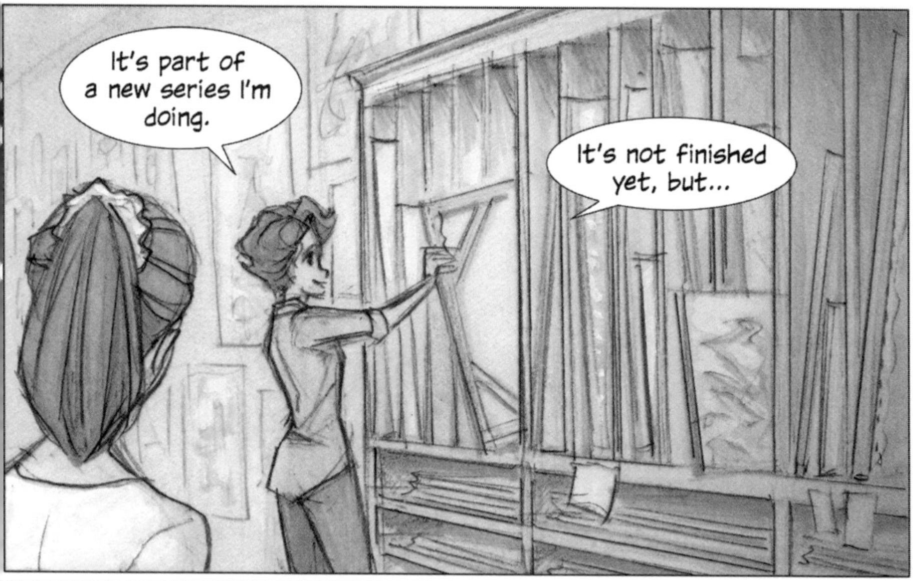
It's part of a new series I'm doing.
It's not finished yet, but...

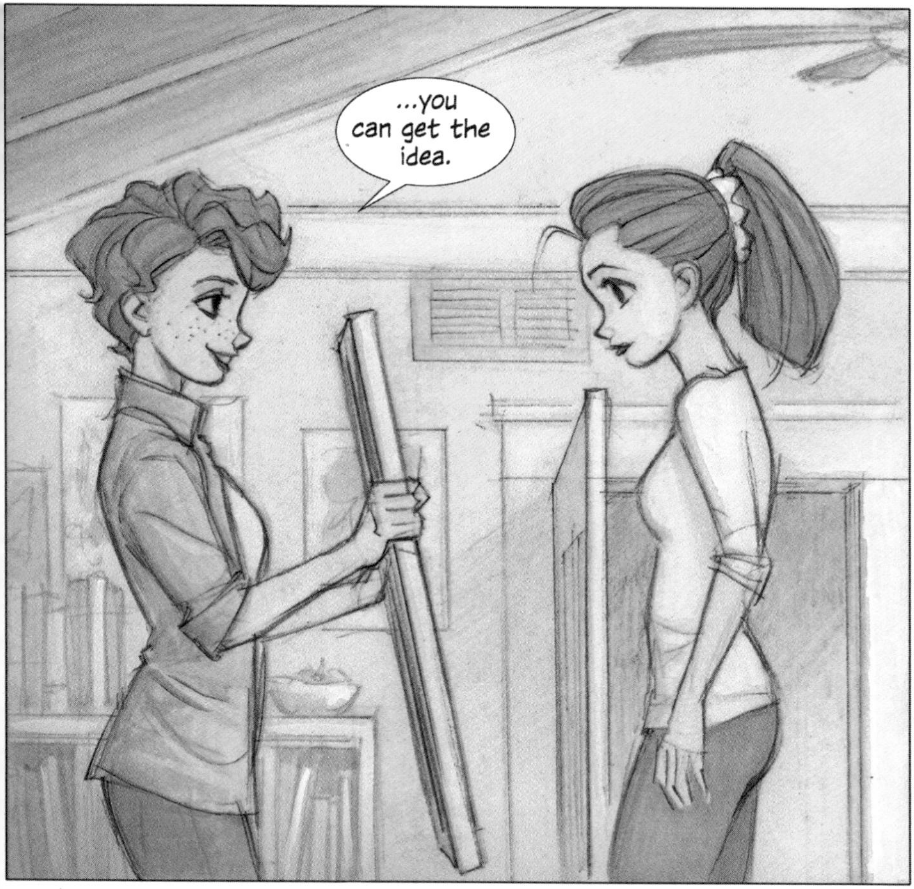
...you can get the idea.

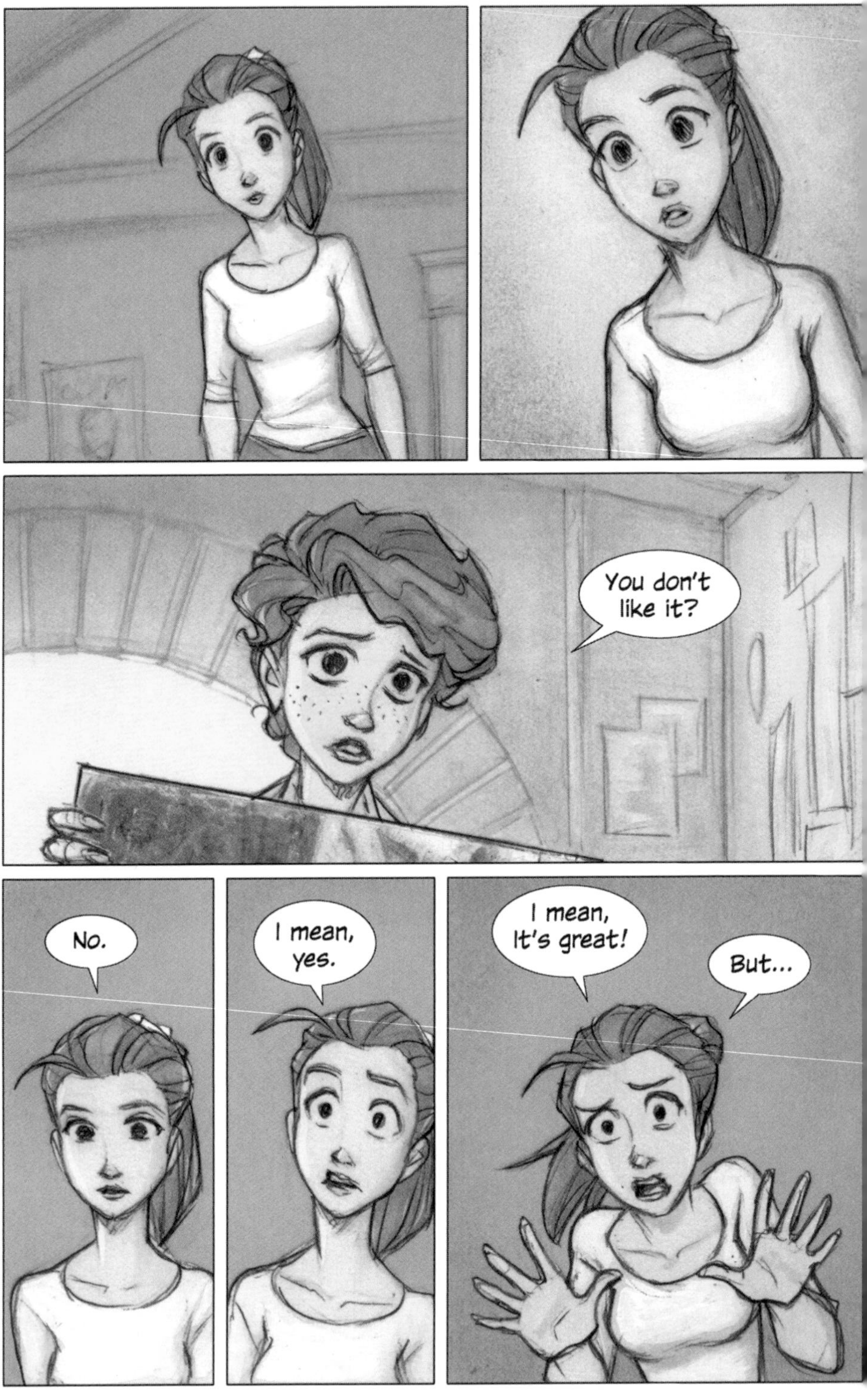
You don't like it?
No.
I mean, yes.
I mean, It's great!
But...

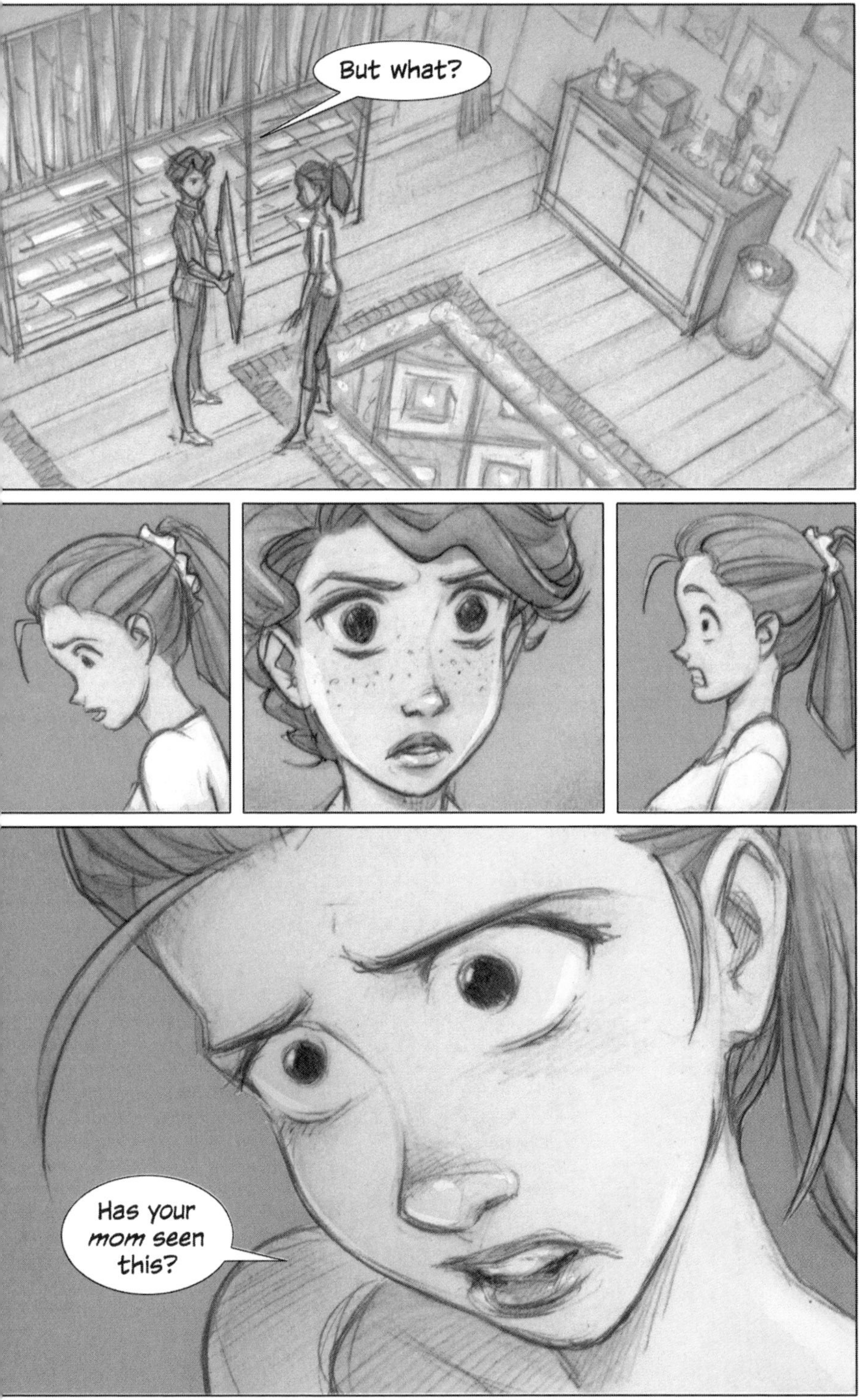
But what?
Has your *mom* seen this?

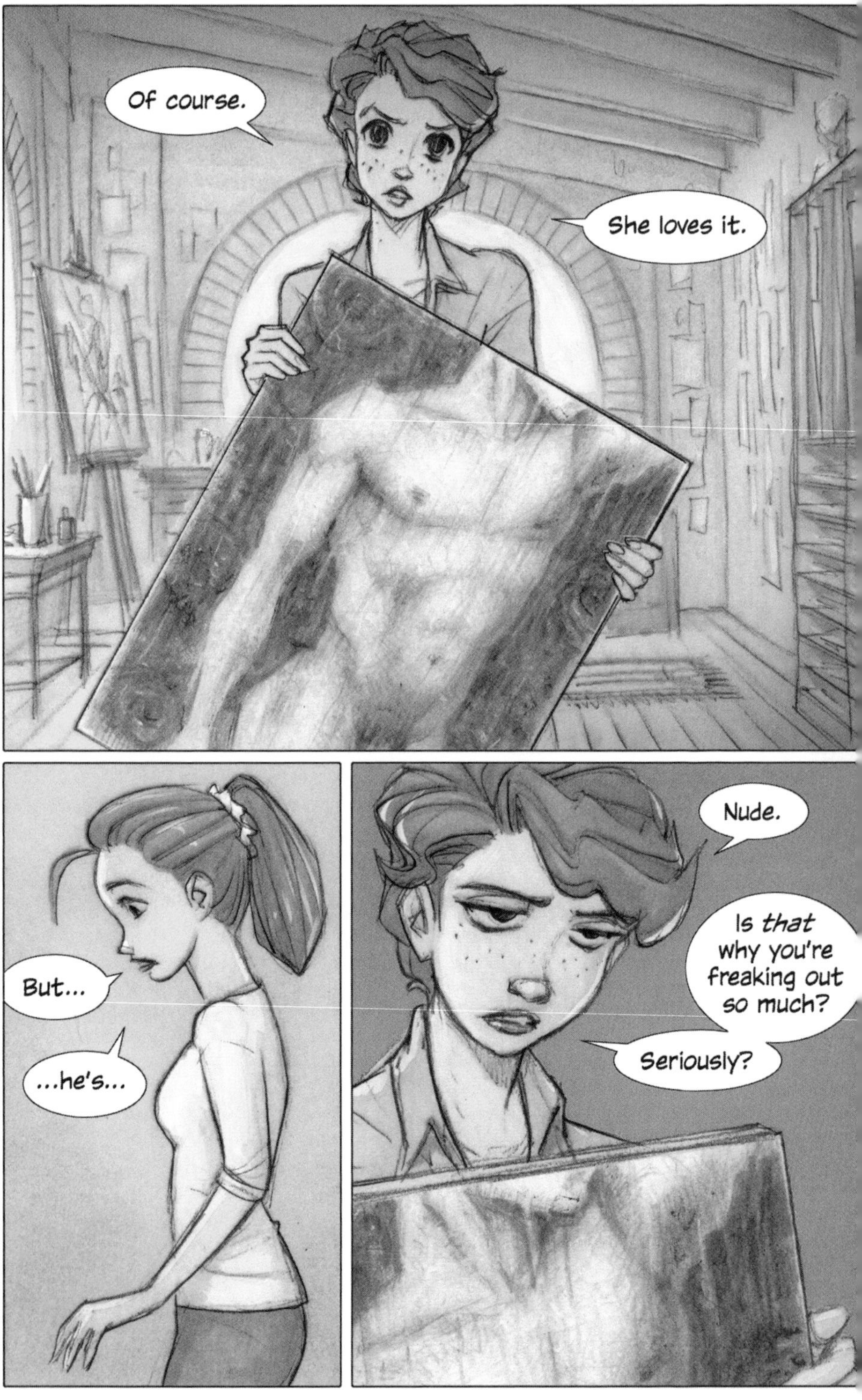
Of course.
She loves it.
But...
...he's...
Nude.
Is *that* why you're freaking out so much?
Seriously?

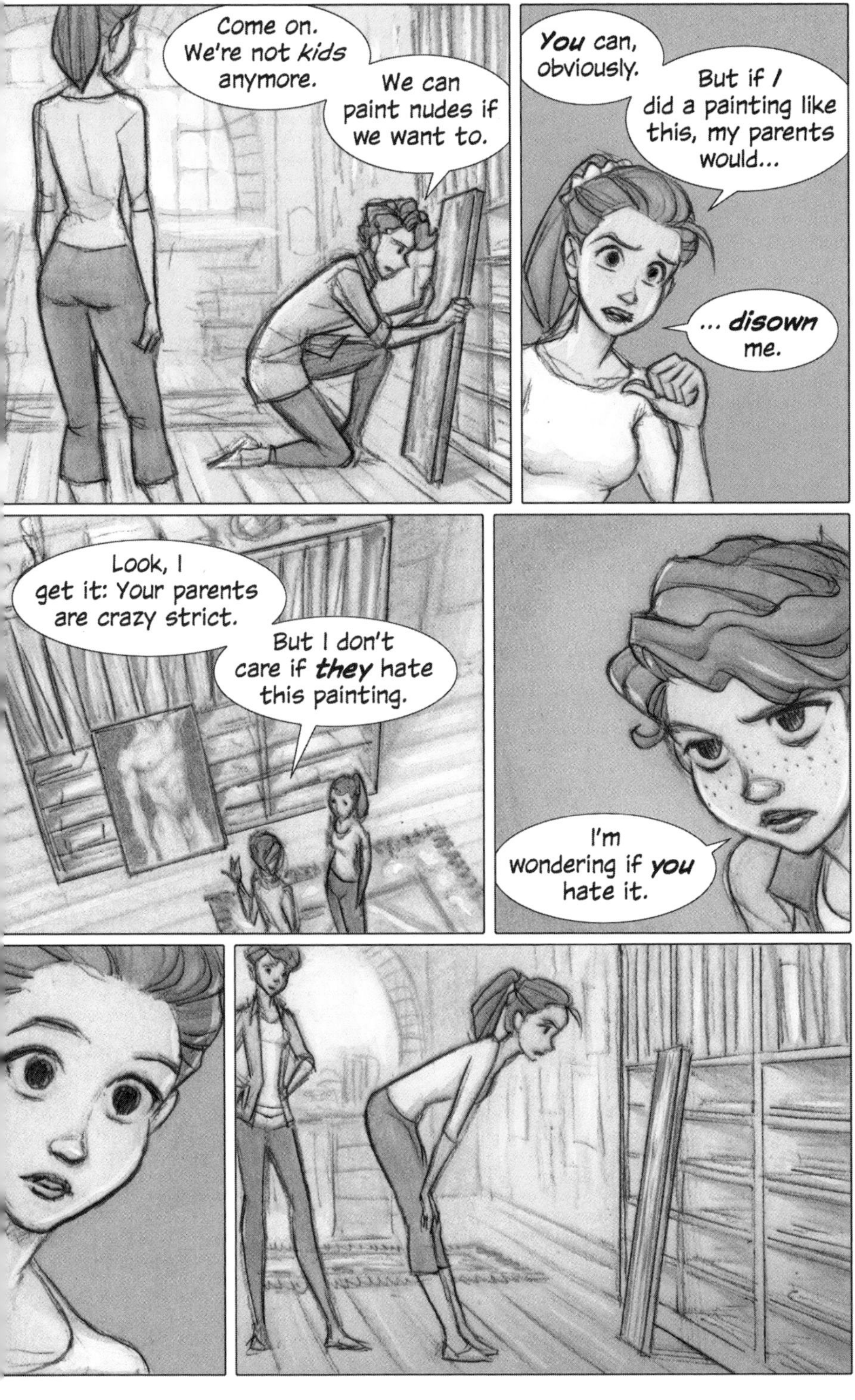
Come on. We're not kids anymore.
We can paint nudes if we want to.
You can, obviously.
But if I did a painting like this, my parents would...
... disown me.
Look, I get it: Your parents are crazy strict.
But I don't care if they hate this painting.
I'm wondering if you hate it.

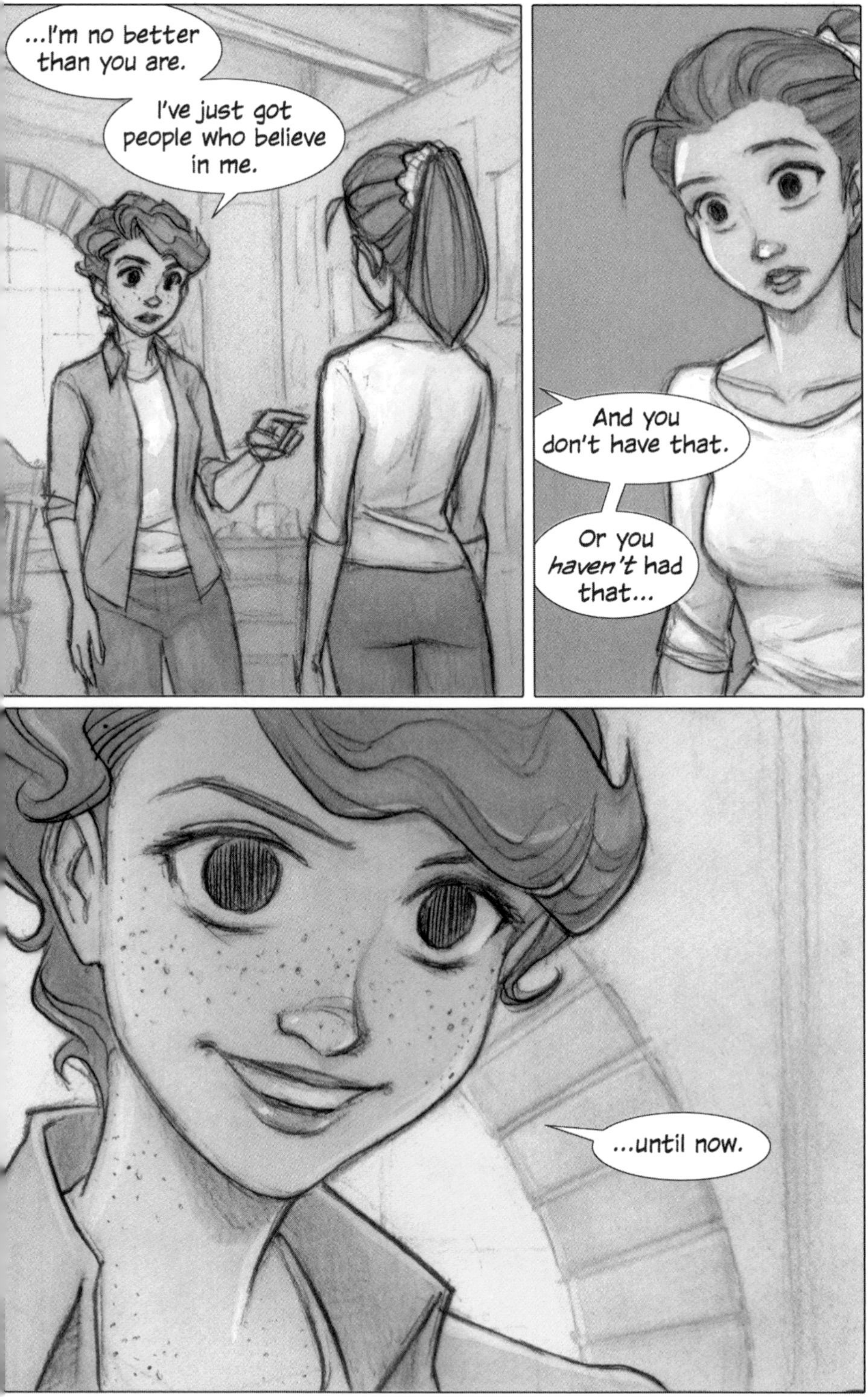
...I'm no better than you are.
I've just got people who believe in me.
And you don't have that.
Or you *haven't* had that...
...until now.

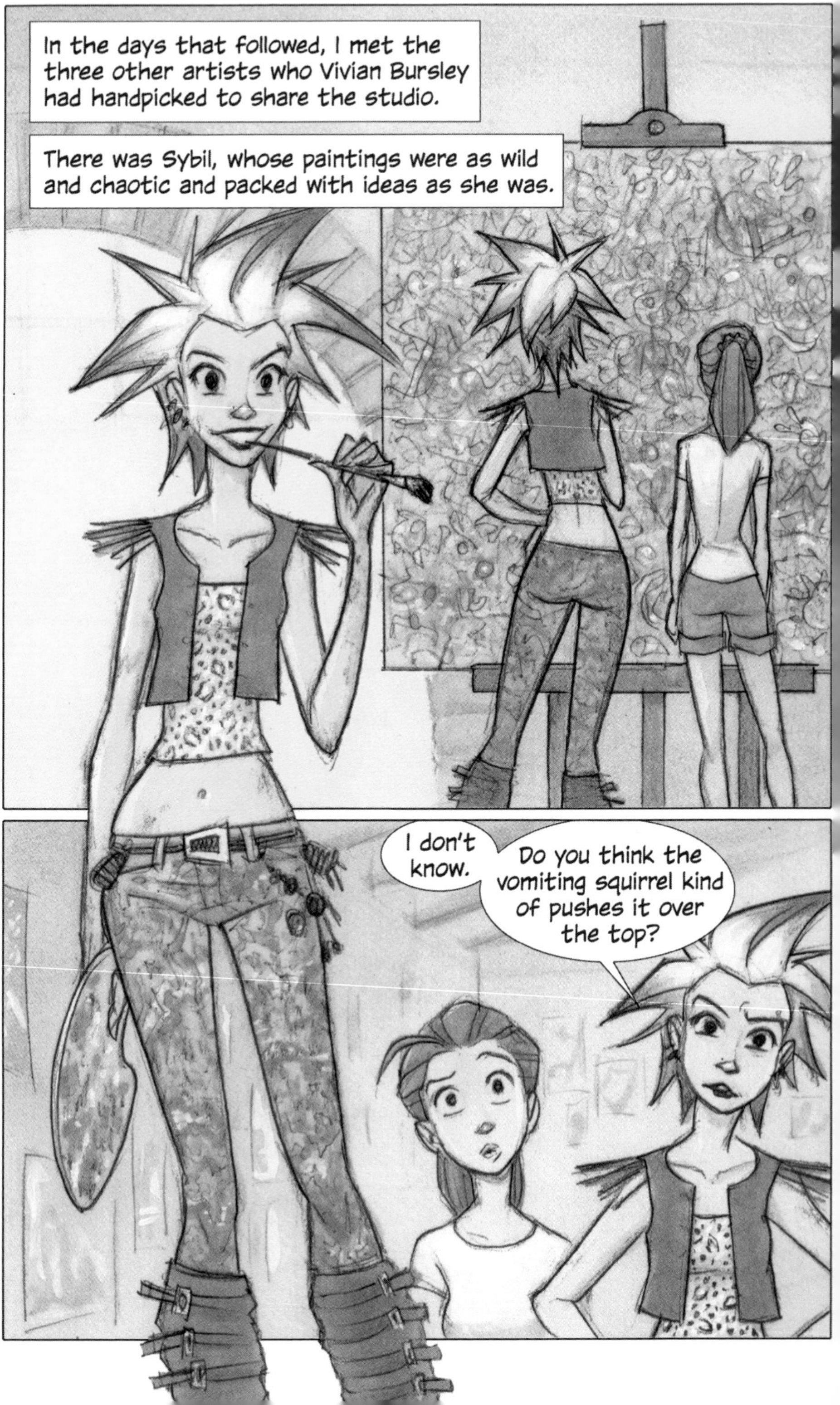
In the days that followed, I met the three other artists who Vivian Bursley had handpicked to share the studio.
There was Sybil, whose paintings were as wild and chaotic and packed with ideas as she was.
Do you think the vomiting squirrel kind of pushes it over the top?
I don't know.

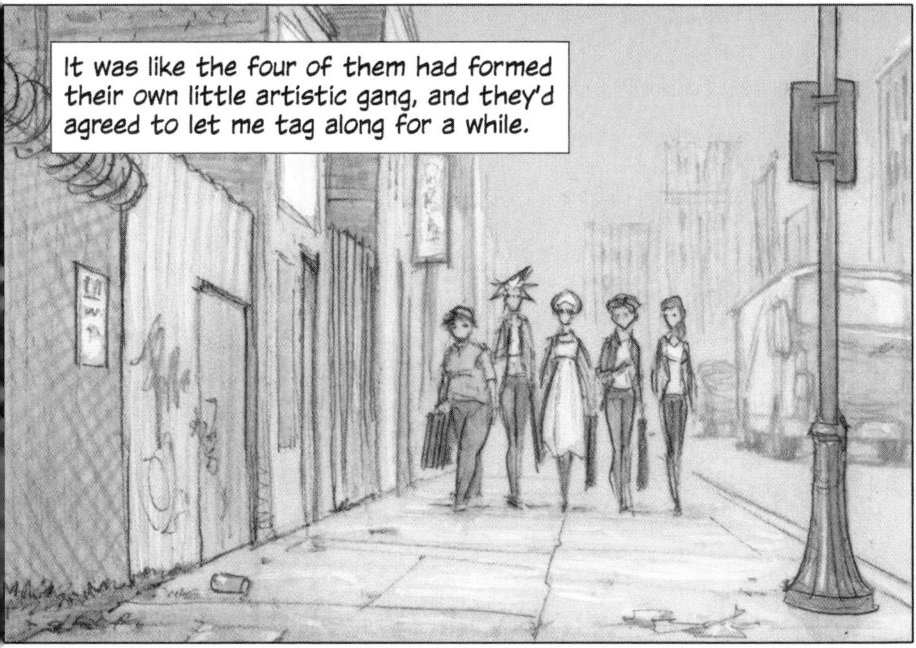
It was like the four of them had formed their own little artistic gang, and they'd agreed to let me tag along for a while.

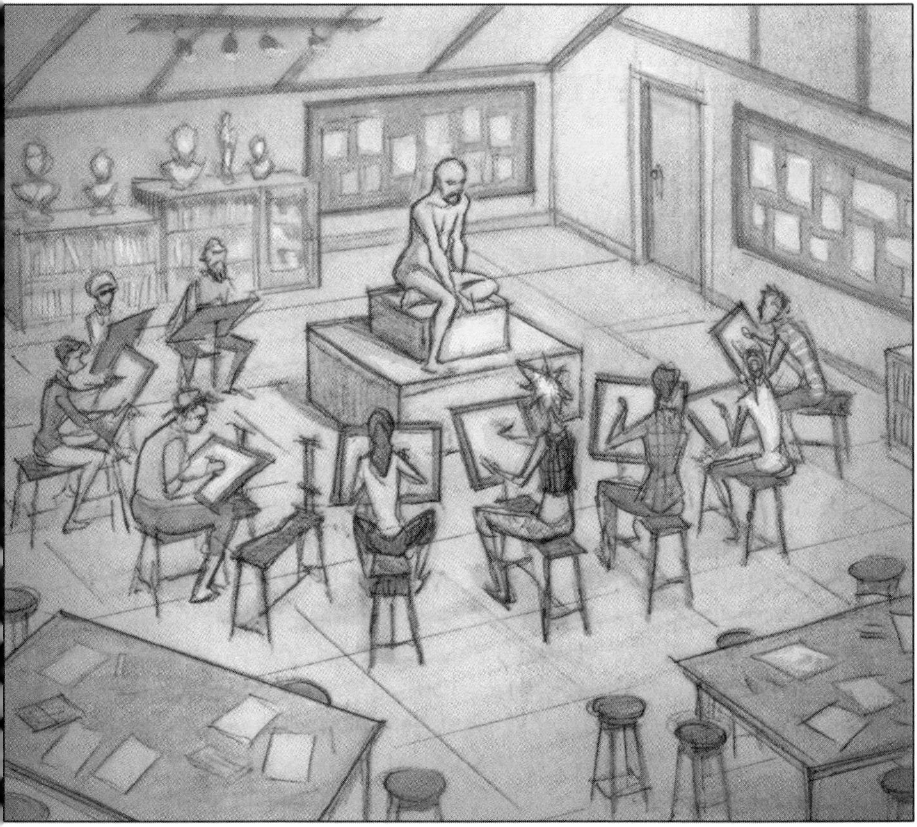

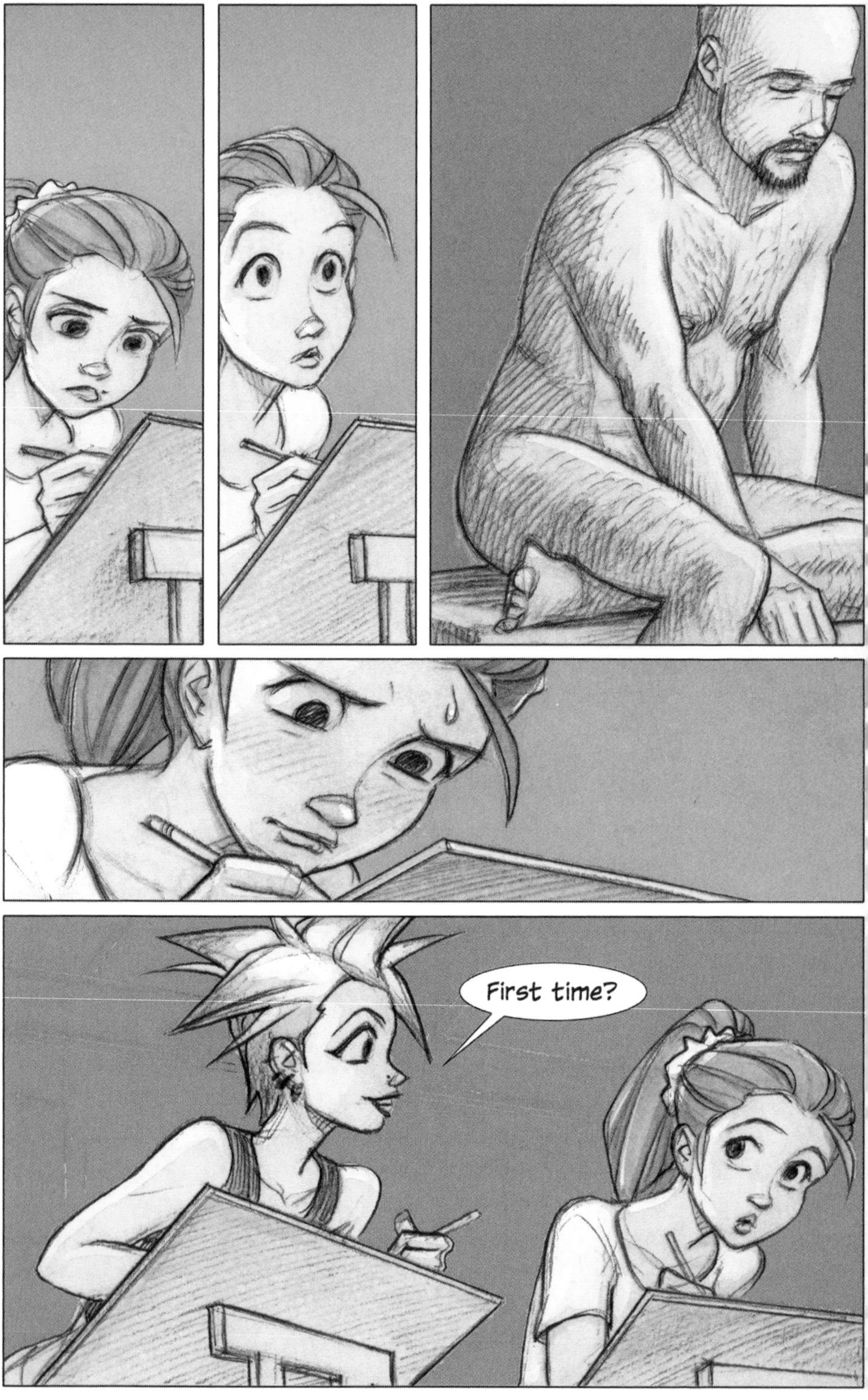
First time?

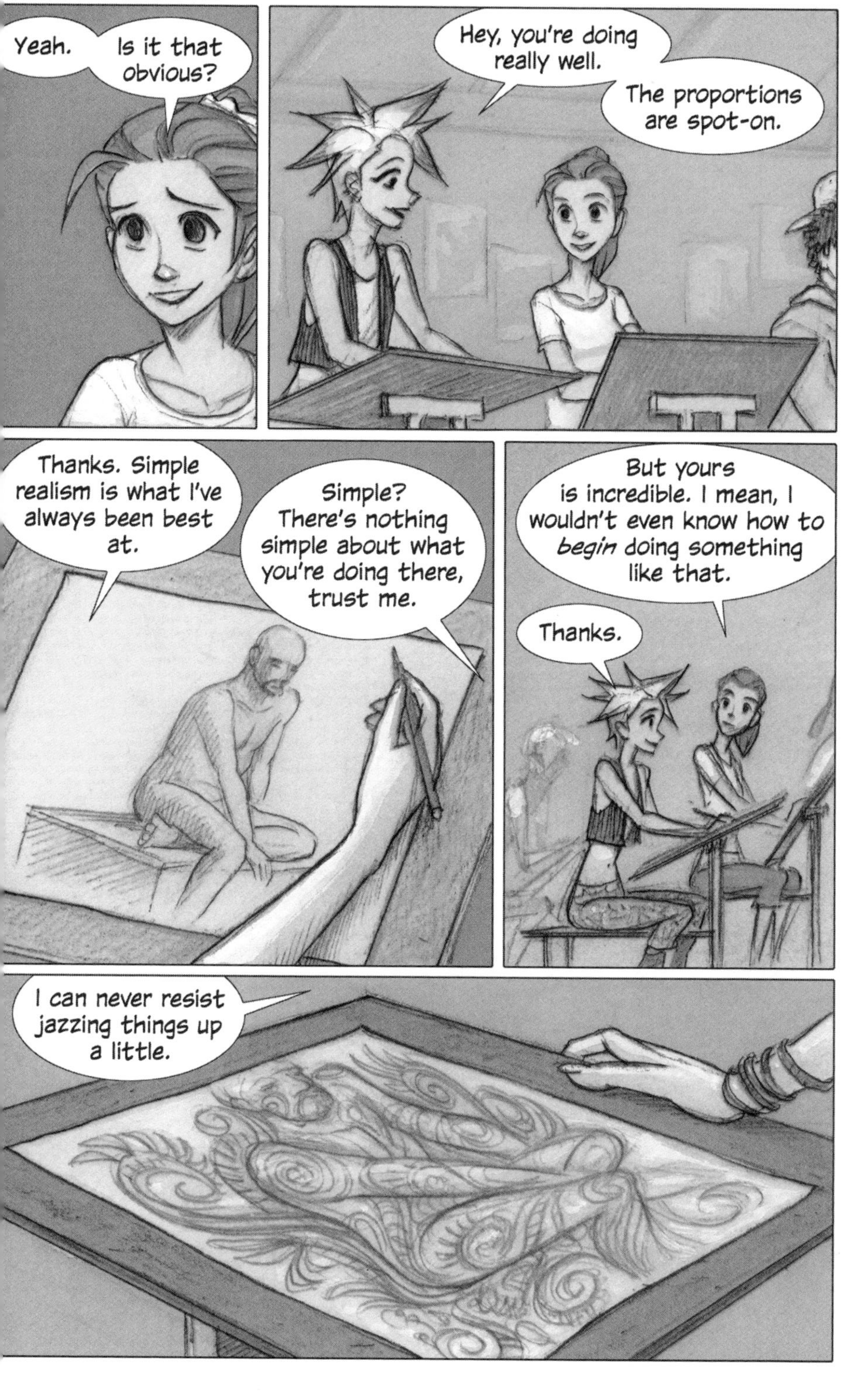
Yeah.
Is it that obvious?
Hey, you're doing really well.
The proportions are spot-on.
Thanks. Simple realism is what I've always been best at.
Simple? There's nothing simple about what you're doing there, trust me.
But yours is incredible. I mean, I wouldn't even know how to *begin* doing something like that.
Thanks.
I can never resist jazzing things up a little.

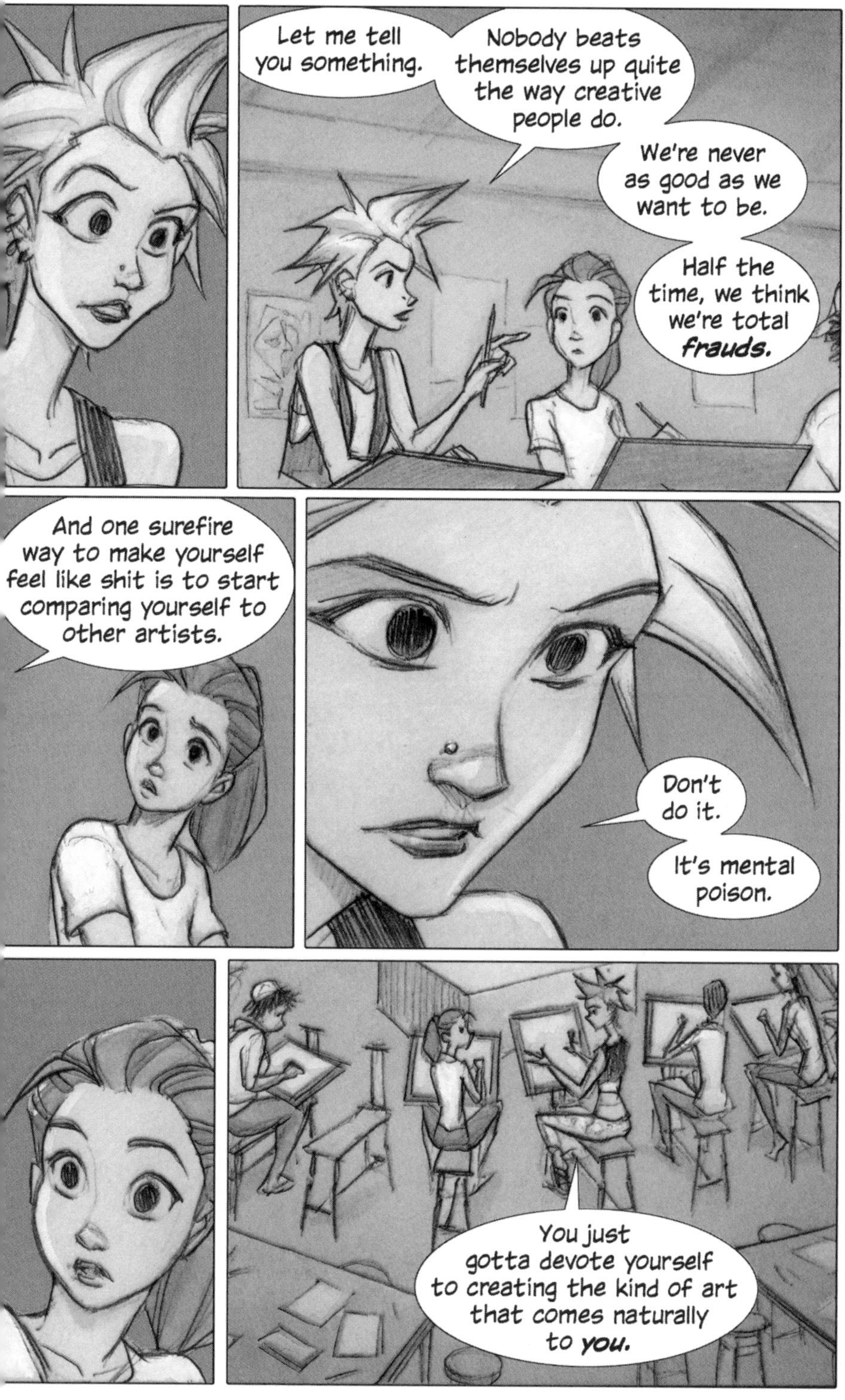
Let me tell you something.
Nobody beats themselves up quite the way creative people do.
We're never as good as we want to be.
Half the time, we think we're total *frauds.*
And one surefire way to make yourself feel like shit is to start comparing yourself to other artists.
Don't do it.
It's mental poison.
You just gotta devote yourself to creating the kind of art that comes naturally to *you.*

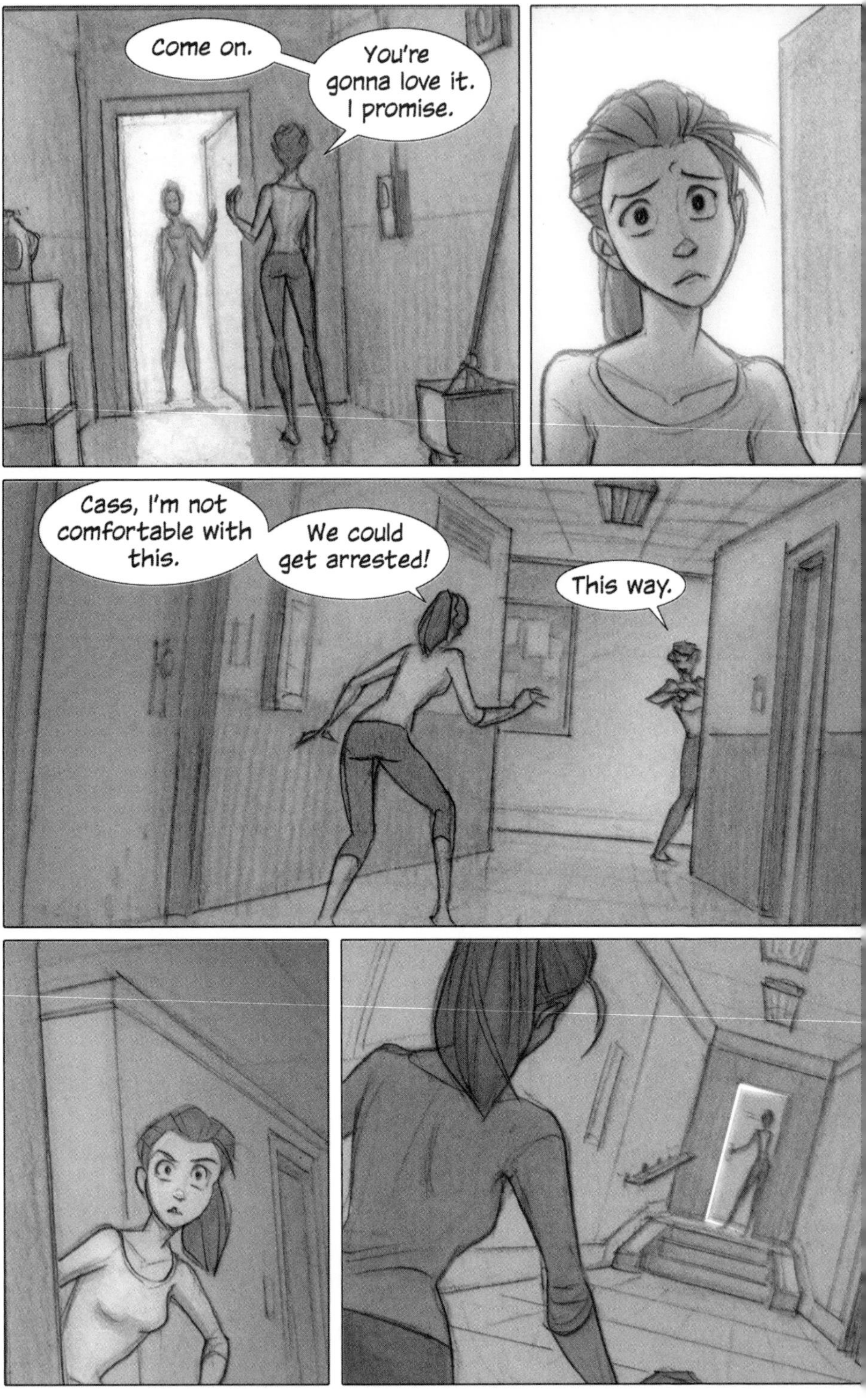
Come on.
You're gonna love it. I promise.
Cass, I'm not comfortable with this.
We could get arrested!
This way.

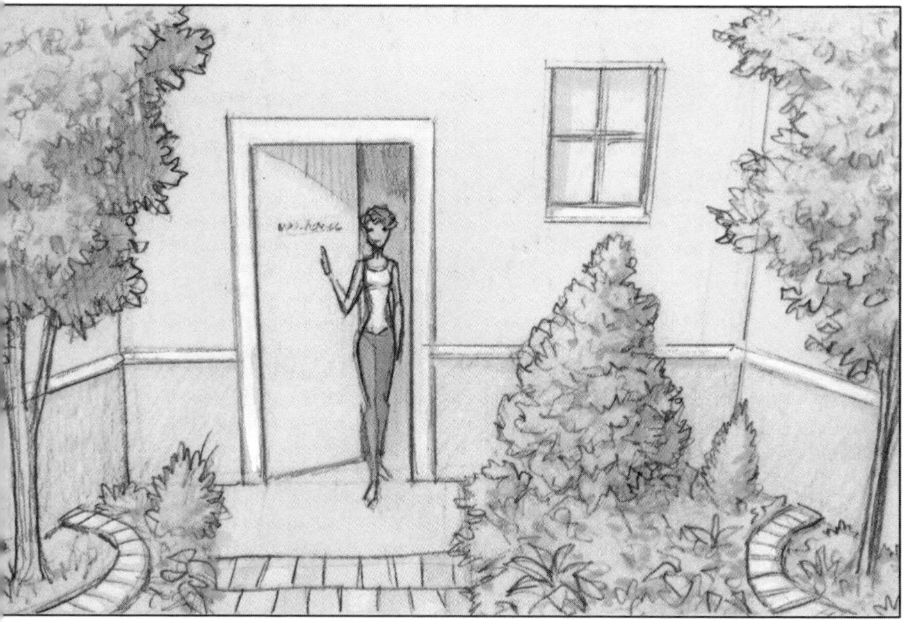

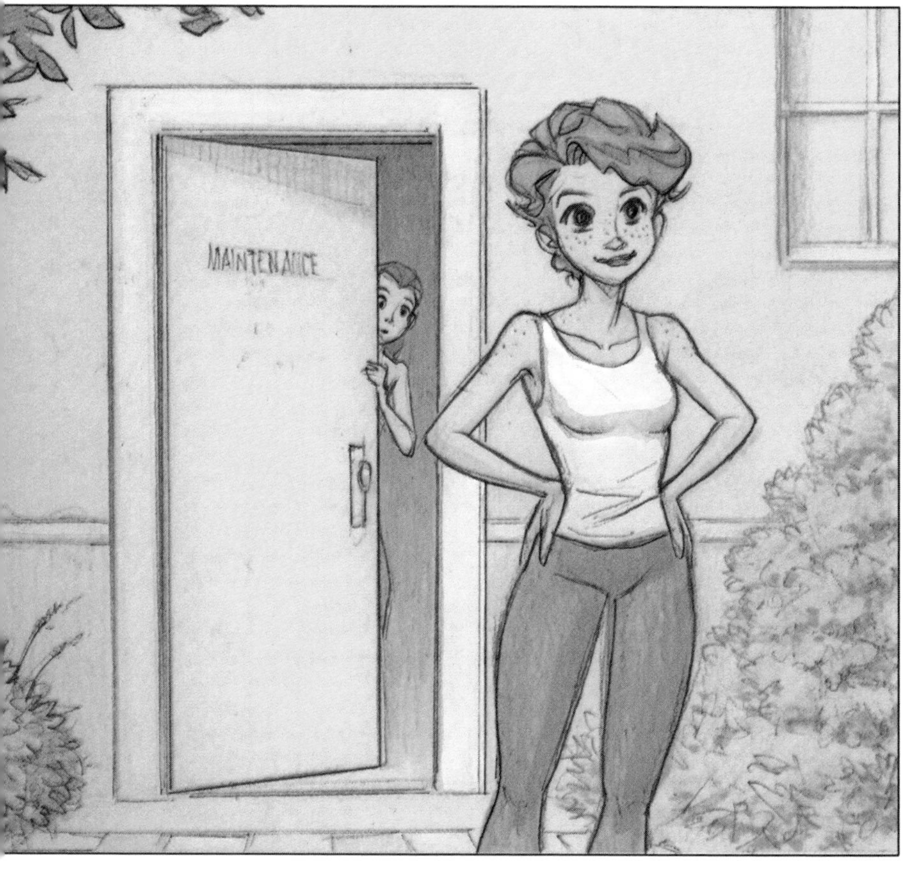
MAINTENANCE

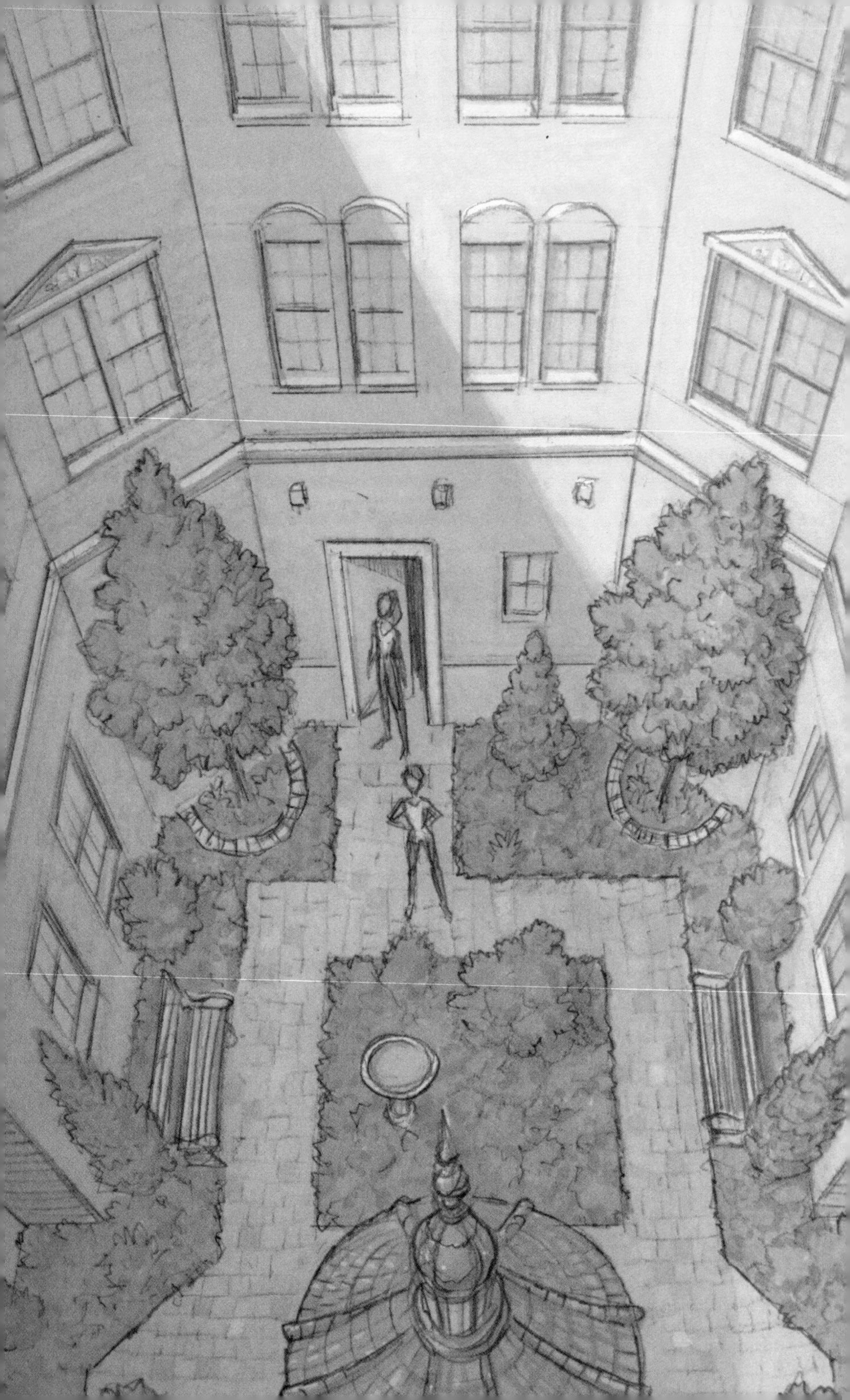

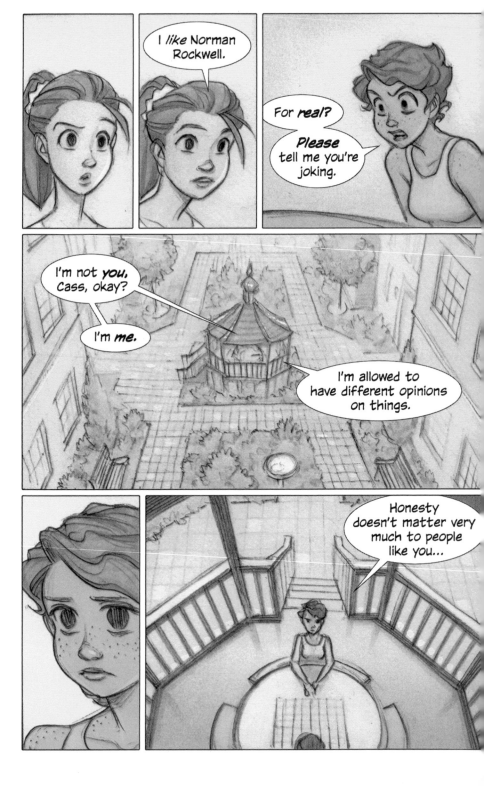

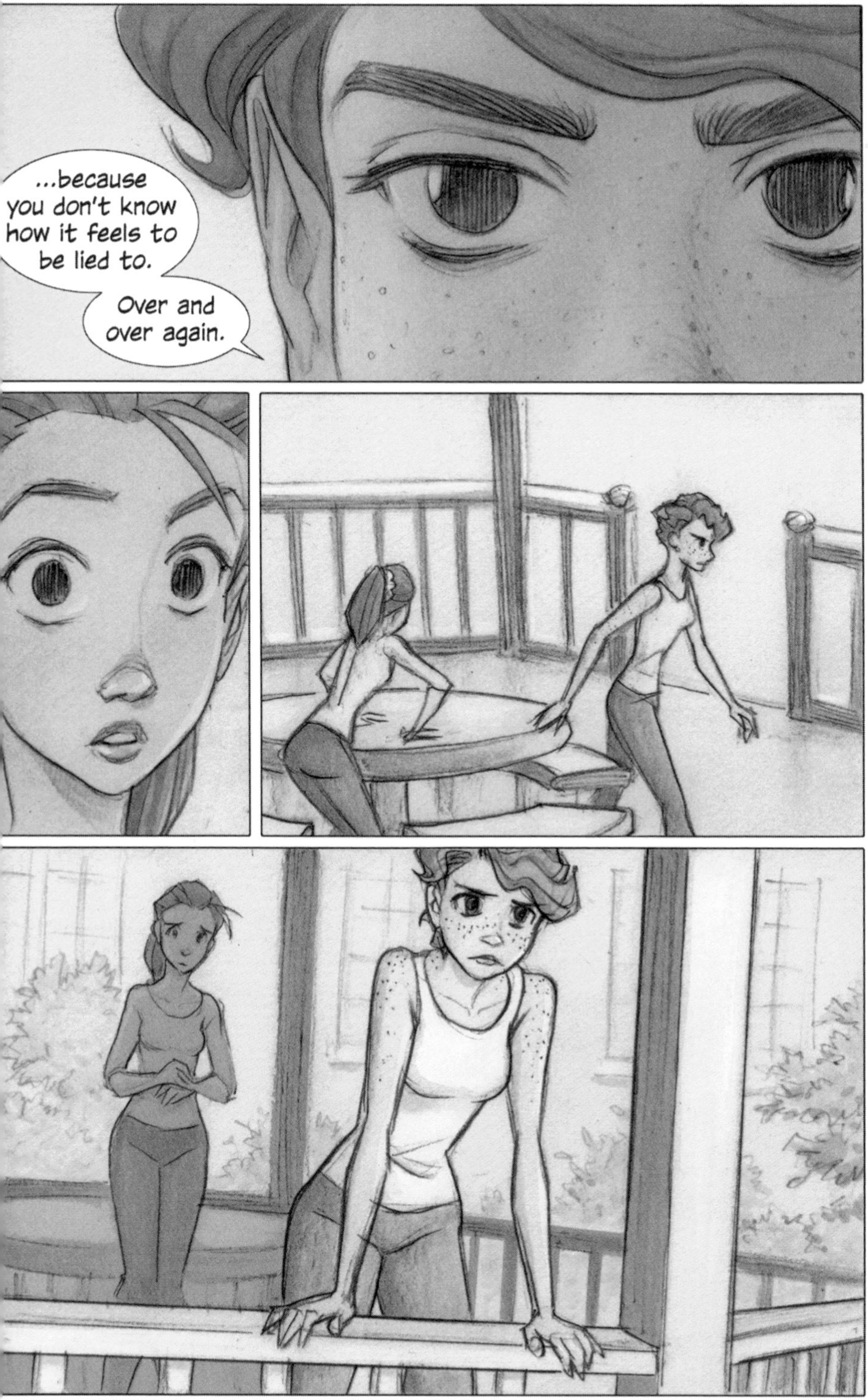
...because you don't know how it feels to be lied to.
Over and over again.

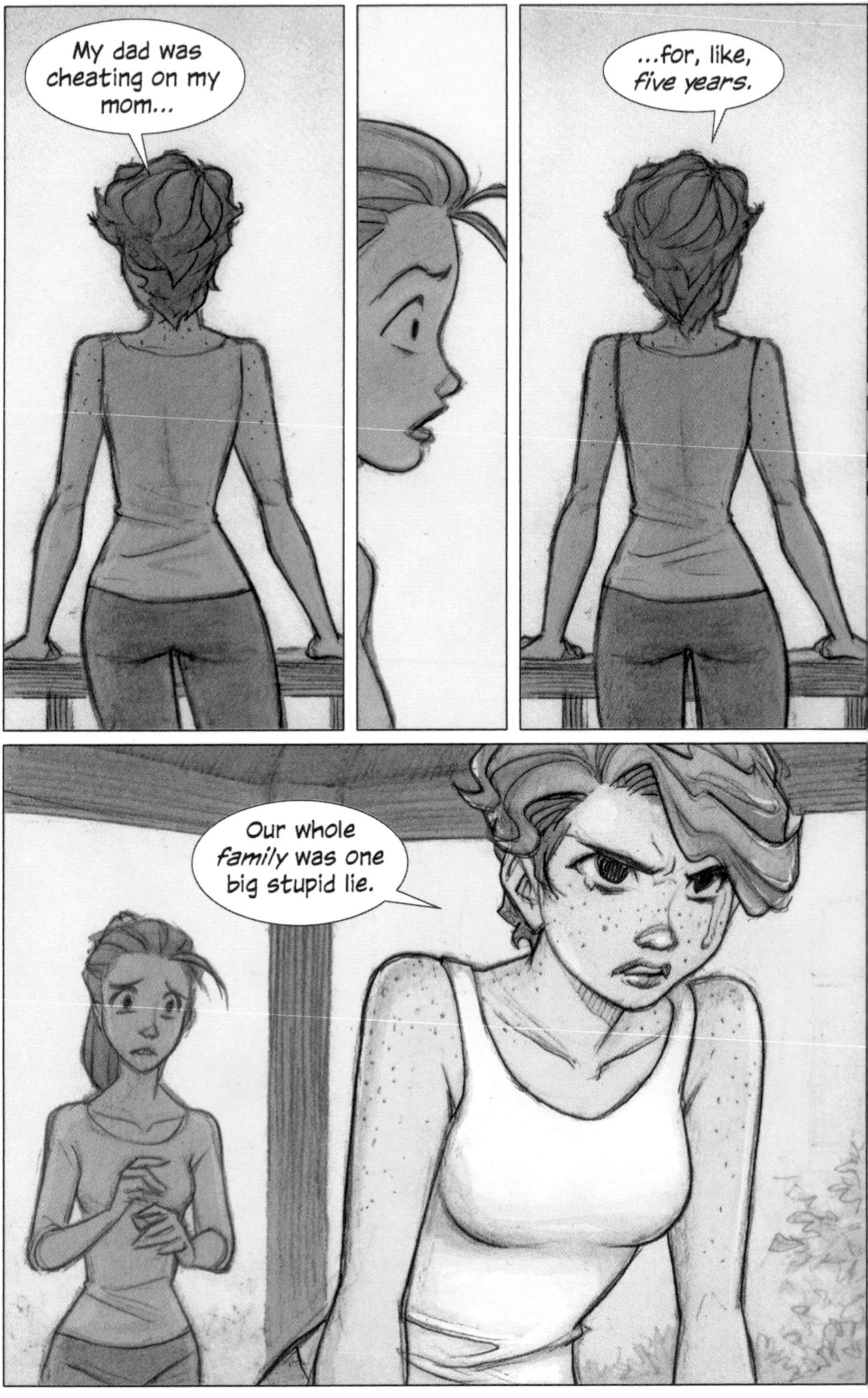
My dad was cheating on my mom...
...for, like, *five years.*
Our whole *family* was one big stupid lie.

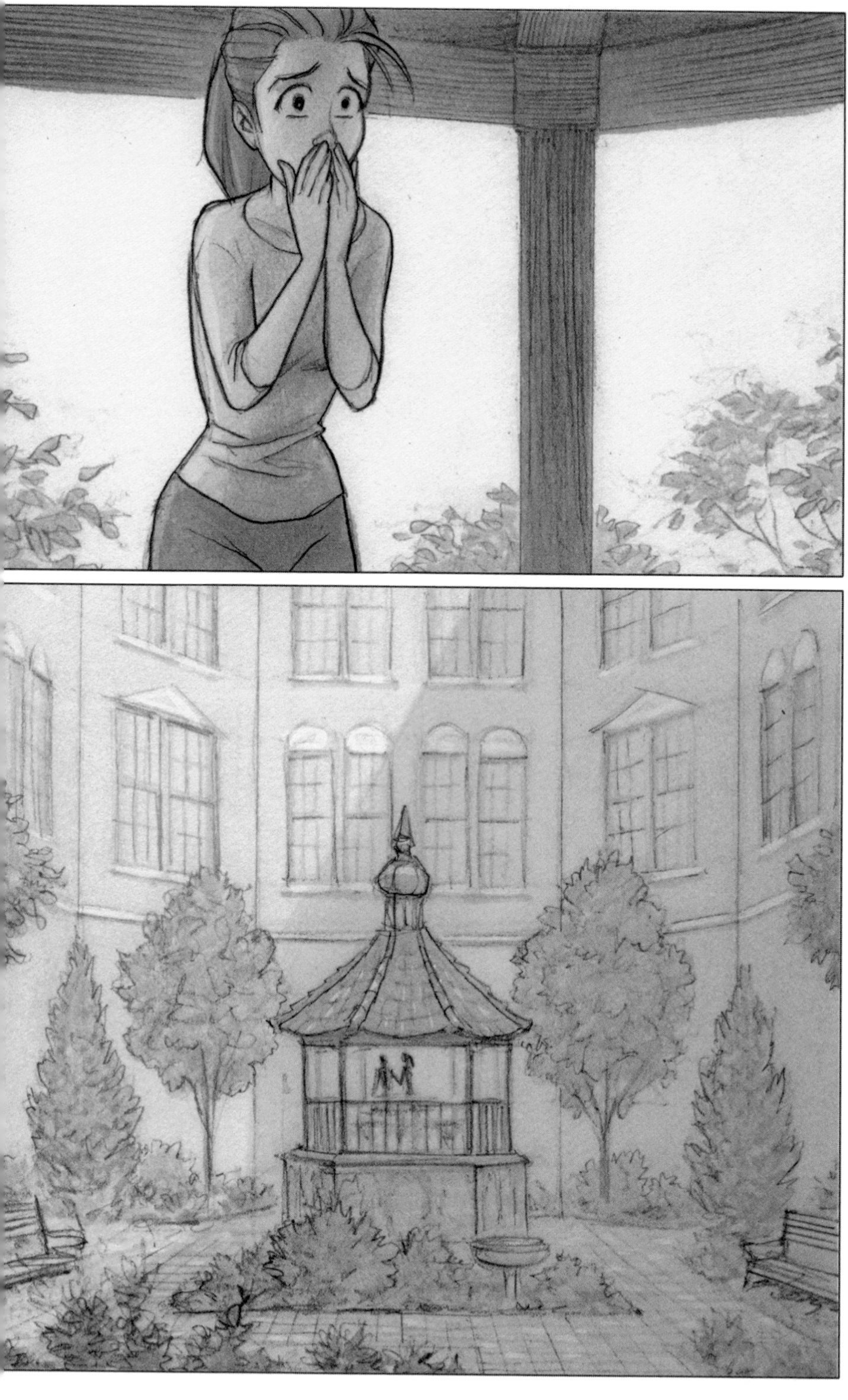

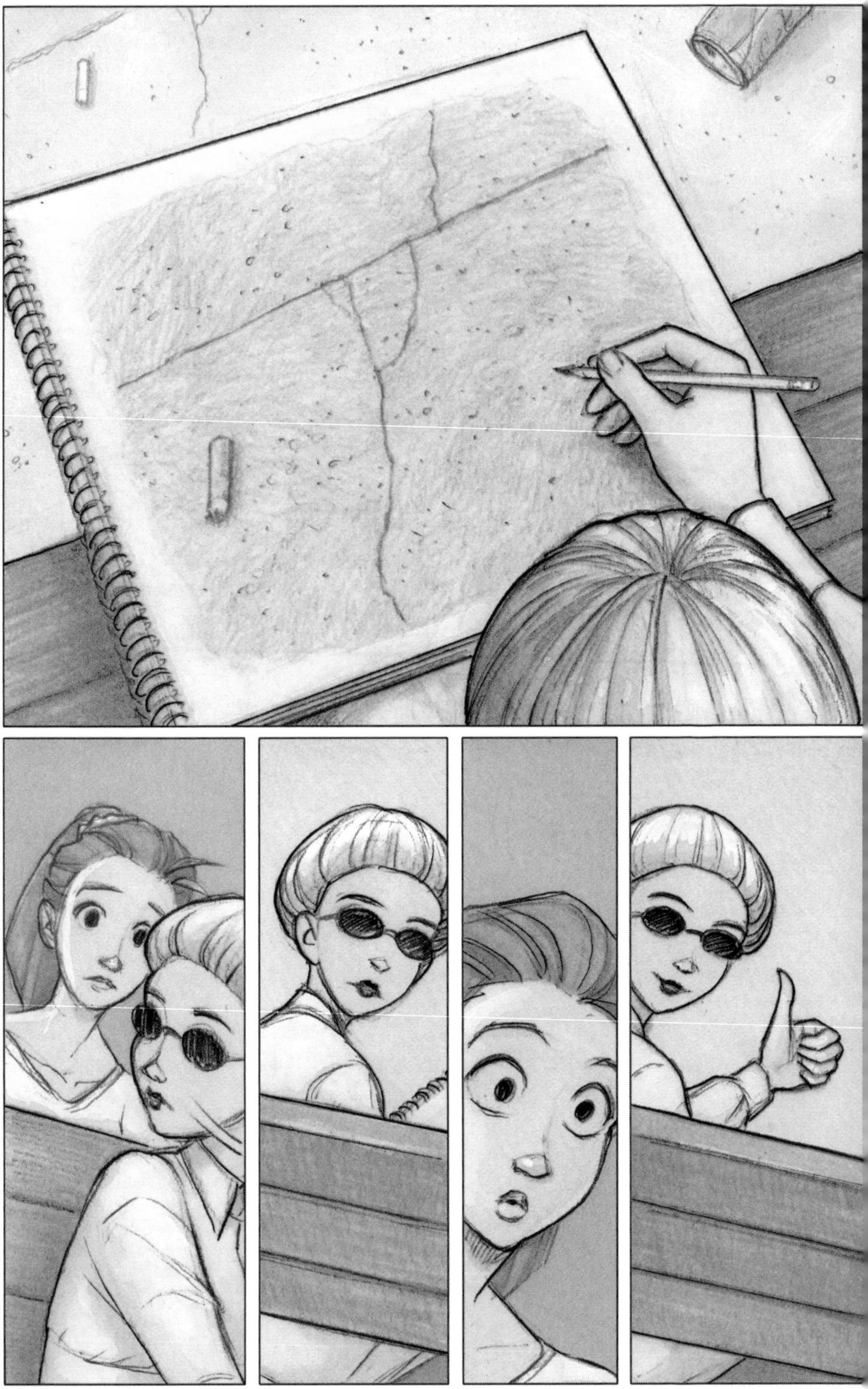

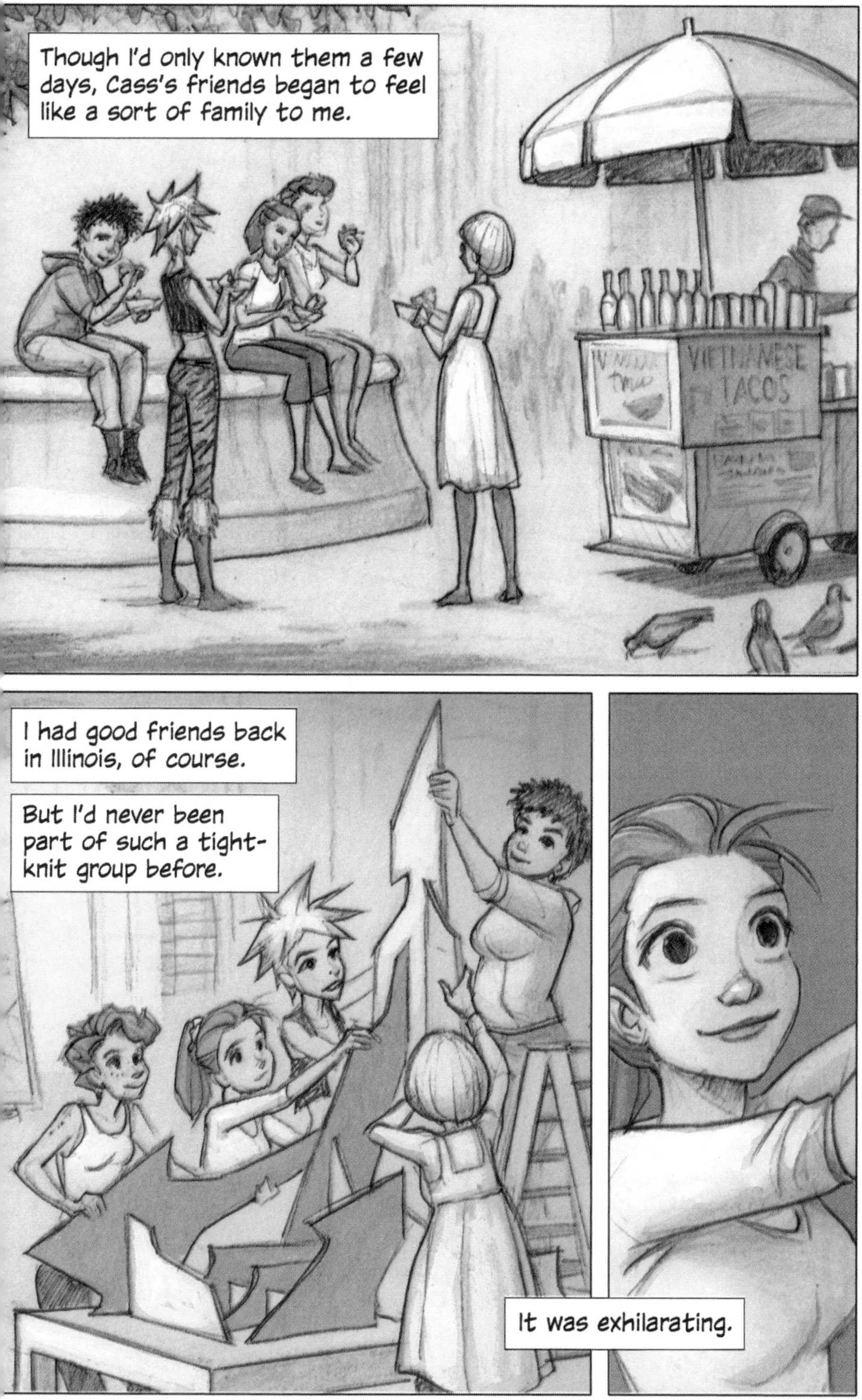
Though I'd only known them a few days, Cass's friends began to feel like a sort of family to me.
VIETNAMESE TACOS
I had good friends back in Illinois, of course.
But I'd never been part of such a tight-knit group before.
It was exhilarating.

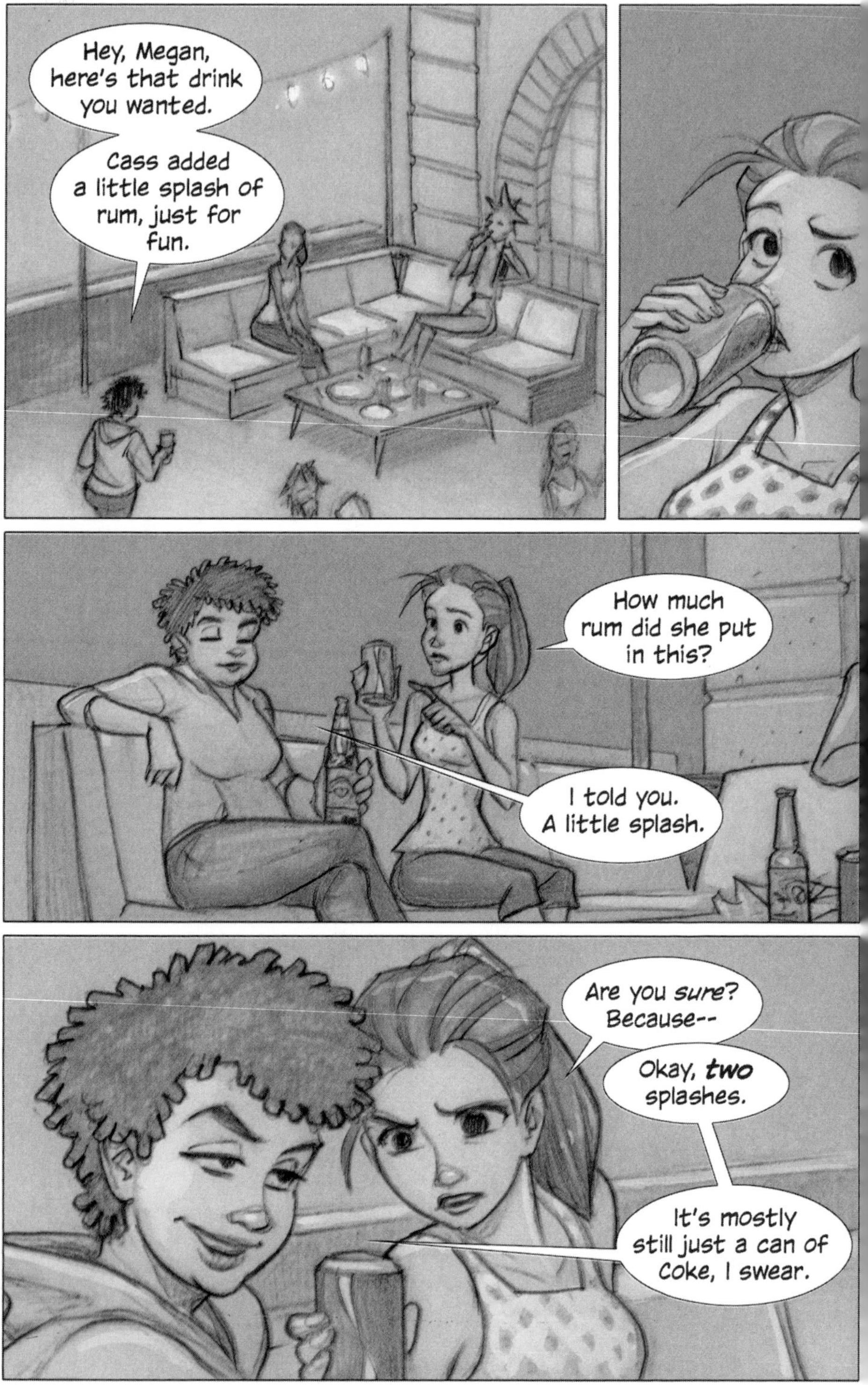
Hey, Megan, here's that drink you wanted.
Cass added a little splash of rum, just for fun.
How much rum did she put in this?
I told you. A little splash.
Are you *sure*? Because--
Okay, ***two*** splashes.
It's mostly still just a can of Coke, I swear.

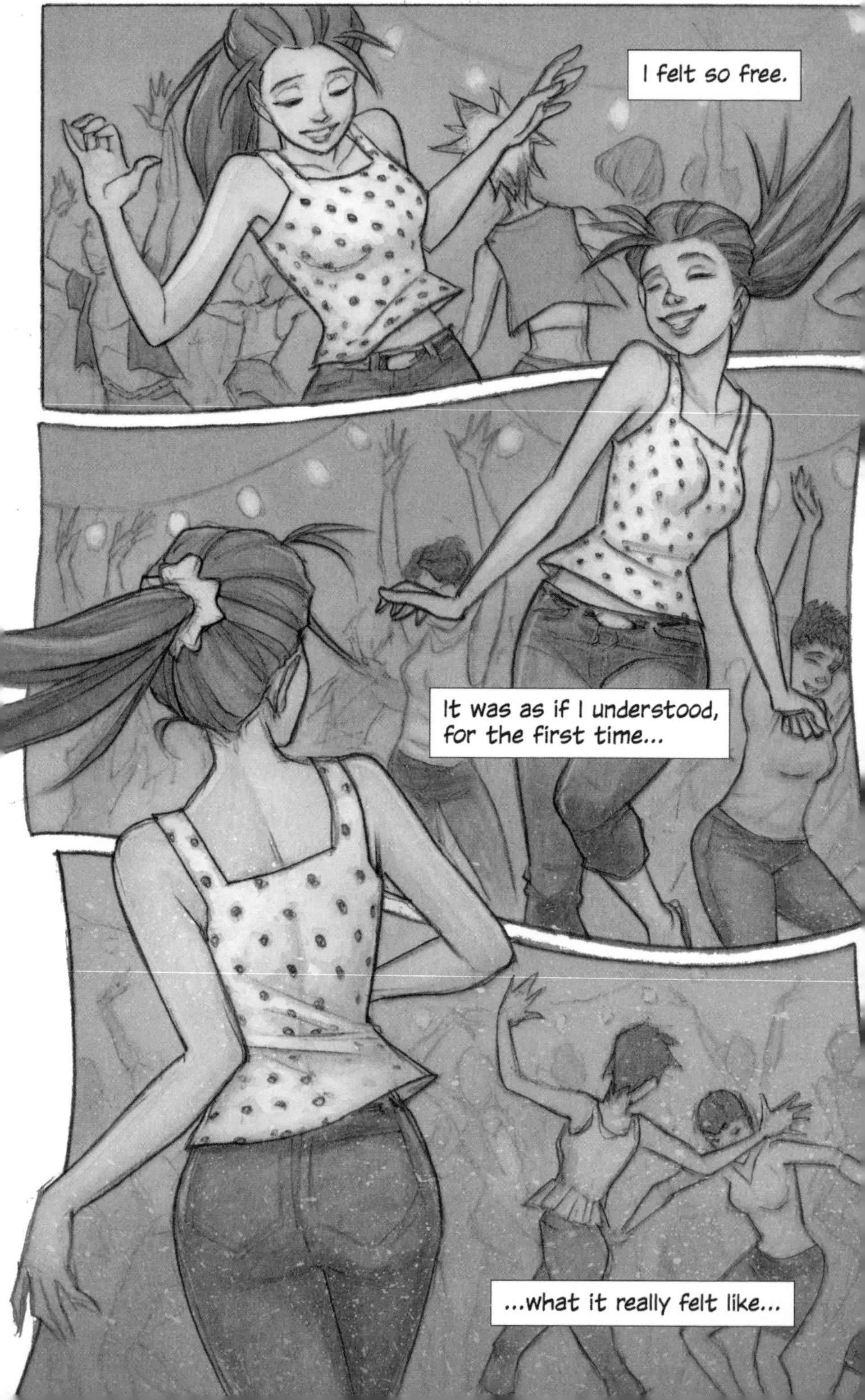
I felt so free.
It was as if I understood, for the first time...
...what it really felt like...

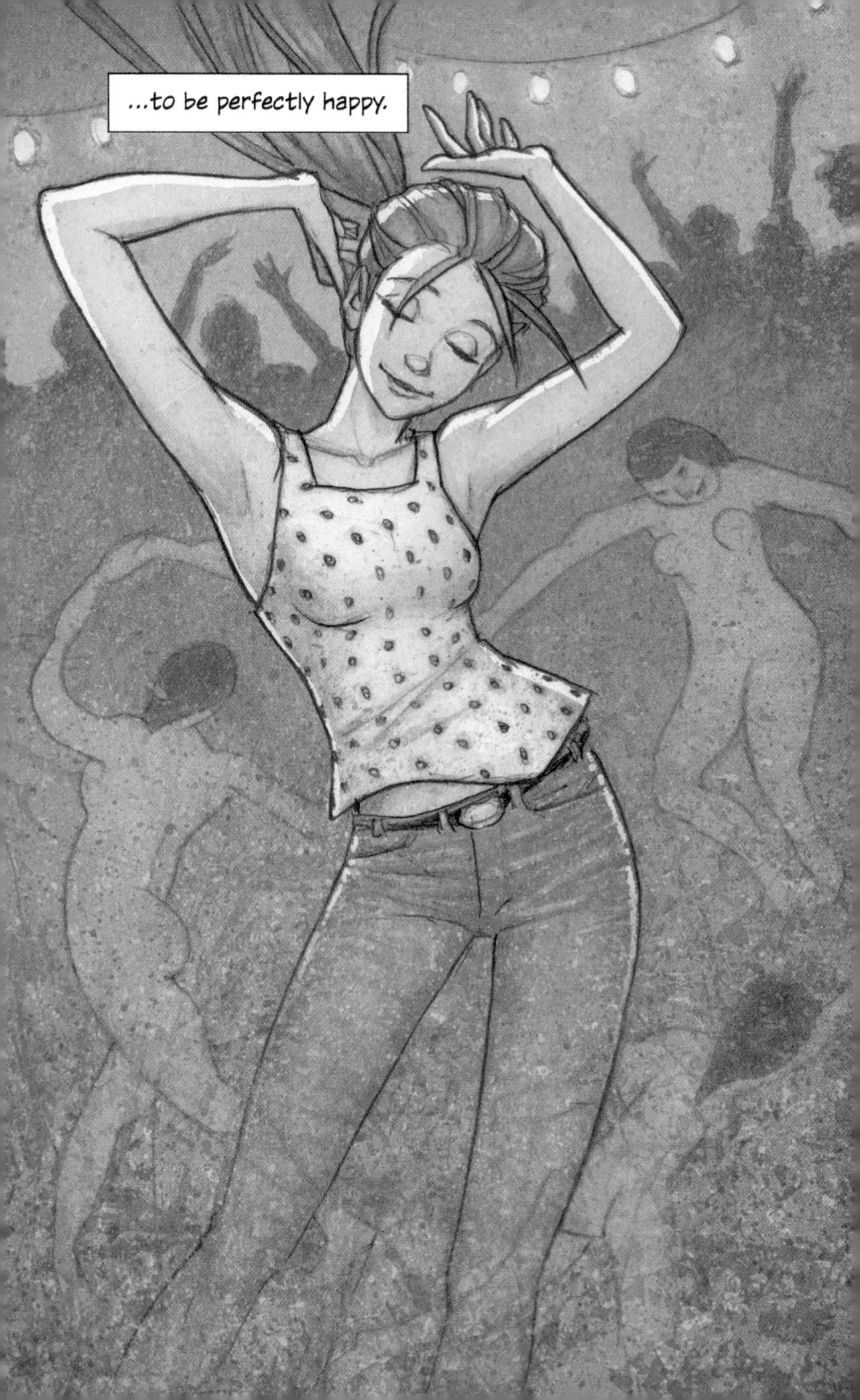
...to be perfectly happy.

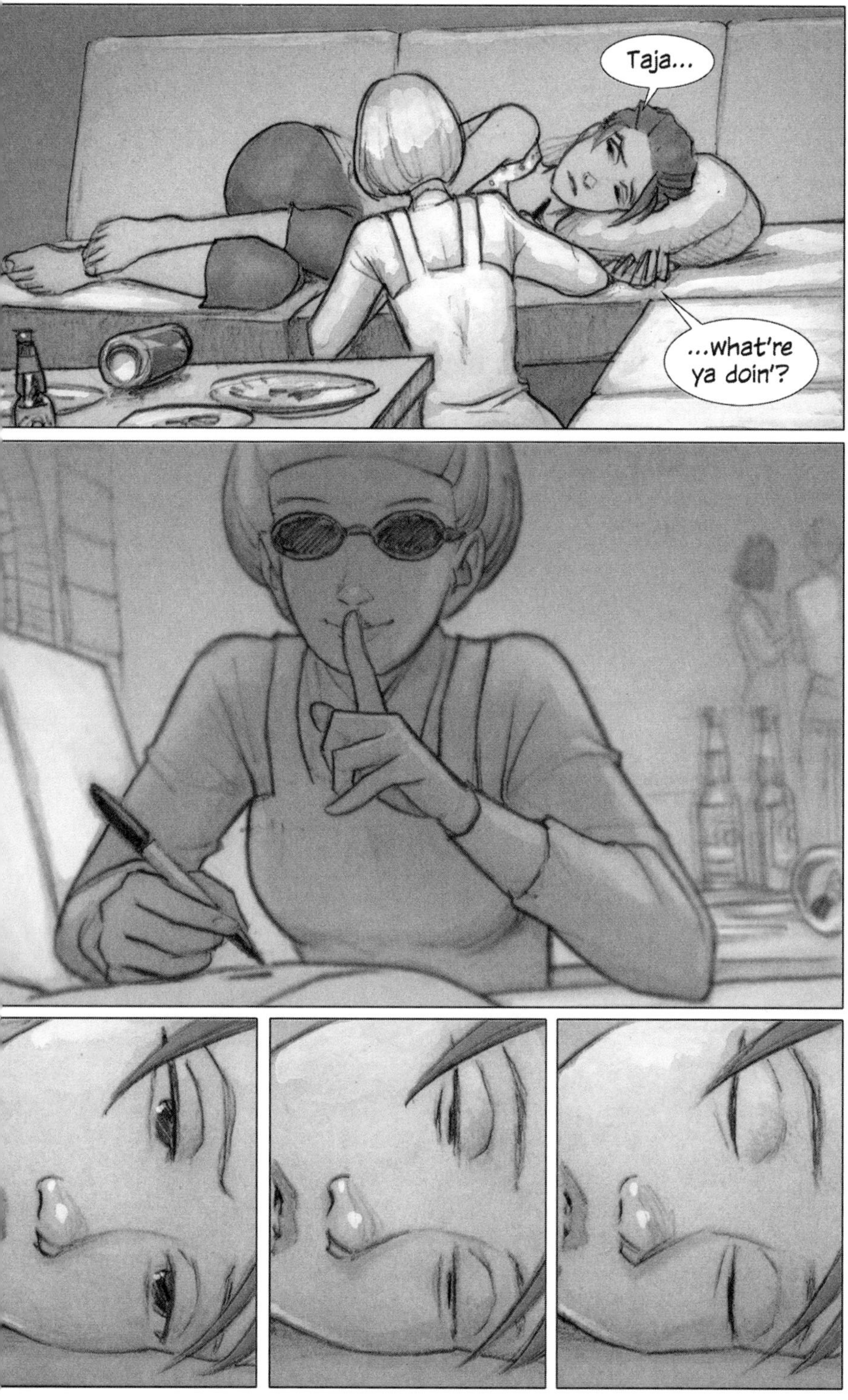
Taja...
...what're ya doin'?

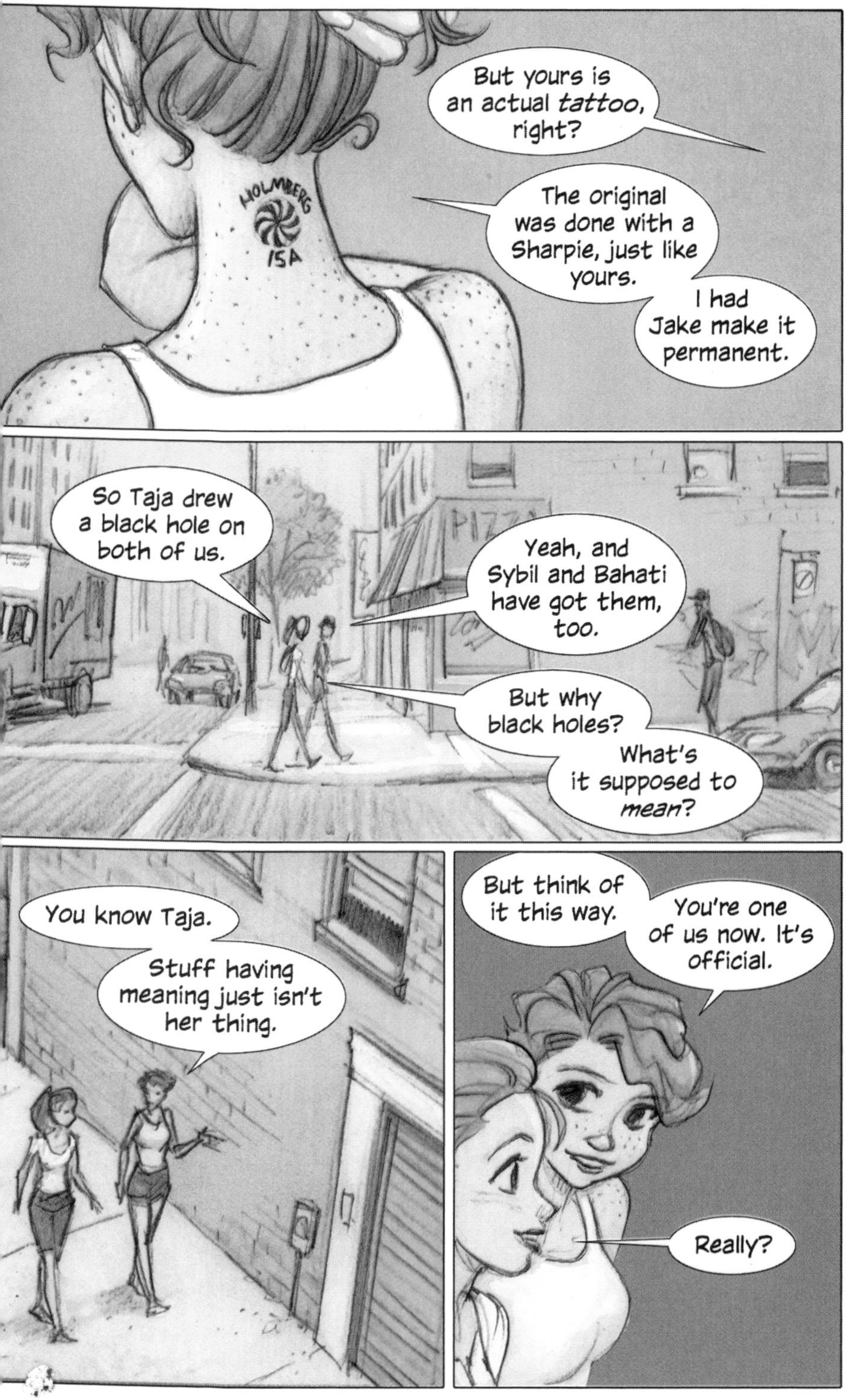
But yours is an actual *tattoo*, right?
HOLMBERG
ISA
The original was done with a Sharpie, just like yours.
I had Jake make it permanent.
So Taja drew a black hole on both of us.
Yeah, and Sybil and Bahati have got them, too.
But why black holes?
What's it supposed to *mean*?
You know Taja.
Stuff having meaning just isn't her thing.
But think of it this way.
You're one of us now. It's official.
Really?

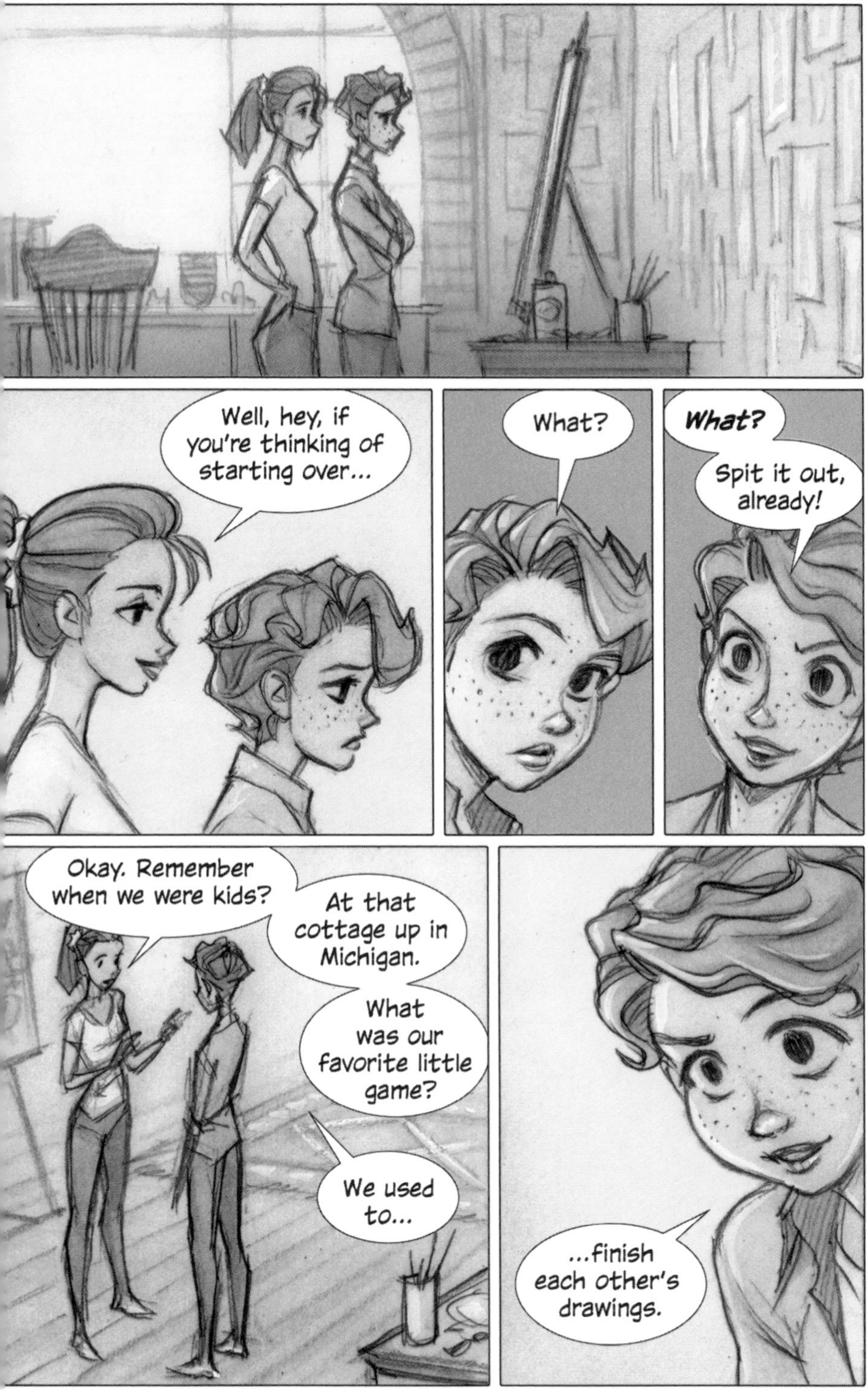
Well, hey, if you're thinking of starting over...
What?
What?
Spit it out, already!
Okay. Remember when we were kids?
At that cottage up in Michigan.
What was our favorite little game?
We used to...
...finish each other's drawings.

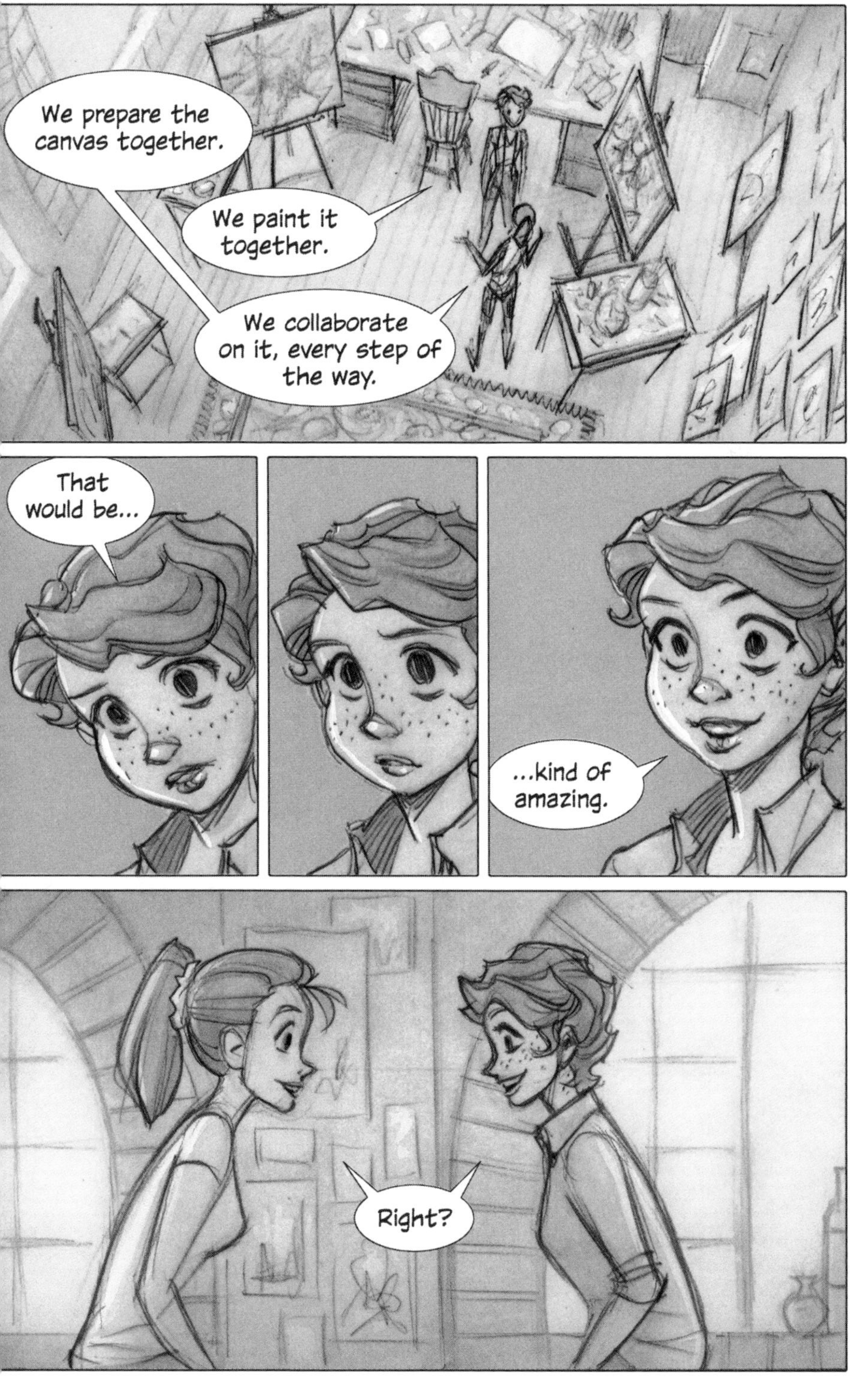
We prepare the canvas together.
We paint it together.
We collaborate on it, every step of the way.
That would be...
...kind of amazing.
Right?

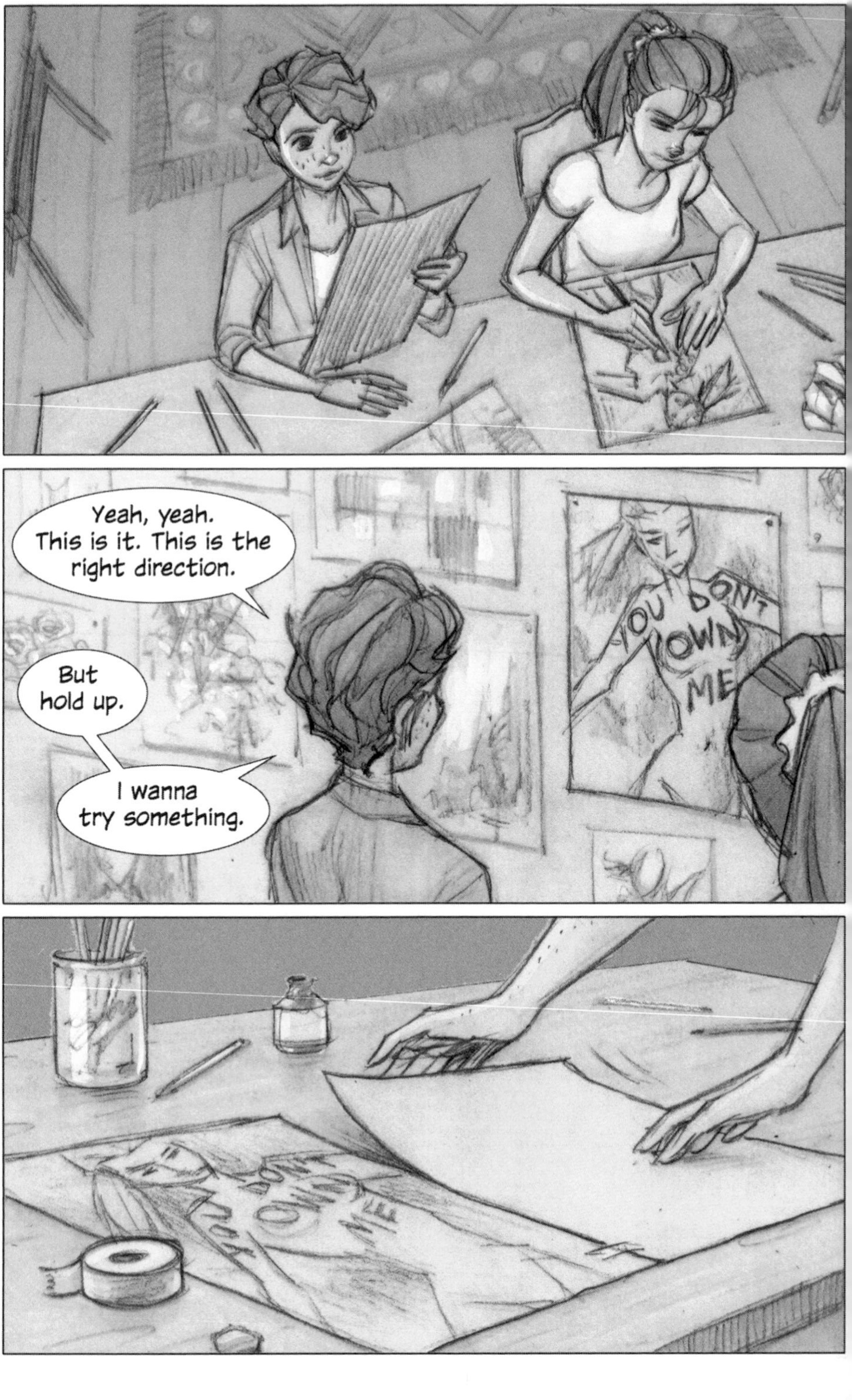
Yeah, yeah. This is it. This is the right direction.
YOU DON'T OWN ME
But hold up.
I wanna try something.

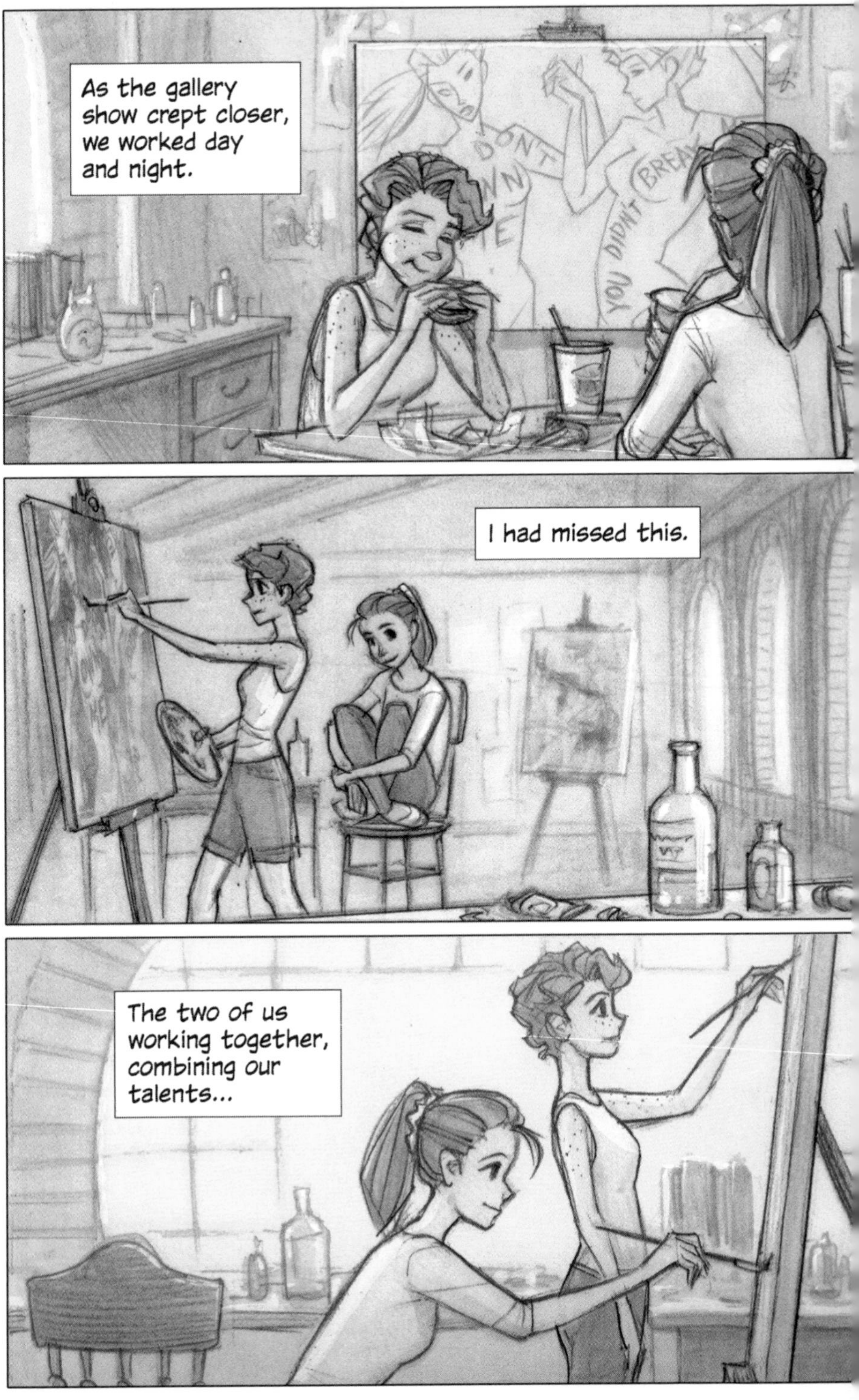
As the gallery show crept closer, we worked day and night.
DON'T
YOU DIDN'T
I had missed this.
The two of us working together, combining our talents...

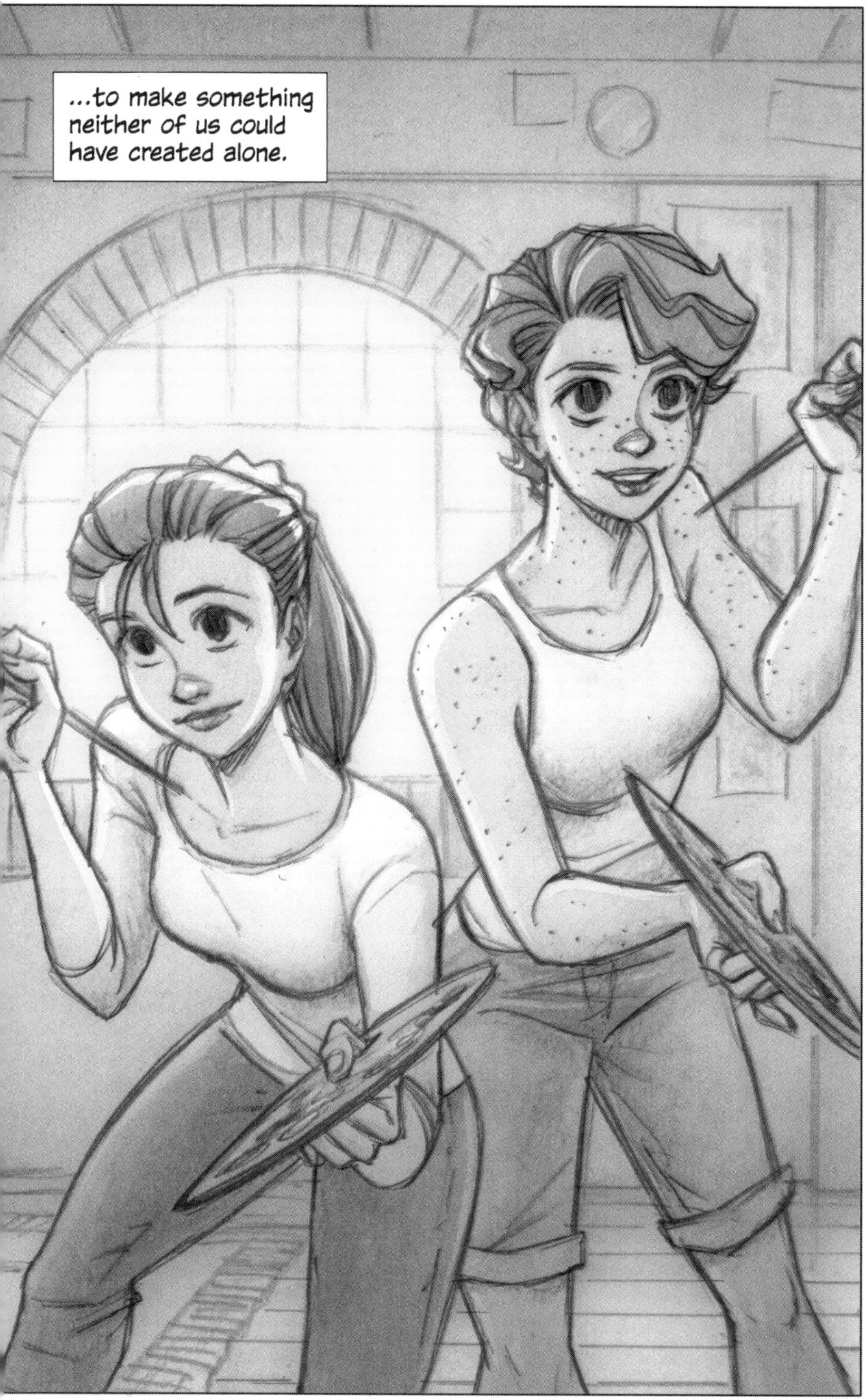
...to make something neither of us could have created alone.

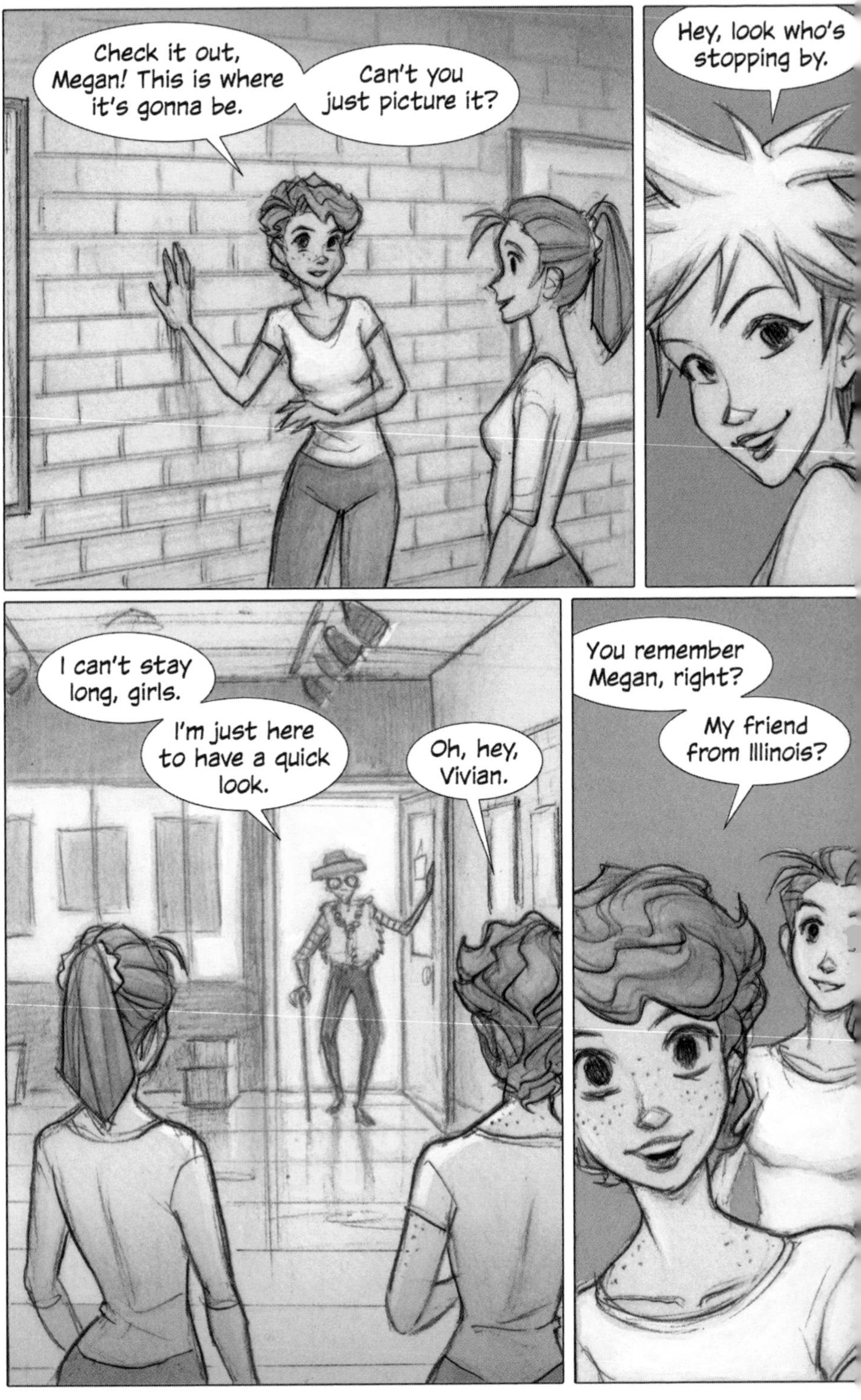
Check it out, Megan! This is where it's gonna be.
Can't you just picture it?
Hey, look who's stopping by.
I can't stay long, girls.
I'm just here to have a quick look.
Oh, hey, Vivian.
You remember Megan, right?
My friend from Illinois?

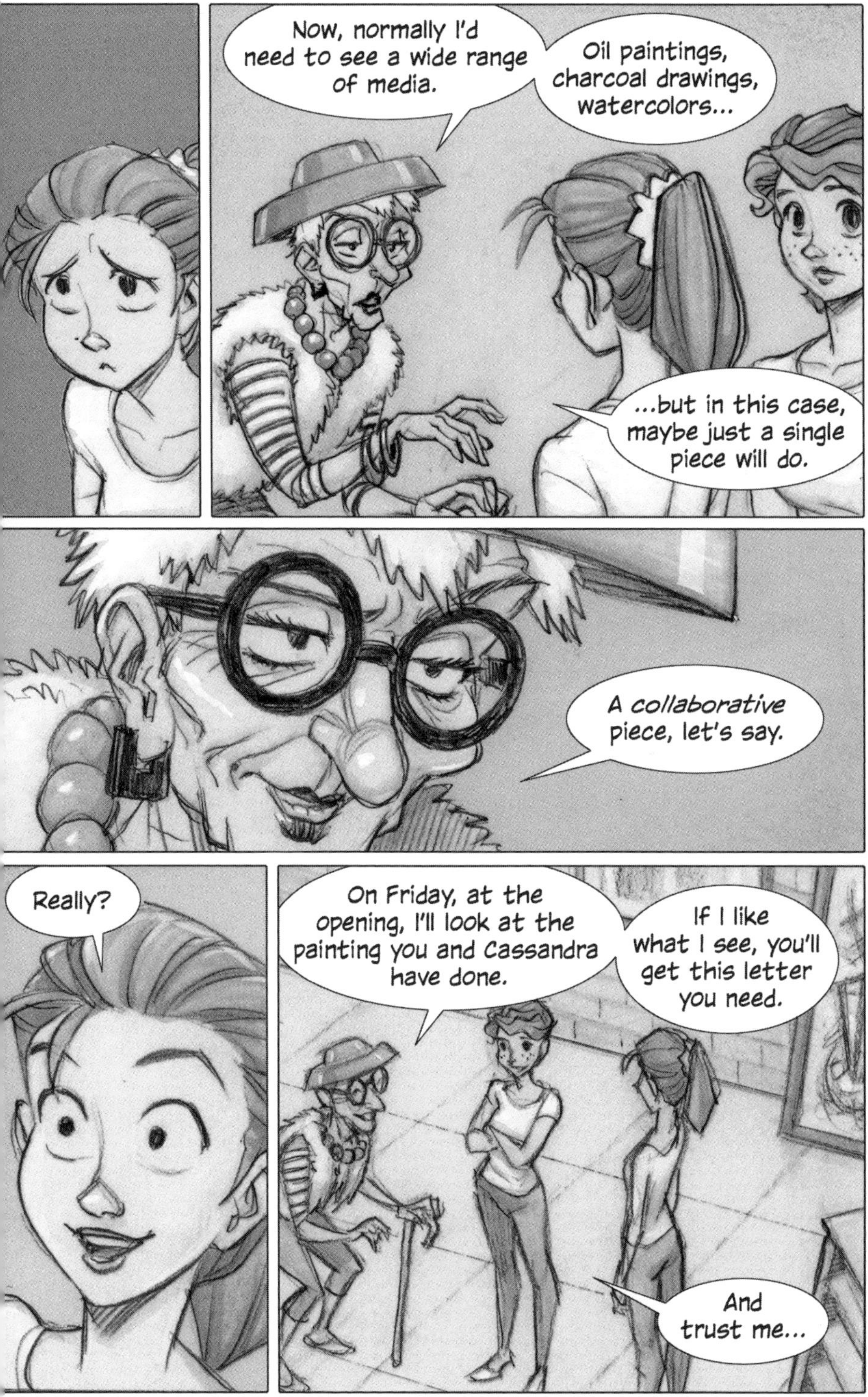

Now, normally I'd need to see a wide range of media.
Oil paintings, charcoal drawings, watercolors...
...but in this case, maybe just a single piece will do.
A *collaborative* piece, let's say.
Really?
On Friday, at the opening, I'll look at the painting you and Cassandra have done.
If I like what I see, you'll get this letter you need.
And trust me...

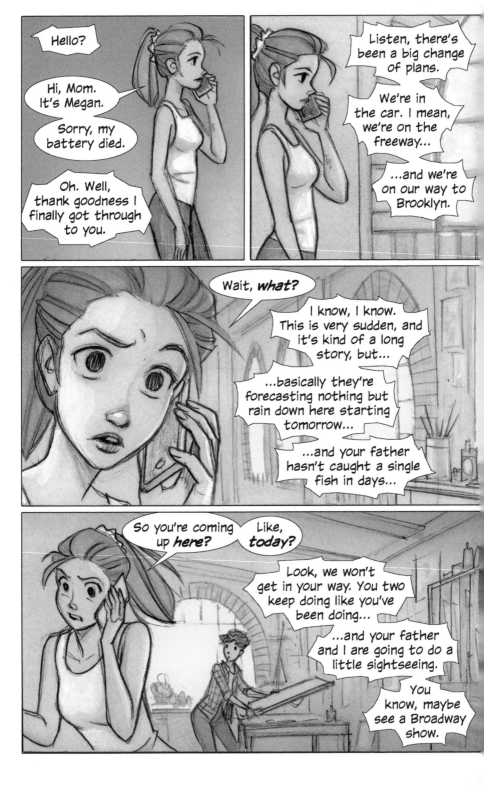

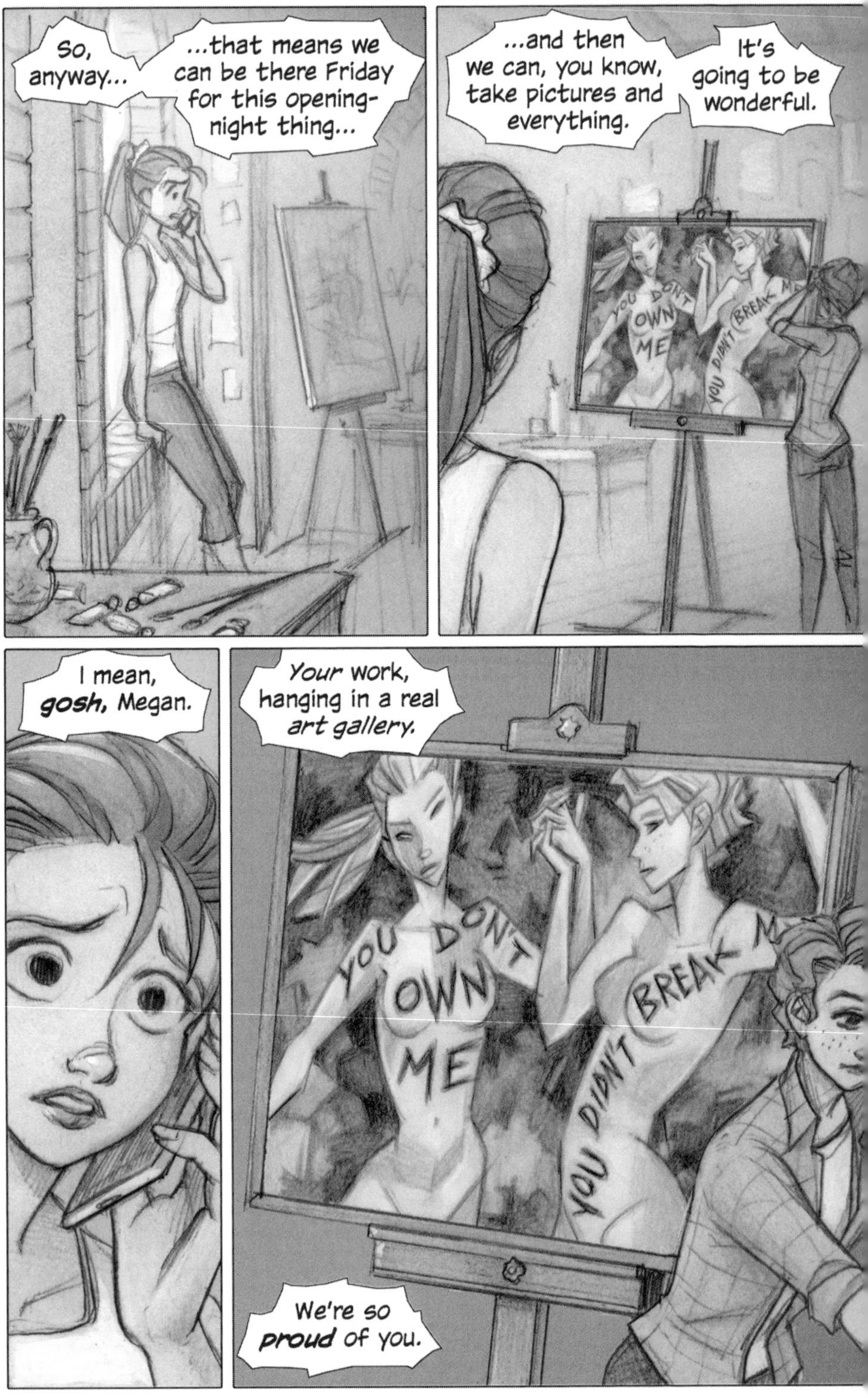
So, anyway...
...that means we can be there Friday for this opening-night thing...
...and then we can, you know, take pictures and everything.
It's going to be wonderful.
YOU DON'T OWN ME
YOU DIDN'T BREAK M
I mean, *gosh,* Megan.
Your work, hanging in a real *art gallery.*
YOU DON'T OWN ME
YOU DIDN'T BREAK M
We're so *proud* of you.

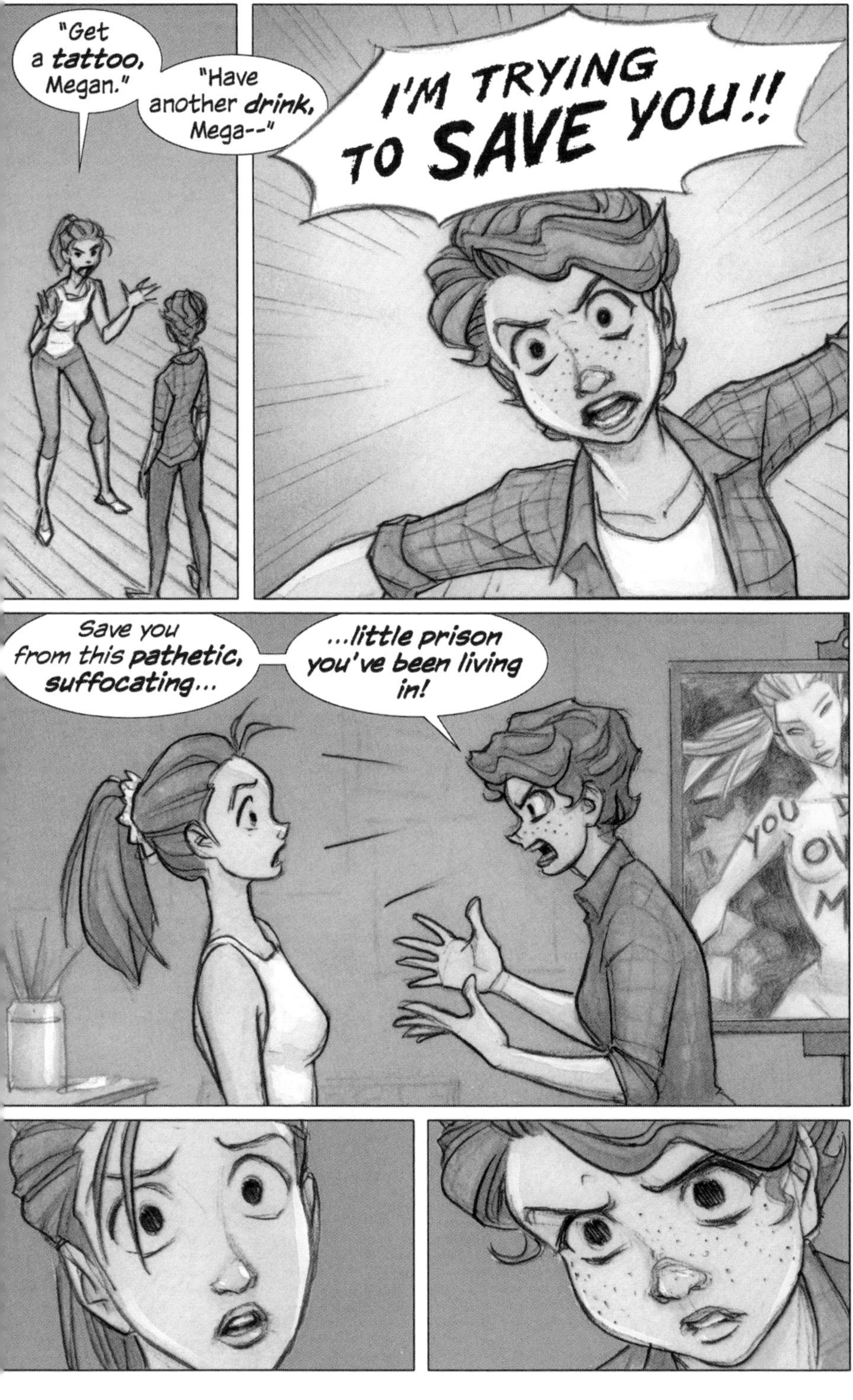
"Get a tattoo, Megan."
"Have another drink, Mega--"
I'M TRYING TO SAVE YOU!!
Save you from this pathetic, suffocating...
...little prison you've been living in!

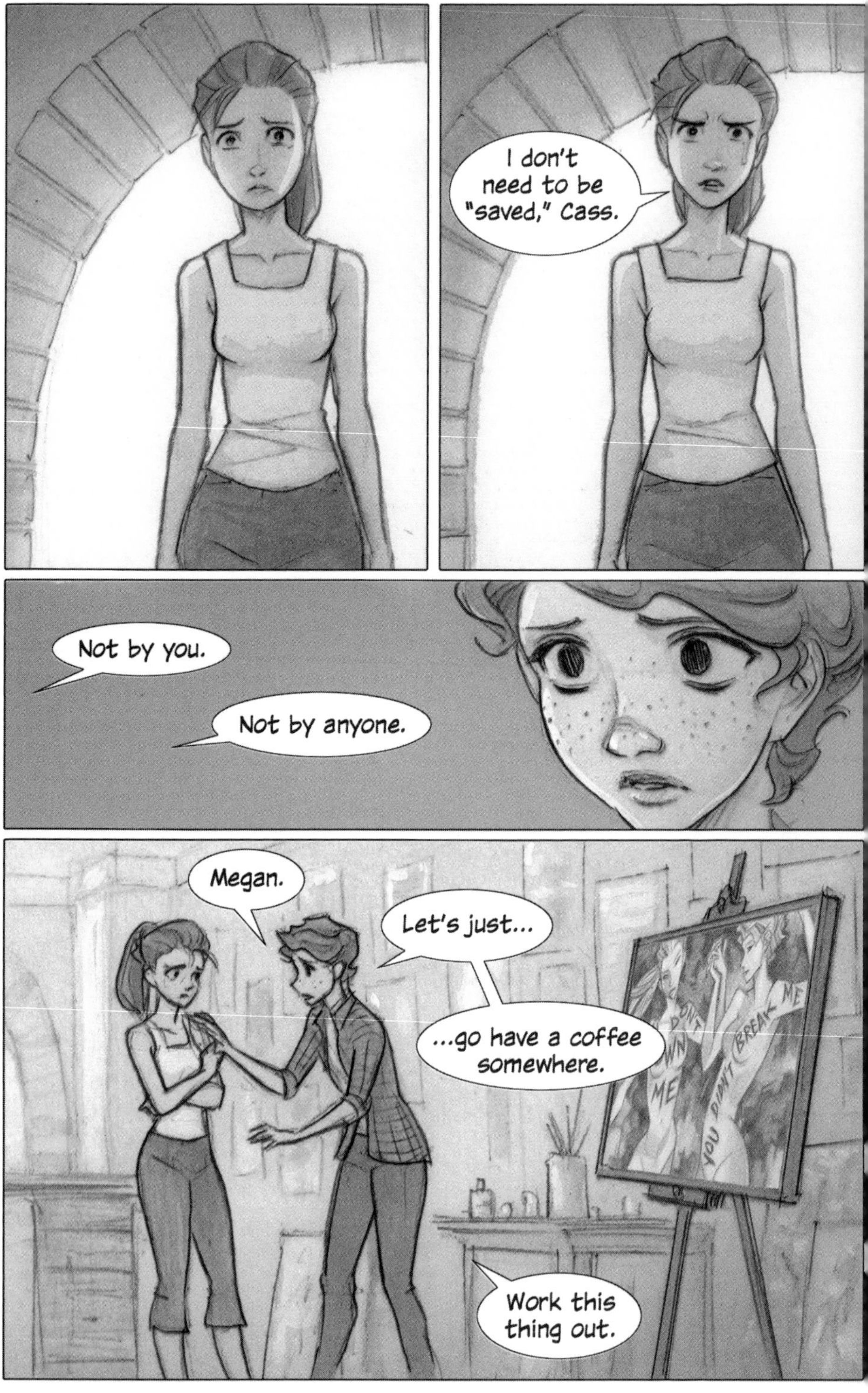
I don't need to be "saved," Cass.
Not by you.
Not by anyone.
Megan.
Let's just...
...go have a coffee somewhere.
Work this thing out.

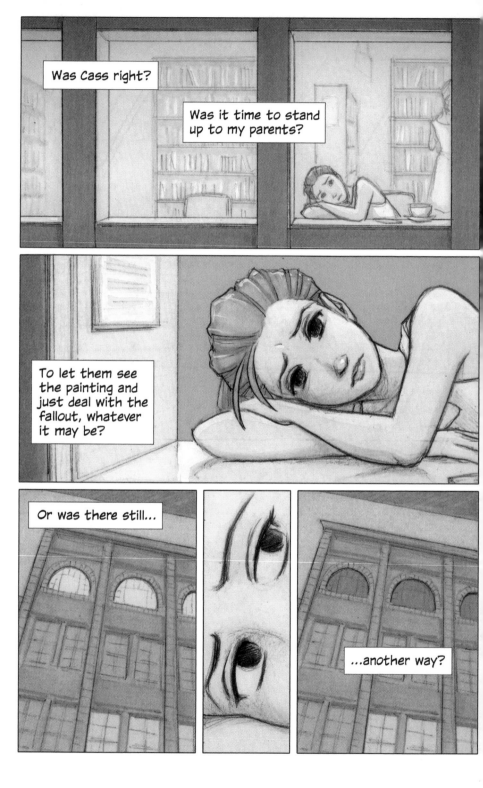

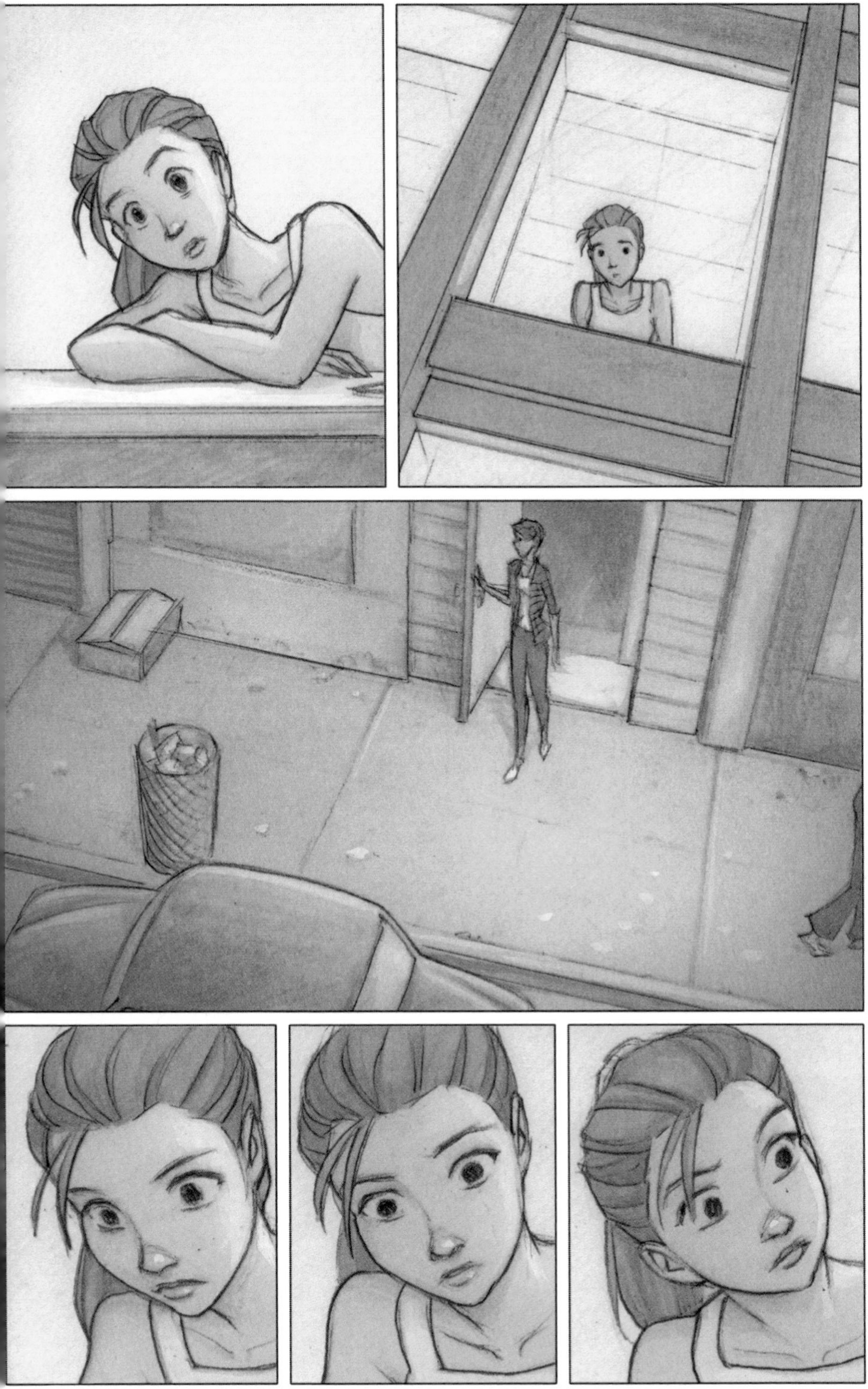

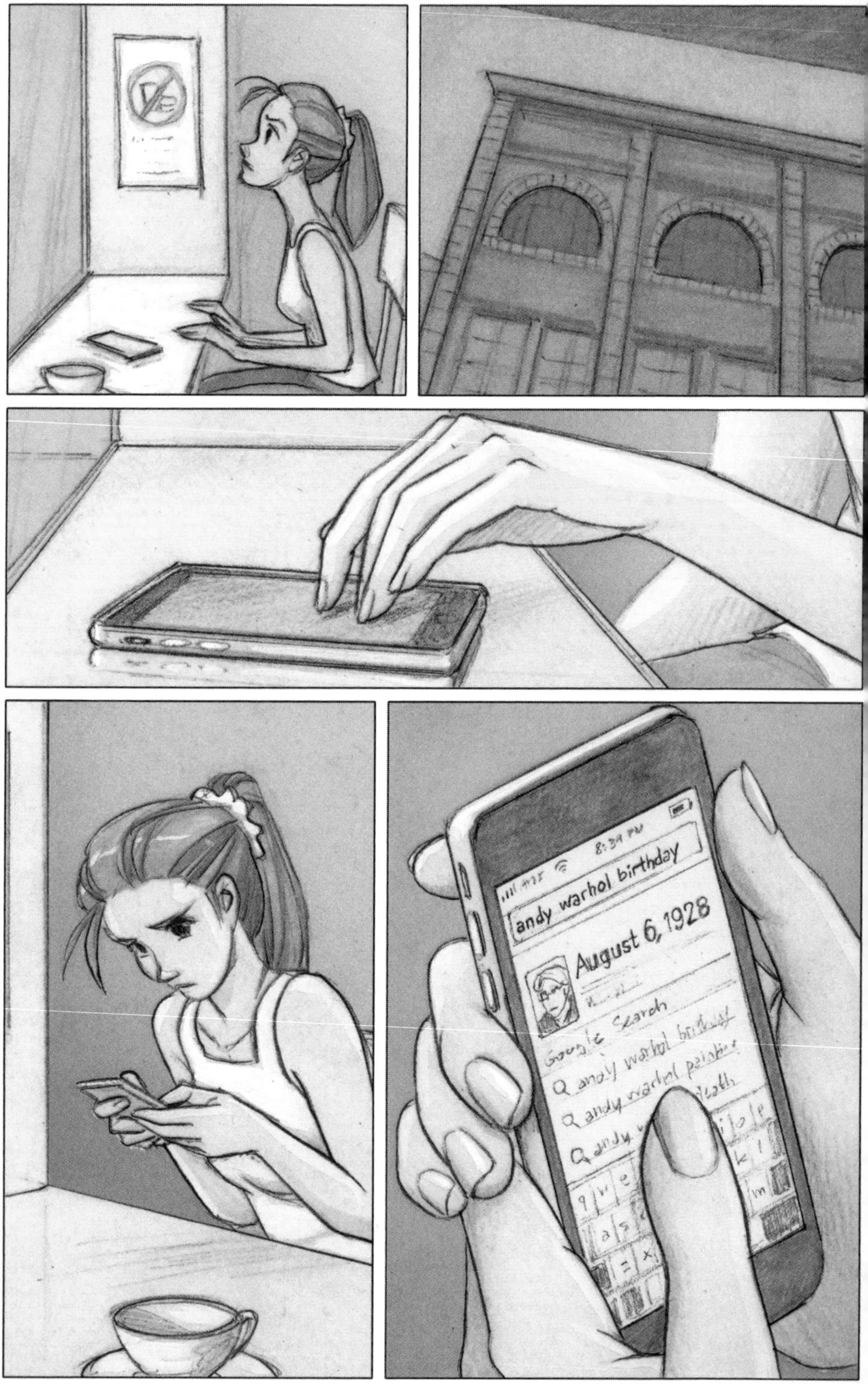
andy warhol birthday
August 6, 1928
Google Search
andy warhol birthday
andy warhol painting

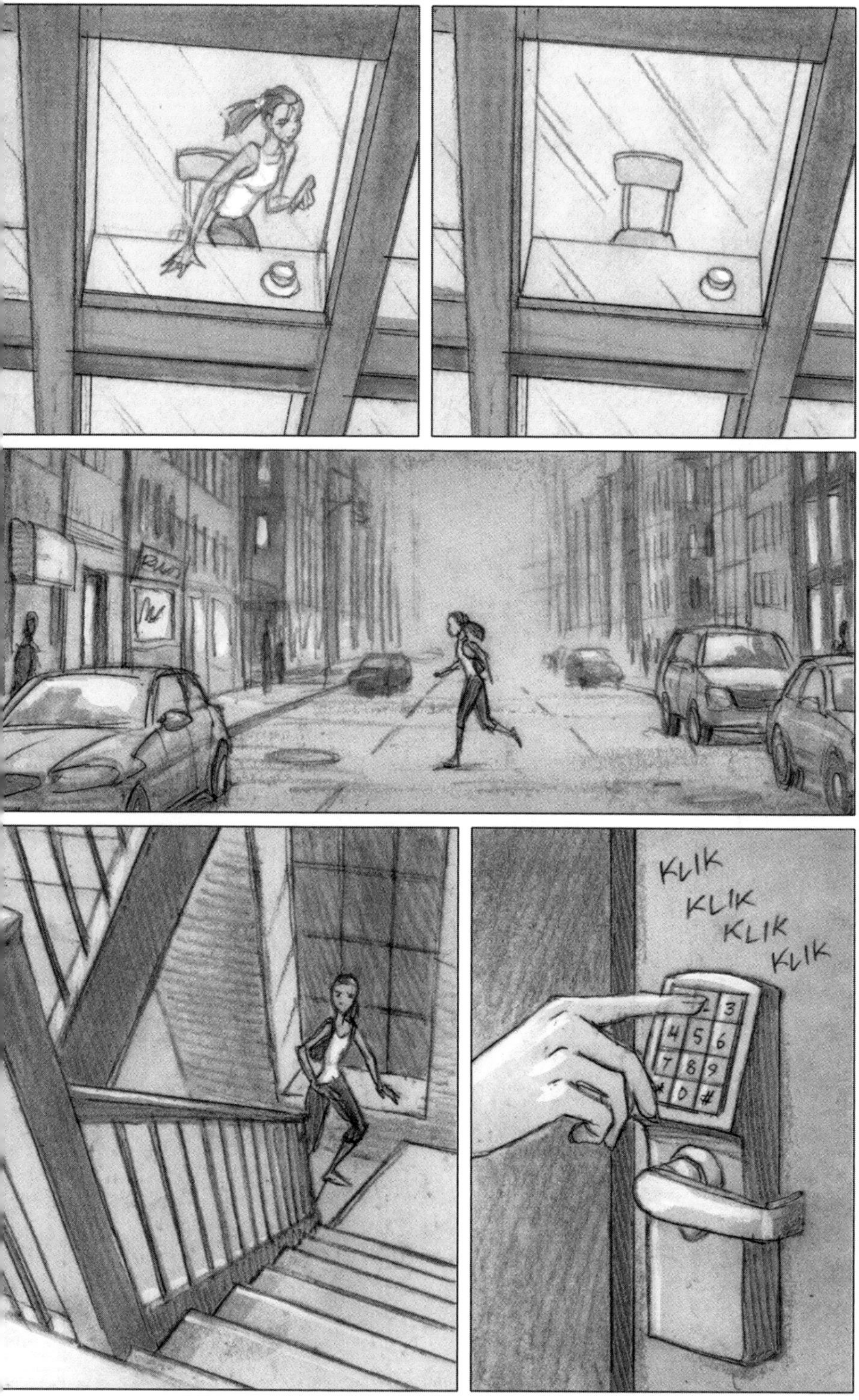
KLIK
KLIK
KLIK
KLIK

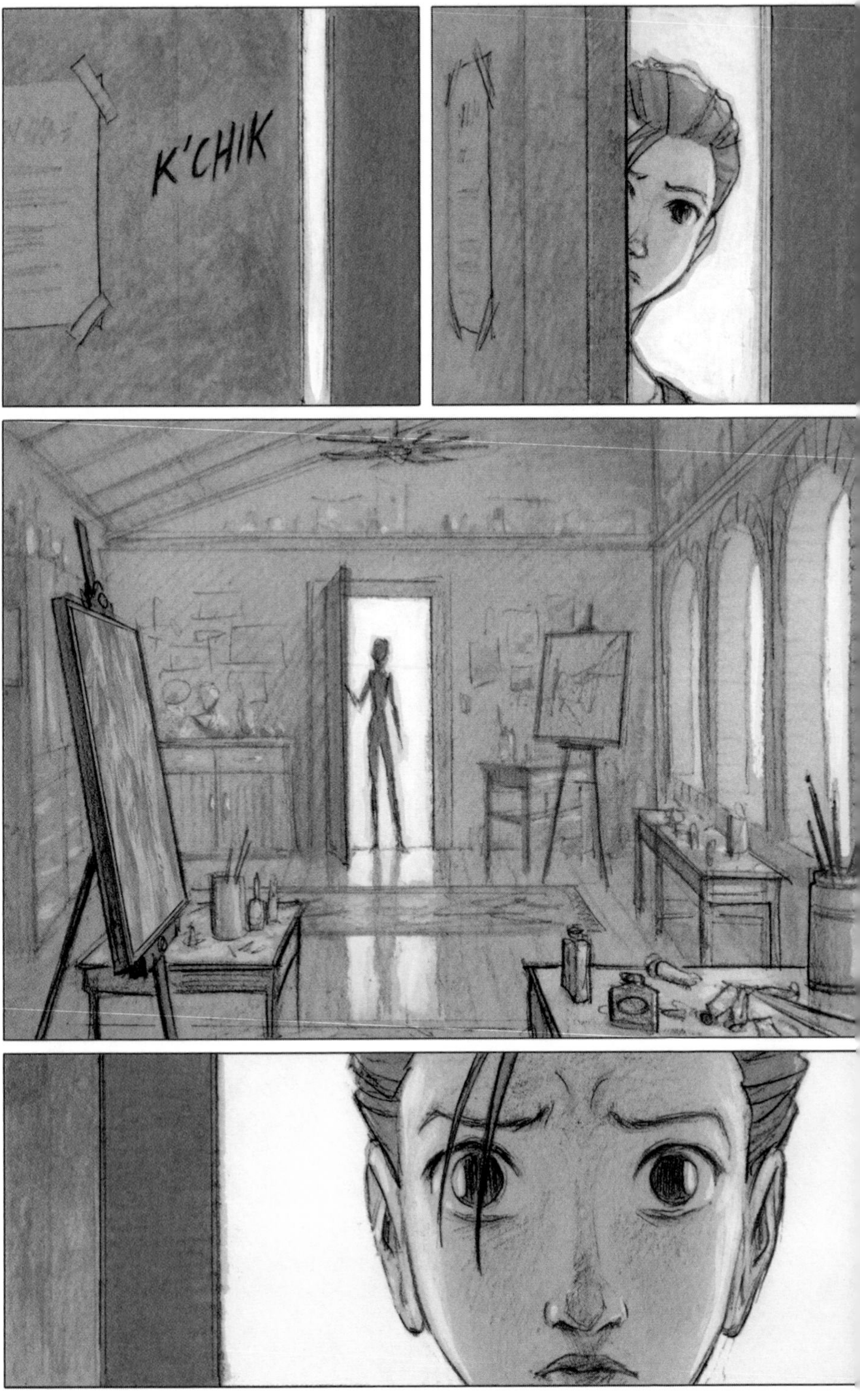
K'CHIK

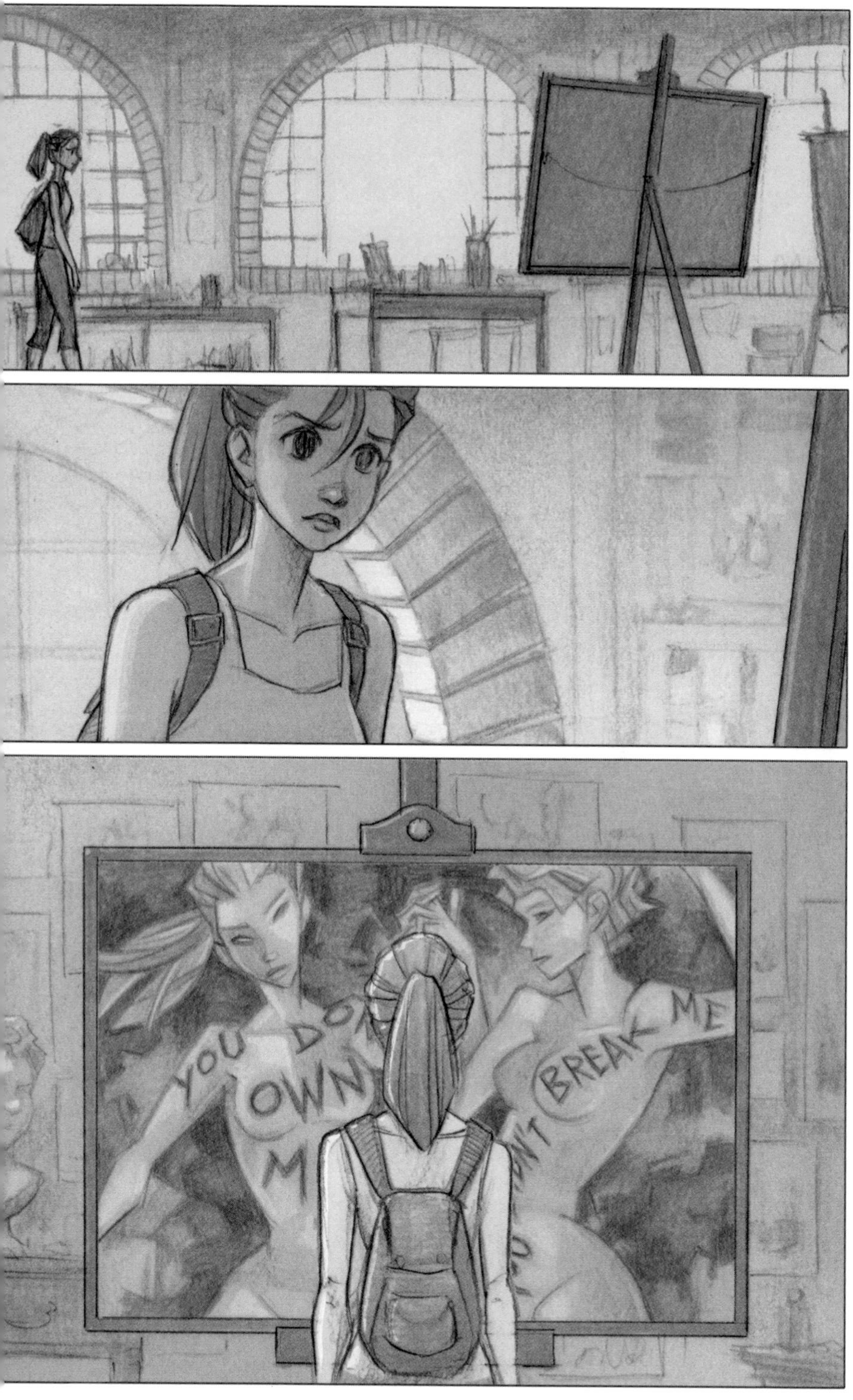
YOU DO
OWN
M
NT BREAK ME

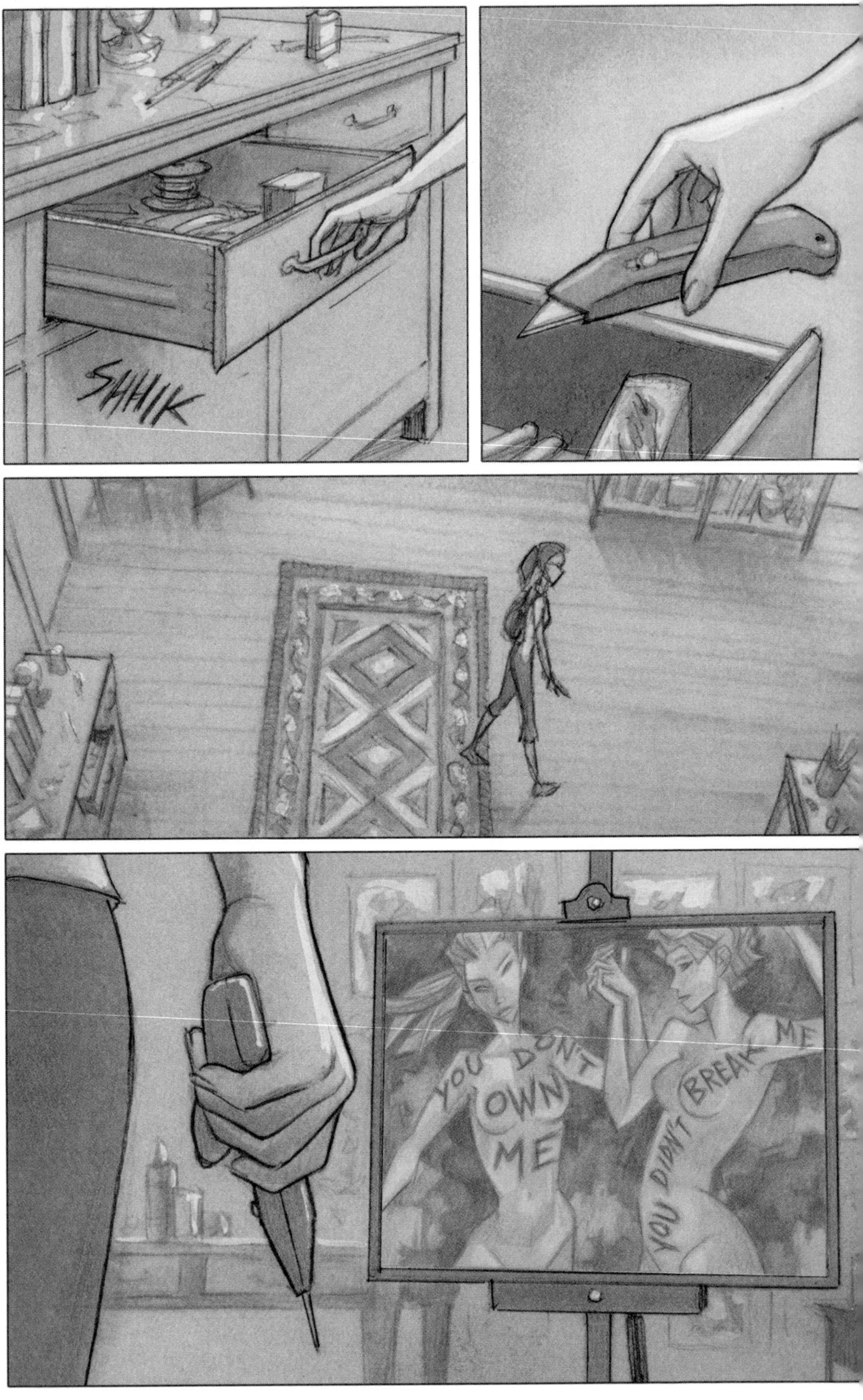
SHHIK
YOU DON'T OWN ME
YOU DIDN'T BREAK ME

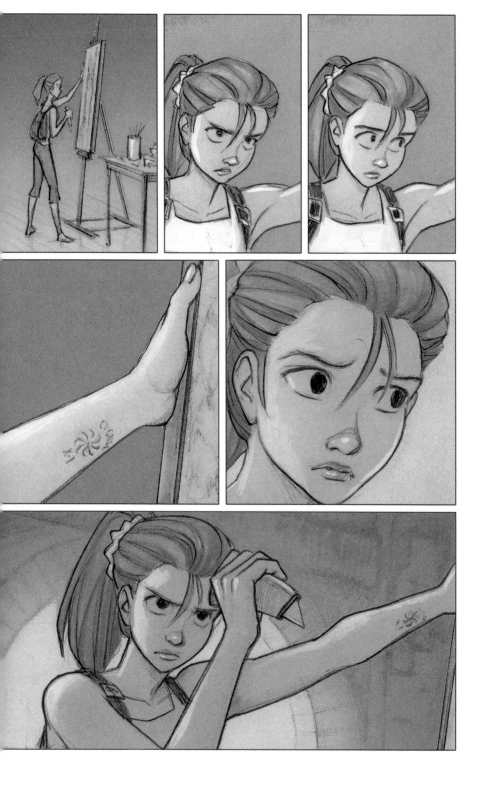

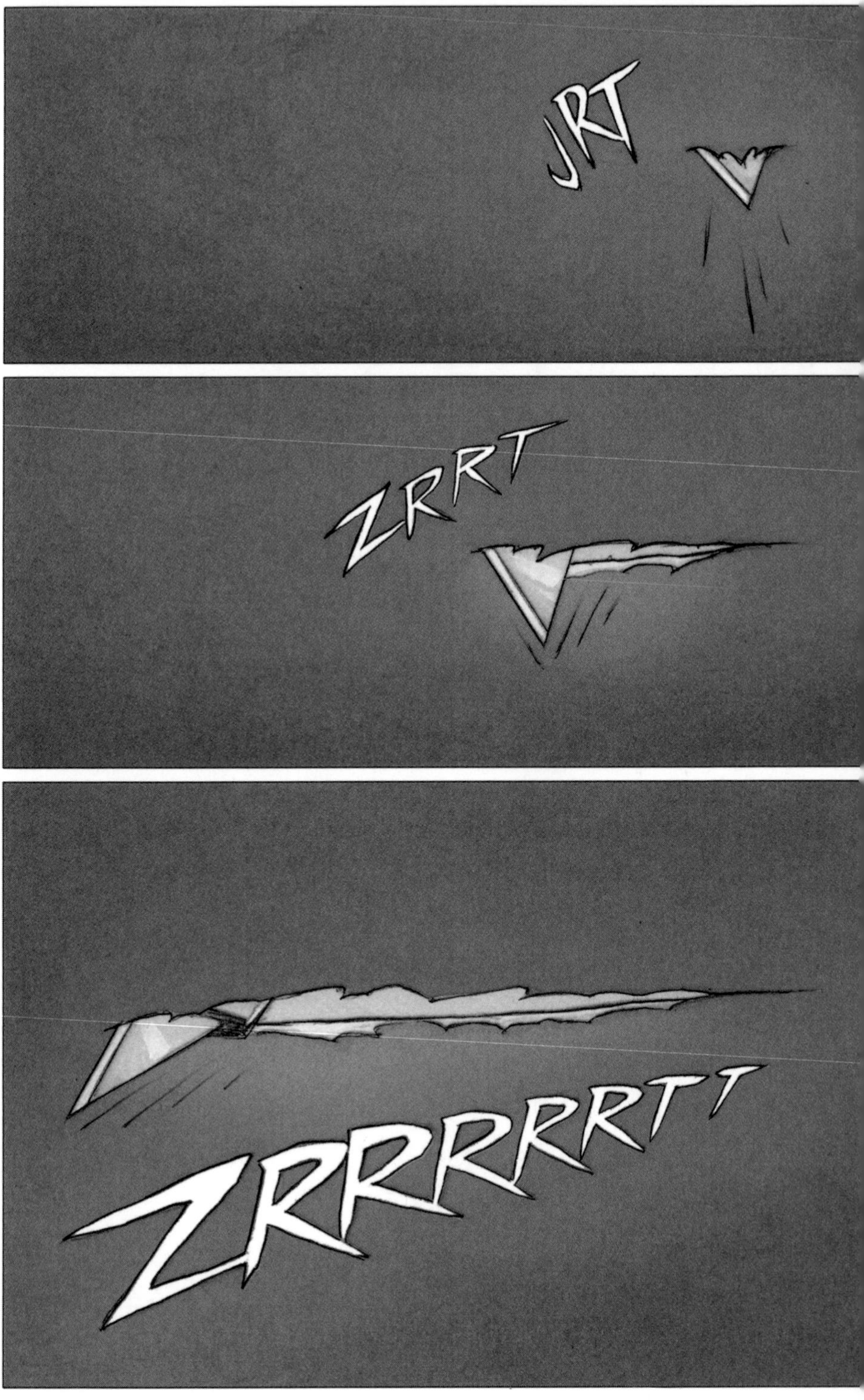
JRT
ZRRT
ZRRRRRTT

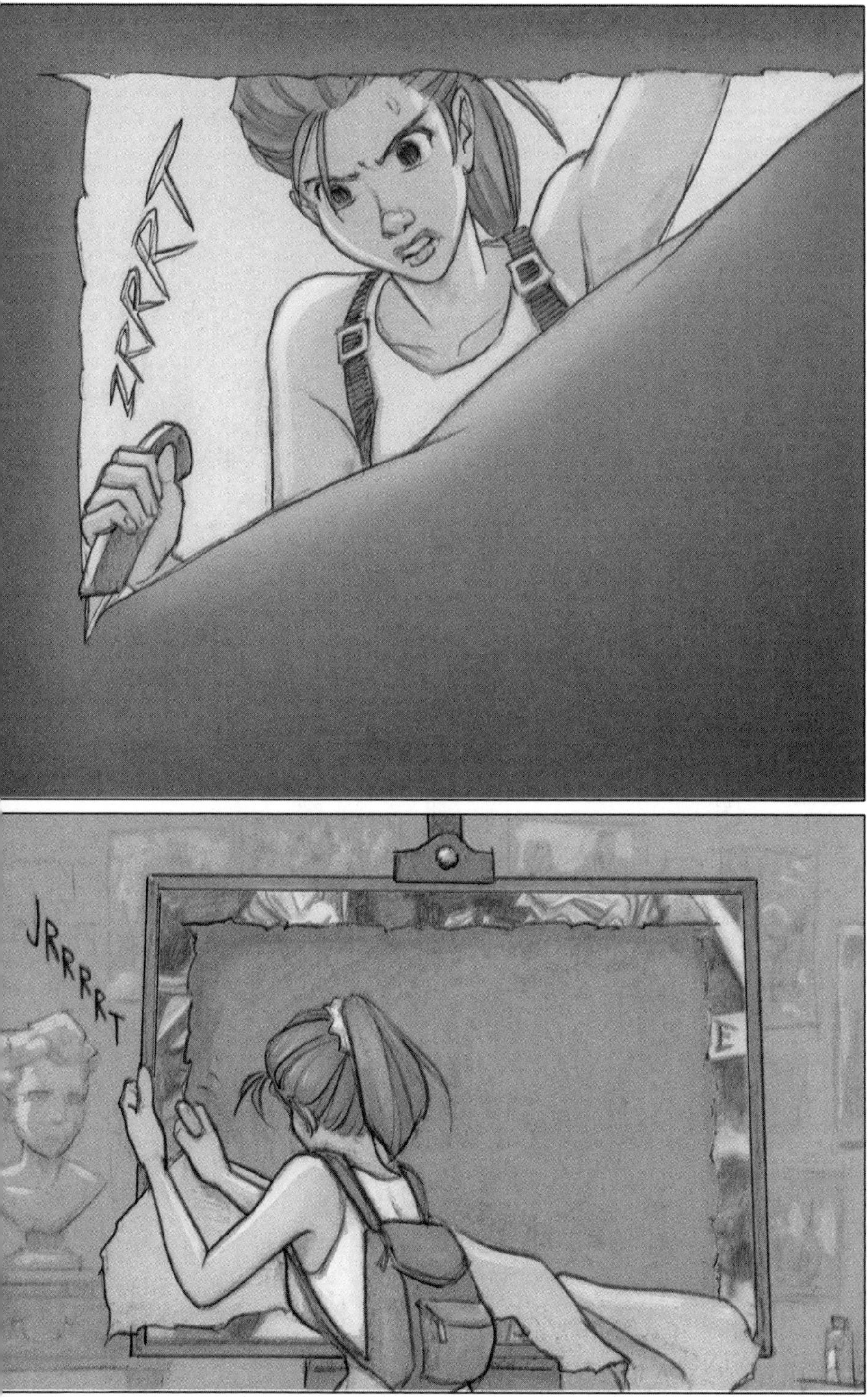
ZRRRT
JRRRRT

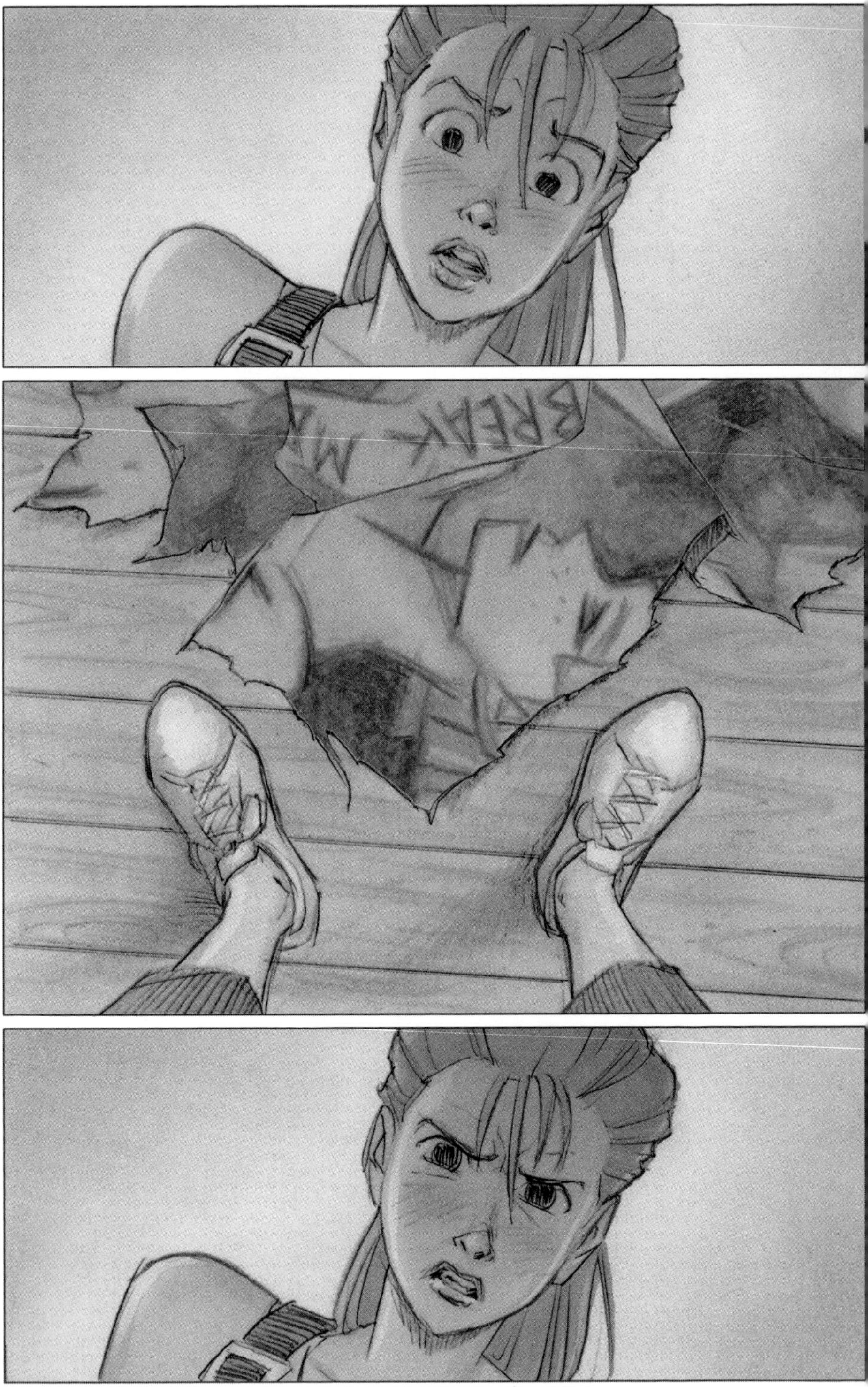
BREAK

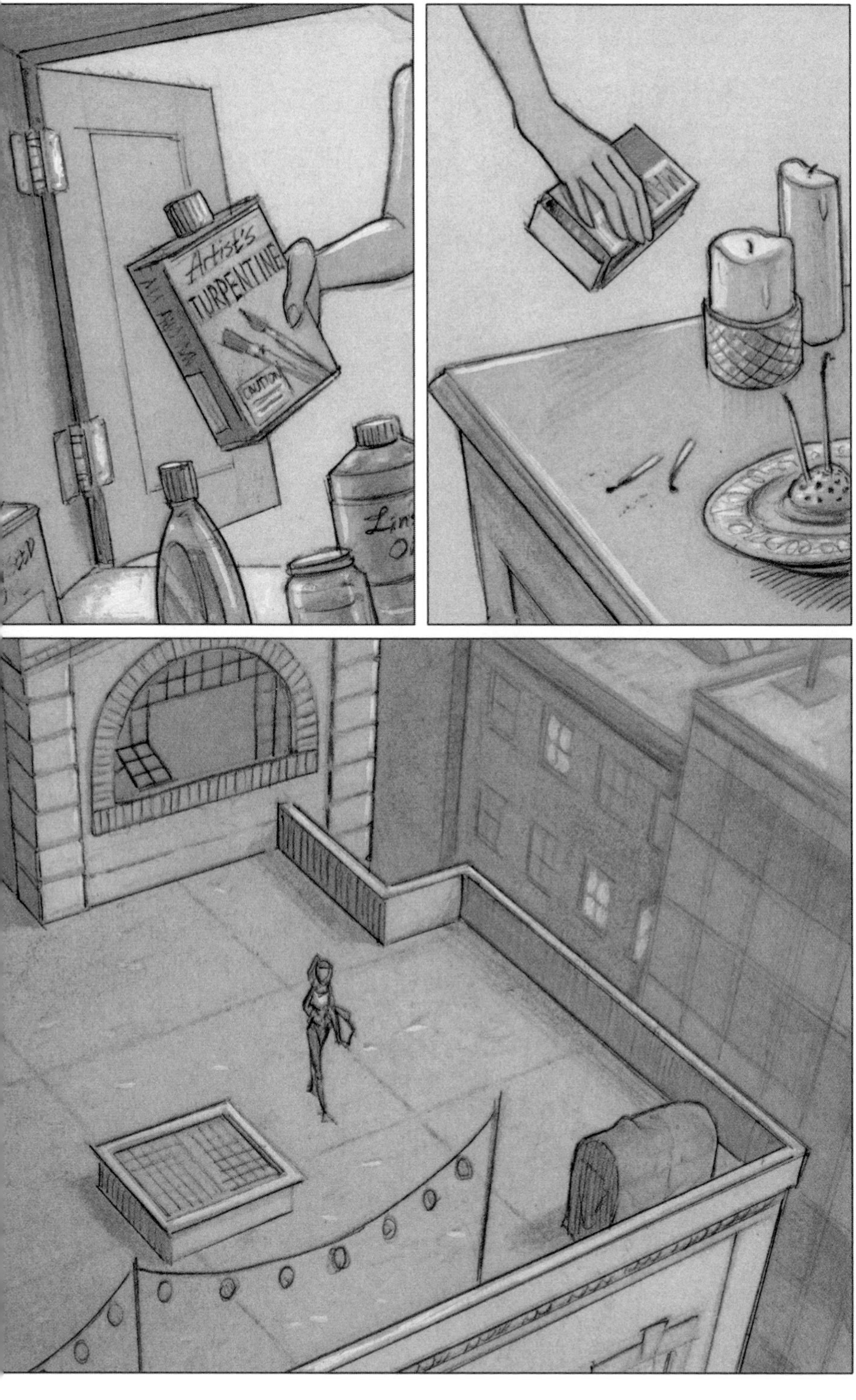
Artist's
TURPENTINE
CAUTION

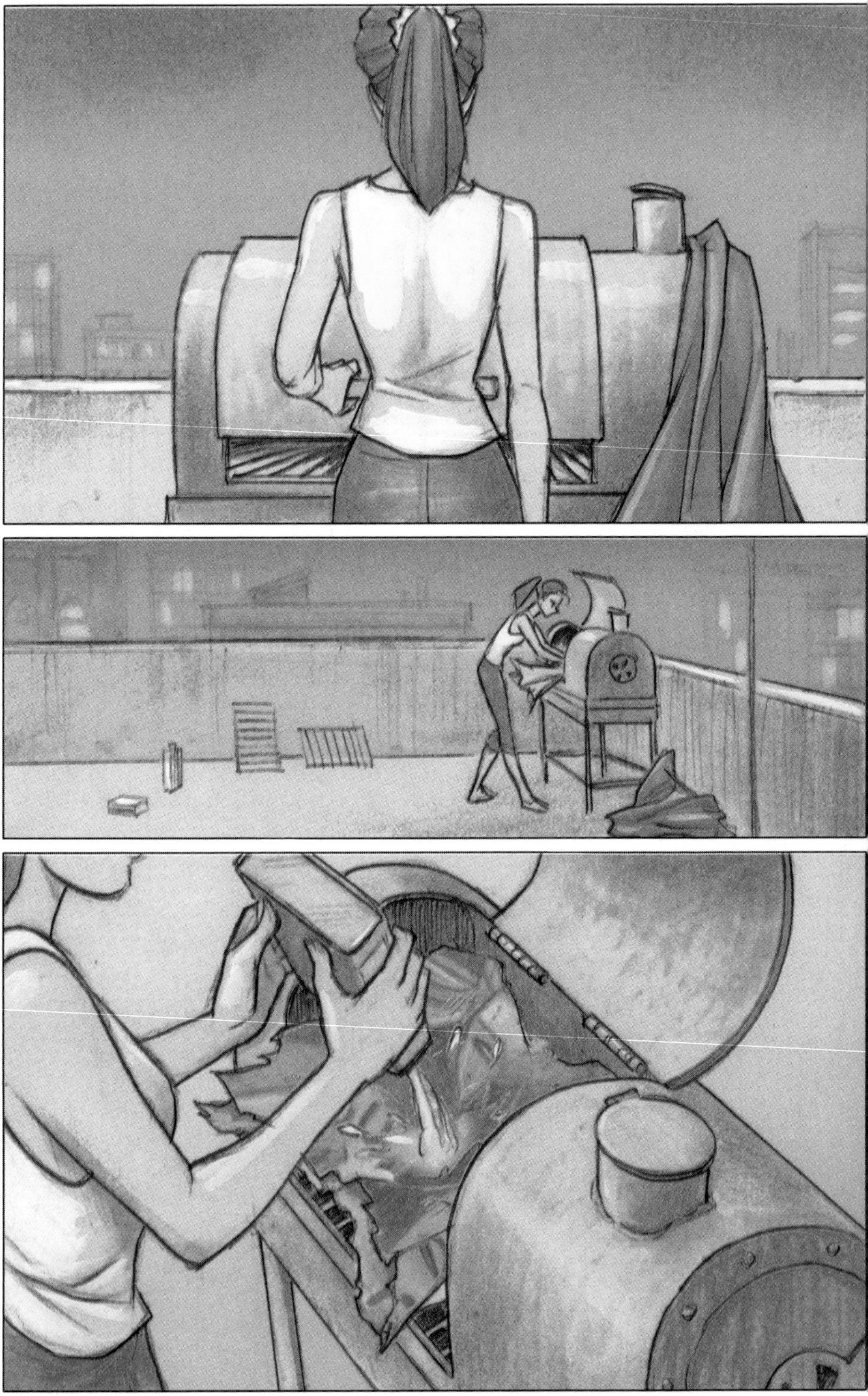

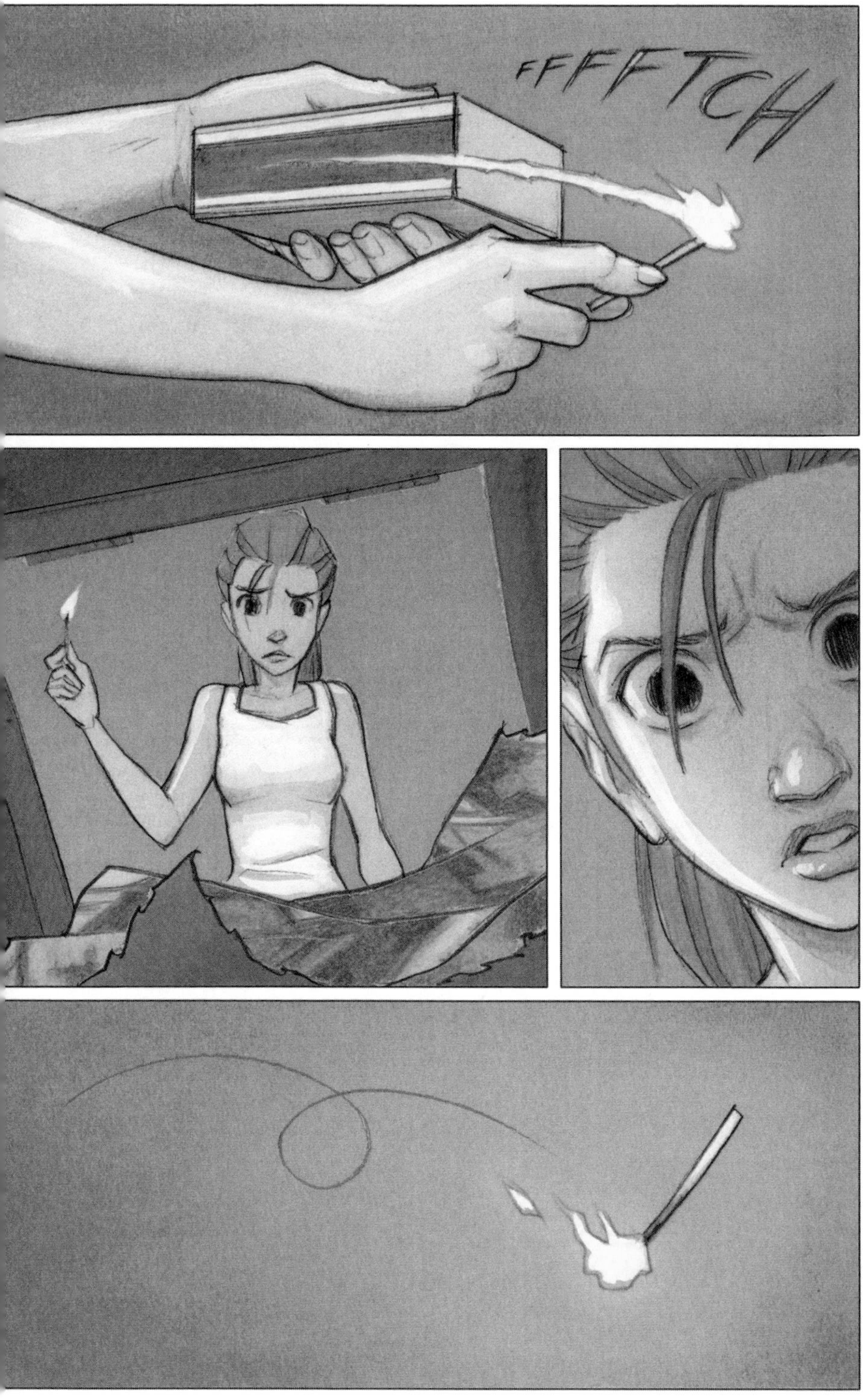
FFFFTCH

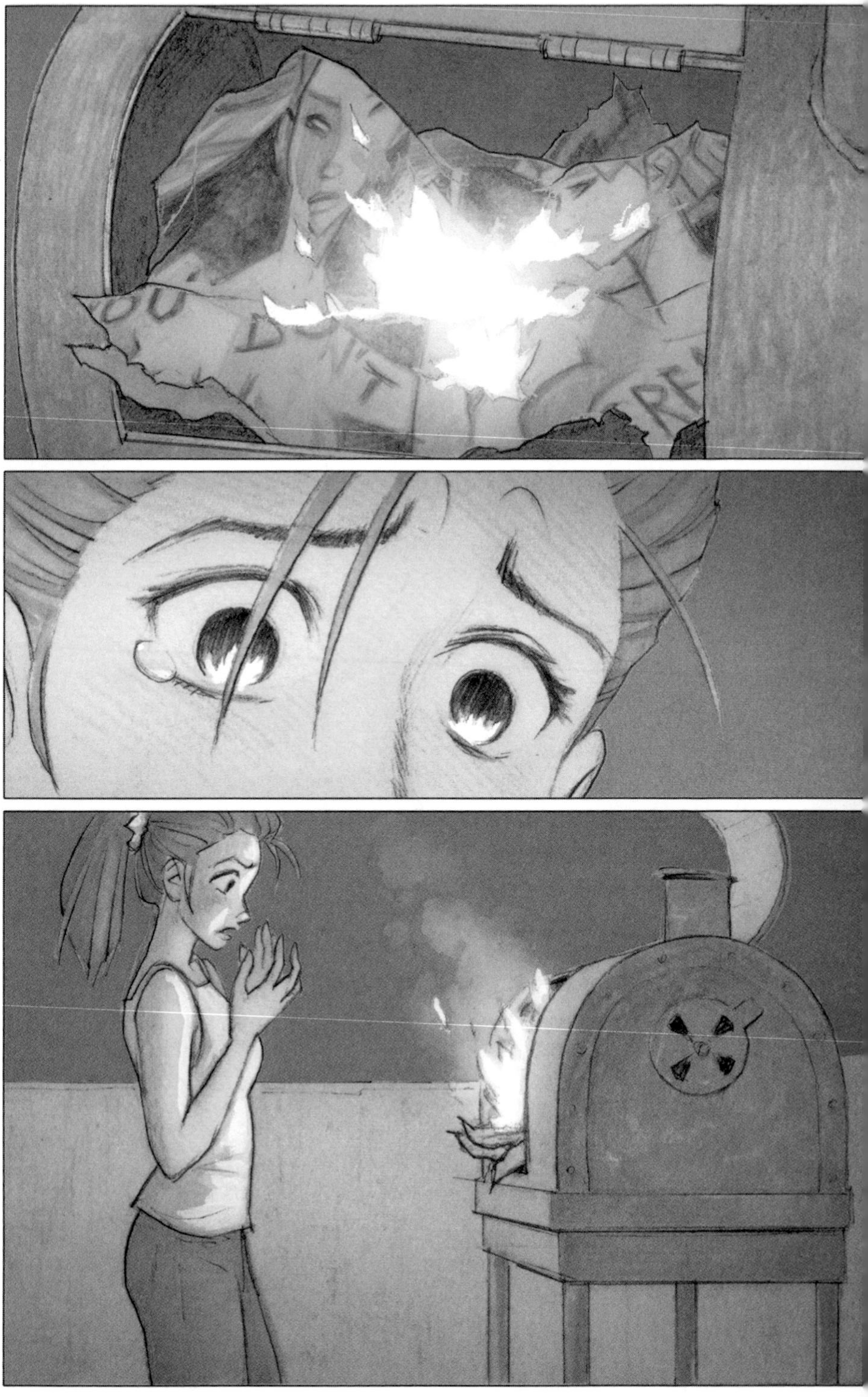

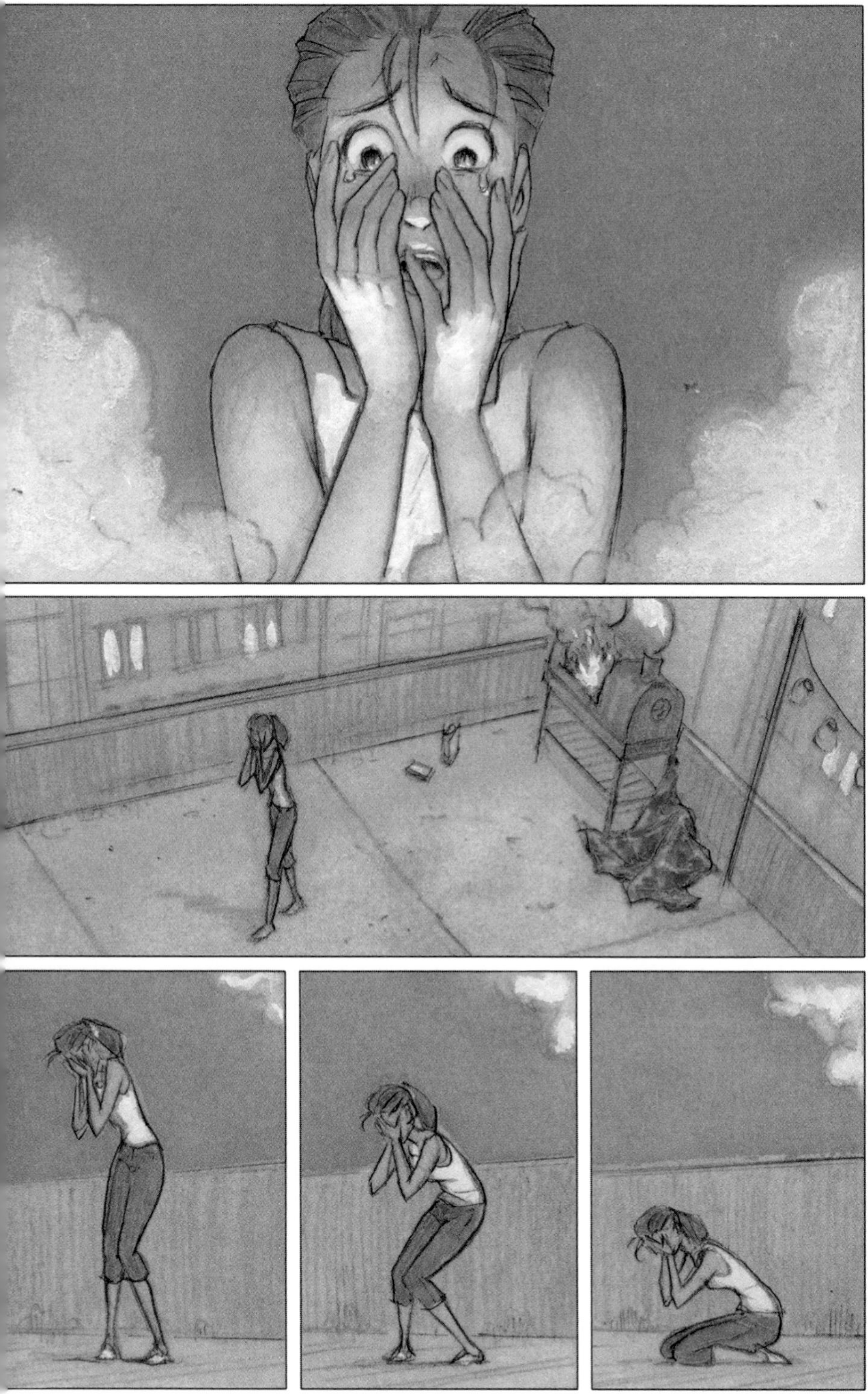

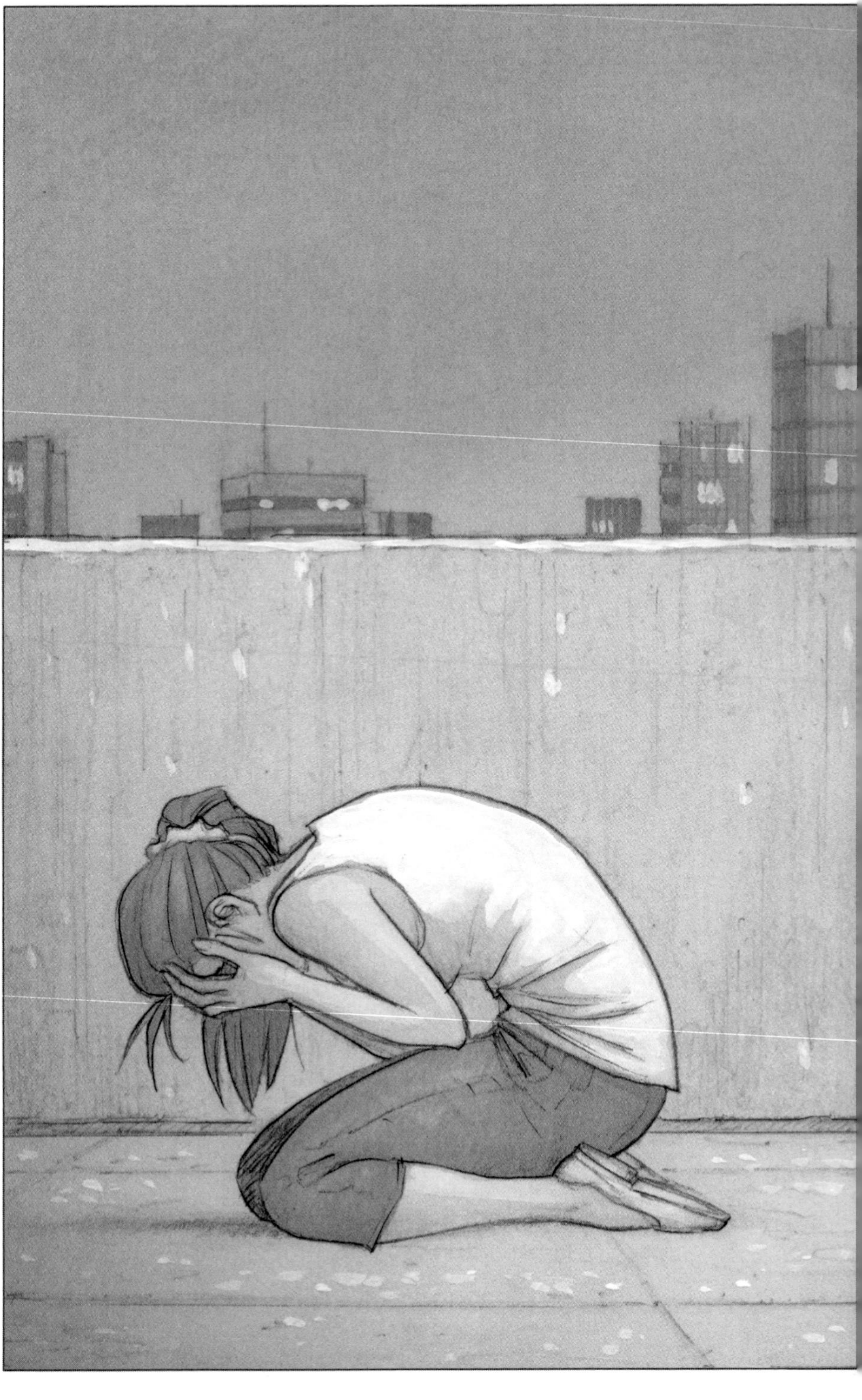

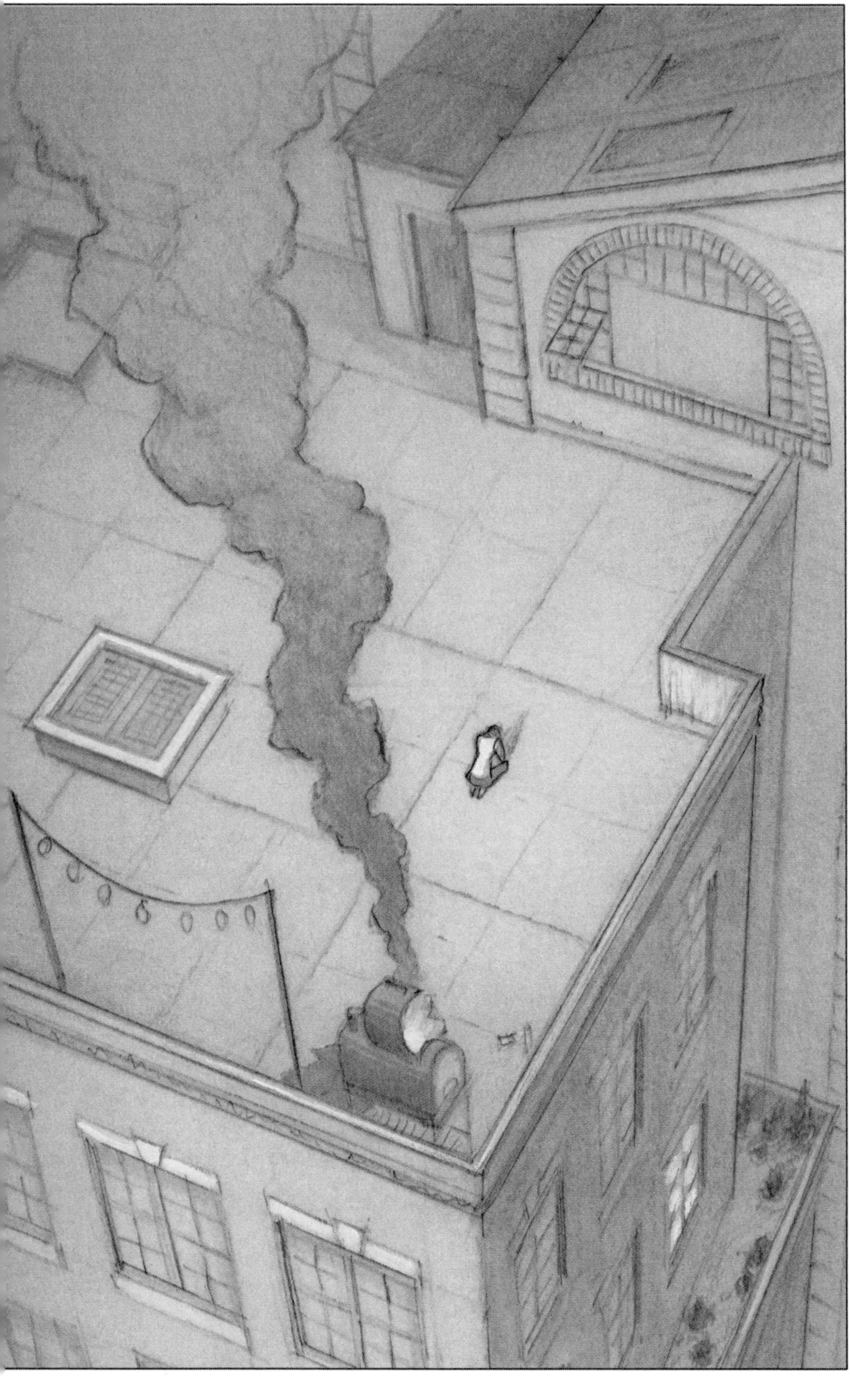

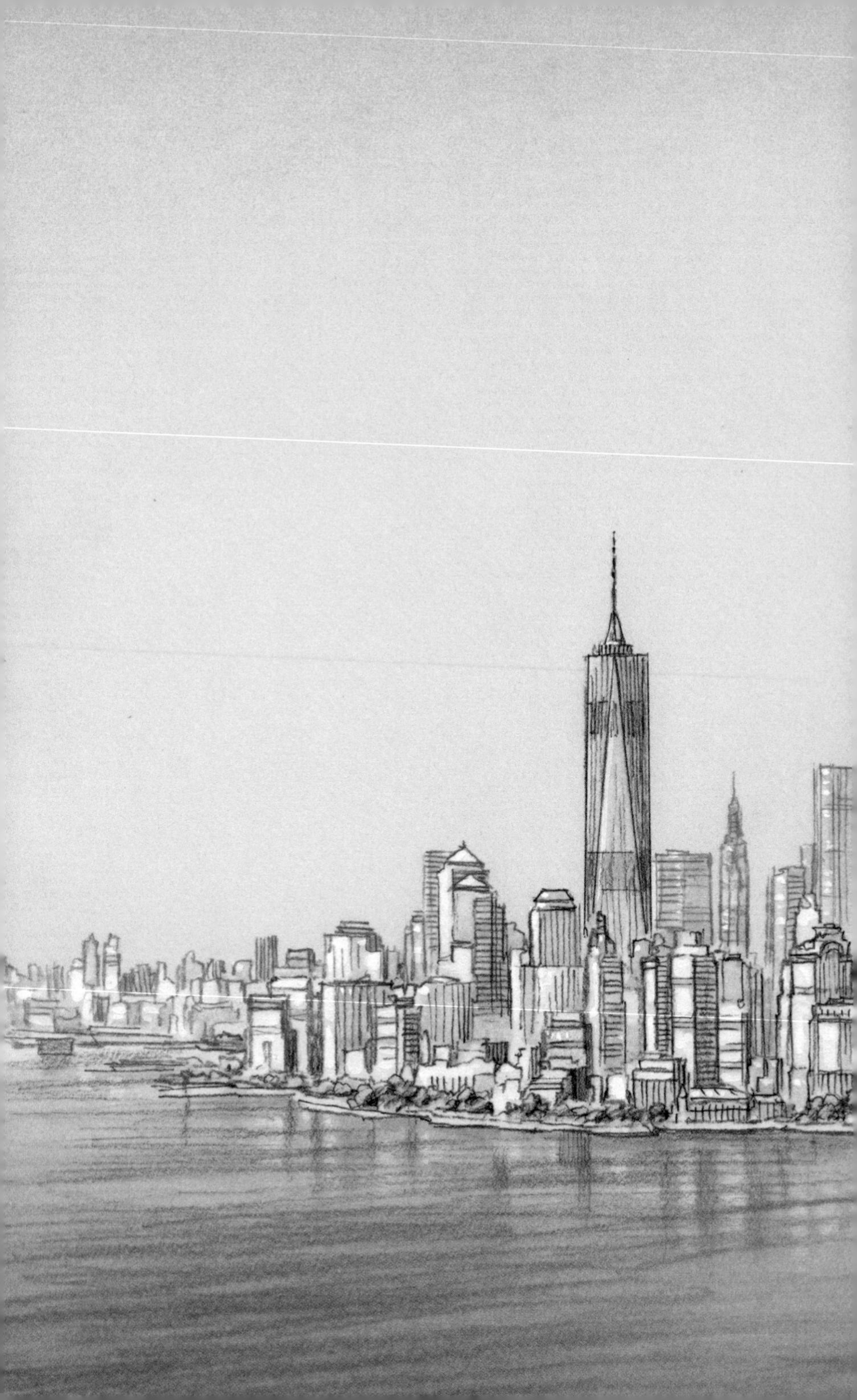

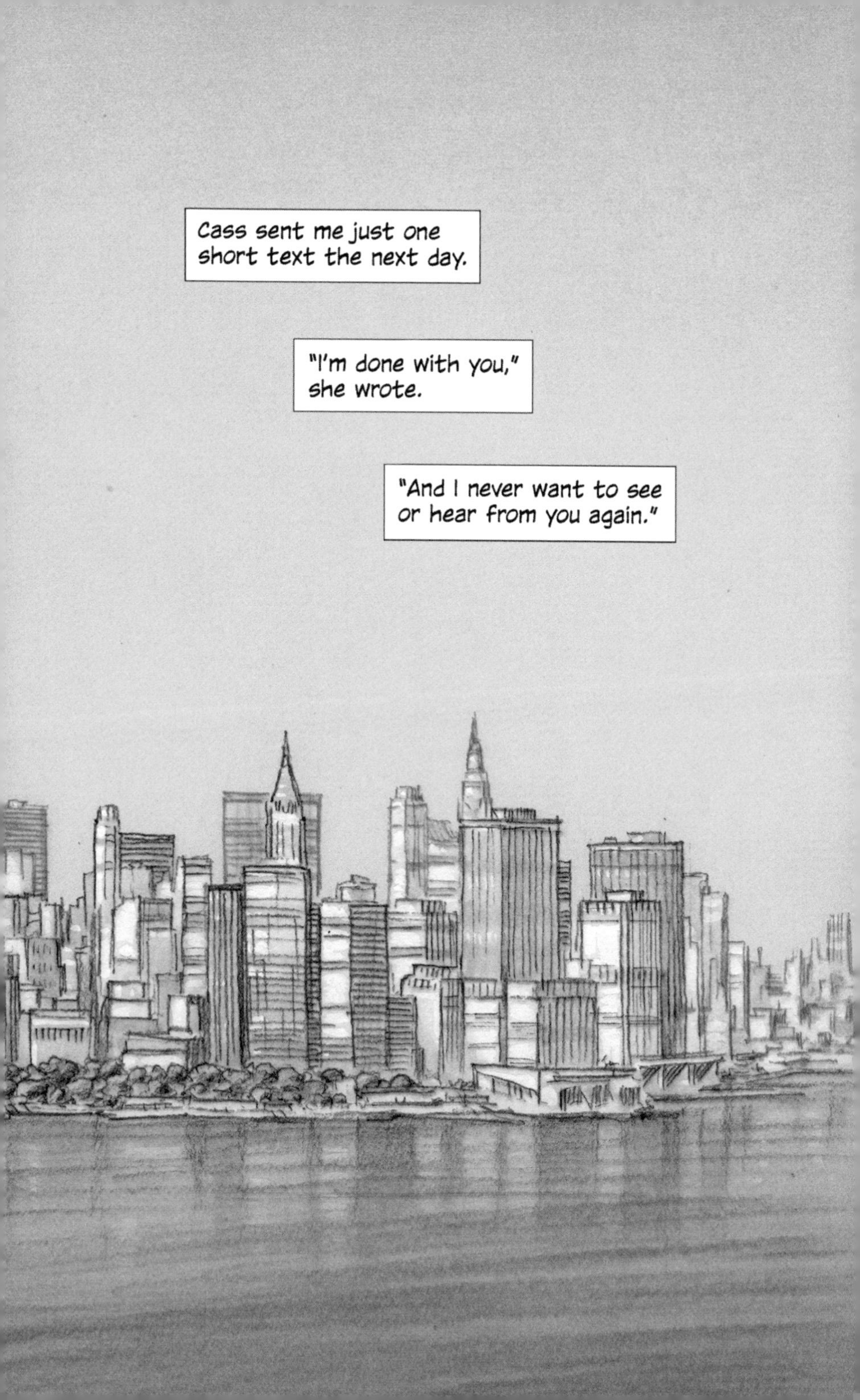
Cass sent me just one short text the next day.
"I'm done with you," she wrote.
"And I never want to see or hear from you again."

Part Three

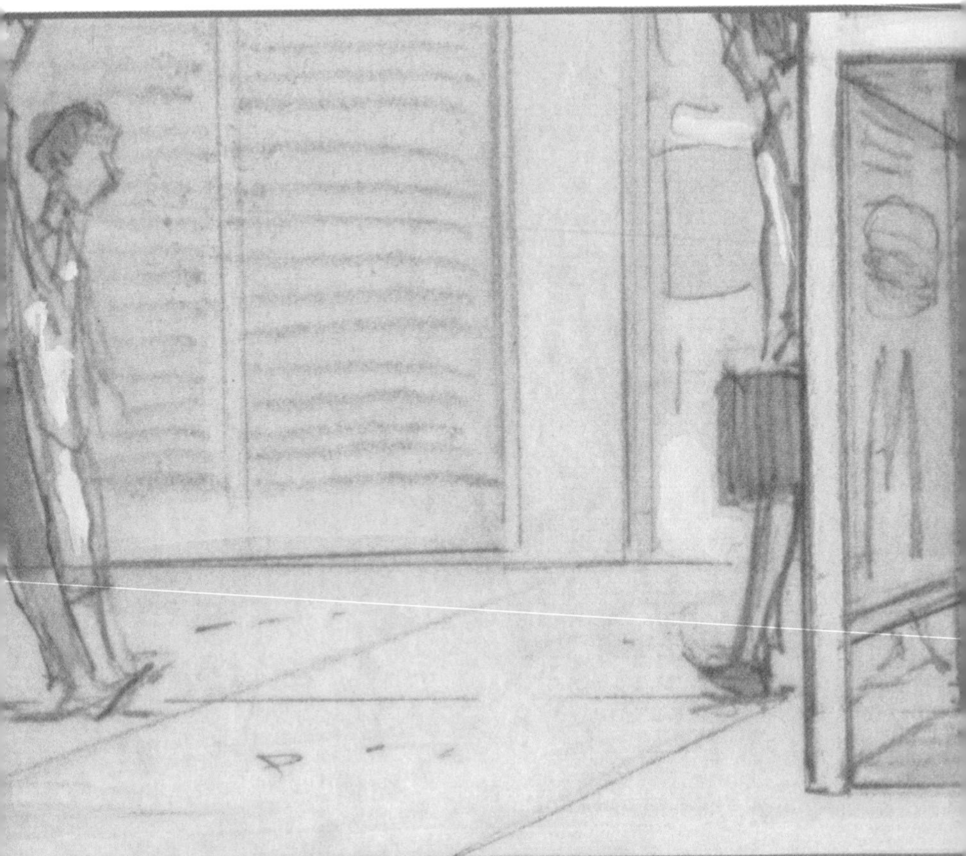

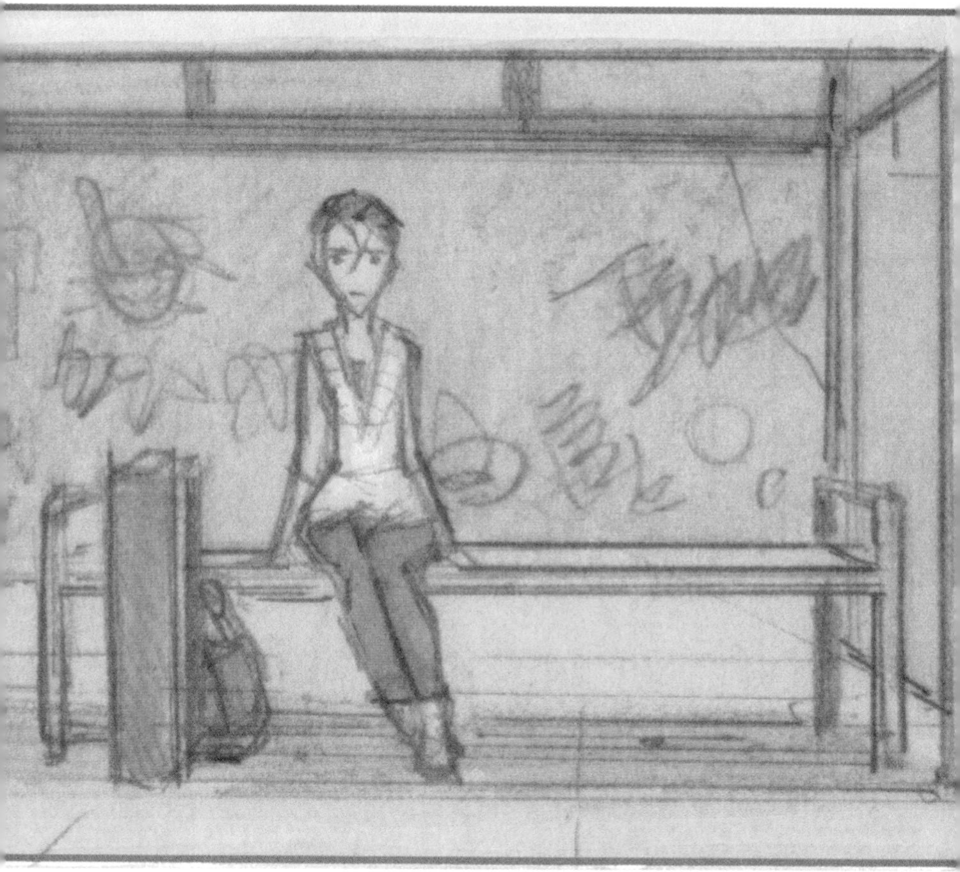

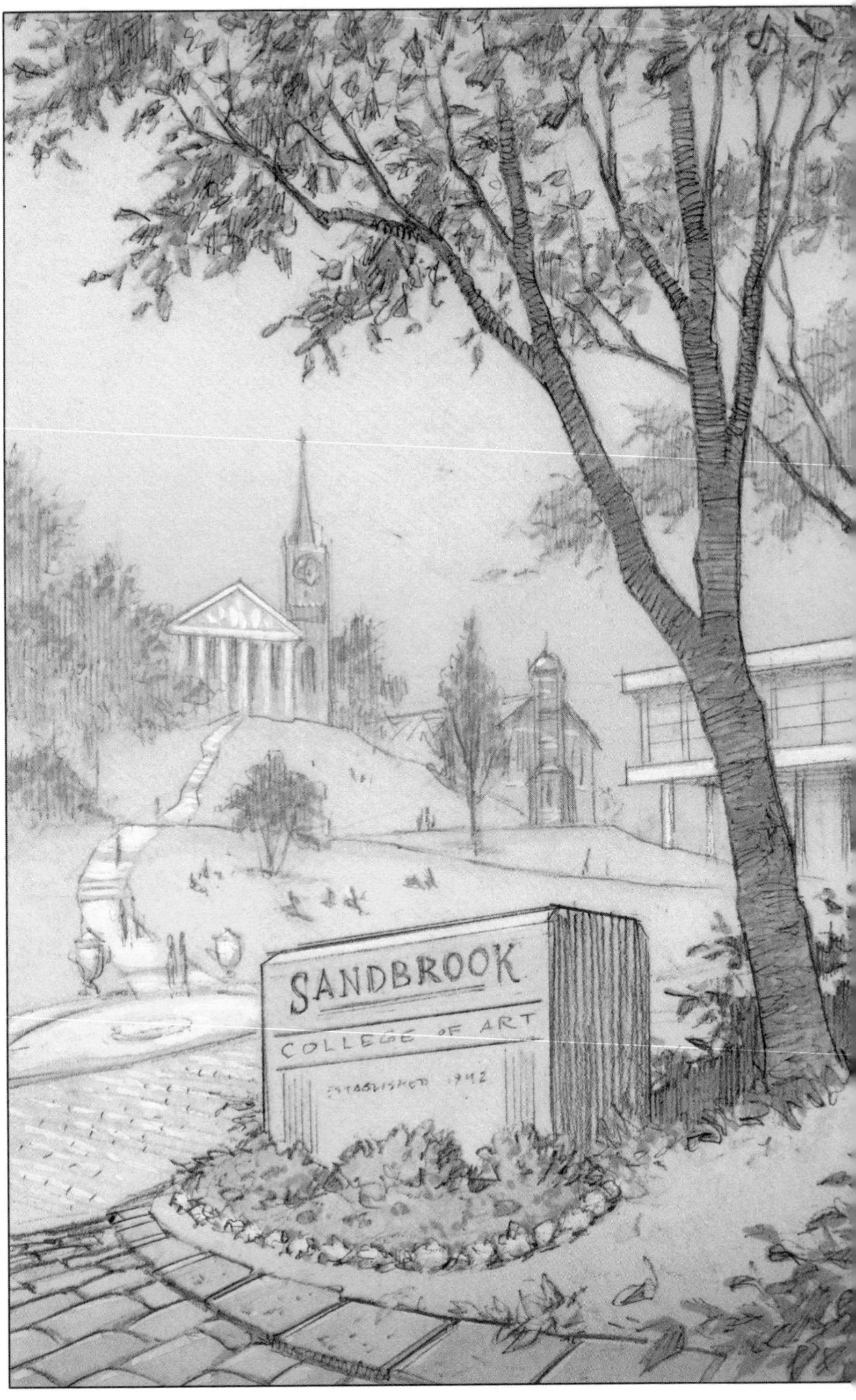
SANDBROOK
COLLEGE OF ART
ESTABLISHED 1942

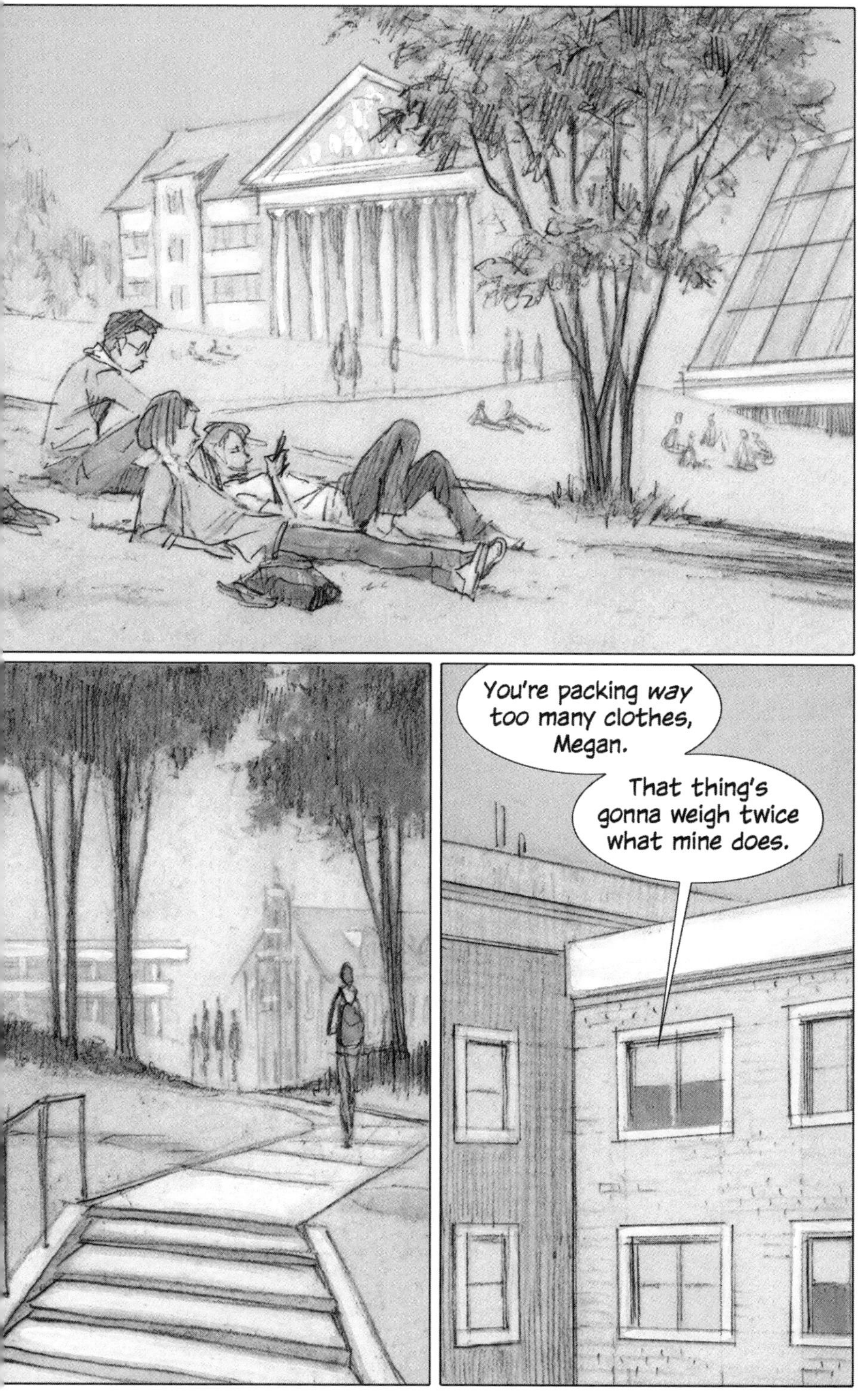
You're packing way too many clothes, Megan.
That thing's gonna weigh twice what mine does.

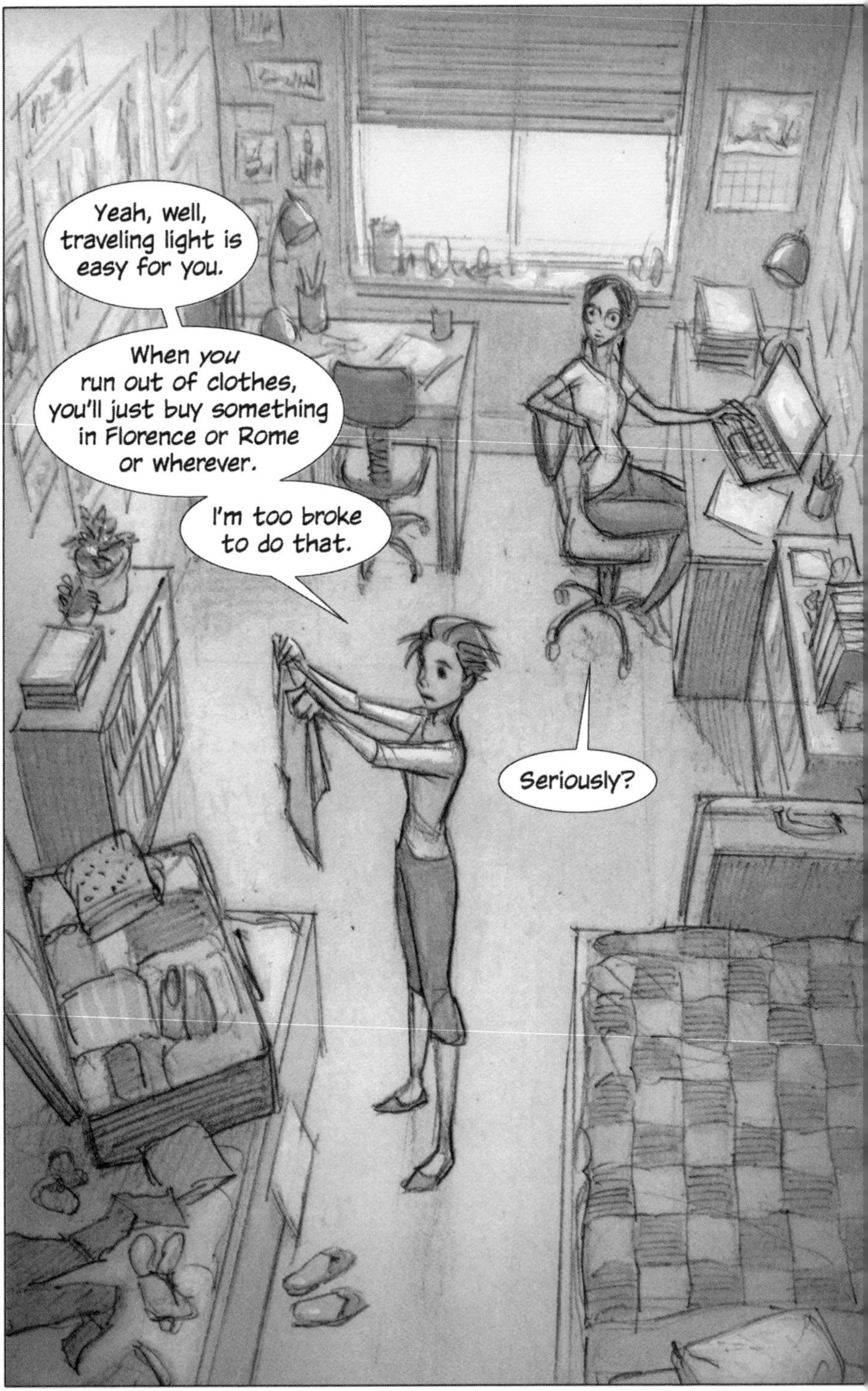
Yeah, well, traveling light is easy for you.
When *you* run out of clothes, you'll just buy something in Florence or Rome or wherever.
I'm too broke to do that.
Seriously?

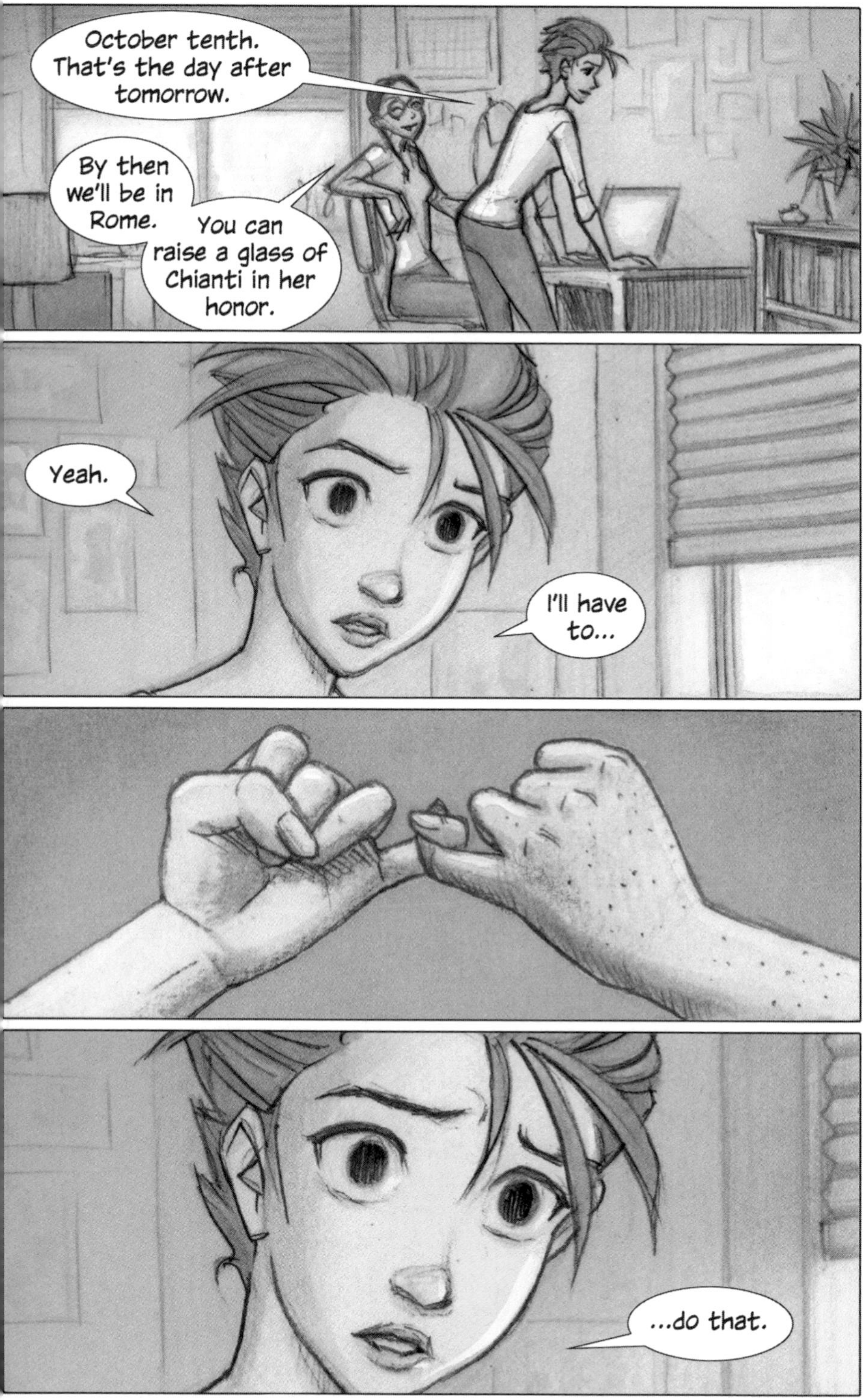
October tenth. That's the day after tomorrow.
By then we'll be in Rome.
You can raise a glass of Chianti in her honor.
Yeah.
I'll have to...
...do that.

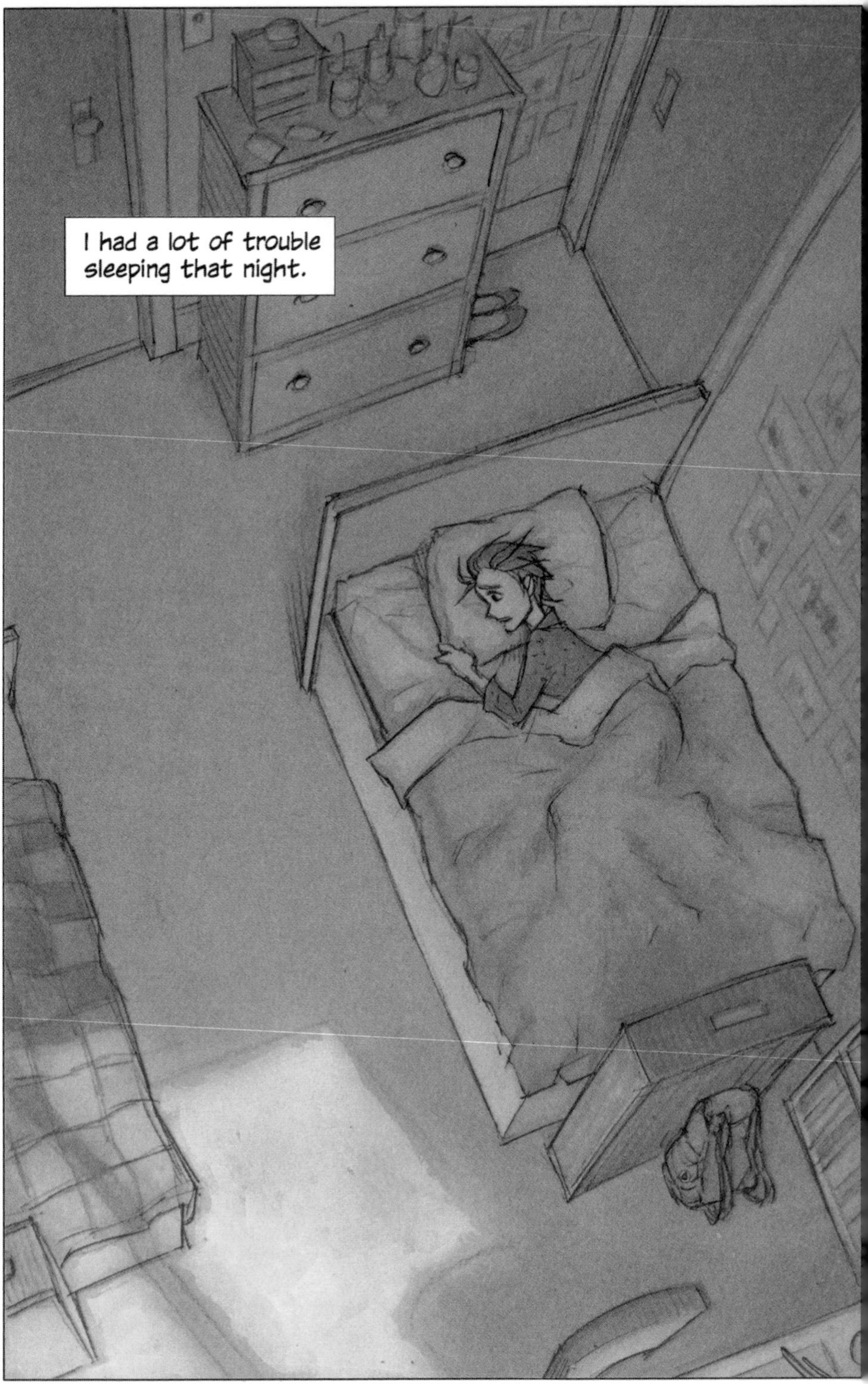
I had a lot of trouble sleeping that night.

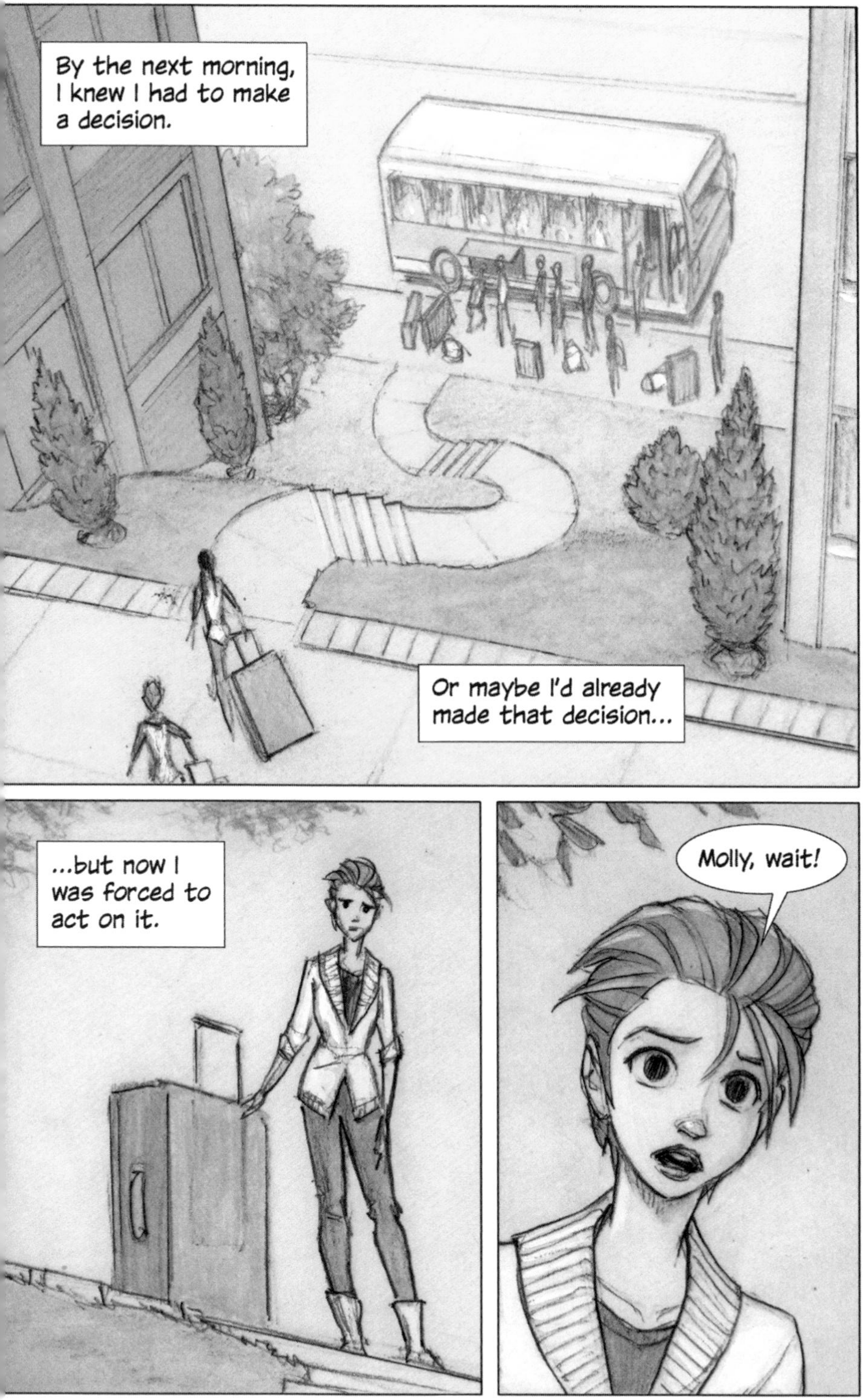
By the next morning, I knew I had to make a decision.
Or maybe I'd already made that decision...
...but now I was forced to act on it.
Molly, wait!

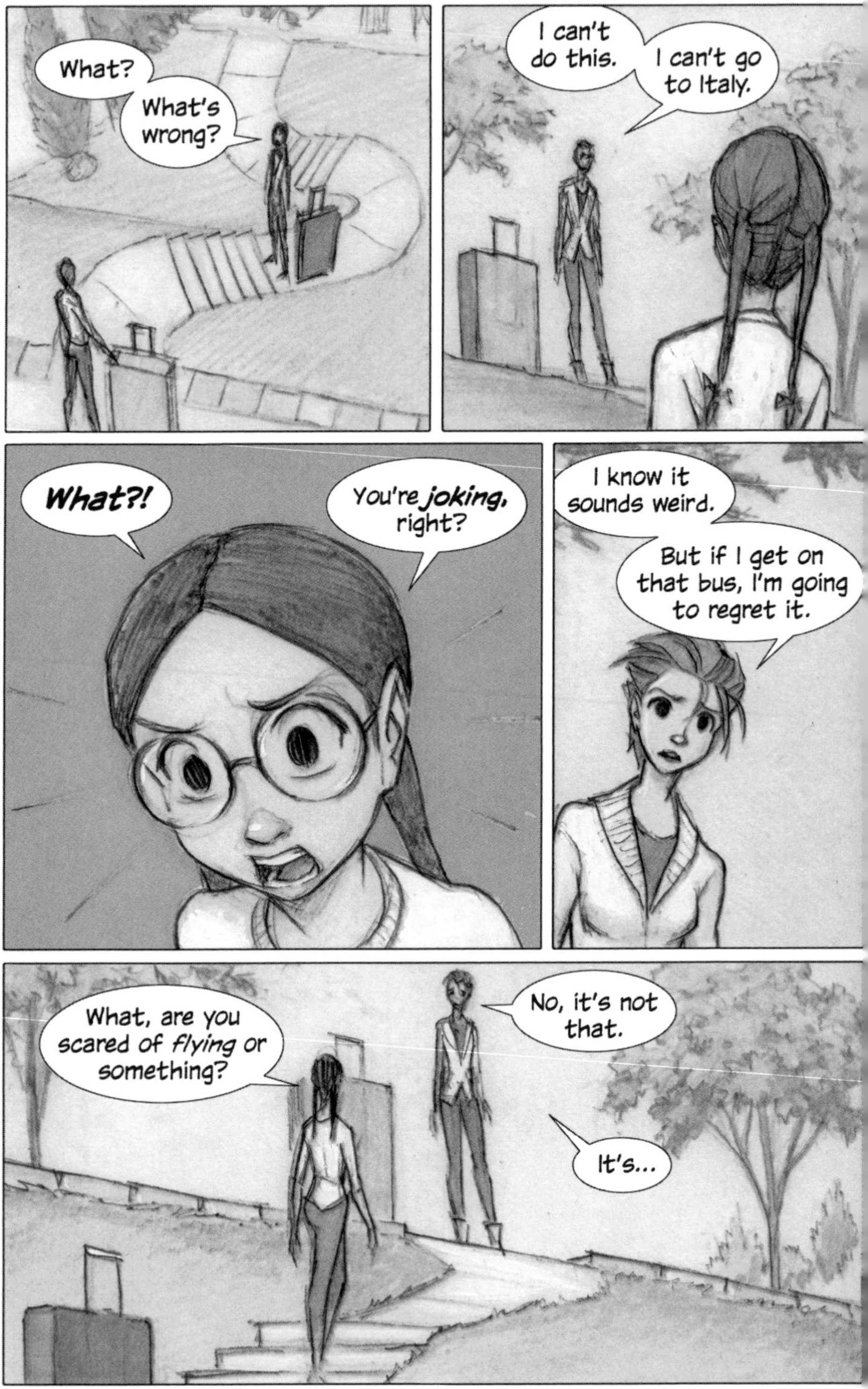
What?
What's wrong?
I can't do this.
I can't go to Italy.
What?!
You're *joking,* right?
I know it sounds weird.
But if I get on that bus, I'm going to regret it.
What, are you scared of *flying* or something?
No, it's not that.
It's...

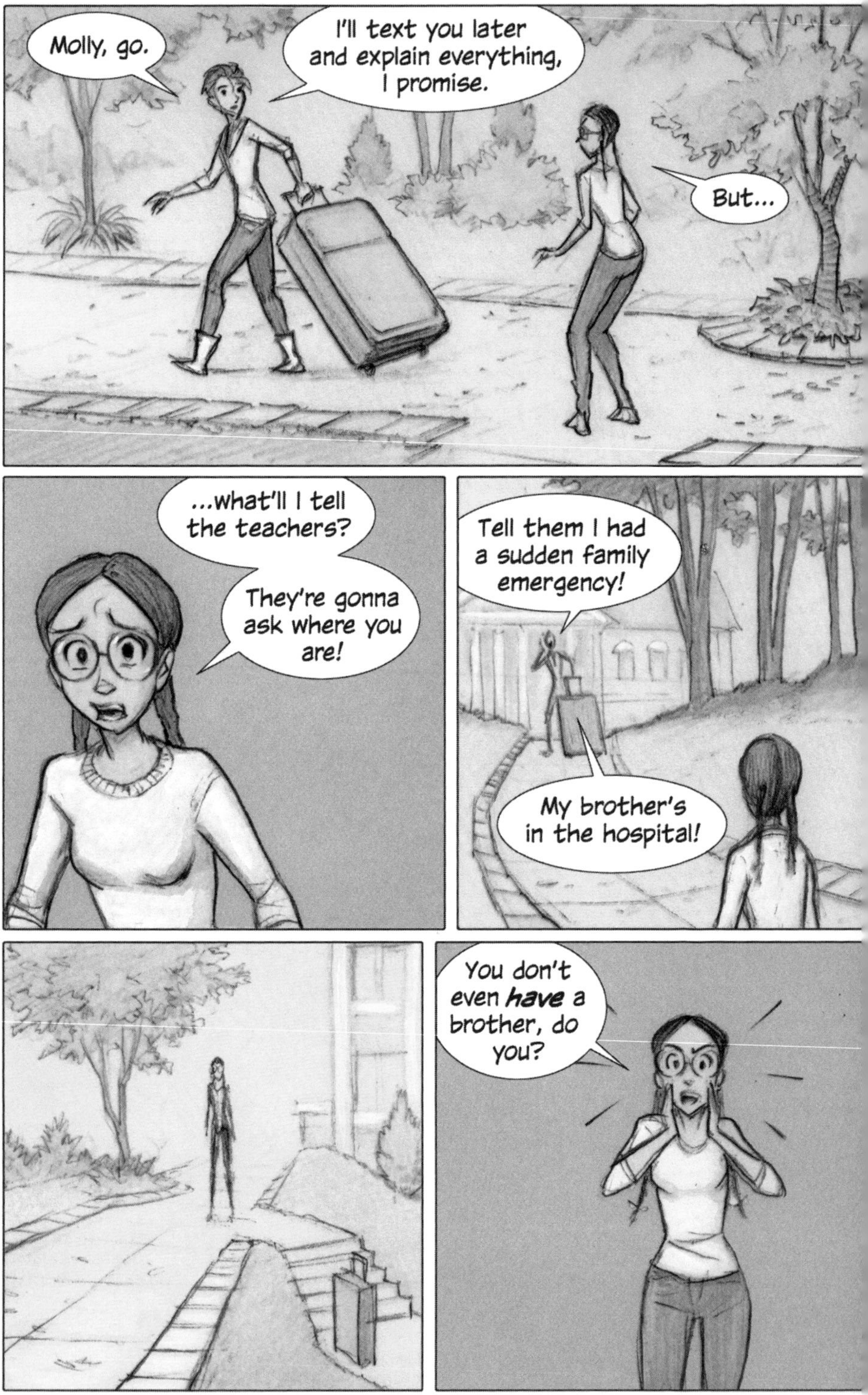
Molly, go.
I'll text you later and explain everything, I promise.
But...
...what'll I tell the teachers?
They're gonna ask where you are!
Tell them I had a sudden family emergency!
My brother's in the hospital!
You don't even *have* a brother, do you?

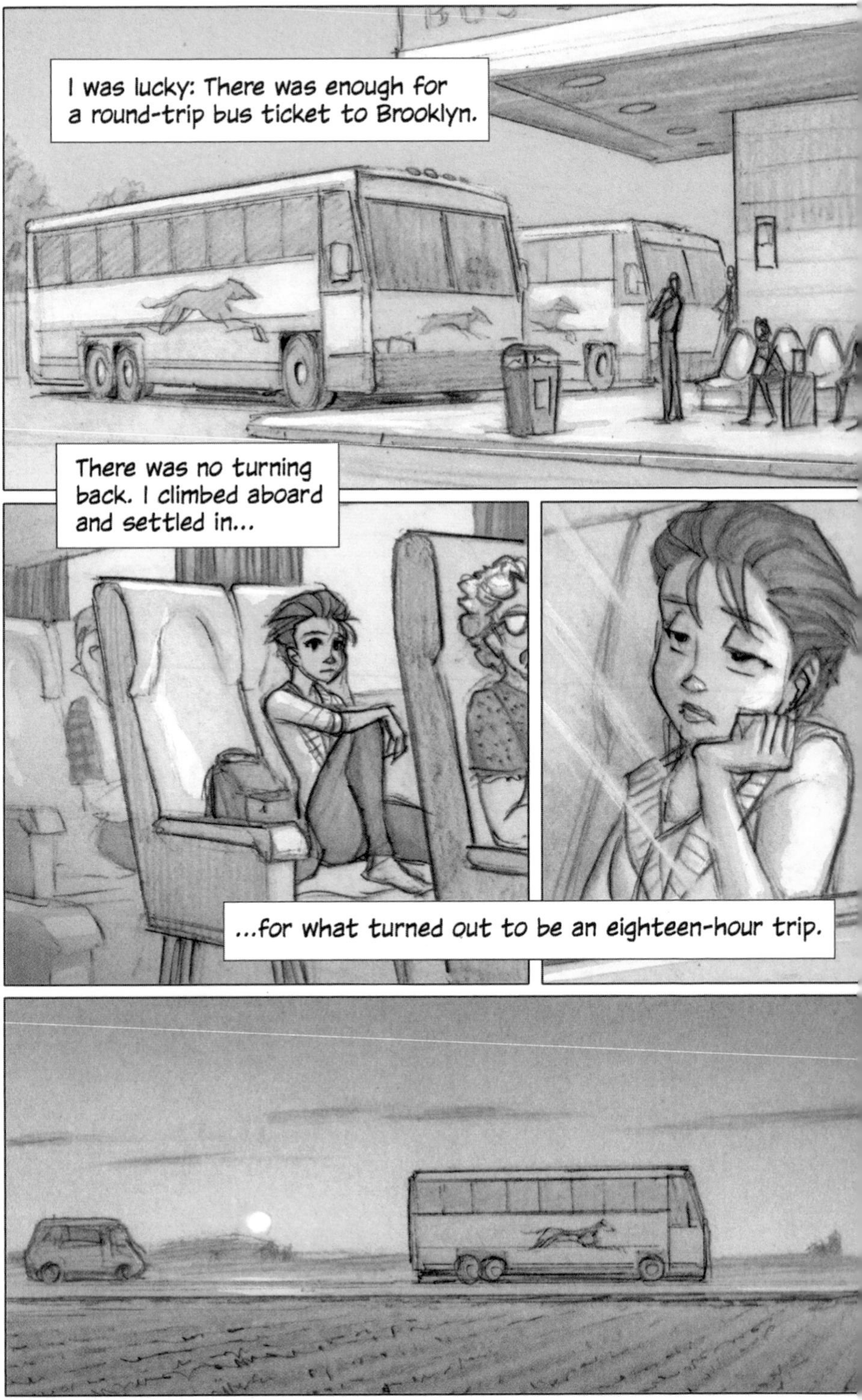
I was lucky: There was enough for a round-trip bus ticket to Brooklyn.
There was no turning back. I climbed aboard and settled in...
...for what turned out to be an eighteen-hour trip.

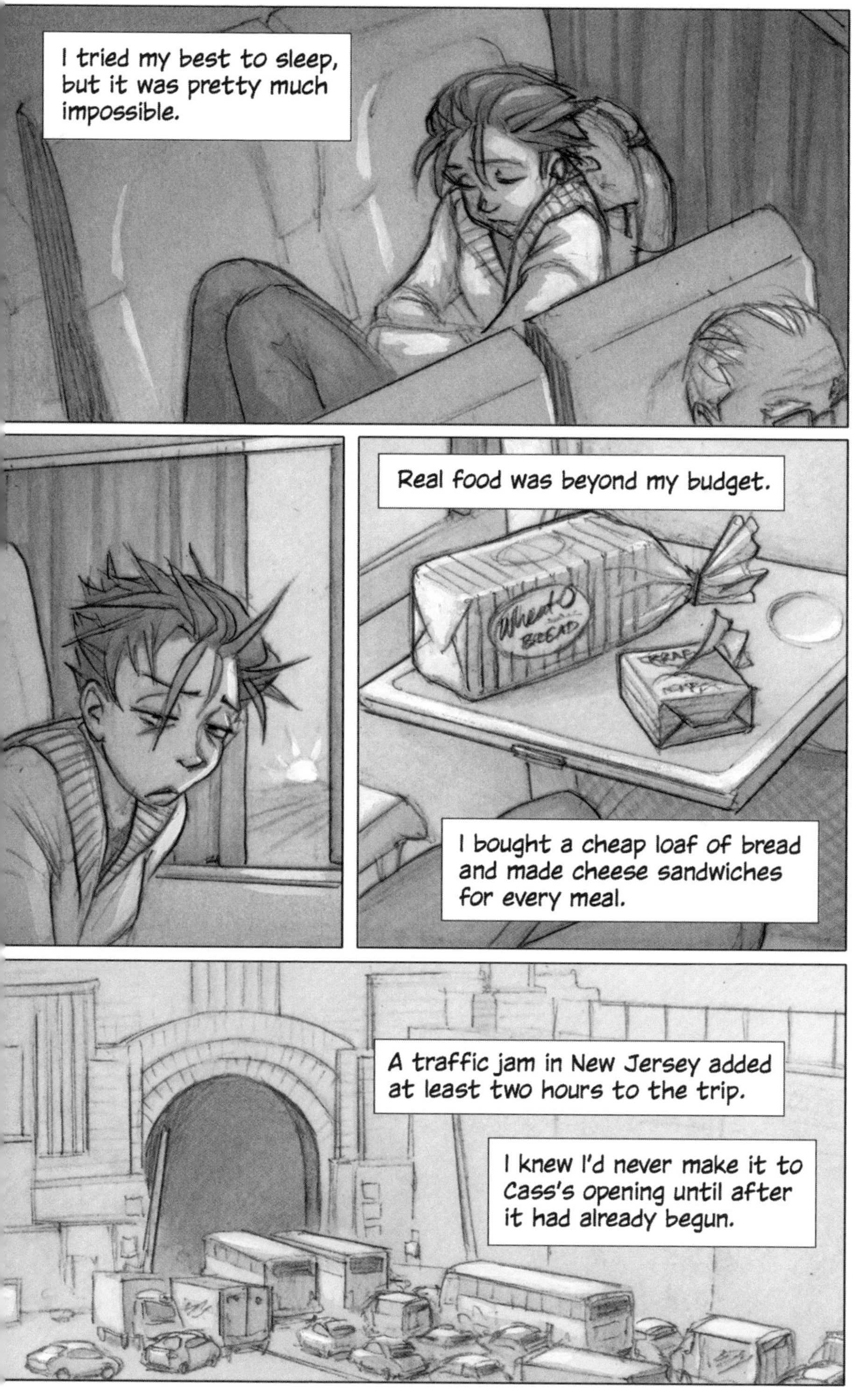
I tried my best to sleep, but it was pretty much impossible.
Real food was beyond my budget.
I bought a cheap loaf of bread and made cheese sandwiches for every meal.
A traffic jam in New Jersey added at least two hours to the trip.
I knew I'd never make it to Cass's opening until after it had already begun.

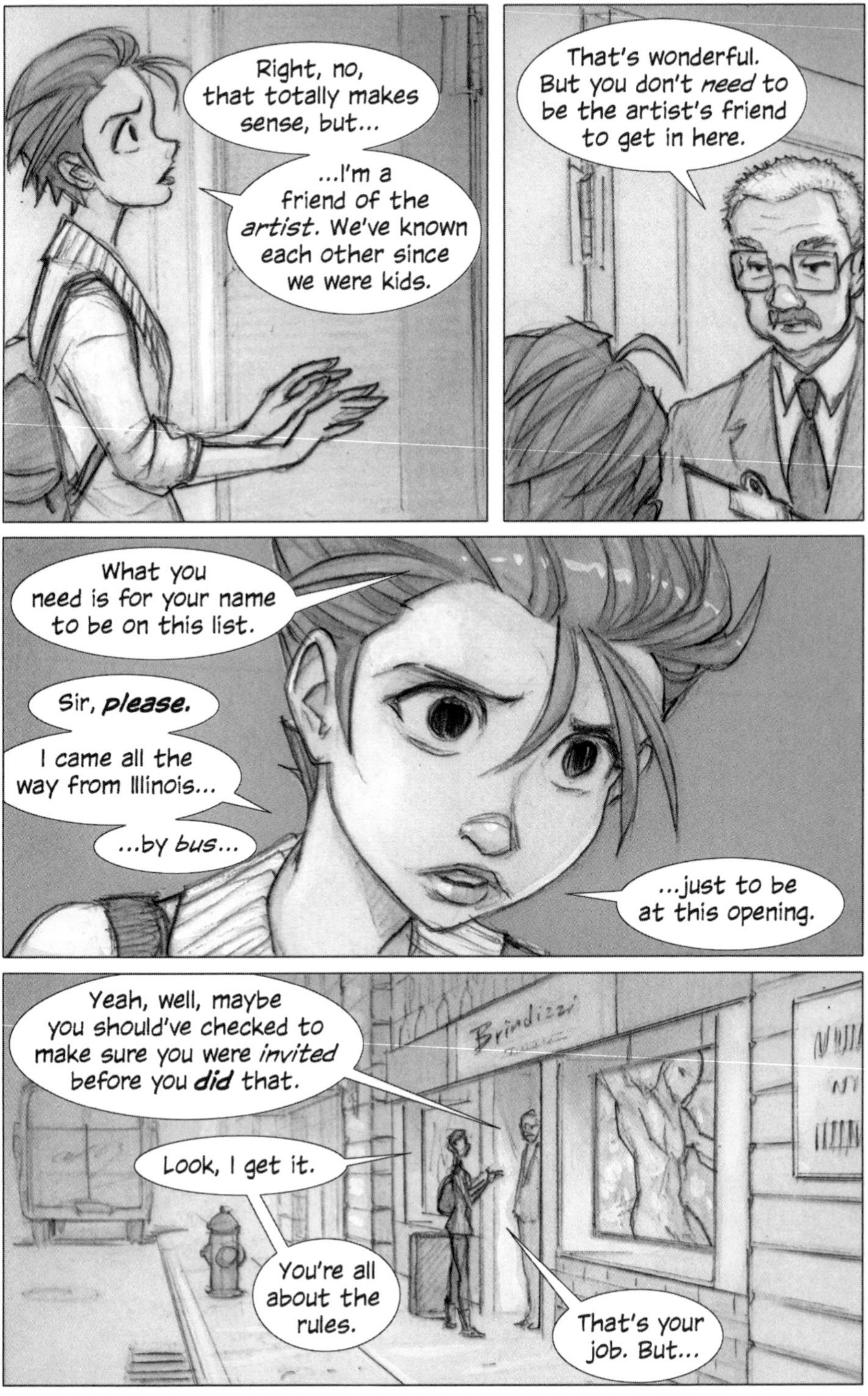
Right, no, that totally makes sense, but...
...I'm a friend of the *artist*. We've known each other since we were kids.
That's wonderful. But you don't *need* to be the artist's friend to get in here.
What you need is for your name to be on this list.
Sir, ***please.***
I came all the way from Illinois...
...by *bus*...
...just to be at this opening.
Yeah, well, maybe you should've checked to make sure you were *invited* before you ***did*** that.
Brindizzi
Look, I get it.
You're all about the rules.
That's your job. But...

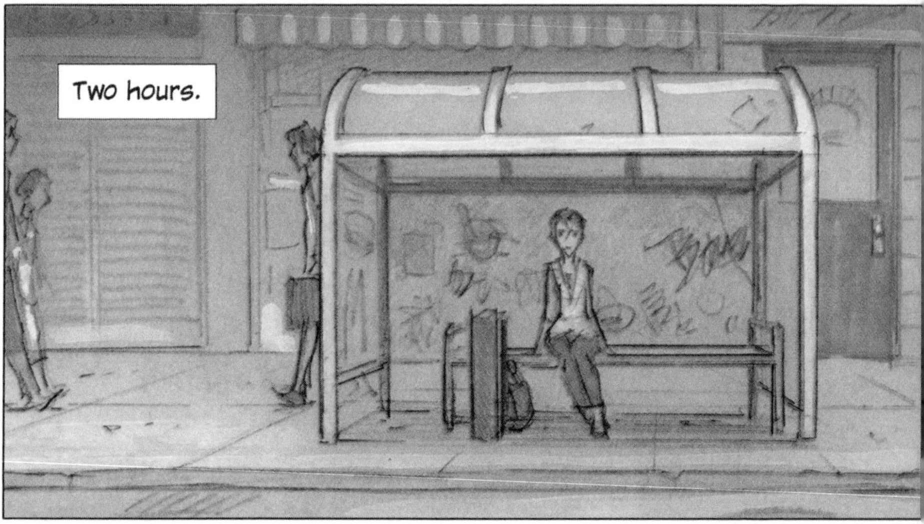
Two hours.

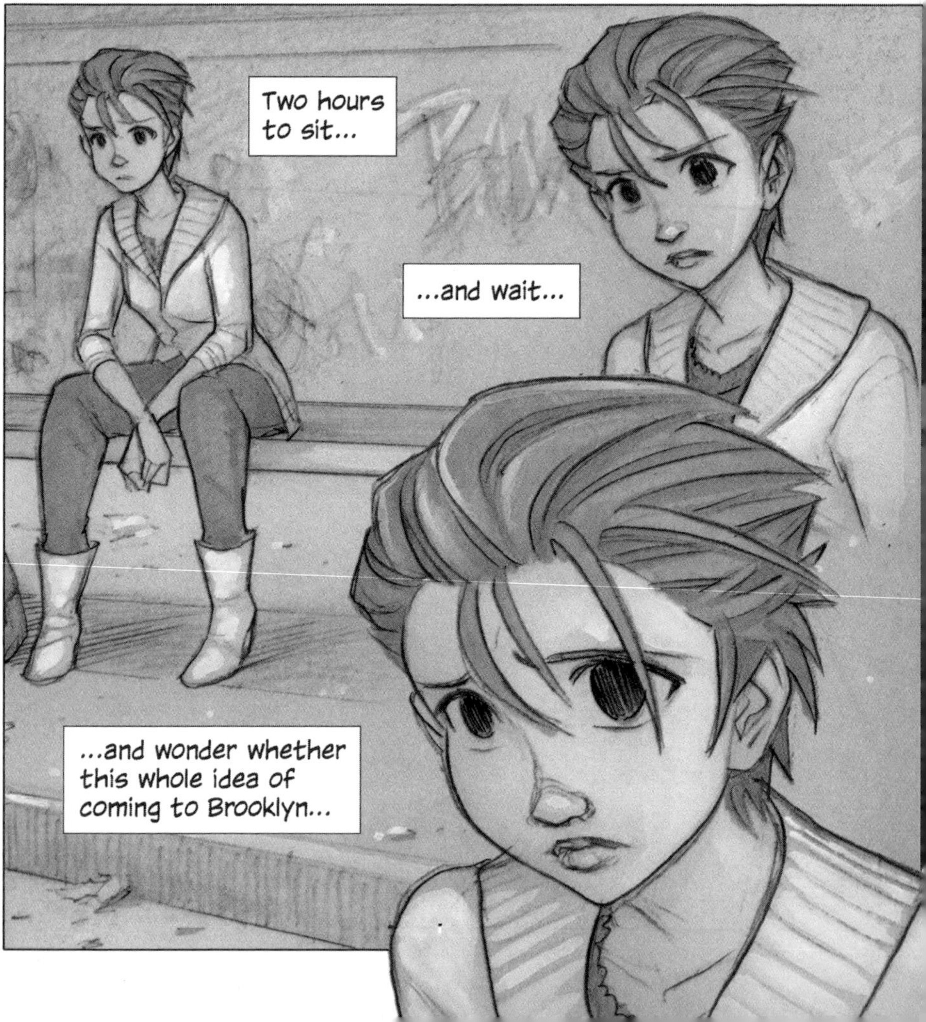
Two hours to sit...
...and wait...
...and wonder whether this whole idea of coming to Brooklyn...

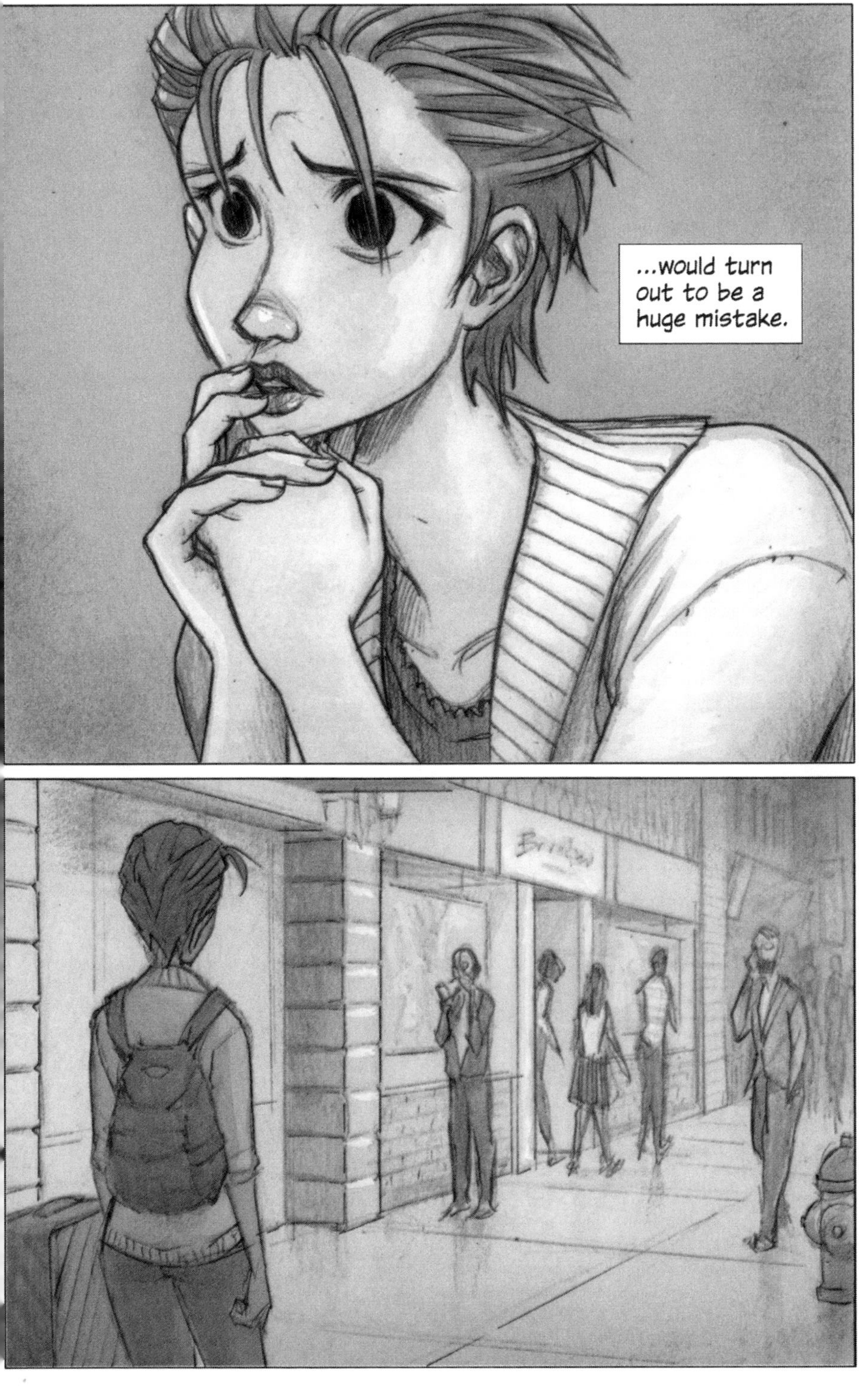
...would turn out to be a huge mistake.

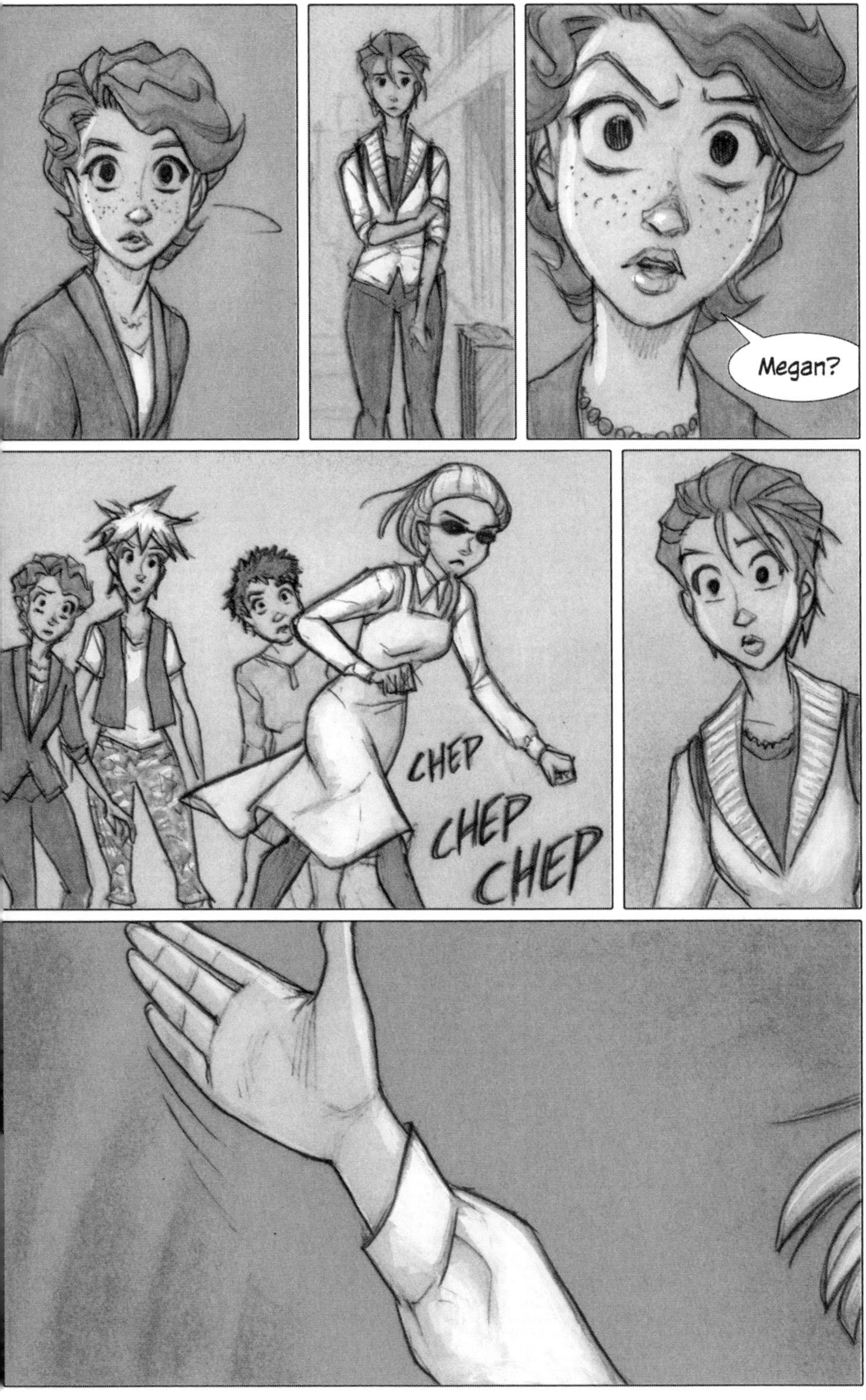
Megan?
CHEP
CHEP
CHEP

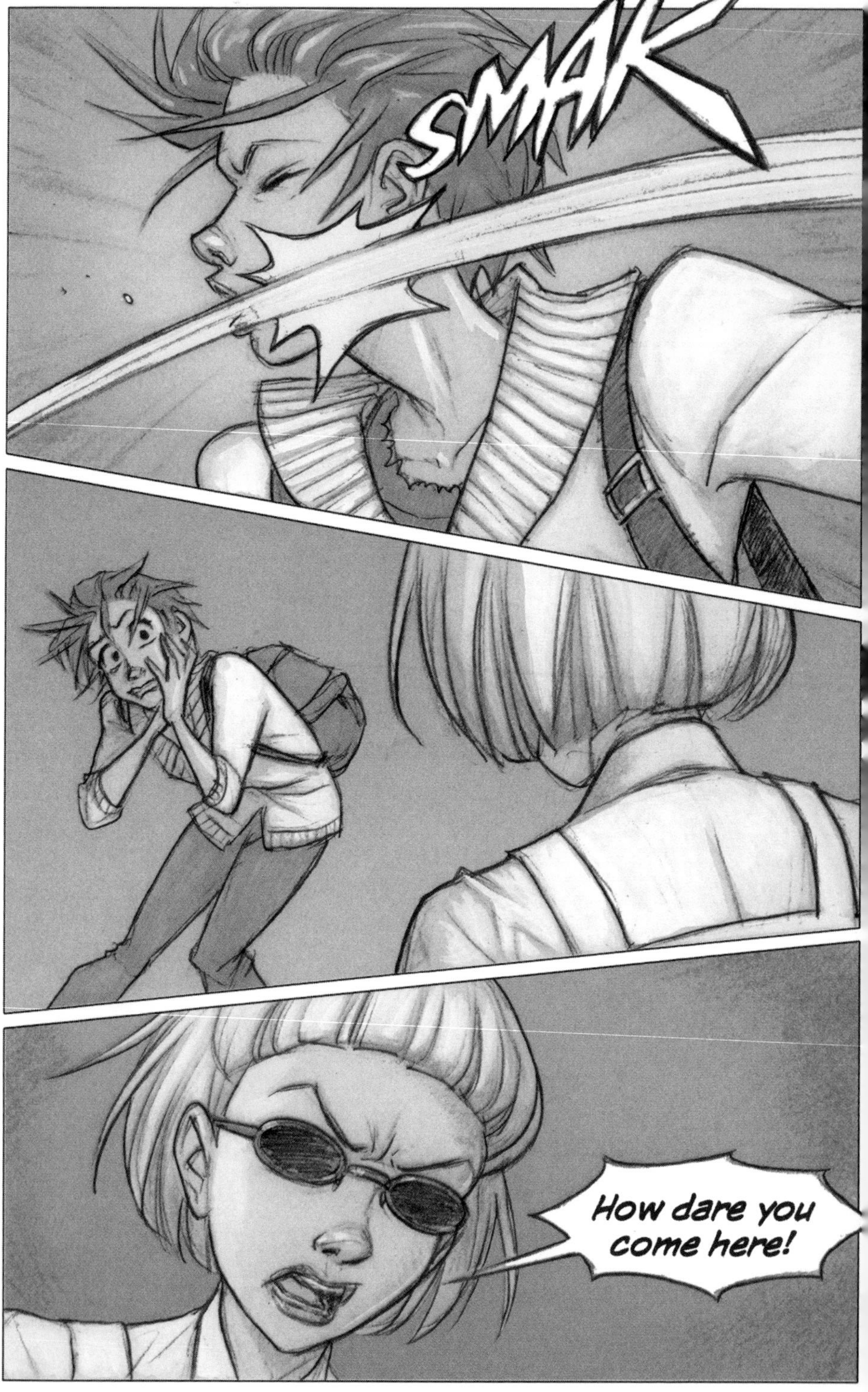
SMAK
How dare you come here!

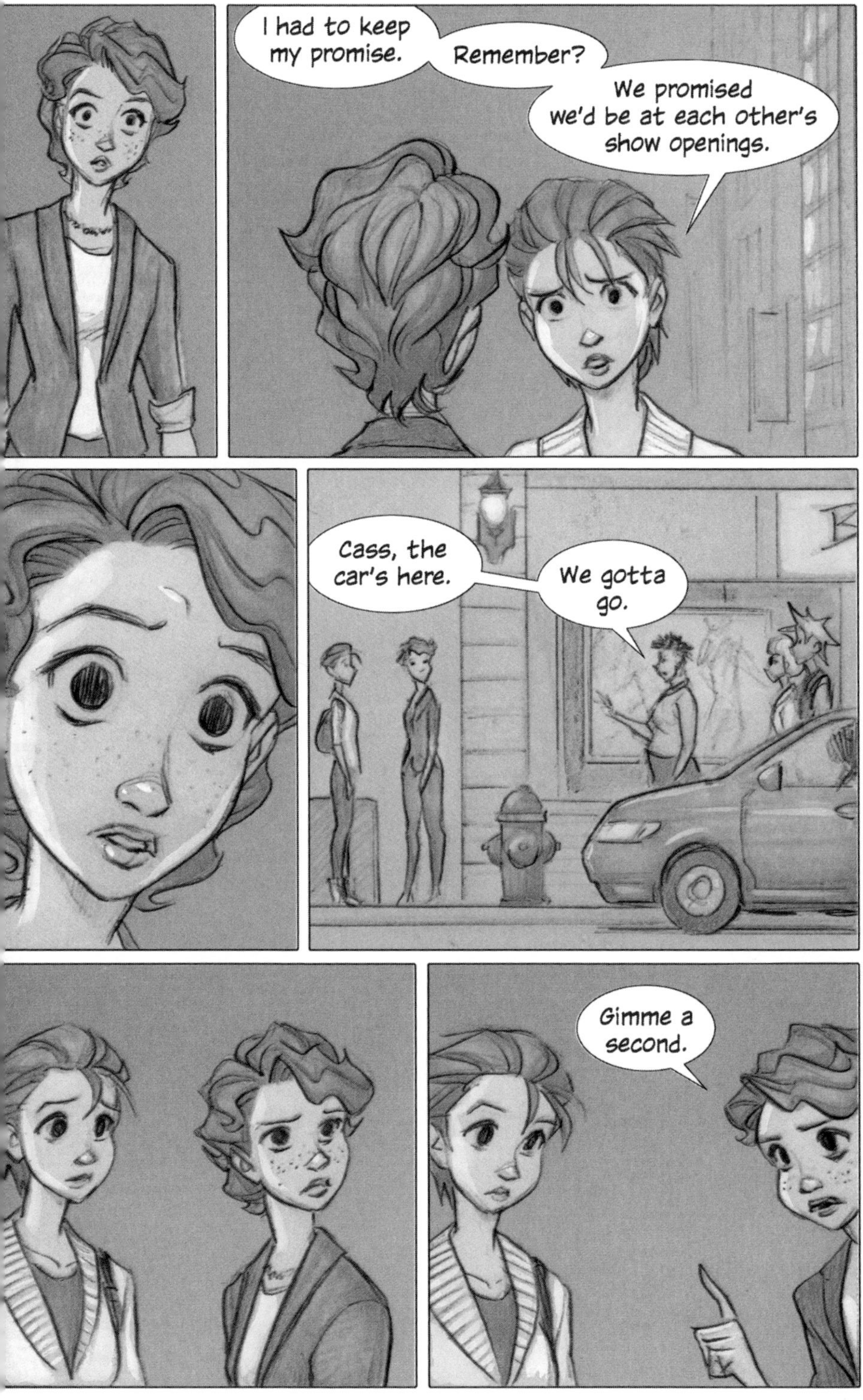
I had to keep my promise.
Remember?
We promised we'd be at each other's show openings.
Cass, the car's here.
We gotta go.
Gimme a second.

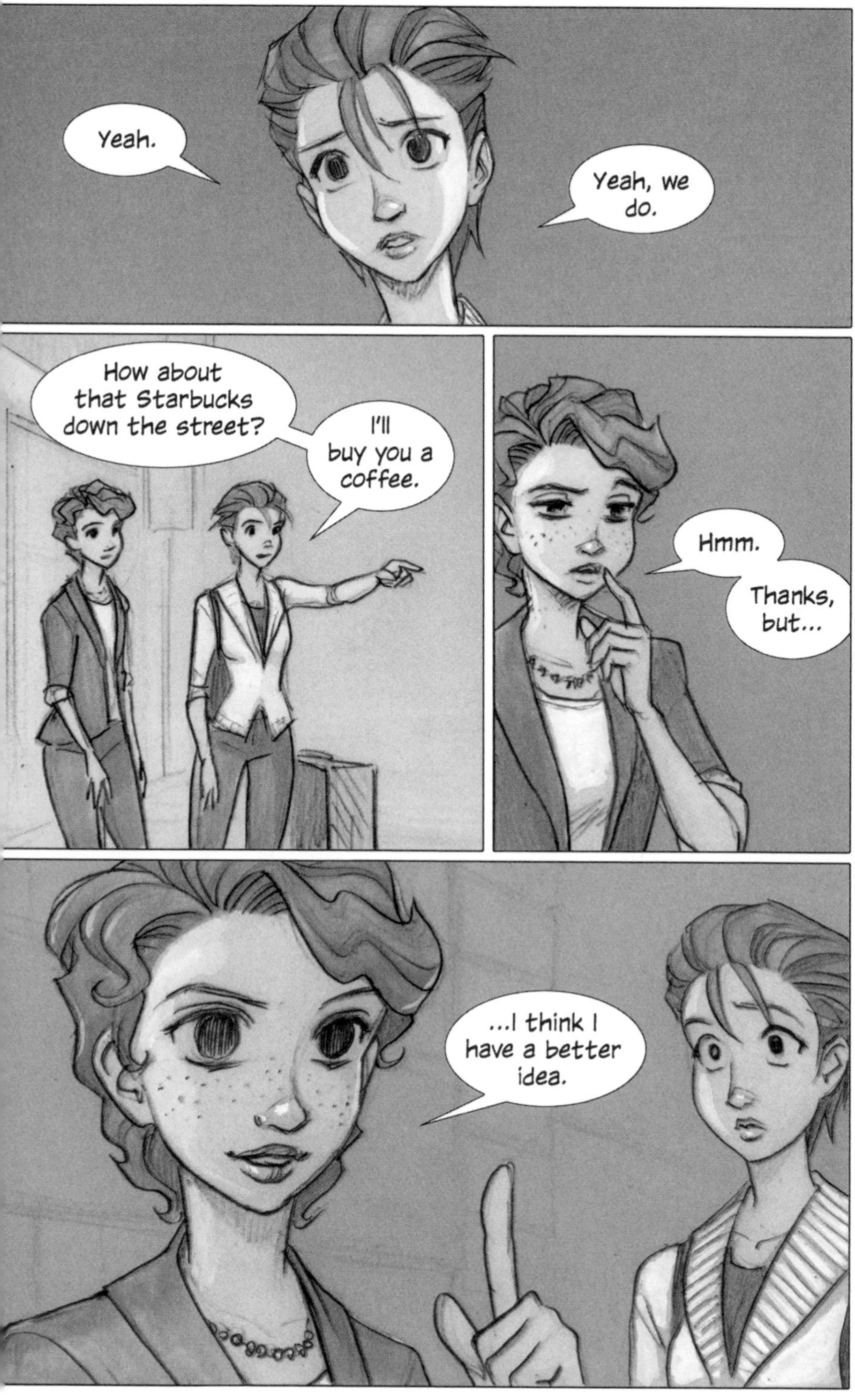
Yeah.
Yeah, we do.
How about that Starbucks down the street?
I'll buy you a coffee.
Hmm.
Thanks, but...
...I think I have a better idea.

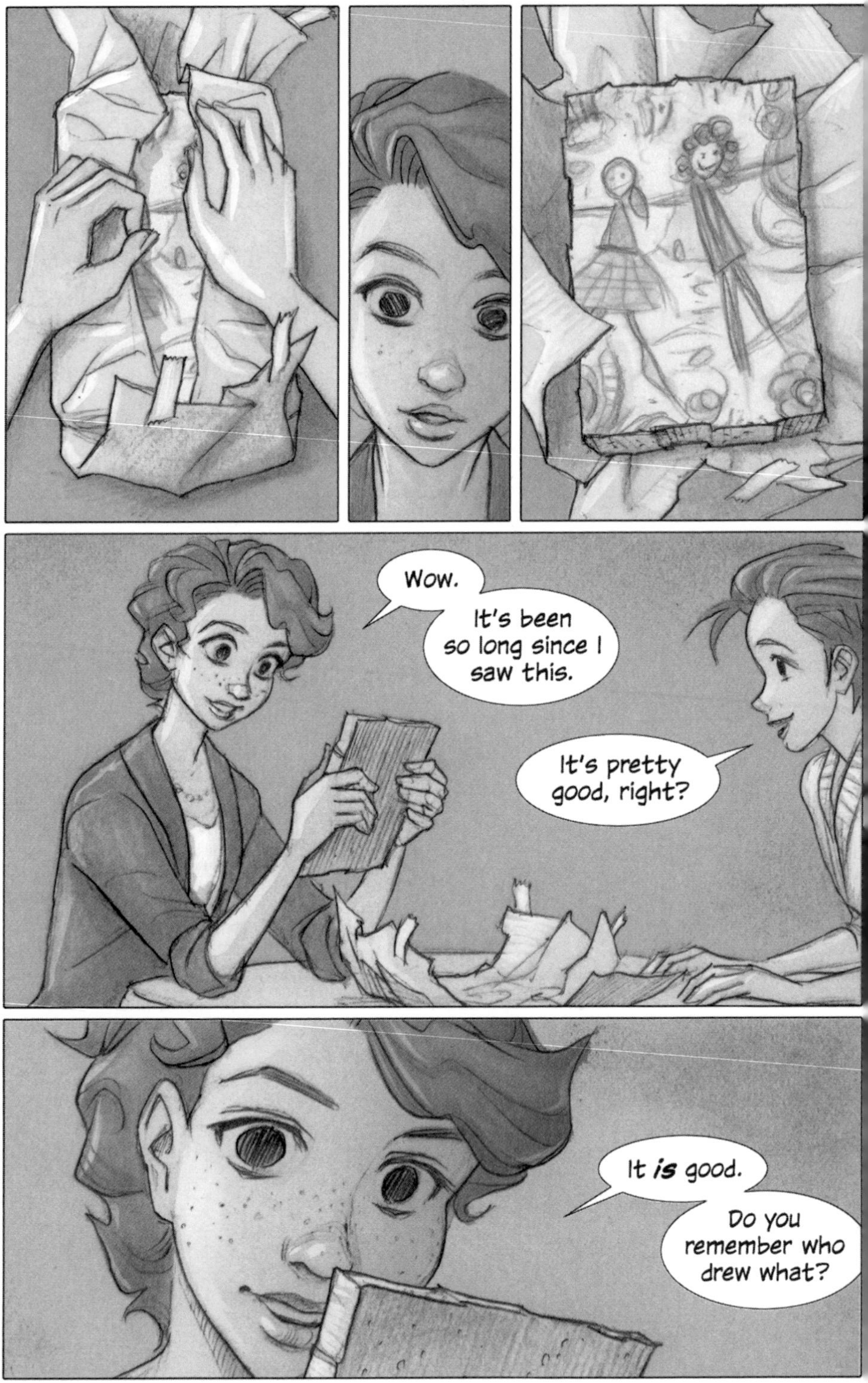
Wow.
It's been so long since I saw this.
It's pretty good, right?
It *is* good.
Do you remember who drew what?

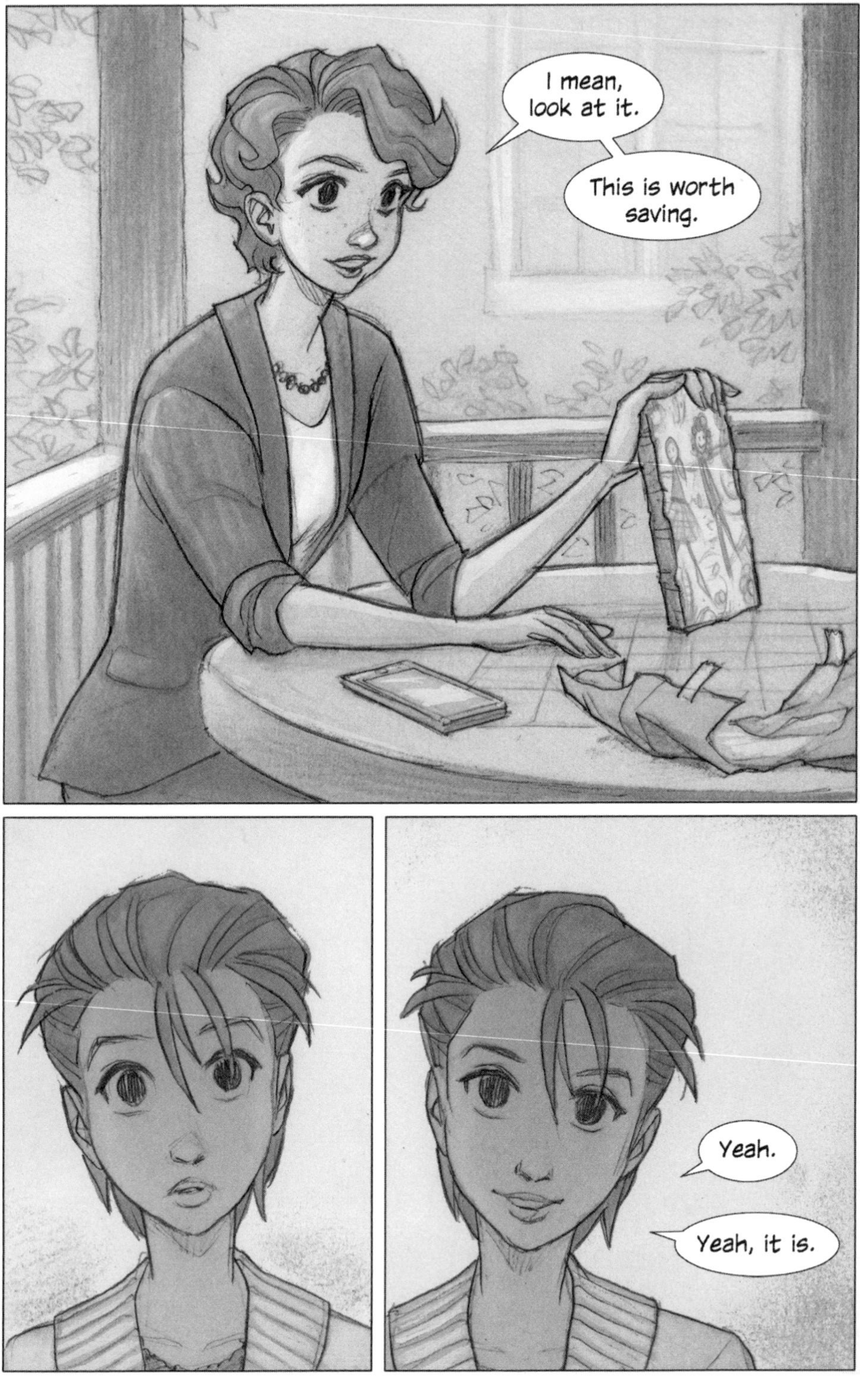
I mean, look at it.
This is worth saving.
Yeah.
Yeah, it is.

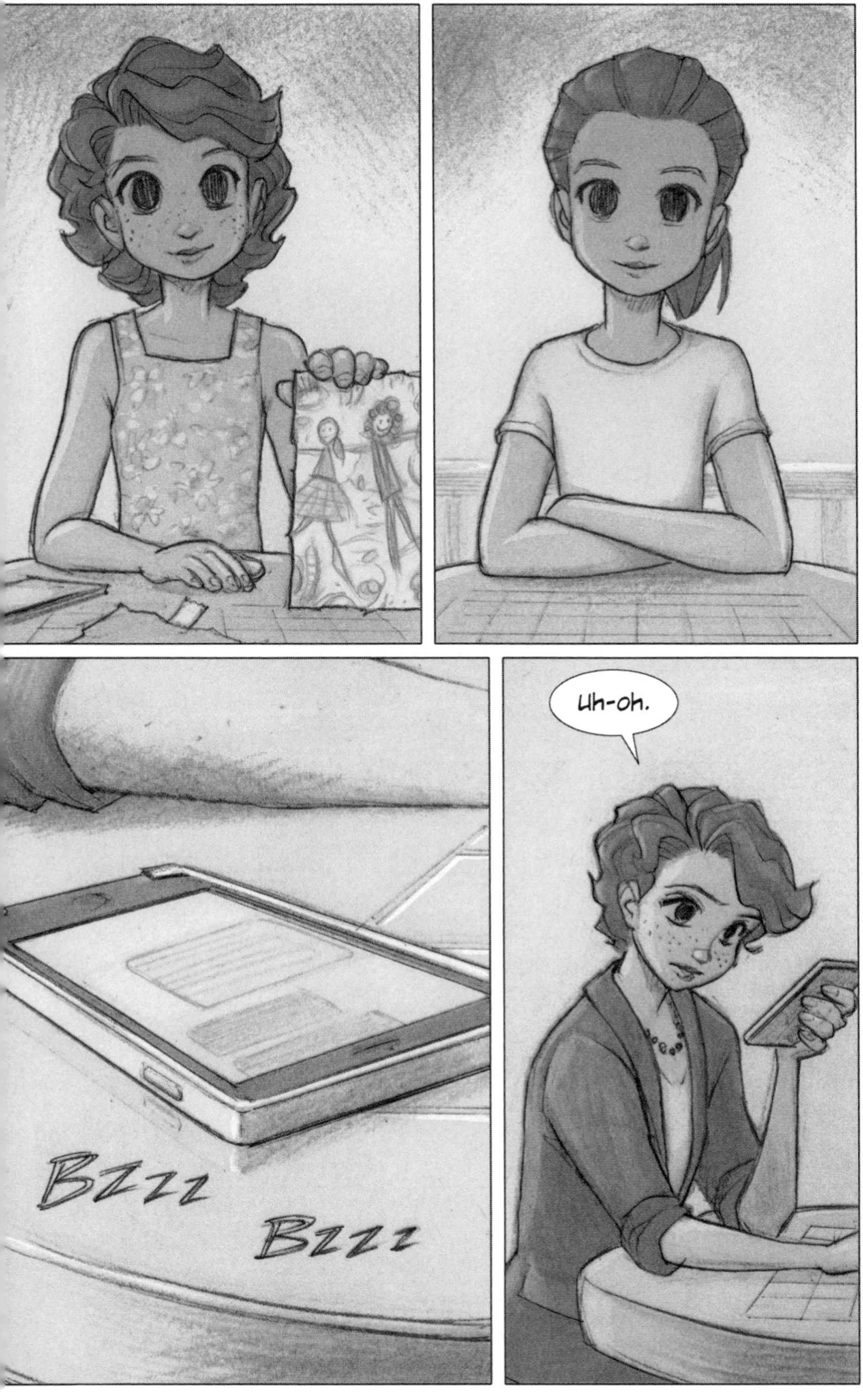
Bzzz
Bzzz
Uh-oh.

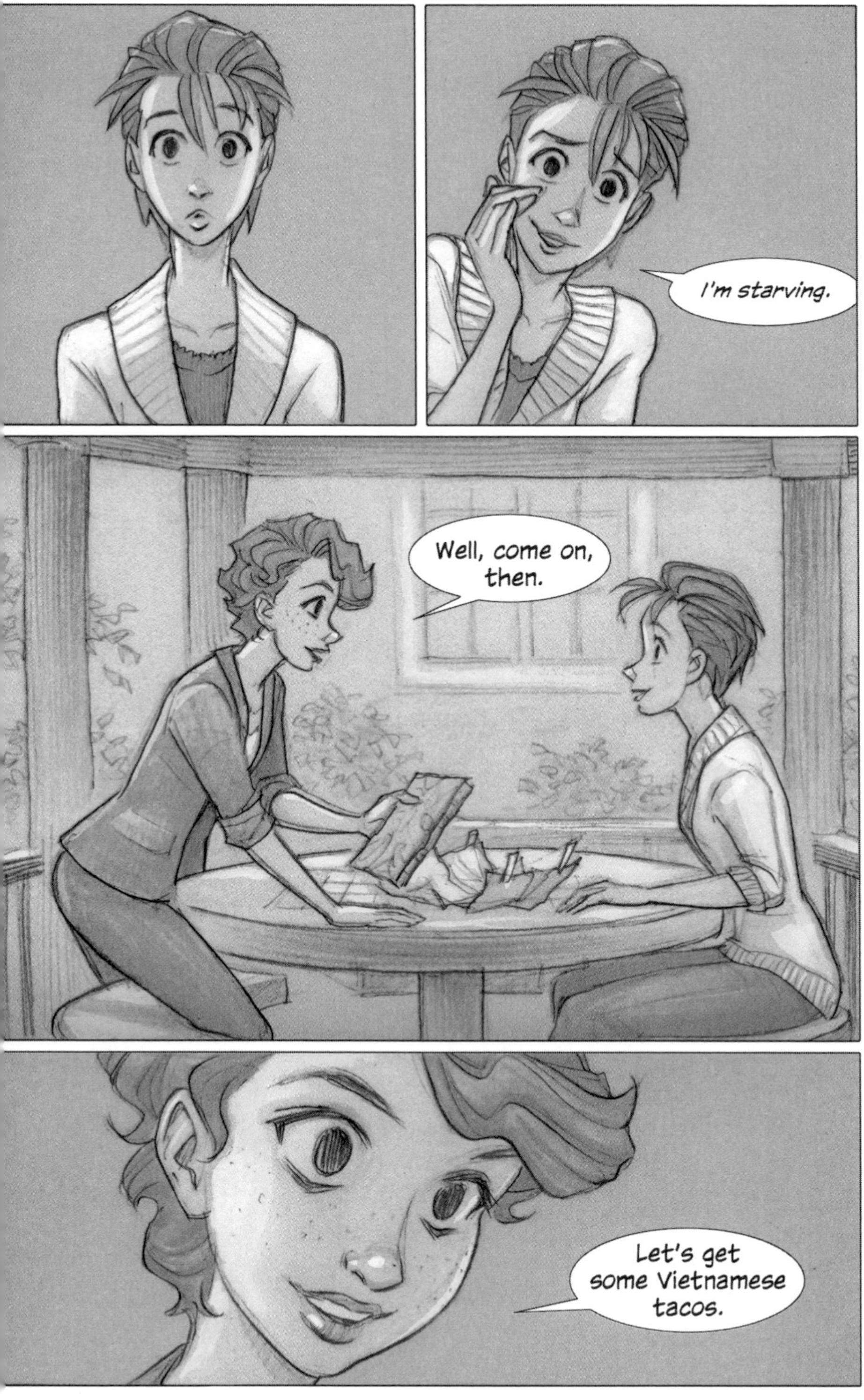
I'm starving.
Well, come on, then.
Let's get some Vietnamese tacos.

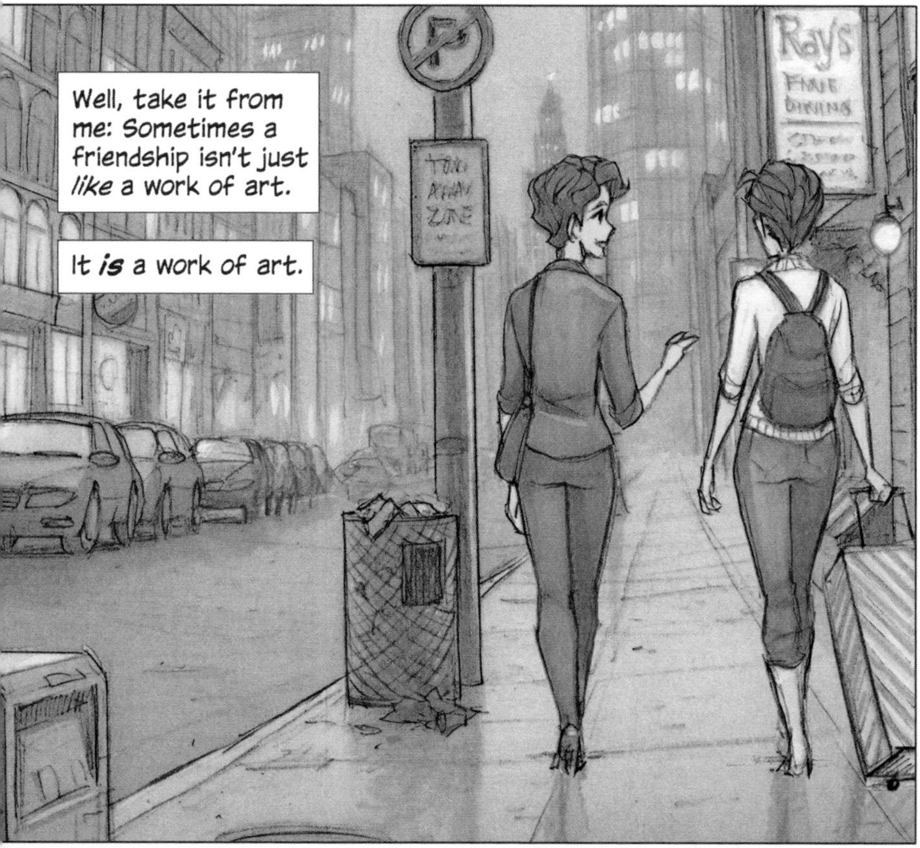
Well, take it from me: Sometimes a friendship isn't just *like* a work of art.
It ***is*** a work of art.
Ray's

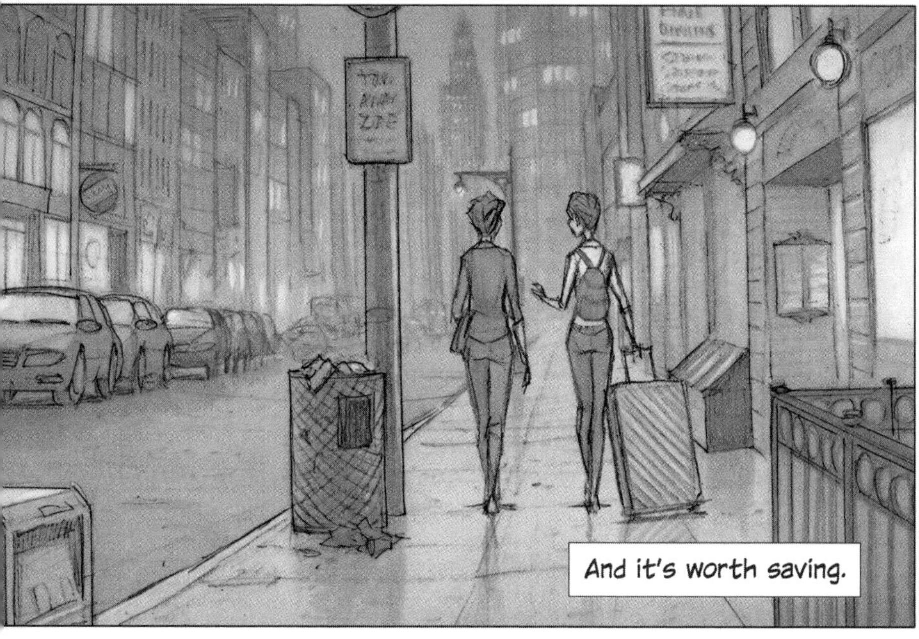
And it's worth saving.

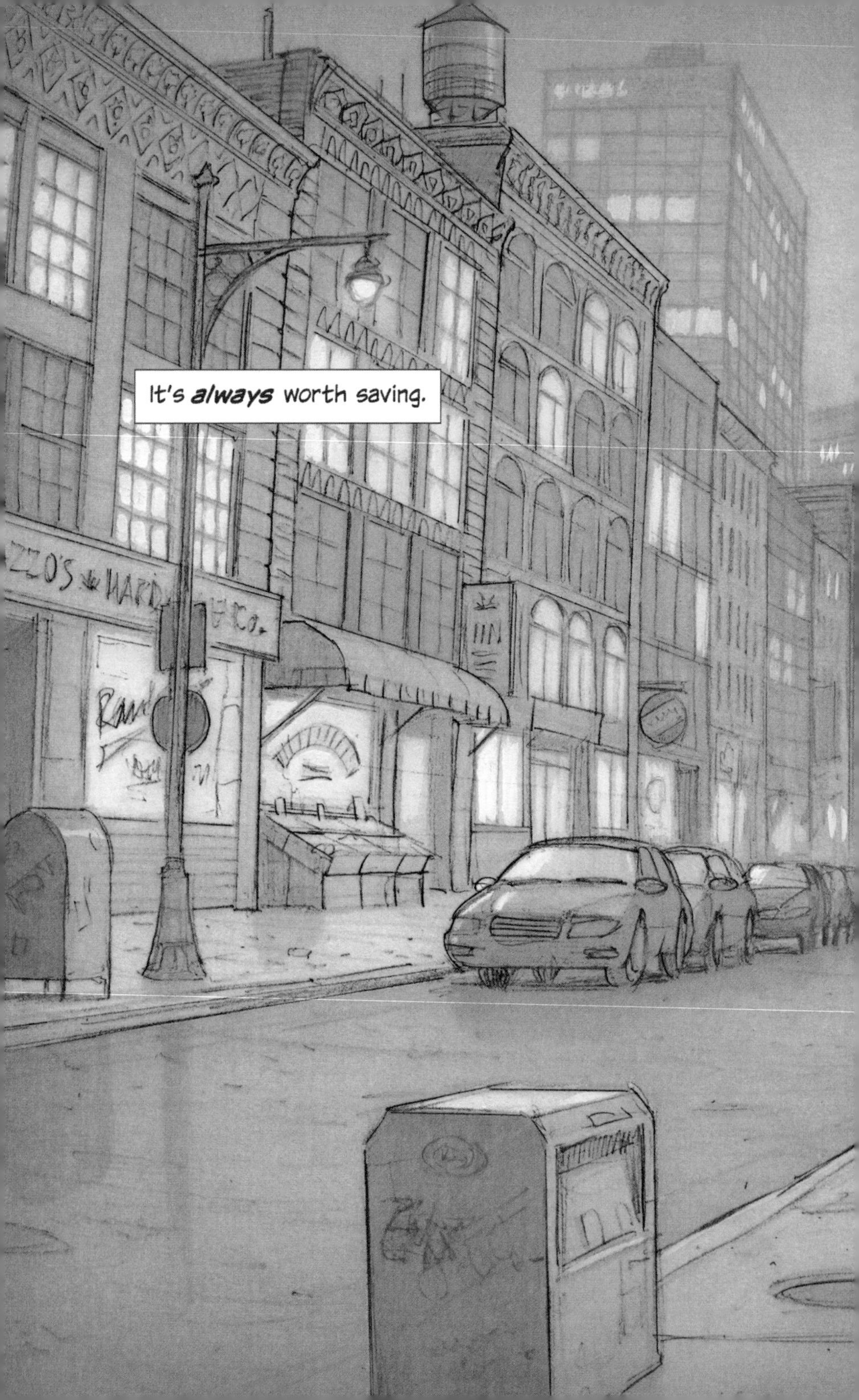
It's *always* worth saving.

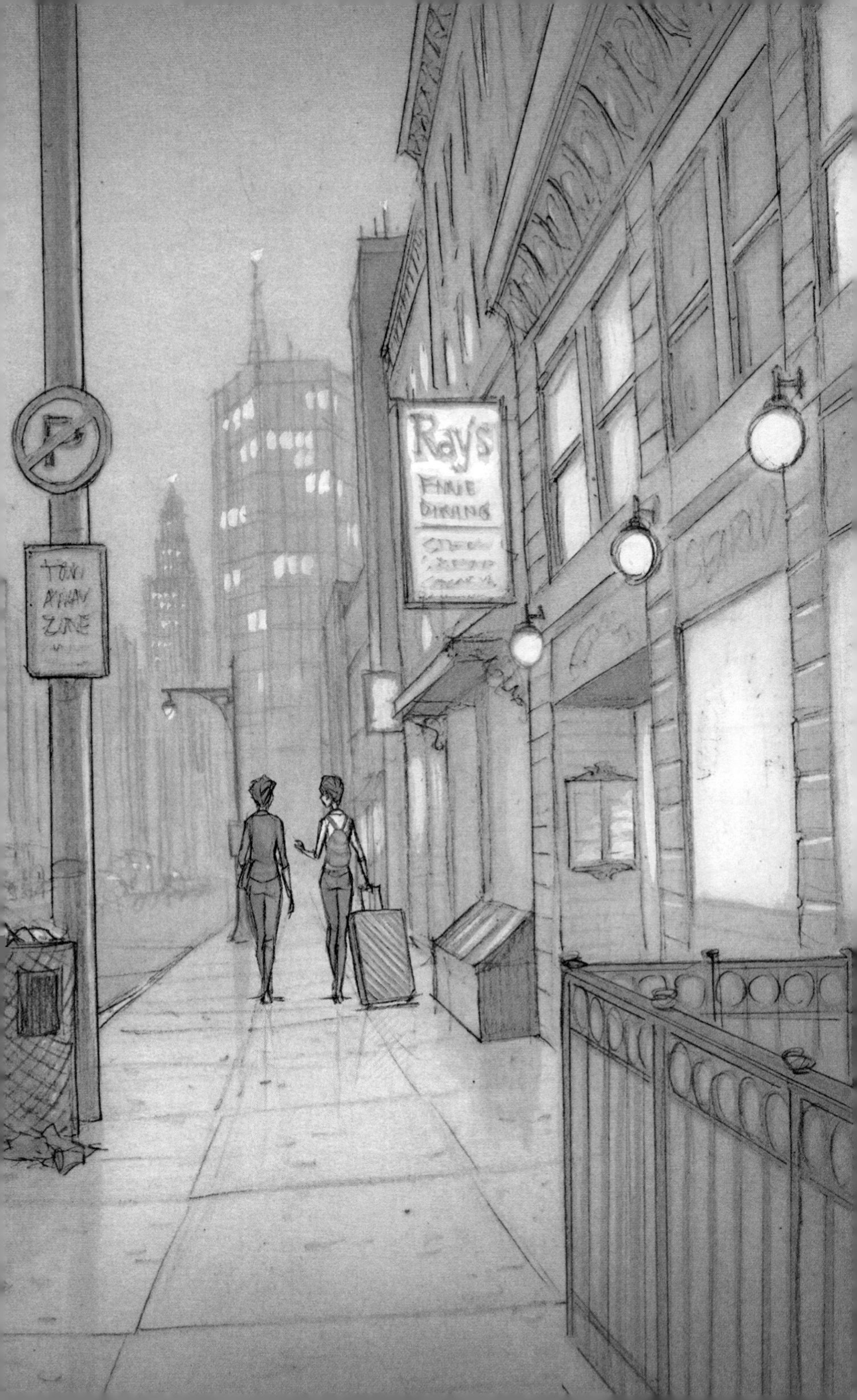
Ray's

ACKNOWLEDGMENTS Thanks to Emily Meehan and Hannah Allaman, whose editorial guidance made a huge difference in both the substance and the style of this story. Thanks also to Andrea Colvin, whose editorial wisdom really saved the day when it came time for me to bring these pages across the finish line in their final form. I must also thank Jenny Kimura, whose design skills made the finished book as lovely as it could possibly be. I'm very grateful to both Kerianne Steinberg and Lindsay Walter-Greaney, whose eagle eyes spotted an awful lot of embarrassing errors—in both the writing and the art—before they slipped through into the final book. A deafening round of applause is due to Ammi-Joan Paquette, my agent, who believed in this book way back when it was just a vague germ of an idea, and who never stopped believing in it. And finally, many, many thanks to my wife, Miki, whose steadfast support stands behind not just this book, but indeed every book I have ever done.

MARK CRILLEY is the author and illustrator of more than forty books, including several acclaimed graphic novels, for which he has received fourteen Eisner Award nominations. His work has been featured in *USA Today* and *Entertainment Weekly*, and on *CNN Headline News*. His popular YouTube videos have been viewed more than 390 million times. He lives in Michigan with his wife, Miki, and children, Matthew and Mio.